# Healing Maddie Brees

*a novel*

REBECCA BREWSTER STEVENSON

Light Messages

Published 2016, by Light Messages
www.lightmessages.com
Durham, NC 27713
United States of America

Paperback ISBN: 978-1-61153-174-9
Ebook ISBN: 978-1-61153-175-6

*for Bill*

# 1

*M*addie was struck that Mr. and Mrs. Peterson looked exactly the same as they always had. Maybe Mrs. Peterson's skin was a bit more folded around the eyes, and Mr. Peterson was more gray, somehow—but it was remarkable, really, that these two who had seemed decidedly past middle age in all her growing up years should look so exactly as they always had. It made her wonder, right there at the door when she and Frank greeted them, just how much she understood about the people she had known back then. Because clearly she had gotten some of it wrong.

The Petersons were passing through town en route from Pittsburgh to Florida. They were old friends of Maddie's parents, and therefore, declared Frank, friends of theirs. They had known Maddie all her life; she and Frank saw them when they went home to visit her parents; and now, for the first time, they were guests in Frank and Maddie's home.

All told, it was a very nice visit. Frank had prepared a lamb tagine for supper, the Petersons had brought ice cream, and Mr. Peterson had astounded Frank and Maddie's boys with his parlor trick: folding his handkerchief into something resembling a mouse and then "disappearing it" (Garrett's phrasing) in and out of his sleeve. All three boys were speechless with amazement, but after they'd been sent to bed, the adults could hear their voices piping down the stairs, suggesting possible explanations to one another. The Petersons laughed and exchanged stories about their grandchildren, and Frank caught Maddie's gaze across the table and held it there with a smile.

Yet it seemed to her that Frank was gone from the table (he was putting the boys to bed?) when Mrs. Peterson mentioned having seen Vincent Elander. In Maddie's memory, anyway, she was sitting alone at the table with their guests when Mrs. Peterson mentioned having seen Vincent at a shopping mall or on the street somewhere. Maddie was sure she had asked very politely about his well-being and had not shown any reaction, except for a kind of bland pleasure, at the resurrection, at her dining room table, of an old boyfriend.

"Ah, Vincent. The Superhero," Frank said when Maddie told him. Their guests departed, their sons soundly sleeping, Frank and Maddie worked together in the kitchen.

"Yes, the Superhero," Maddie replied. She felt a vague irritation that she put down to fatigue.

The Superhero was an old joke, Frank's nickname for Maddie's first boyfriend.

"Come on, Maddie," he would say. "I could handle you dating the star quarterback or the captain of the swim team. But *this* guy? You've got to be kidding me. The guy had superpowers."

It was a joke: the girls he had dated against the guys she had dated, and always her list had this little asterisk, this little first and last item: that Vincent Elander, her first boyfriend (who happened also to have been a quarterback), could heal people.

Frank got tremendous mileage out of this. He might look at her, his head turned to one side, or call to her as he was coming up the basement steps, or mutter when he was climbing into bed: "Did I ever tell you about Lisa? Well, she was the captain of the cheerleading squad" (or girls' soccer team or dance line) "*and* she had this uncanny ability to fly!" So the joke went, and Maddie had learned to laugh at it, and to play along in company when the conversation went that way: "Hey, did Maddie ever tell you about her first boyfriend?"

In truth, it was a great story, that incident of the homeless man who came out of nowhere in a torrential Pittsburgh rainstorm to be hit by a car right in front of them ("Right in front of them!" Frank

2

would always repeat after her). People loved the story: it was bizarre and fantastic, but it ended well. And Maddie always finished it the same way: of course her old boyfriend couldn't really heal people. Of course he couldn't.

—∞∞∞—

He was hit by the car. It was night, the rain was pouring down, and he had crossed the intersection when he shouldn't have. Everyone was waiting for the walk signal, but he came stumbling heedlessly through the crosswalk. Drunkenness will do that to you, and it was drunkenness he exhaled when, after being hit by the car, after rolling off its hood and falling to a crumpled heap at their feet, Vincent helped him up. Maddie cringed and backed away, but Vincent bent down to him and then called him by name, and it was this gesture almost as much as the healings themselves that with disturbing insistence was forever in her mind Vincent: he was seventeen years old; a drunk, homeless man had been hit by a car; and Vincent reached forward to help him, uninhibited by fear or distaste. Vincent had leaned down to see if Willy was all right.

They had talked with him that afternoon before the baseball game—"Willy," he called himself, gesturing with his one good hand to his chest. Maddie first spotted him as they were approaching the stadium, walking under the last vaulting leg of the bridge, and she was feeling magnificently independent and in love until he was calling out to them ("Hey! Hey!") from his square of tattered blanket. Maddie clung closer to Vincent, hastening her steps, awash in sensible descriptors (homeless, dirty, mentally unstable), but Vincent didn't ignore him the way anyone else would. Rather, he turned and, drawing Maddie along with him, walked over to where Willy was standing to his feet. And then he was emerging from the shade of the concrete column, making his way toward them, his gaze steadily fixed on them. Maddie tried not to shadow Vincent like a child. What was there to be afraid of? They were just going to have a conversation.

She had stood there taking him in. The whites of his eyes were yellowed and his light blue T-shirt was stained. Once upon a time the shirt had a pocket on the chest, evidenced by a darker patch of fabric in the pocket's place and a small hole. His jeans were dark with dirt, he wore a black Pittsburgh Pirates ball cap on his head, and his right arm was withered: permanently bent at the elbow and impossibly thin, as if all the muscles had long ago atrophied into dissolution. The fingers of that hand, too, were lifeless and stiff, curled inward, and Vincent talked to him as though he saw him every day, or at least every time he made his way downtown to a Pirates game—a not infrequent occurrence.

Maddie no longer remembered what they had talked about, but Vincent called him Willy. He seemed to know his name before Willy had even identified himself, but Willy hadn't known Vincent's name or hadn't seemed to. He called him "Buddy."

"Buddy?" Maddie said as they were walking away.

"Yeah," Vincent answered, "he calls everyone that."

---

When one is a freshman or even a sophomore in high school, it's possible that upperclassmen can seem a bit like superheroes. The contrast of anonymity and celebrity does it, and Vincent Elander had this celebrity in spades. He was only a year older than she, but this narrow divide made no difference. Maddie would never have considered a crush on him: his status was just too great. The beauty, accomplishment, charisma, and fame fixed him permanently out of her league. Other than knowing who he was, Maddie never gave him a second thought.

And then he showed up in her church on a Sunday evening—a Sunday *evening*, when even some of the faithful Sunday morning worshippers didn't bother to come. And he had that heart-wrenching something-or-other of an experience at the altar, the one that could never be compatible with what Maddie felt surely was a godless life before that. It was in the wake of that momentous spring evening that she learned he was number 22 on the baseball team, that he always crossed the school parking lot on the way to baseball practice, and that once (she remembered it like she had a photograph) she had caught his eye.

A relationship with someone like Vincent Elander can wrench one forever from anonymity, and the fifteen-year-old Maddie had been shocked by the draw. Add to that drastic change this about

Vincent's healing people, and Maddie sometimes wondered that she had weathered it so well. She saw herself in retrospect emerging from that year, her head raised and eyes wide, shaking the dust from her feet. Only later had she been able to recognize Vincent's presumption in it: the celebrity-status confidence had been all it took to woo her, and the fact that she succumbed to it would have been the first of many Vincent-related embarrassments had she not told herself level-headedly and many times that it wasn't her fault.

She was only fifteen at the time. Almost anyone would have been taken in.

---

She was a long time getting used to it: the lighthearted humor with which Frank regarded that strange year in her life. She had been guarded in telling him about it. How much is wise to say, anyway, about previous loves? But even from the beginning, Frank was the sort who wanted to know everything. There could be no secrets, he said.

And so she had told him as he was taking her to meet his parents for the first time, and he was driving in the rain. She felt reckless in the telling: this brief year in her history was suddenly the hinge on which their entire relationship seemed to hang. The drive was a long one and she unraveled it slowly, careful with the details, wishing it merely the story of the complicated joy and bafflement of a first love. But her resentment of the story itself rang in her voice no matter how she tried to suppress it, and she finished rather abruptly as they got off the turnpike.

"So what happened after that?" Frank asked. He wanted to know the breaking up part, the predictable end of all the stories in the genre.

"Nothing, really. He went to college. His family moved away. I went to college. I met you. We don't keep in touch," she said.

"Does he still heal people?" Frank asked her. They were sitting in his parents' driveway and he had turned off the headlights. The rain was loud on the roof and it fled down the windshield, obscuring her view of the house.

"He never *could* heal people, Frank," Maddie told him, She felt strangely frustrated with him. Had he not been listening? "It was obviously a mistake."

"I don't know how obvious it was," Frank answered, all unguarded interest.

Despite the fact that they were sitting in his parents' driveway, despite wishing desperately to change the subject to anything else, Maddie felt compelled to revisit some important details of the story—which Frank was more than happy to revisit with her. To her rising dismay, he remained unconvinced that Vincent *hadn't* healed *anyone*, and the two of them sat arguing in the car until his father finally emerged, bearing a flashlight and two umbrellas.

Maddie had tried to be cheerful all evening. Her anger gradually waned in the company of Frank's parents, but it returned when, much later, the two of them stood whispering in the hallway outside the guest room door.

And that was when Frank had taken her face in his hands, holding it so that his thumbs curved around her cheekbones, and he told her he was sorry they had argued, that he realized she had been there and he hadn't, and that she would be the one to know if her old boyfriend had been able to heal people.

His words went a good way toward assuaging her anger that night, but it took her a long time, nonetheless, to be able to laugh when Frank joked about that year and her superhero boyfriend. She had always had an excellent sense of humor, but some things were just easier to laugh about than others.

---

Maddie told Frank that what was strange about the mention of Vincent was that she had recently seen him in a dream.

"Isn't that odd, Frank?" she said, and handed him a rinsed bowl for the dishwasher. "Don't you think that's odd?"

Frank agreed that it was weird; he affirmed that dreams are always weird. He told her he'd dreamed about his childhood dog the night before and he hadn't remembered the dream until now. "Rover, his name was," Frank said absently, knowing Maddie knew this. Maddie smiled. Frank liked having reason to mention that dog: he was pleased to have owned a dog named Rover.

Then Maddie said that she hadn't dreamed about Vincent in years. Maybe not in ten years, she said.

But last week there was the morning that was colored throughout by Pittsburgh. Her mother called during breakfast and Maddie was caught off-guard by how suddenly vivid her hometown appeared, despite the fact they hadn't been home since last summer. All morning she felt vaguely shrouded in that city, in the hilly streets of the town, hearing strains of old hymns from her childhood church. The sense of these things hung about her with a hazy insistence, as if she'd inadvertently walked through a web and now felt but couldn't see a gossamer thread still clinging to her hair, now draped over her forehead, now falling across the lash of one eye.

It wasn't until early afternoon, heading to pick up Garrett from pre-school, that she recalled without knowing why the dream she'd had the night before. She had seen Vincent.

In the way of dreams, Vincent had appeared but hadn't been recognized as Vincent: she and everyone with her in the dream had known him as Charlie Reynolds, whom she had dated for a short time while a college freshman. In fact, the dream seemed to have taken place when she and Charlie were at school together at some sort of picnic, and he was wearing a ball cap with the brim tucked down to frame his face, the way that Charlie always wore it. Maddie was standing with friends in the shade when he came up to them. There was a definite sense of an intrusion by an outsider, yet everyone acknowledged him as Charlie, who was being friendly, the way he always was. He had nothing particular to say—nothing practical, as in real life, entreating them all to a game of ultimate Frisbee or asking what time they were expected back on campus—but nothing wildly impractical either— no bizarre, dreamlike non sequiturs like a comment about firemen or the taste of salt water. He was just present, smiling at Maddie from under the brim of his cap. And it was there, at that moment when he smiled at her, that Maddie and no one else saw that here was Vincent and not Charlie Reynolds at all.

"Isn't it strange," she said to Frank, "that I could see it was Vincent, and no one else could?" They had finished in the kitchen, had turned off the downstairs lights. Frank was checking his email at the bedroom computer desk, and Maddie was flossing her teeth.

"Dreams are weird," Frank said again, and Maddie thought so, too. How was it, she silently wondered, that she should so vividly recall Vincent's face? How does memory work that she should clearly remember the details: the curl of his lip, the shape of his nose, and the line of his jaw? And how was it Vincent then, Maddie wondered, and not Charlie that she had seen? Because in every way—demeanor and behavior and context—it made sense to have been Charlie. And yet she had awakened with that very strong sense of Vincent, of his having joined her and some college friends there in the shade.

Once she and Vincent had stayed up late watching Rocky movies at the Tedescos' house, a marathon, Nicky had declared. They would watch all three of them in anticipation of the debut of *Rocky IV*, which would be coming out in only a few weeks. Maddie had said she had never seen a Rocky movie, not one—an innocent comment, a bald truth—but Nicky found this status untenable. Maddie countered that she didn't care if she ever saw them—too much violence, she said— and Nicky and Vincent declared that her current state of ignorance could not be allowed to continue. No, Nicky said, this could not stand: Rocky was a cultural icon! Could Maddie even call herself an American? And he rented a VCR and the three videos for the occasion.

All the others fell asleep after midnight, just after the third movie began, and Maddie was left to watch the hero duke it out with Mr. T. on her own. She was so enthralled with the boxer at this point that she was unaware of her solitude until the movie finished, when she turned to see Nicky and Amy fast asleep, nestled like spoons on the sofa, his hand resting over hers on the quiet swell of her pregnant stomach. And Vincent, wedged next to Maddie in the recliner, slept with his face turned toward her.

She had sat for a moment and studied the geography of that face: the long, straight bridge of his nose and the curve of his dark eyelashes on the tender skin beneath his eyes. His mouth—the lower lip fuller than the upper one, his high cheekbones. He had a white scar, barely visible, that cut across the pores on his left cheek, from a tumor, he'd told her, that had appeared when he was seven years old. It was benign, and Vincent didn't remember what reason, if any, the doctor had given for its sudden presence on his face. But they had removed it easily enough; he scarcely remembered the details, in fact.

Maddie had felt almost possessive about that scar. Other than his mother, she thought she might be the only person in the world who could see it, who got close enough to trace its faint white presence dividing his face at a cross angle to the line of his nose. We don't get close enough to most people to know them like this, she thought, to understand the topography of the skin or to learn the landscape of a face.

So how could she mistake Charlie Reynolds—whom she'd dated so briefly—for this boy she had known when he was seventeen?

⸺ ∞ ⸺

Maddie had a hard time falling asleep that night. It was a weeknight; they were both tired. Frank had fallen asleep almost instantly, and Maddie was glad for him and slightly jealous all at once. She lay there in the faint glow of the alarm clock and listened to him breathe.

Certainly the Petersons' news didn't bother her: Mrs. Peterson's report—and Mr. Peterson's nodding agreement—that they had seen Vincent Elander, that he was very well, married with three children and working for an accounting firm in Pittsburgh. It was fine news, normal news. It was not, in fact, news at all. Except for the fact that it had only been a week or two before that they had seen him.

Was this what unsettled her? The imagined proximity? She and Frank lived 500 miles away. And besides, Vincent Elander and family could live anywhere they pleased. It made no difference to Maddie.

Or was it the proximity of time that was somehow alarming? This person who was years removed, in terms of her history, had apparently progressed along with the rest of the world into the 21$^{st}$ century, had continued on with sleeping and waking and eating and so had arrived—along with the Petersons—in a shopping mall one day just a week or two before.

Lying there in the near-dark, Maddie felt encroached upon.

She told herself she was being irrational. She reminded herself, moreover, that none of this mattered at all.

And yet her vague unease and sleeplessness persisted. The minutes slid by, time Maddie filled with heedless visits to long-neglected history and innumerable looks at the clock. Although she lay safely in her bed, Maddie nonetheless perceived a terrible instability beneath her. It was as if, treading carelessly in a field, she found her footing uncertain. Instead of grass and solid earth beneath her, she had slid suddenly on gravel that had given way and poured out from under her feet. As if she had stumbled upon the edge of a well, an invisible and deep space surrounded by stones.

She moved closer to the sleeping Frank, pressing herself against his body, and was gratified by his impulse, even when sleeping, to wrap an arm over her. But the precarious sense of sliding stone continued, as if the edge of the mattress were the edge of the well.

Maddie didn't sleep until sometime after three a.m., and even then it was with a continued disquiet. She focused on Frank's steady breathing; she stroked the familiar hairs of his forearm. And as she drifted into sleep, she told herself that she had slid but hadn't fallen, that she could sit and catch her breath at the edge of the abyss and listen—for days, it seemed—to hear the loosened stones hit the bottom.

# 2

*T*he lump, when she found it, was small. Like a raisin or smaller; a dried currant, only firmer; like a cherry pit, only less uniform in shape. Maddie stood dripping in the bathtub, the shower turned off, the curtain flung open, her voice breaking as she called Frank to come, come feel this, did he feel it, too?

She waited anxiously—not breathing—to hear his verdict: nothing was there. She stood on the edge of his answer, knowing he wouldn't lie, her mind not yet—still not yet—embarking on the journey it might imminently take: she was fine.

He felt her breast and was detached, she thought, almost clinical in the way he probed for the lump, his eyes focused somewhere toward the ceiling, to where wall and ceiling met, maybe, trying to see with his fingers what she had discovered. Yes, he felt it, and immediately he took her in his arms and so had to find another shirt to put on for work, as the one he was wearing became soaked by her wet body, her wet hair. He had held her for a long time, saying nothing, waiting for her to speak, perhaps. And then finally, when she didn't, he drew from some reservoir of confidence that he wasn't entirely certain was there and told her it would be okay.

The appointment was scheduled, a biopsy discussed, the possibilities alluded to and then put down. No need to worry about it before we know anything. Why worry? It's probably nothing. You are far too young for this. Maddie steeled herself to believe him. Frank's strength, for now, would have to be enough for both of them.

And so the rest of the day was a matter of warding things off, of dodging the thoughts that flew at her like wild things, like wild, ravenous birds she had seen in a movie once. She called Frank countless times at work: Don't worry, Maddie. Don't worry. Whatever it is, we'll face it together.

For now, for the course of the day, Maddie was very much alone. How should she confront this unknowing, this waiting, except to counter it with a rational response? Should she tell herself that it is a gland, swollen? A duct, infected? The doctors will look and find nothing. They will diagnose it away. Or, after pre-school, when Garrett would be quietly watching a video on the living room sofa and the other boys still at school, should she go to her bed and let the wild thoughts come and then give in to crying? Or should she sit silently, not crying, a study in abject terror?

⁂

Frank pushed his chair away from the desk and leaned back, stretching his arms over his head. It was always a challenge to concentrate at this point in the writing stage, but today it was far worse. He had hated leaving Maddie that morning—despite her insistence that he go in, her reassurance that she'd be fine, that she had plenty to distract her. Already she had called him twice, and he could hear her trying to sound brave, apologizing—as if she needed to, as if she would ever need to—for interrupting him. No matter how she had protested, he thought, he should have stayed home. He should have worked from home today.

He told himself it wasn't time to get up: he knew without counting that he hadn't yet written 400 words. At 400 words—even if he was in the middle of a sentence—he could get his third cup of coffee. It was a firm line he drew for himself when he first started working as a journalist, and he wasn't about to break it over this column, a little weekday number about high school soccer.

Frank gazed briefly at the small paragraphs on the screen, then closed his eyes and made a silent guess: 332. He leaned forward again and hit the keyboard, getting the official count: 348. Mixed reaction: glad he underestimated and disappointed that he had more than 50 words to go. 400 words. That was the goal. The office coffee wasn't very good, but at least it gave him something to do.

Meanwhile the cursor blinked steadily at him. Some might call it rhythmic, but Frank found it mind numbing. His deadline was 1 p.m., and it was now going on 10:15. The lucid cleverness with which he had sketched the column in his head last night (while doing dishes, while playing catch with the boys) had understandably dissolved, draining from him like so much bathwater as he had stood holding Maddie after her shower. She was a strong woman, but that morning as he held her naked and dripping, Frank had felt acutely aware of the smallness of her frame. When she folded her arms against his chest and tucked her head into his shoulder, his arms had easily spanned her back. He had grasped his own elbows behind her.

The column, he thought, trying again. He was sure it had something to do with the history of the term "off-sides," but whatever specific link it once held to this piece was gone.

Of course, they should make no assumptions. The lump certainly did not spell disaster. Even if it was cancer—and it almost certainly was not cancer; what were the chances?—it would certainly be treatable. Almost certainly.

At any rate, there was no need to get ahead of themselves here. The appointment was tomorrow, which was soon enough. There was no need to make more of this until they knew for certain what they were up against.

Fifty-two words before that second cup of coffee, and after that he would need to write a good 200 more before he could begin to know the shape of the thing. That's how writing worked, he knew: you spit the words out and then you ground them down, picking the best ones, throwing away the bulk of it. With writing, Frank thought to himself, you had to make your own building materials before getting down to the building itself. Tedious discipline and necessary process: there was no way of getting around it.

But this morning, discipline was hard to come by. His attention was snagged again and again by the black-and-white photo on his desk: Maddie reading to the boys. They were on the sofa together,

Garrett on his mother's lap, Eli sitting on her left and Jake, standing on the sofa cushions, on her right. All three of the boys looked unsmiling at the camera, their gazes just lifted from engrossed attention to the book. Only Maddie was seen in near-profile, her head still bent to the page, mouth open, reading, the photo snapped mid-sentence.

Today that familiar photograph could nearly bring Frank to tears. Today he felt acutely, uniquely absorbed in love for his wife, and he focused for a moment on the slenderness of her bare arm in the photograph, imagined he saw the freckle above her left elbow that was invisible in the photo but that he knew was there.

And in his memory he saw Maddie, cold and dripping, standing in the bathtub with fear in her eyes. In the back of his mind there echoed those conversations he'd had with Father Tim about "living the dream," those late-night basketball-shooting conversations in the light of the alleyway lamp. He and Tim would head out there in the cold and dark in their sweat suits. The ball wasn't so loud on the packed earth of the alley, and around shooting balls at the hoop, Tim had painted the picture of what a marriage could be: best friends, thick-as-thieves, an almost other-worldly union of body, mind, and soul. How the couple would be young together, would grow old together, would make a life out of working through tough times together.

Maddie's appointment was tomorrow.

———— ⚭ ————

She decided that she wouldn't take Garrett home after pre-school. She had been home all morning, rattling around the house with the thoughts that rattled in her head. Perhaps being out was the thing she needed, something to distract her from the uninformed fears she had been entertaining all morning.

They went out to lunch—she and her four-year-old boy—eating fast food that he loved and that she fretted over. She tried to lose herself in his pre-school prattle, his short-term delight over the toy that came with his meal. And inwardly she scolded herself again and again for her distraction: she didn't hear much of what he'd said for competing thoughts of diagnosis and treatment, words like prognosis.

She realized it had been months since she had taken Garrett to the playground, but the weather was growing warmer. It was a sunny afternoon. They could wait there for his brothers to finish school.

Maddie sat in the shade and watched Garrett playing, first digging in the sandbox and then navigating the lowest rungs of the jungle gym. She listened as he negotiated the use of a toy dump truck with a little girl she'd never seen before. And she remembered there had been times like this with the other boys when they had been Garrett's age and younger.

Without working to summon the memory, she saw Jake, age two, legs spread wide, feet braced against the edges of the slide to slow his descent. Maddie hadn't been able to help him. She had sat on the bench opposite, nursing a colicky Eli, coaching her cautious toddler from the sidelines.

When he reached the bottom of the slide, Jake hadn't acknowledged his mother with a grin or sat still for a moment in contented relief. Instead he had taken off immediately for other adventures, making his way to the see-saw, where he stood for a moment in mute admiration of two older children playing there. Maddie had fixed her gaze on him, watching his brown head and blue jacket move among the other children.

That was the day she'd imagined she was knitting—though she had never actually learned how. But she had imagined that she could, and that as she sat, her knitting needles clicked in her hands, binding together the softest yarn into a ribbon and then a square, and then an oblong sheet that grew so long it fell to her feet. Still she knitted, calmly, efficiently, so that the blanket (for this is what it was) pooled onto the ground and then, by the force of her knitting, began to move away from her and toward her son where he sat in the sandbox or walked toward the swing. This great blanket of her affection followed him over the playground, flowing up the ladder behind him and then piling around him as he sat on the platform at the top. It followed him down the slide, too, and she could see in her mind's eye the way that it surrounded his torso and flowed over his legs that, once again, he used to brace his body against gravity. Such was her love for this child, and such was the way that she willed it to cover him.

Sitting watching Garrett, a lump newly discovered in her breast, Maddie again summoned the image of the blanket. It flowed after her son over the playground, it flowed through the fence-gate toward the parking lot, it flowed into the school and found her other sons, who any minute now would be dismissed.

◦◦◦

It was after midnight. Frank had planned to call sometime after work, but ended up waiting until Maddie was asleep. Now he stood at their back door and looked into the darkness of the yard. He could make out the legs of the swing set and the saddles of the swings, but beyond that the lawn receded into nothing. There was no moon. The light from the door where he stood fell in the pattern of windowpanes down the steps, and there in the middle was his own distorted shadow—recognizable shoulders and torso, a head, a phone held to the ear. Beneath the door's window hung his other hand, gripping a glass of scotch.

He had already decided what he wouldn't do when calling The Priest: he wouldn't chat him up, wouldn't catch up about things, wouldn't describe what the kids were doing and then, just when it was time to hang up, mention that Maddie had found a lump in her breast. He would come out with it cleanly. He would tell him how it went with Maddie all day and evening and about the planned visit to the doctor tomorrow and how he was sure it was nothing, but God, he's a little scared.

The conversation went well. Just hearing Tim's voice on the other end shored up in Frank the calm he'd been trying to impart to Maddie all day. And what else could The Priest bring him, really? He couldn't administer a miracle through the phone lines, but he reminded him that perhaps this time a miracle wasn't needed.

He repeated to Frank the welcome, if overused, reminder that God is good, and he told Frank to get some sleep and to be sure and call him after they'd seen the doctor.

Frank felt immeasurably better after this. He took in the last gulp of his scotch and forgot the feeling he had earlier, that sense he'd had, coming home in traffic, of being about to enter a tunnel, a long and winding tunnel whose other end was someplace new and conceivably terrifying, a place he'd never meant to go. No, now he knew he'd be able to sleep, and he was glad, when he climbed into bed next to his wife, to see that she was already sleeping soundly.

Once upon a time when she was a child, Maddie had watched Matthew, her friend Justine's younger brother, suffer horribly in treatment for leukemia. From her perspective, Matthew's two-year battle with the disease was marked only by pain for Matthew and a terrible sadness for his family—a sadness that extended well beyond his death at age four. Maddie had considered that the brief years of his illness might have been better lived in ignorance. What if they had simply let the disease take its course?

The adult Maddie understood this to be foolishness. Of course the best approach was diagnosis and treatment. Who knew the efficacy of those painful treatments in also extending his life?

But she wondered, too, at the time that might elapse while in ignorance of disease—the carefree days one might enjoy before an illness took noticeable effect. One could, for a time, live with the reality of the disease without suffering from its realization, so to speak. A thing could be true without one having to reckon with it.

Take rain, for example. One could drink it, bathe in its overflow, close a window against its coming in without ever having to consider high or low-pressure weather systems, evaporation, condensation or the vital functions of the water cycle. The science of rain could be true and a person ignorant of it even while opening her umbrella.

And anyway life—and rain—brought so much to consider without science or other truths weighing in. The night she told Frank about Vincent, it was raining. And it was raining the night she and Vincent watched Willy get hit by a car. Rain, both times. Pure coincidence. If any larger truth inhered in this fact, Maddie had never been bothered to find it.

She remembered well how it went. For starters, there were the many retellings: Frank had been fascinated by the story from the first, and it wasn't uncommon for him, even now, after seventeen years of marriage, to ask for it again when at dinner with friends or the holiday office party, any time the conversation went the way of remarkable exes or the miraculous and strange. And, of course, Maddie obliged him. On the surface, at least, it was a great story and nothing more.

But even if Maddie hadn't rehearsed it for Frank dozens of times, even if she hadn't told it at the occasional party, she wouldn't be able to shake the memory if she tried.

Rain in torrents had ended the game. The management had made a valiant effort: multiple delays, the field covered with tarps. Fans, players, officials alike watched the sky, hoping the game could be resumed. But hours passed and the rain was unrelenting, and finally they had to give it over. Maddie and Vincent left the stadium together drenched, walking without umbrellas or jackets into the sodden night.

There was some light: glowing stadium, streetlights, ambient light of the city. And at the intersection was the light from the oncoming cars and the glow of their taillights behind them.

Still, they didn't see him right away. He came from the darker side of the street, and no one would have expected him. If you weren't one of the fans spilling from the stadium, why would you be out in this weather? And yet he came, stumbling and anonymous, his face obscured by the enormous hood of a mustard-colored parka. By the time they noticed him, he was already weaving his way across the intersection.

Maddie saw him still: the sleek wetness of his hood, his stumbling progress, the traffic that was against them and so had them all hanging back at the curb, waiting for the walk signal.

He had made it more than halfway to them when the car came from their left to round the bend. It wasn't going very fast, but it hit him with a screech of brakes and a loud and dreadful thump. The faceless figure bent a little bit and rolled up onto the car's hood, then slid to the ground.

Here, Maddie's audience would usually gasp: what a terrible thing to witness! What a dreadful accident! But Frank would silence this interruption with a raised finger and a slight smile. There was more.

Maddie continued: the figure didn't remain in a crumpled heap, but instead began immediately to uncoil. A hand and legs extended from it as it began to make its way into an upright position, reaching with one hand for the curb, then grasping Vincent's sneakers and then the leg of his jeans, reaching as if this frame were leverage by which to draw himself up.

And there was Vincent *not* stepping away from this man but

leaning forward to help him, bending forward at the waist as one might do to take up a small child. He grasped the crumpled figure by the upper arms and helped him to his feet.

In telling the story aloud, this was the part she would emphasize—and Frank, the writer, the real storyteller of the family, might break in to underscore it further: "The kid was holding the guy by the *arms*."

"Right. By the *arms*," she would repeat again with a knowing grin. She was nodding and complicit, fostering the story and Frank's clear enjoyment in it, pausing to let this moment have its full effect.

Maddie had no memory of the crowd, of the comments of onlookers; she only barely remembered how the car that had hit the man was now parked at the curb. She could see streaks of rain in its taillights. Was the car white? The driver had gotten out and was standing anxiously next to the climbing man. Was there mention of the police? Surely someone ought to have called the police.

Drawn fully now to his feet, the man gained identity. He was Willy, the homeless man, the one with the crippled arm who had accosted them earlier in the hopes of selling them tickets to a game they already had tickets for. He raised his chin and looked Vincent in the eye, with Vincent's hands still gripping him by the shoulders.

"Willy, you okay, man?" Vincent asked.

But Willy's only answer was to reach back, take hold of his flung-back hood, and pull it again over his face. He exhaled heavily, sounding as if being hit by a car in the dark rain was for him—what with all the climbing to his feet—a great bore or perhaps (and this did seem more likely) an exhausting enterprise. He exhaled directly into Vincent's face while seeming also to take no notice of him and then stepped up onto the curb only to continue walking, making his way through the waiting crowd as if it were nothing to be hit by a car. Nothing at all.

That was when Vincent turned to Maddie and said that that guy was seriously drunk. There was nothing more to the incident.

Here her audience invariably laughed: the group at the party, heads leaning in, faces alight; Frank, bemused, listening.

The inevitable question came: Had no one called the police? She herself had wondered this many times. Perhaps someone had done so, but she and Vincent, in their ignorance, had continued on their way without such responsible thoughts. What could she tell her fascinated listeners? The shock of it all had been enough. They were only children, really.

But they must have talked about it together, Maddie thought now. Surely they spoke to one another about it in low voices as they rode toward home in the trolley. They must have talked about it, because she was sure they both knew that it was Willy who had been hit by the car.

Which was why he had only used one arm as he had climbed to his feet.

She had asked Vincent about this; she recalled this part of the conversation—or did she reconstruct it, setting it there in the yellow glow of the trolley's interior as it made its lumbering way into the dark and drenched suburbs? Because she could see him—Vincent—sitting in his wet jeans and T-shirt beside her, and she asked him if he had known it was Willy coming toward them in the rain?

Vincent said he hadn't known it was him until Willy had looked him in the eyes and breathed all that alcohol into his face. He looked around the trolley car as he said this, not looking at Maddie because they were sitting side by side. She sat by the window and he held her hand; outside it was dark and wet, and all she could see was the occasional streetlight and the beaded water sliding down the pane.

⁂

The doctor said it wasn't a very big mass—only about one centimeter—but the biopsy was clear: it was cancer. Suddenly all the conversation was of treatment plans and radiation and chemotherapy. A lumpectomy, a mastectomy (Maddie gasped at the mention of it; Frank squeezed her hand); she'd have her lymph nodes out. The doctor wanted to do some scans to be sure that the cancer wasn't elsewhere. He would be sitting down to discuss her case with other doctors; they would decide together on the best course of treatment. And they had caught it early—very early. Good for her for doing her self-exams. Well done.

Maddie and Frank walked out into the day and, when Frank asked her how she felt, she said she didn't know. Stunned, maybe. That was the best word for it. Maddie knew nothing of the return to their car;

she felt she could take nothing in—not the feel of her feet in her own shoes. This news was enough to absorb for a day, enough to absorb for a month or longer, and already there was so much immediately ahead that was meaningless terminology: lymph system, CT scan, MRI. How to proceed in the vague unreality that was now to be her life?

Frank was talking. He hadn't thought it would be cancer; he really hadn't thought it would be.

Why not? Maddie suddenly answered aloud. What were the chances? No family history—but what difference does that make, honestly? They were far too happy. Things were going far too well. Of course the disaster must come to their family, the happy one, the family screaming for fate to hit them. It's like, in all our happiness and contentment, Maddie said, we'd volunteered for this.

Frank reached over and took her hand and reminded her quietly that it might not be that bad. We found it early, he reminded her. We'll get through this, he told her again.

Maddie said nothing more. For now there was the yard to face, the house, the sunlit kitchen. The maddening normalcy of the entire world lay cheerfully indifferent before her, immune to diagnosis and its terrors. Soon enough it would be time to get Garrett from school; soon enough it would be time to get Jake and Eli. She ought to call her mother. But all of the ensuing conversations would only make it more terrible: if no one talked about it, then surely it would be less true.

In the end, Frank was the one to handle all of that: telling her parents and his, The Priest, other friends and family. He did it gently, over a series of days. And as for their children, he said there was no sense in telling them more than they could handle or even understand. The five of them sat together on the living room sofa, Garrett in his father's lap, Jake and Eli flanked by their parents. The boys listened with interested expressions: Mommy was sick, but she was going to get better. It just might take some time. They departed from the conversation with the pleasant instruction to "go play."

Later, she considered her instant bitterness in the car, all of that anger about their happiness and fate. Frank had let it slide, eager, she thought, to soothe her, anxious to be of comfort, to let her respond with whatever shock this sudden grief might raise. All of it had been nonsense; both of them knew it. Cancer wasn't a weapon in fate's hands; this was no time to be feeling sorry for herself. She should move forward in strength; she should be optimistic. But Frank, wanting to be gentle with her, she supposed, hadn't said any of that.

Still the thought pricked at her. She thought there might be something to it. There was something to the notion of fate here, or maybe vengeance. Don't they say that everything happens for a reason? A kind of punishment, perhaps. How else to explain it? The ground shifting beneath her feet.

In any event, there it was: resolute fact. The certainty of the cancer rushed to the fore, obscuring everything else. Suddenly there were only possibilities that included cancer and its treatment, and for several days Maddie felt that the world had taken on an unaccustomed, terrible brilliance, its hard edges grown perilously sharp. For a time, thoughts of the future—both immediate and distant—were subsumed in the reality that was cancer. She could not remember anything having been so true as this.

---

The trolley in Pittsburgh's Bethel Hills leaves the parking lot near the mall and follows the line of the road. Small businesses and suburban shopping centers top hills and climb the rises here, but soon enough the trolley slips behind these and is lost in a tunnel entrance lined with cement blocks, and then the dark tunnel itself. On emerging again, the view is all backyards whose far reaches are bounded by the trolley line.

In her childhood days, Maddie had loved this: the surprise of the landscape's unfolding. What would lie behind that tree, beyond this rise, on the other side of the tunnel? It was delightful variance; each emergence meant new and sudden insight, all of it life-sized. But from the vantage point of the trolley, these yards and houses were magically diminished, somehow taking on the properties of the miniature. She liked to imagine that she herself had shrunk and climbed into the electric train display her father had once taken her to see, the one where the track ran through the artificial green grass and was here and there bordered by plastic trees; the one where the little houses had the occasional plastic dog or person in the front yard, and the houses, though small, were lit by electric light.

The houses from the perspective of the trolley gained this quality of stillness, of waiting to be seen, of having been prepared for this moment when the trolley would go sliding past. So whether the yard was newly mown or had, at the back, a neatly stacked pile of firewood, a swing set, or some things discarded—an old bicycle perhaps, a broken ladder, a pile of indistinguishable and clearly unused rubbish—Maddie imagined it whole and entire, established and set just so: this was how it was intended to be seen. A decoration, a life imagined, something distinct and safe, set apart just for the looking.

The houses were old and generally tired, but many were well-kept nonetheless. Yellow brick predominated here after the aluminum siding of her neighborhood, yellow and red brick and slate roofs. And then another tunnel, perhaps, and the green slope of a nearby hillside that, along with a row of trees, obscured the backyards and would have kept her guessing, except that there wasn't time to guess, there was only the next thing to see, which was that now the houses were closer together, or here they were in what almost looked like the city but really was the suburbs more grown-up. So now there were storefronts with apartments above them, a bar replete with neon sign in the window, little restaurants, a tailor, a store for coin and stamp collectors, and all of it in yellow or red brick or very tired-looking aluminum siding. And everywhere, at every corner, the gray concrete of sidewalk, the black pavement, the cars lining the streets, and weeds and grass and gravel collected in the cracks between.

It all went by quickly enough; here was nothing permanent. It was a memory composed of impressions. That Pittsburgh's suburbs should be spread like a wrinkled skirt on the other side of the mountain was nothing at all remarkable; every city might be like this. But there was always the last, dark tunnel, the long one at the nearly end, when they went through the mountain and then emerged into downtown—into the narrow, flat strip abutting water, and then the river, and then the city itself. That much Maddie knew or thought she knew—that and the day when she and her parents took the trolley into the city in the early autumn of her junior year and Maddie, fixed as ever to the view outside her window, saw the pedestrians going by and saw among them Willy, the man who had been struck by the car.

This was where she would resume the story, the miracle tale that Frank loved her to tell. It was months later, she would explain, and she really only caught a glimpse of him from the trolley window, but there he was: Willy, unmistakable. It was fall now, cool, and Maddie noticed first the mustard-colored parka as it moved down the sidewalk. She studied the figure wearing it as the trolley approached, observed the dirty blond hair, recognized the rapid walk. And as the trolley neared him, she watched for his face—the same set and focused gaze, staring straight ahead. Willy was pushing something—what?—a cart, something piled with garbage bags. But what held Maddie's gaze was Willy's arms: both of them straight and strong.

She would remind her small audience of the crippled arm, the muscles' obvious atrophy; the preceding year or two during which Vincent had seen him multiple times, always in the same impaired state; the clear unlikelihood of medical intervention for a person like Willy; the inability, at that time or even now, for medical science to improve such a condition.

The glimpse had been fleeting even though she did what she could to hold it, sitting up in her seat and twisting round to stare at his disappearing figure. The bags on the cart were not so high as to obscure his hands: she saw them, well and whole—both arms, both hands, fingers strong and wrapped around the cart's handle.

# 3

*T*hey were going in very early for the surgery, but Maddie was awake before the alarm went off. She didn't think she had slept at all; she hadn't slept much in the days and weeks between her diagnosis and this surgery. After this, she thought and had been telling herself. Things would be better after this. After this, they would know where they stood. The cancer would be out; it would be a simple process of discouraging it from ever returning again. She just needed to get through this.

Before the alarm sounded, Maddie reached over and shut it off. Frank stirred and turned over. She sat on the edge of the bed in the dark and marveled at his ability to sleep. Then she went into the bathroom.

The water was warm but still shocking: wet on a body that wanted to be dry, stimulating to a body that needed to sleep. Frank had encouraged her the night before to sleep later: Why get up so early tomorrow? You need your rest.

But he didn't really know that she hadn't been sleeping at all anyway. What is the point of lying there, thinking? And she wanted to get up early. She wanted to shower and do her makeup and hair and present herself to her surgeons in the best possible light. If she wasn't going down without a fight—and she wasn't—there was no need to be less than vigilant here in the first battle.

She showered, she shaved her legs, she washed her hair, and she allowed herself, for the first time since she discovered it, to feel for the lump. From the time of her diagnosis, she hadn't felt for it again until now. The doctors knew it was there, and Frank had felt it too. What was the point of palpating it again, of closing her fingers once more around that tiny knot?

What if it's gone, she wondered? Hadn't she heard of stories like this before, of bodies riddled with cancer that, when opened on the operating table, were clean? Patients presenting with all sorts of problems and then, tests run, showing themselves to be pictures of perfect health.

The water streamed down her face, the pressure of the water ran over the lashes of her right eye. The lump would be gone now, she imagined, but she wouldn't tell Frank. Let them put her out, put her under the knife, and let the doctor tell an amazed Frank, while she was still coming out of her anesthesia, that Maddie was clean, that they couldn't find the lump, that his wife didn't have cancer after all.

Standing there in the shower, she envisioned Frank sitting next to her in a sun-washed hospital room, and she opened her eyes, and Frank was smiling and telling her there had been a mistake, that she didn't have cancer—that it was a swollen lymph node and, by the time they'd gotten in there, the swelling had disappeared and she was perfectly healthy.

But Maddie reached for it and the lump was there. She would finish her shower and get dressed. She would do her makeup and her hair and she would wake Frank, and while he was getting dressed, she would walk silently into the boys' rooms and kiss their heads. Jake would be sweating, and his hair would be plastered against his forehead. Eli would be lying on his back with his face turned toward the wall, and Maddie would have to lean over to reach his cheek. Garrett would be curled on his side, and when she kissed him, he would tuck up his legs just a little bit and his thumb would find its way back into his mouth.

In the kitchen she checked again to be sure that her list was on the table. She had typed it out for her mother, describing the boys' routines and their favorite dishes and snacks and what they were allowed to watch on television. Her mother, arrived two days ago from Pittsburgh, would already be up, wrapped in her bathrobe and leaning against the counter, waiting to see them off. She would put her arms around her daughter, and she would hesitate only for a moment before beginning her audible prayer. Her voice would break only a little as she asked for God's protection, for wisdom for the doctors, for her daughter's complete healing from cancer.

The prayer over, Maddie would not need to resist any urge to cross herself: even after all these years, the old ways remained familiar. Then the two of them would talk for a few minutes while waiting for Frank to appear, and when he did, he would carry her bag for her and together they would go out to the car. Frank would not eat anything because he knew Maddie wasn't allowed any food before the surgery and, to whatever extent it was possible, he wanted her to know that he was with her, that they were in this together.

⁂

Her mother liked Frank, but it wasn't always that way. She had held a grudge against him for a while, believing him to be a frat-boy, party-animal, state-school kind of guy, and Maddie had some work to do in convincing her otherwise. But some stories are too good to be true, and maybe that was why her mother couldn't believe it at first when Maddie told her that she'd met Frank in the library.

It was the beginning of her second semester at college. He worked in the media department and she'd had to do a paper on propaganda during World War II. Frank had helped her locate a few newsreels and then held her in conversation, pushing his glasses up with his forefinger as he turned his head and pointed her in the direction of the microfilm desk. He'd asked her out some time later, after she borrowed some films by Leni Riefenstahl, and she'd been completely caught off guard. She had fumbled around until she hit upon a way to say no: she had a test on Monday that was going to be huge; she would be studying all weekend (*All* weekend? Really? Not even time for dinner? After seventeen years of marriage, Frank still teased her about it).

Of course, what she couldn't have told her mother was that detail about the conversation in the bar—that shouting match over the band's din that convinced Maddie to give Frank another chance. She couldn't tell her mother about that until later.

But at bottom, Maddie knew that her mother's resentment—and, indeed, her father's initial caution—was Frank's Catholicism, which made no difference at all to Maddie. And, thinking further, this was ultimately her explanation to Frank himself: her parents were disappointed that she wasn't "taking her faith seriously." Catholicism, they felt, wasn't taken seriously by anybody. Catholics just pick and choose when they go to Mass, they said; they squeeze it in on a Saturday evening, getting it out of the way before they spent the rest of the night drinking, sleeping in (and sleeping it off) on a Sunday morning. They felt that her interest in Frank despite his Catholicism was symptomatic of Maddie's "backslidden" status, of her disinterest in God.

Frank's response to this was baffled amusement. Catholics don't use words like "backslidden," and Catholics are Christians, does your mother know this? Catholics were the first Christians, for Pete's sake. And also, of course you do take your faith seriously, don't you, Maddie. The last bit coming as more of a statement than a question, to which Maddie had responded nonetheless: yes.

More privately still, Maddie realized that all of this was symptomatic of her parents' resistance to change. They hoped that, having started a family, Frank and Maddie would be like themselves: attending a Protestant, evangelical, even fundamentalist church, and gathering with the faithful at said church every time the doors were open: Sunday morning for two hours and again on Sunday night for one and again on Wednesday evening for the prayer meeting, not to mention the bridal showers and baby showers and all other events in-between. But Maddie knew better. It was unreasonable to think that life could carry on like this for her own family, and unreasonable, too, to go to church so often. She liked it that Catholics—many of them, anyway—went once a week: confession and Mass, said and done.

In truth, Maddie felt there was something refined and tidy about Catholicism, something less-than-filled with expectation that had its appeal. To be sure, there was the incense, the sing-song sort of chanting, the statues and icons that lent an air of mysticism to one's basic Sunday morning (or Saturday evening) experience—an air so different from anything she had known at the Bethel Hills Church of Holiness. But there was something, too, that she found less intrusive about the Catholic faith, as if Catholics understood something more about God than other people did: that He was doing His own thing and was, for the most part, letting you do yours. Maddie had observed and felt strongly and honestly preferred that, with the Catholics, God was never on the brink of getting involved.

He was forever getting involved with the people of the Holiness Church. Or they expected him to, anyway.

---

By the end of the fourth grade, Maddie had memorized the knots in the pine ceiling of the church sanctuary. Had she been old enough or perhaps a more artistic child, she might have appreciated their beauty, too: the parallel blond planks, the dark veins and swirls of the timber. She might have admired the modern austerity of the room's architecture, a Puritanical plainness influenced by a 1960's sensibility surfacing in modest touches: narrow windows glazed in amber glass, white cylindrical light fixtures where, in another building, with a different aesthetic, one might expect chandeliers.

But these thoughtful details were lost on her. Instead, her powers of observation were put to preventing boredom. During the long Sunday evening services, she counted rather than admired the light fixtures. Lying down the length of a pew, her head in her mother's lap, she studied ceiling planks and traced constellations among the knots in the wood. She knew she was too old to be lying down during church by the time she hit fifth grade, and shortly after that she knew without looking that there were sixteen ceiling planks between the far wall and the first support beam, and then sixteen more to the next. She guessed this was the pattern throughout, but here again maturity prevented her turning around and craning her neck to count them, so she focused her energies on the number of pews or people in them, the number of hymnals per row, the number of Christmas hymns (or Easter hymns or Thanksgiving hymns) in the hymnal.

It was here, during the Sunday evening service, that the Holiness belief in God's imminent involvement reached its feverish pitch. Every week, the sermon wound to its emotional conclusion. The organ began to throb the quiet strains of a familiar hymn. And then the pastor made his plea: that anyone—anyone at all—who felt the need to draw close to God come to the altar to pray.

Pause. Collectively, the congregation made an almost indiscernible turn from passive and listening receptivity to one of poised expectation. The room took on a silence distinct from that experienced during the sermon, which was one that accepted cleared throats, shifted weight, or whisperings, and instead became gravid and still. The organ's intonation continued, and the pastor rephrased: If you feel a need of God—any need at all—just slip out of your pew and come forward.

This was the part Maddie dreaded, for who could know how long the wait might be? The movement of God's Holy Spirit was, at best, unpredictable. Sometimes a dozen or so came forward, sometimes only two or three. Sometimes the needy ones came forward immediately, and sometimes multiple hymns were required to elicit a response. Meanwhile, the organ poured forth one hymn after the other in plodding succession, dying down at the end and then, just when Maddie thought it was over, resurging with yet another refrain.

She was young—maybe nine?—when she learned to hope against God's involvement in this portion of the service. Her ideal Sunday would find the congregation sated by the sermon, joining their voices in a single, upbeat closing hymn, and making their way to the parking lot within five minutes.

Unfortunately, someone nearly always did feel a need for God, and then a new kind of waiting began, for the custom was that the entire congregation sat it out, presumably praying along in their seats, until the one or ones at the altar were finished. And some pray-ers needed more time than others.

For a time, Maddie could and did find in this a distraction: guessing what the praying might be for. A transgression against one's neighbor, a spat with a spouse—these might only require a few minute's kneeling before the red-eyed return to one's seat. But larger issues—long-term battles against pride or lasciviousness maybe, the release of one's soul to the saving powers of Jesus—these could take a very long time indeed.

Some of the needs were relatively obvious. There was Mr. Taylor, grossly overweight, at risk of losing his left leg to amputation and diabetes. For a time, Mr. Meyers could be expected at the altar because he'd lost his job, and it was understandable to see Mrs. Wahler up there because her husband had left her for his secretary. And there was Susan Sweet, a young woman in her early twenties, possessed of an awkward gait due to a birth defect. She might pray for her leg to be healed or for a husband—both were fair guesses.

That people like these should be praying out in the open was, to Maddie, somewhat reasonable. But there were weeks, too, when it seemed—for some precious, hopeful moments— that the altar would remain empty.

Except for Mr. Gillece—and Maddie would swear to you even now that Mr. Gillece was kneeling at that altar every blessed Sunday night. He really was. It got to the point that she would count, eyes closed, to see how long it would take Mr. Gillece to make his way to the front.

She liked Mr. Gillece. As was true with almost everyone in their small congregation, she had known him all her life. From all she could see, he was a successful and happy man: two healthy children, an apparently happy marriage, a successful business career, good health. He was always friendly, greeting her by name, sometimes chatting with her father after church, doing his part by serving as an usher on Sunday mornings. So his weekly Sunday evening vigils mystified her. What could he possibly be praying about? What was the issue that had to be raised again and again with the Almighty, as if He might have forgotten, from week to week, whatever it was that drove Mr. Gillece to his knees right in front of everybody?

This irritation incited her, with all the daring she could muster, to ask John Gillece about it once. She was in the fifth grade at the time, and John was in seventh—a significant difference in age that Maddie felt keenly. But this was also the height of her annoyance with Mr. Gillece's prayers, and John Gillece was kind of an awkward kid, so it was with some boldness that she asked John flat-out about it one Sunday morning after church, when a bunch of the kids were hanging out on the rusting swing set over on the parsonage lawn.

"Why does your dad pray so much?" she had said to John from the swing, calling him into dialogue with her when they had been minding their separate business.

"What do you mean?" John answered.

31

"On Sunday nights, at the end of church. Why does he always go up front and pray?"

John's face had reddened, and Maddie detected within herself a rising confidence. She had not anticipated his embarrassment, and now it occurred to her that John was harboring a family secret. Perhaps she was on the verge of discovering something; perhaps John would come out with it.

"What do you mean?" John said again, faltering. Other kids around them were noting the conversation.

"I mean he always goes forward for the altar call." She was pleased by the attentive listeners who, she suddenly imagined, might also be irritated by Mr. Gillece's insistent praying. "Why does he do that? Why does he need to do that? Every time?" Somehow, adding the "need" to her question empowered her further; it suddenly and clearly made her father superior to John's father; it even made her superior to John. John looked weak. The whole Gillece family looked weak, and Maddie was more successful than she had imagined, and she pumped her legs harder on the swing.

John stammered and fell silent.

It's probable that Maddie would have forgotten this conversation, along with countless other childhood conversations in which she exerted subtle domination over others. But this conversation was burned in her memory due to Mrs. Gillece's sudden and dismaying presence. Unknown to Maddie, Mrs. Gillece had been coming up behind Maddie to call John to go home.

"What was it you were asking, Maddie?" she asked.

On hearing her voice, Maddie suddenly grew hot—and this despite the near constant breeze from the swinging. "I just asked John a question," she said, all innocence.

"What was it you wanted to know?"

Maddie considered silence: What would happen if she said nothing? She pumped her legs.

"Maddie," Mrs. Gillece said. Maddie had to answer.

"I just wanted to know why Mr. Gillece always goes up to the altar to pray," Maddie said, and she was glad that the swing kept carrying her away from Mrs. Gillece so that she didn't have to look at her face.

Mrs. Gillece responded with the same patient tone she had used since she appeared on the parsonage lawn.

"Prayer is a conversation between a person and God," she said, "and so I guess you could say that this is none of your business." She said it gently enough, but Maddie felt the reprimand. She had been put in her place, and before so many witnesses, which left her no option other than to scud her swing to an almost halt and walk away without saying a word.

She had a hard time talking to—or even looking at—Mrs. Gillece for a long time after that, while Mr. Gillece persisted in his weekly vigils, which now managed to incite guilt in Maddie along with the original irritation.

By the time she was in high school, she was relatively sure that Mrs. Gillece had forgotten the incident, though recalling it still made her insides twist. Occasionally she found herself in mental discourse with Mr. and Mrs. Gillece or John or even Pastor McLaughlin, presenting a kind of defense: she wouldn't deny anyone the opportunity to pray. She knew that praying was a good thing. But why make everyone else wait it out? The altar call extended the Sunday evening service to unpredictable and sometimes dreadful lengths. People have to work and go to school on Monday morning. Perhaps Mr. Gillece—and the others—could do some of their praying at home, or more privately, at the very least?

She rehearsed this many times in her head, but never voiced it to John Gillece or anyone else. She feared her practical argument would ultimately be indefensible. For what was there to doubt in such focused and fervent prayer? Certainly God loved prayer like this: the humility, the kneeling, the apparently earnest emotion that so often seemed to accompany those bent at the altar. More precious still the members of the congregation who, moved by compassion or God Himself, left their seats to pray for and with the one so kneeling. Moreover, she should want these people to come forward for prayer. She should be actively praying for the people who were praying themselves. She should consider going forward herself—at the very least in repentance for bullying John Gillece—except that she couldn't bear the thought of the exposure.

And she couldn't imagine—or understand—what would come of it.

But if she had needed convincing of God's genuine involvement in all of this, then there was that singular Sunday night to show for it, sometime in the spring of her sophomore year of high school, the night that Vincent Elander came to church.

She hadn't seen him come in. Neither did she notice him right away when the service began. But somehow in the course of things—maybe when they all stood to sing the first hymn?—she saw him there across the aisle, just a row in front of hers. She had a clear shot of his profile, and the moment of recognition was a spasm through her core.

Vincent Elander. She would recognize him anywhere. The football quarterback, the baseball team's star pitcher, heartthrob crush of most of her friends freshman year—until each of them realized with a slowly dawning despondence that he was fixedly out of her league. As a freshman, he had been the starting quarterback. As a sophomore, he had steadily and somewhat predictably—except for the age difference—dated the captain (a *senior*) of the cheerleading squad. The best parties always included him. Recognition by him—no matter how small the acknowledgement—was the quickest route to the fast crowd. The most intriguing rumors—imparted to her by the all-knowing Justine—always included his name in its cast of characters.

Now Maddie was wrapping up her sophomore year and he was ending his junior, and if she was certain of anything at all in life, it was that Vincent Elander had no idea of her existence. Yet here he sat in the fifth row on the left-hand side of the Bethel Hills Church of Holiness on a Sunday evening. Moreover, he was alone, a truth almost as strange as his presence, because Vincent was always surrounded by a coterie of friends and friends of friends, ex-girlfriends and hopefuls. Tonight he was an island, alone in a pew that had, otherwise, four hymnals to show for it.

Maddie was stunned. How had he come to be here? Had someone invited him? His solitude argued against that. Then what was he doing here? How had he come to choose—of all available Sunday evening church services in Pittsburgh's Bethel Hills—hers? Her persistent disbelief brought nothing to bear on the situation. Vincent was unmistakably present. Certainly she could get confirmation from Justine.

Except that Justine wasn't there. She had given up Sunday evening church some months ago. After years of church-twice-on-Sundays, Justine had told her parents, the pastor, Maddie, and anyone she perceived might question her decision that twice a week was enough. Which meant that Sunday nights were out.

And now here sat Vincent Elander. How could Maddie ever get Justine to believe this?

She spent the remainder of the sermon convincing herself, casting careful looks in Vincent's direction, taking care that they were balanced with looks elsewhere: the ceiling, the preacher, even her hands. Meanwhile, it seemed nothing could distract Vincent from the church service—not even the prolonged crying of little Tony Martin, whose mother finally carried him out of the sanctuary. But Vincent never even turned his head at the height of that ruckus, when half of the congregation watched Tony's red-faced departure from the room. Instead, Vincent seemed fully focused, taking part in singing hymns and then, when the preaching began, never shifting his gaze from the pastor's face.

Maddie began to entertain the options, trying to figure out what drew him: he was here to do research, some assignment from sociology class; or—horrifying and far more believable—he was here on a dare, a strange bet of some kind. It was all a huge joke, and later he would laugh about it with his friends: the hymns, the standing, the sitting, the preaching, the wails of Tony Martin, the endless altar call.

She resolved that she would need to escape quickly after the service. If Vincent Elander were ever going to recognize her, it couldn't possibly happen tonight. If he saw her tonight, if she were to register at all in his wonderful mind, it would most certainly be as "that girl from that church that one time," an identity that would brand her in a most undesirable way, almost as ignominious as if she'd been wearing glasses, or straight hair, or bell-bottomed jeans.

For perhaps the first time in her life, Maddie wished that the Sunday evening service would not come to an end. As the pastor reached his sermon's conclusion, she felt her palms grow sweaty and her heart begin to pound. She supposed she could exit the pew on the far side of the aisle and avoid eye contact. She would have to urge her parents out in that direction too, hastening them before her with no explanation, and then she would make for the exit and wait for them at the car. It felt like terrible cowardice, but also her only option.

With dismay, she realized that the hymns had begun. The pastor was making the first entreaty, inviting anyone who might think he needed Jesus to just step out of the pew and come forward. Maddie stole a long look at Vincent, watching for a tell-tale smirk, but he sat as before: straight, still, inscrutable.

Then a new hymn surged from the organ and the pastor made the next appeal. This Sunday night ritual that she had always found annoying had just become an embarrassment. Maddie rolled her eyes and buried her face in her hands. In all of the Sunday nights she had endured, never had there been one as dreadful as this. She stole another look at Vincent, just between her fingers, wondering how he was managing.

He was gone.

He'd had enough; Maddie was sure of it. She turned to watch him walking away down the far aisle, but he'd already left the room. That was fast. He might be halfway to the parking lot by now. He might have reached his car.

Maddie felt envy, and also sweet relief. She returned her gaze to her hands, folded in her lap. He hadn't seen her; she hadn't been recognized. Her greatest fears went unrealized.

And then the sounds began—sounds of committed crying, somewhat akin to those of Tony Martin, but deeper, and adolescent in their breaking. The crying was enclosed somehow, coming to the congregation as out of a tunnel, the cries of a young man in the throes of grief. It was a horrible sound, a second shock on what had become a very surprising Sunday evening. Involuntarily, Maddie looked around to see where it was coming from.

Her fellow congregants seemed unmoved. They were in their typical altar-call attitude of prayer and expectation. A few men had left their seats and were making their way to the front, and Maddie's gaze was automatically drawn there, to what she realized was the source of the sound.

It was Vincent Elander, crying between his hands. His body was bent at the altar, head down between his shoulders. He alone was kneeling there, but already a few men stood near him, their hands resting on his head, his arms, his shoulders. Maddie was stunned, her mind blank. She knew only this tableau: his broad shoulders and bent head, the golden turn of his splayed elbows, his red T-shirt, his jeans. More men came forward to pray alongside him—even Mr. Gillece found a place nearby—and together they formed with their bodies a kind of shield or covering for Vincent. Soon enough, all that appeared of the stranger was the soles of his shoes.

Maddie had forgotten her fears of Vincent's seeing her. Awareness of his potentially recognizing her between the pews fell away. Instead, the boy at the altar wept on in pain that quietly awed her, and soon enough the pastor dismissed the congregation—something he did only rarely, when it appeared that the one praying at the altar would be doing so for a very long time. Vincent was still praying when she left.

From the distance of time, Maddie could see how characteristic, how typical this was. Not that Vincent prayed in such a way every day, but that Vincent should shock or surprise her should have ceased to be a shock or surprise. For surprise was integral to his language; shock seemed to have been a means to his being. He certainly surprised them all when, just a few weeks later, he came to church again. That Sunday morning, Vincent Elander entered her Sunday school class with every confidence, not even stopping in the doorway to ascertain that he was in the right place. He entered as though he had done this every day, all his life.

And that, right there, was the beginning of everything. Vincent had sat next to Maddie in Sunday school and also in the ensuing church service, and afterwards had walked with her into the spring sunshine, squinting and holding her in conversation while he leaned against the side of his car.

She and Justine had parsed it all out on the phone that afternoon, Maddie was sure, but she no longer remembered the conversation. She could recall the novelty of it and the excitement, but the feelings themselves were long gone. Human beings have that uncanny knack for becoming accustomed to almost anything, and a year or so of dating Vincent Elander had been enough to erase the squeals and elation of a first love. And if that hadn't been enough, that strange year, then other years had ensued, years full of novelties of their own. There was Frank, for example, and her boys.

And cancer.

⚬⚬⚬

The surgery had been going on for some time when Frank remembered the book in his lap. It was almost weightless there, having become like an extra appendage over the hours that had seen Maddie's check-in and subsequent wait in pre-op. He had forgotten it even before that endless hour in which they had light-heartedly talked about the boys and about Maddie's mother, about Jake's tee-ball season, and even, somewhat, the surgery, which he had assured her again would be over in no time. Only now did he realize that he was worrying the book's cover, pulling it and the pages back repeatedly as one might play with a flipbook.

He had wondered whether to bring it. He didn't know the protocol. What does one do in the waiting room while one's wife is undergoing surgery for breast cancer? Surely one doesn't read. It seemed to Frank that it wouldn't be right to sit by reading something unconcerned with anesthesia and incisions, something indifferent to the sudden, unforeseen turn their lives had taken—or might soon be taking. His wife lay unconscious on a steel surgical table just down the hall while he sat on comfortable upholstery in a waiting room, perusing a sweeping, brilliant work that took nothing else than the whole of human history under study.

Yes, the book suddenly struck Frank as irrelevant, and he wished he'd brought something different, something on art or theology—even science would have been preferable to this. Reading this history of the world seemed callous, at best. How to escape into a meta-narrative of human civilization while this intimate and staggeringly significant story of his wife's illness unfolded before him?

Calm reading of any sort with Maddie in surgery seemed callous. He wanted to be *there* for Maddie. Even in his best efforts, he didn't know how better to say it: he wanted to be *present* with and for her throughout this process—if dealing with cancer could be thought of as a process. Yet he didn't know if it *was* thought of as a process;

he rather wished it *were* a process—but if he had learned anything about the disease in these incipient weeks of Maddie's diagnosis, it was that cancer seemed to call the shots, and the doctors decided how to deal with it as they went along. He felt very keenly—without ever saying so to Maddie—that they might only just be at the beginning of dealing with cancer, though he hoped he was wrong. Once again, as had frequently been the case in this past week, the image of a tunnel came to mind, and he was standing with Maddie at its threshold, peering into the dark.

But they had found it early, right? They had found it early. So yes, these recent days had been difficult ones, as it was clear that Maddie was afraid. He, too, was afraid. And who wouldn't be? Though he was sure—he was quite sure and so must tell himself—it would be nothing. They would get through this, as he had said to her time and time again. It would be quick and relatively simple. They had found it early.

He sat on the upholstered chair in the waiting room and the book was unopened in his lap and Maddie was not helped by his sitting there, moping. To sit and do nothing was to acquiesce somehow—to what? To fear, to worry, even to sadness—and there was certainly no guarantee that this story would be a sad one. To sit and ponder—that was a kind of giving in. To read, as one might do in one's living room, or in one's bed, or on the beach—this was to continue life in the face of sadness, or in the face of potential sadness, or in spite of it. It was living with hope.

Hope was what Frank had been championing all week. Hope and, of course, a sense of humor. "Well done!" he had said to her when they were talking of the diagnosis. "Well done," he said, because he perceived the slightest softening of her mood and he had been watching for it—the crack where some light might come through. "They'll be wanting to take your picture, I would think," he said.

"What for?" she had asked him, and he should have noted her subdued tone.

But he had plowed ahead, foolish, thoughtless, so strong a believer in this best medicine. "To take your picture, Madelyn! Haven't you heard? You're the new poster child for self-exams!"

Her stony reaction spawned his immediate and continued regret.

So early in the process and already he had blundered. That premature effort at hopefulness—for that was what humor was, wasn't it? Hopefulness? And he and Maddie had hope. They had a great deal of hope, didn't they? Frank cast about him. Surely, he felt, there was reason for hope, there was reason for faith. Now, here at the beginning, was not the time to give in to fear.

The diagnosis—as anyone would expect—had been very hard on her. She was scared, and it was hard—unreasonable, even—to argue with her. Cancer—the big "C"—is frightening for everyone, and Frank had told her this. Of course you're scared, he'd said to her countless times, taking her into his arms the way he'd done it that first day when she stood dripping wet from the shower, her whole body curled into him. He tried to be understanding—he *was* understanding—but he also wanted to be sure that she didn't give in to fear. He wanted to keep her hopeful, keep her positive.

That said, Frank had also thought more than once that, if indeed hope and a positive attitude were the best way to approach her diagnosis, Maddie was maybe not a great candidate for cancer. It wasn't that she was a negative person; he wouldn't say that. It was just that she was so thoughtful about things. She took things almost too seriously. It was chronic with the boys. Everything would be going fine. The boys would be going to school without complaint, getting to bed on time, cheerful—and Maddie would come to Frank with a random concern, such as how Jake hadn't learned to floss his teeth yet. Frank's bemused reply would be casual but sensible, something like how he had plenty of time to learn to floss his teeth and how he hadn't flossed his teeth when he was Jake's age, and Maddie would counter that she was concerned the boys weren't developing good habits in general, of which flossing was just an example. Frank would then trouble his brain a bit to bring forth comforting evidence: Jake makes his bed, Eli puts his dirty laundry in the hamper, and Garrett has already learned to hang up his bath towel. See? Good habits. But then Maddie would respond with something about how Frank wasn't all that faithful a flosser himself and she wanted them to have good gums.

It was exasperating. Things were really going so well; they had so much to be happy about: the boys were healthy and happy—and she had to trouble herself about tooth decay. Always something.

Frank teased her that she was a pessimist; she answered that she was a realist; Frank said that all pessimists say they are realists: people never want to call themselves pessimists.

But he didn't think she was a pessimist, he really didn't. Yes, she sometimes approached things in a way that seemed negative, but in fact, she was trying to get at the heart of the thing, and she didn't want to be blinded from what was true by some Pollyanna-rose-colored self-deception and so miss it—miss what mattered. It was like when Eli had colic as a baby and he would cry for hours at a time, usually in the middle of the night. It was unbelievable how awful it could be. Frank would cover his head with the pillow, or he would get up and offer to take the baby, but Maddie was up with Eli from the minute the wailing began, pacing the floor with him in her arms. She wouldn't let Frank take him from her—she said it wouldn't make any difference to her if he did; she still wouldn't be able to sleep. But through the three months or so that this crying went on—and all the while with two-year-old Jake to parent during the day—she never minded, she never complained.

Frank marveled at it. It wasn't that Maddie was always cheerful; it was just that she was accepting. Some babies have colic, and this is what you do to help them, she said. There was nothing more to the matter. And she said she was glad that she couldn't sleep through it—even though, God knew, she was exhausted—because she wanted to experience it. If this was what it meant to be Eli's mother, she told him, then this was what she would do. Period. And anyway, some parents have far worse to deal with. I'll take a colicky baby, thank you very much.

That was Maddie in a nutshell. She recognized that bad things happen, that things don't always go the way you want them to, and that you deal with it, because dealing with it is part of life, and you don't want to miss part of life, do you? It was, in a way, Maddie's own way of living with hope.

Frank had liked this about her from the outset—her serious way of looking at things. After the girls he'd spent time with in high school, after the girl he'd dated in his first year of college, Maddie was refreshingly earnest. Of course Francesca had served to bridge the gap, in some ways. In many ways, really, Francesca had prepared him for Maddie. But he didn't want to think about Francesca now.

Maybe the classic example of Maddie taking things too seriously was the story of consuming the host. God, even now it made him smile. Maddie, not yet confirmed in the church, unfamiliar with Catholic ways; the priest all aflutter, his robes swirling about him as he turned to go after her, pursuing her in that small interval as she made her way to the wine. Frank had laughed, and later Father Tim had chuckled about it, but it had been a challenge to get Maddie to find the humor in it. She was so appalled at herself; she was angry at Frank: "Why didn't you tell me? Why didn't you *tell* me, Frank?"

He *had* told her. He had coached her, albeit hurriedly, as to how Catholics received communion, but this likely had come too late. By the time he had explained it, they were already standing in the aisle of the church, waiting their turn to receive the host. He told her over her shoulder, whispering into her ear, and he had forgotten some essential details.

"It was your own fault, Maddie," he had tried saying to her, a small defense against her mortification.

"I don't see that, Frank," she said. "I wasn't raised Catholic. You know it. I didn't know what I was doing."

Which was when Frank tried to explain to her—and Father Tim—that if she had only agreed earlier in the day to receiving communion, he wouldn't have been in such a hurry when telling her how to go about it. As it went, they had argued about it in hushed voices throughout the entire homily, and she had only finally agreed while the priest was blessing the host. Frank hadn't meant to leave out any important details. It was an accident.

That was spring break of her junior year in college, and against her parents' wishes they had gone to Florida together for the week, where they were amazed to find themselves talking about getting married. Maddie had determined that she wouldn't marry until her mid-twenties at the absolute earliest, but their casual dates had turned into something very nearly overwhelming, and suddenly it seemed that marrying Frank—and soon—was the only thing to do.

It was Frank's idea that she should go to Mass with him then. It was like asking for a blessing somehow, he said—like a tacit agreement before God, a submission of their plans to his blessing—and it couldn't matter to God that she hadn't been confirmed yet. But Maddie had hesitated about the receiving communion bit. She would go to Mass with him. She had done it a time or two already, and now, their plans laid, they would find some Catholic church neither of them had been to before, something—she specified—looking Floridian and missional, overhung with Spanish moss. They would go to Mass together, this time with the intention of her conversion and of their becoming husband and wife. A beautiful, vaguely symbolic plan.

Maybe it was beautiful. Maybe some symbolism inhered in it, but this was lost to them now, the entire event devolving instead into the frantic priest and Maddie's ensuing mortification. It had all gone well enough at first: she stood before the priest as she was supposed to, hands open. He said what he was supposed to say ("The body of Christ"), and Maddie said what she was supposed to say ("Amen"), and then she had turned to get the wine—without the all-important ingestion of the bread. Which led to the now famous line from that episode, delivered by the priest who had come after her, abandoning his post and whispering loudly enough that Frank—and perhaps others in the congregation—heard it: "Aren't you going to consume the host?"

"It's not such a big deal, Maddie," Frank had tried to reassure her as they resumed their seats, as they drove away from the church, as they revisited this episode and her embarrassment time and again. Maddie went on about how she must have seemed disrespectful at best and at worst sacrilegious, how she had no business receiving communion before her conversion and how her error had made her sin apparent to everybody and how it wasn't fair to laugh at the priest, it really wasn't.

Father Tim had helped at both ends, which was his way. He agreed with Maddie: she really should have been confirmed first; and he chuckled with Frank: the whole scene was amusing; and he defended the priest's panic: "One can't have one's parishioners carrying the host around with them in their pockets!"

But ultimately he sided with Frank. He told Maddie to relax about it. He reminded her that her intentions had been nothing but good. And he encouraged her to remember that God has a propensity for looking at the whole picture, a view far larger than any of us are accustomed to—or even able to see. He felt certain that the Almighty was not offended by Maddie's error, and that she should probably let it go.

Eventually Maddie was able to laugh at it—it just took her a while. And that was the way it was with Maddie, Frank knew. She thought hard about things, she prepared herself for the worst, and she believed, ultimately, in the best. Sometimes Frank found it bewildering, sometimes it drove him crazy, but he loved her for it.

———

Frank did not think about the weight of Maddie's body in his arms as he climbed the stairs. He did not consider that the first time he had carried her was laughing through the door of their hotel room on their wedding night. He thought only of her comfort, of the site of her incision and the potential of his arms to pull against it, and of the doctor's injunction that she do nothing—not climb the stairs, not push a vacuum, not drive a car.

He hesitated a moment when reaching their room: the bed was made, and now he wanted to lay her down, but not on top of the covers. He stood there just looking at the bed, his arms laden with his wife's body, and then she spoke to him in a faltering laugh, "Anywhere will do."

When he was certain Maddie was asleep; when he had fully debriefed his mother-in-law on their enlightened understanding of the cancer; when he had ensured himself, through a careful inspection of refrigerator and pantry, that they had healthy and good foods that Maddie would like to eat; when he had dispatched his mother-in-law to get the boys from school and had once again checked on his sleeping wife, Frank sat down heavily at one end of the living room sofa.

On the coffee table stood a glass of lemonade and the sandwich his mother-in-law had made for him. Condensation beaded on the glass, its base fringed in water. They kept the coasters tucked into a drawer in the end table, just next to the TV remote. Maddie was forever after him to use a coaster, and now Frank looked toward that drawer, suddenly too tired to get up from his seat.

What was so fatiguing, he wondered. He had slept well enough. It was only just three in the afternoon, but it had been an enormously long day.

Remaining seated, Frank stretched toward the drawer, pulling it open awkwardly, at an angle and with his middle finger. With the tips of his fingers, he prized a coaster from the stack and then slid it under the sweating glass, wiping at the ring of water with his palm. For now, this, at least, was something he could do for his wife.

⁂

Maddie slept for a long time, dreamless. When she awoke in the late afternoon, it was to a quiet house, and she herself lay motionless on her side of the bed, wondering where the children were, but not wanting to call out to anyone yet: they thought she was asleep.

At four o'clock the shadows from the birch tree in the front yard played across her bedspread. She was never in bed at this time of day, except maybe in the earliest days of the boys' lives when, after her difficult deliveries, Frank insisted on her getting rest. Lying there, she remembered Frank carrying Jake in, how his hair stood up over the top of his blanket. She remembered him in his newborn infant skin, how a scratch in that soft and perfect flesh, accidentally inflicted in the morning, would by noon be only a reddish line and, at his bedtime, would have all but disappeared.

The healing from this lumpectomy shouldn't take too long; she'd be feeling much better within a few days; it was too early in the process for her to be an invalid. She would be on her feet and managing things in a day or two; tomorrow afternoon Jake had soccer practice and she would ride along in the car. She would drive him herself next week. She had to do these things now, because it was likely (so now it seemed) that times were coming when she would not be able to.

She hadn't been free from anesthesia long when the doctor came in. He had stood by her bed, grasping his clipboard and frowning faintly, speaking in low tones. Frank sat next to her, his fingers tracing the tape that secured her IV, absorbing the news without looking up: the cancer was much larger than they'd thought; they hadn't got it all. They would revisit her case and make a new plan of treatment. And when the doctor left, closing the door softly behind him, Frank had leaned over her bed and rested his cheek on hers. She felt his breath in her hair.

The dim and inevitable future asserted itself: more surgery and yet another recovery, chemotherapy and its sickness, radiation, maybe hair loss, nausea, exhaustion.

It was unwise to dwell on such things.

Dust clung to the picture frame and crucifix on the wall. She liked the picture—a cross-stitch celebrating their wedding—and the crucifix paired together, as if Jesus was keeping watch over their marriage. Now she could see that Jesus' bent knee was, yes, dust-caked. She sighed audibly, a small sound in the silent house.

The shadows moved over her body—never a distinct, serrated birch leaf, but only suggestions of leaves and branches. The shadows had dark centers and paler edges, but a shift in the breeze made the shadows seem to exchange those dark hearts again and again, passing them back and forth to one another in untraceable, effortless action.

Her body was a strange constant in this mutable light: solid, motionless, and block-like under the white bedspread. Present and invisible. This body under the blankets could belong to any number of women. She could be almost anyone.

Yet there it was again, the fact of the cancer lying over top of everything, unavoidably true. Here under the spread was her body and no one else's, invisibly diseased, potentially dying. The calendar she kept in her mind, labeled like the one on the refrigerator with color codes for lessons, field trips, practices and games, now appeared before her in long, blackened segments, marked out by regular treatments and the days and weeks of recovery between them. And far off, unknown and impossible to guess, the day when she would be recovered and utterly well.

Then Frank and the boys came in. Maddie wiped her tears away on a corner of the bed sheet and Garrett climbed up next to her, entreated by his father to remain on her right side. He had brought his stuffed kitten, a grey and ragged thing that he held by its tail while he sucked his thumb. He lay there beside her for a long time, content to lean against her shoulder, and she stroked his hair and studied the scab on his round knee, an injury he'd happened upon last week in the driveway. It was only a shallow abrasion, but Garrett had a very low pain threshold, and he had cried for a long time.

# 4

*M*ore and more, Frank found himself thinking of shooting hoops with The Priest behind the Catholic church in their little college town. He listened for the ring of the basketball as it pounded the dirt in the alley. He heard the clang and rattle as the ball hit the hoop and the sagging metal net beneath it. He and Tim had shot hoops together for hours at a time, starting in those dark months of his freshman year. They had been out there in the snow; in February, the ball cracked the ice in the alley's ruts. In the spring, they had played even in the rain, both of them drenched to the skin, firing the ball at the hoop as they fired questions at one another: so often The Priest returned Frank's questions with questions, forcing Frank to think.

He had first come upon The Priest because of the rain, driven to the church in a sudden downpour. His roommate had warned him to take an umbrella, but Frank hadn't cared and his roommate hadn't been surprised: by that time, he had grown accustomed to Frank's solitary, nightly rambles, his skulking around on the small town's streets "like a dejected Heathcliff." Frank's roommate was a lit major, and Frank had rather liked the allusion. He felt it lent gravitas to his grief, the greatest loss he had known at that point in his life: Francesca's sudden transfer to another school and her consequent departure from his life. It wasn't until he sought refuge from the downpour and stood dripping on the carpet of the Catholic church that he was aware he might also bear some guilt, might even owe a confession or two. Since arriving at the little Protestant college in August, he hadn't acted at all like the good Catholic he'd been raised to be.

But happily for Frank the open church building appeared to be empty, and Frank thought he would wait out the rain in solitude. Until, that is, Father Tim startled him, appearing suddenly from out of a dark hallway. He didn't seem at all surprised to find Frank standing there, and Frank couldn't remain startled for long: Tim was decidedly warm and welcoming, young and tall and rosy-cheeked, and his pale hair, thinning, seemed to stand up an inch or two over the top of his head. He seemed to harbor no suspicion that Frank was in want of confessing anything, but immediately invited the dripping Frank into his study for tea and then (when the rain stopped) out into the alley to play basketball in the mud. Frank keenly remembered that first walk out to the hoop with The Priest, how cold the November air felt on his still-wet clothes, and how Frank asked himself what in the world he was doing. It was after midnight, and he had spent the last hour or so discussing with Tim all things *not* Francesca—which felt strange, as she had occupied his waking thoughts and much of his dreams since September.

But he didn't want to talk about her with The Priest. He needed no conversation with a man of the cloth to inform him that with Francesca he'd been feeding his lust, that sex outside of marriage was strictly against the rules. He didn't want to hear the inevitable: that he had sinned, that his pain was his own fault, that his recent fornication-with-abandon was meaningless, was wrong, was an act of the body against the soul, and he needed to repent.

Frank rather believed, while first crossing the parking lot to the solitary hoop, that he must get through this strange encounter without raising Francesca's spectre at all.

But then, despite these reservations, Frank began to talk about her. There was something about Tim that invited confidences. He was, in the first place, disarmingly young and unassuming, friendly and even jovial, for lack of a better term. And then there was the fact that, at that time and for a few months prior, Francesca had very nearly become Frank's identity: her approval, her opinion, her affection, her body—these were all that Frank had appetite for. By the time he and Tim reached the basketball hoop, Frank had exhausted his capacity on any subject that wasn't Francesca.

That was how it began: the many-times-weekly dialogues with The Priest, when Frank pitched his newborn grief against existential beliefs as old as centuries, grappling with what he'd been taught, confronting it as if for the first time.

Perhaps what made Frank go back for more was the fact that The Priest met almost none of his expectations. Tim didn't dismiss outright his relationship with Francesca. He didn't tell him that he was making too much of this lost love, that fornication had brought him his just desserts. Where Frank anticipated—even felt he deserved— remarks about sin, confession, repentance, Tim instead had helped him explore what it was he loved—or imagined he loved—about her. And what was it about her body, about their bodies, about the union of them that Frank loved and missed?

It was The Priest, not Frank, who suggested that maybe it wasn't that sex was wrong, but that sex in the wrong way was wrong. Perhaps one wasn't intended to have sex with someone who might arbitrarily disappear, that the loss Frank was suffering was perhaps more real— not less—than he realized. That their physical union perhaps mattered far more—not less—than Frank had earlier conceived.

It was those conversations under the basketball hoop—not his first communion, not years of Catholic religion classes, not his confirmation—that made Frank a Catholic. He and Tim banged the ball into the dirt; they passed it back and forth to one another until their hands were seamed with dirt or numb with cold. Under a sky so often leaden in that little nook of western Pennsylvania, Frank thrust his sadness and anger toward the hoop, toward Tim, toward God. They talked about theology, sex, women, about what it meant to be a spiritual being within a limited, corporal frame. The Incarnation, pounded out on the dirt. The unlikely miracle of the Eucharist.

And could it be that sex with Francesca was somehow connected to the Eucharist? Frank was shocked, when Tim raised it, at the possibility. Could one link something so earthy and—for lack of a better term (they both laughed at it)—*hot*, with the death of Christ? It was Tim who made Frank see the terrible physicality of the crucifixion, the blood and sweat, the torn flesh. No, not at all the same in terms of passion, but passion nonetheless. All of it so physical, Tim said. The body matters, he said. It signifies.

So what could it mean that communion might be more than symbolic, standing in weighty contrast to the clear belief of the Protestants? Frank and Tim hashed out the possibilities: Transignification; Consubstantiation; or the actual daily, hourly renewal of the crucifixion, made real in Holy Mass all around the world? Frank pondered the possibilities as he palmed the ball. The transformation of wine and bread into actual blood and body, nourishing body and soul. The incarnation took on new and near-frightening implications, all of it punctuated by the ball hitting the ground and the rim, and Tim's open laughter, and the worn-out sweatpants he always wore, the ones Frank laughed at because, based on the wrestling logo riding up the leg and Tim's own admission, The Priest had worn them even in high school. Sweat beaded and then dripped down their faces, ringed their armpits, drenched their chests, backs, stomachs, leaked into their drawers. And the talk was of "Christ with us," a thought horrifying and wretched (how to bear the scrutiny?) but also—miraculous in its simultaneity and in Frank's inexplicable hunger for it—infinitely comforting.

Afterward, Frank walked back alone to campus, chilled with perspiration. The sky was invariably dull; his mind teemed. He could reconcile none of it. Belief was audacious at best, with repercussions he couldn't conceive of. Maybe belief was even stupid. And it wasn't a sudden revelation, in the end. It wasn't a specific conversation that did it. He can't remember which time it was—the day or even the month—when the leaden sky was peeled back at the corners and Frank was able to see.

Now, in the days surrounding Maddie's surgeries, Frank found himself wishing he could remember more of the hope he had found in those days. He longed to shed some light into the gloom of Maddie's sadness. And certainly he tried, but words seemed empty. The second surgery was plainly profound loss, and he knew from his long ago grief—so trivial now—that there was no way around it. She would have to be sad—and angry, and in denial, and all the other things—

until she wasn't anymore.

So the night before that surgery, he just told her that he loved her. What else was there to say? They fell asleep together with his arm over her shoulder and his hand at her waist, a shelter insufficient but earnest.

---

When Maddie knew he was sleeping, she lifted Frank's arm and laid it along his own side, then lay still for another moment to be sure he wouldn't stir.

She didn't turn on the bathroom light until the door was closed, and then she stared at herself in the mirror, studying the way her shirt lay over her body. She studied her profile, too, then lifted her shirt over her head and let it fall to the floor.

Her breasts weren't large, but they were shaped well enough, given the breast-feeding. They were flat at the top now; their fullness resided underneath. Maddie cupped them in her palms and studied her reflection, trying to summon the thoughts she had saved for this night: thoughts of nursing her babies, for example, of wearing her first bra when she was twelve, other memories, too—sexual ones. First times.

Since knowing she would have a mastectomy, Maddie had tucked away these aspects of her loss in her mind, hoarding them as if in a box or journal, to be drawn out and reflected on when she was alone. Now she could think of none of it. She was just there with her body, staring at her own reflection, all of it the same as always.

She pulled her shirt back over her head. Disbelief, she realized. That's what this was. It was shock and disbelief. That one breast would be gone by this time tomorrow was as believable as her own death, or Frank's, or any other terrible unreality that she had never known.

---

In October the day finally arrived when the humidity was gone. Standing in the backyard on a Saturday morning, coffee cup in hand, Frank felt the clear air in his lungs. For the first time since May, the damp blanket that was the summer air had been rolled up and heaved into some celestial attic. Never mind that it was October, that this delightful shift would have—and had—taken place up north a month ago. Frank was a southerner now, or trying to be one. The summertime heat and its vicissitudes were integral to a southern life. He couldn't hold Raleigh's weather against her.

He inhaled deeply, taking in the crisp air and the expanse of the newborn weekend. Things were better now. Maddie was doing well—well enough, anyway: almost completely healed. The second surgery had been brutal—as one would expect with an amputation. This, of course, was a word he would never use with Maddie. It was a mastectomy, a lateral mastectomy—but Frank felt that official euphemism was not effective. In his more objective moments, he wondered at the nomenclature. Perhaps it wasn't called an amputation because reconstruction, in this case, could be effected—more so, anyway, than in the amputation of a limb. Maddie's reconstructed breast would be prosthetic, but it wouldn't look artificial in the way, say, of a peg-leg.

Before the surgery, he had pondered whether she someday might allow him to give the reconstructed breast a nickname, something to privately amuse them both. But now this seemed like something he might have done in another lifetime, to a couple who did not as yet live under the weight of diagnosis. He couldn't imagine anything about this surgery or its after-effects taking on humorous proportions. Not ever.

It had actually been horrible to watch her come out of the anesthesia: violently sick to her stomach, her face deathly pale. The pain and how she fought against it. The drains dangling at her side, filling with red liquid—not blood entirely, the doctors said, but yes, blood and other fluids. Frank had emptied the drains himself, working to be cheerfully untroubled by the task, by the tubing's disappearance into Maddie's side. This was a small duty—this and the others: getting her meds, helping her bathe, all and anything it would take to help her.

If she decided to undergo reconstruction, they would have to go through this yet again. If that's what she wanted, Frank knew, he was more than willing. And if she didn't want it? He didn't care. He told her often that she was beautiful, and he meant it.

Now she was nearly healed, which meant they would be moving

on to the next phase of treatment. Chemotherapy didn't sound good, but to Frank—and to Maddie, too, he thought—it meant progress, moving forward, getting on with this phase and thereby, eventually, getting past it. The waiting had been tiresome despite its necessity. They were both ready to move on.

And yet. He hadn't been able to help himself: he had spent more than enough time researching this next phase that they were supposedly ready for. The potential side effects to chemotherapy were legion and ranged from bad to horrible. Meanwhile, doctors couldn't tell them which ones Maddie would be likely to face; one couldn't predict how an individual would react. He had read the good news: stories of women whose treatments had been a relative breeze. No side effects to speak of, carrying on with work and life in an almost normal way. And he had read the horror stories. They were mostly horror stories on the Internet.

Standing there in the yard, Frank considered mowing the lawn and pruning the bushes between them and the neighbors. Through the open window at his back drifted the sounds of running water as Maddie cleaned up after pancakes and the mania of Saturday morning cartoons. Who knew what they were headed for? Already they were moving forward, driving toward God-knew-what and there was no turning around, no escape hatch into the bright and open air. In sickness and in health. His wife had breast cancer.

Maddie would scold him if she knew, but Frank thought of it often: a story of the Superhero, her old boyfriend, Vincent. He had been playing football and an opponent had been injured—his neck, his back, something awful. Vincent had prayed for him right there on the field, and the kid had gotten up and walked off unassisted to the sidelines. Completely fine. A miracle on the gridiron.

But Maddie would protest—and had, so many times—that this, like all the other stories, was a misunderstanding. "He couldn't really heal people," he heard her saying. "It just didn't happen."

⸺ ❧ ⸺

The thing to do was not to think about it. Mind over matter, that was Maddie's philosophy. Let the incision heal; let her body recover. Move on with her treatment and kill the cancer. There was no need to shed

53

tears over what was already done.

She need only look at her boys, at her boys and Frank, or even, while they were all gone to school and work during the day, to look at the little pieces of their lives: Garrett's stuffed kitten, lying lopsided by his pillow; Frank's array of favorite pens on his desk; Jake and Eli's Lego empire waiting for their return. All of it spurred a keen tenderness within her. Whereas she used to see these and other things as merely part of the household, now it was all hung with profound and ineluctable meaning. Everything pointed to the demand of her recovery—which meant looking forward, not back.

Still, mind over matter wasn't effective in all arenas. Once upon a time Maddie had worked to push thoughts of Vincent from her mind, and she had largely been successful. But lately the memories sabotaged her. They volunteered themselves, each a small eruption triggering another that—chronologically or causally—was completely unrelated to the one before it.

Kneeling next to her on the pavement, the sky pale around his bent head. He had taken off his baseball hat and his hair was pressed in a ring. His profile, his silence, his deliberate attention to her leg and the center of the pain where the car had hit her. He hadn't even known her name.

Her photo, cut unevenly from the yearbook page and stuck inside his locker door. It was a terrible picture. She didn't think until much later of him leafing through the book to find her picture, wielding the scissors, finding tape—or maybe chewing gum—to hold it in place.

Standing after dark in the pouring rain, allowing his own body to be the means by which a drunk and homeless man righted himself, even reaching down to take hold of his shoulders and helping the man to his feet.

His patient progress through the oncology ward of the children's hospital and the way the sunlight streamed through the room, falling on and between the beds of the little sick children, their eyes over-wide and dark.

His head bent over Mr. Pavlik, his hands on Mr. Pavlik's swollen head. His hand on Mrs. Senchak's head, her body curled and shrunken on the hospital bed, her breath grating like a shovel over pavement.

How much of it was certain? It had happened so long ago. The scenes were isolated but clear—and who was to say which ones were true memories and which imagined, things she envisioned then and now envisioned again, as clear and acute as memory? And which of them was accurate? Was that the way it happened? He said it, and in this way?

At home, recovering from the surgeries, Maddie had these quiet hours to regain her strength. Yet the memories plagued her; she was almost angry: she had left this wretched territory behind her long ago. Cancer was more than enough, thank you. Must she spend its treatment combing through this layered sediment again?

She considered talking it all out with Frank. Yes, she had other friends she could talk to, but she found her husband was the best candidate for helping her assess the sometimes swarming contents of her mind. He had certainly heard this stuff before, or much of it, anyway, and maybe that prior knowledge would be insightful. But that was reason enough, too, not to mention it to him. Why drag him through the old narrative when they had so much else to deal with?

At the very least, she could set the record straight in her mind, the simple and exonerating order of events. For none of it could be claimed to be her fault, could it? Vincent—of his own mysterious accord—had visited her church in the spring of her sophomore (his junior) year. His loud repentance at the altar had engendered natural curiosity in Maddie, and it was this that led to her innocently observing him over the ensuing week at school.

She had wondered what to expect from a boy like that, wild party-er that he famously was, after his bone-chilling display at the altar. What happened, exactly, in that interaction with God?

It was because she had been watching for him at school that she had been hit by the car. She had been staring at Vincent Elander—but this time they locked eyes, and she had been unable to look away. So she hadn't seen or even heard the car coming, the one that should have, for all of its speed and impact, broken her leg.

That Vincent knelt to pray over Maddie as she awaited the ambulance was *his* choice. She hadn't asked him to do that. Had she known what would follow after it, she would have done everything in her power to send him away. Not that it would have worked. And then this memory: "You shouldn't worry about what other people think." His first words to her, just a few days after her accident. And she might never have believed it was Vincent Elander who had said it if he hadn't turned his head and looked at her as he was going inside, if he hadn't looked right at her with those deep blue eyes and smirked before disappearing behind the door.

That was when Maddie seized on the idea of Vincent's having healed her.

A miraculous healing was not the sort of thing that one could recount easily to Justine who, like Maddie, had been raised in the Bethel Hills Church of Holiness. Justine had some time ago come to the conclusion that the people of their church were too readily inclined to look for miracles, so Maddie knew she would have to keep her mouth shut on that score. But Maddie wasn't one to remain silent, and so she said something different. She said, "Vincent Elander says I shouldn't worry about what other people think."

"When did you talk with Vincent Elander?" Justine asked. Immediately Maddie wished that she *had* talked to Vincent, and could see again, as she had imagined it so many times already, the way the conversation might have opened up in the hallway before class, could imagine leaning against the wall with, perhaps, one knee bent, the sole of her shoe pressed against the wall, and Vincent standing perpendicular to her, his shoulder pressed against that same wall, looking down at her, talking to her, listening. If she had only come down the hall sooner, maybe that's how it would have gone.

But honesty was one of Maddie's strengths. "I didn't talk to Vincent," she said. "He talked to me."

Justine had no patience for this cryptic response. She wanted immediate and full disclosure, and so Maddie immediately disclosed it.

"Well," Justine said, and Maddie noticed how she moved effortlessly past any surprise, "he's right. You shouldn't worry about it, Maddie. You just have to let it go." To which Maddie responded that she knew this was true, but she did not say aloud how difficult she found it: to reject or be unconcerned with other people's responses.

"Did he say anything else?" Justine asked. Maddie said that he hadn't, and then went on to say that the bell had rung, creating and leaving open the possibility that, had the bell failed to ring, the conversation during which she would have leaned against the wall enjoying Vincent's perpendicular attention might have taken place. She did not mention that he hadn't paused, hadn't stopped, but had spoken as he was walking and then had walked away from her.

"I wonder what he thinks of the whole thing," Justine said.

"I thought that you shouldn't care what other people think," Maddie said.

"Ha, ha," said Justine in that way she had of sounding as if she thought something were funny while showing you that it wasn't really funny at all. "I mean," she went on to say, "that you should ask his opinion as to what went on that day. Why did he come over to you in the first place? Why didn't he stay with the team? And why did he touch your leg like that? How did he know? You should ask him," she said.

Maddie was certain that she couldn't ask him and never would. In the first place, she couldn't imagine the circumstances under which she could put such a question: Does one walk up to a person like Vincent in the hallway or the cafeteria and just start asking questions? Or does one first have to say, "Can I ask you something?" and then proceed to ask while all the friends, girlfriends, and general entourage stand by to overhear? She said as much to Justine.

"I think you should ask him anyway," she said, without offering suggestions as to how. Maddie was easily influenced by Justine. She was easily influenced by lots of people; it couldn't be helped. She was only fifteen, after all, and most of the people she knew were nice enough. But Justine especially, despite her gruffness, was someone who could be trusted. She had a level head; Maddie's parents had said this before, and Maddie had observed it to be true.

Still, Vincent Elander would be difficult to talk to. There remained the whole question as to when and how to approach him. And there remained, too, (although this she did not say) the way that Vincent Elander looked in his baseball uniform, and the way that he had met her gaze from under the brim of his baseball hat. And there was the way, too, that she had heard him cry out from the altar at the front of the church only a few weeks before that. All of this informed her intimidation. All of it made Vincent Elander, of all people, particularly difficult to approach.

Now Maddie shifted her weight, making to stand up from the sofa where she had been resting yet again, and felt only the slightest twinge at the incision site. Swinging her legs gently to the floor, she sat, hands on knees, and contemplated getting to her feet.

Frank would laugh with her at this narration, at what had been adolescent insecurity laced with puppy love. Naming it with Frank would put it in its place.

Except that she wasn't sure they would agree on it. The insecurity, yes; the infatuation, sure. But what of the healing? From their long dormant conversations about those miracles, Maddie guessed that Frank still might wish to talk with Vincent if he could.

Frank simply had more faith than Maddie had. She knew this. Or, at the very least, he was more open to possibility. And now, of all times, was *not* the time to get him thinking that way. Neither one of them needed to be hoping for miracles now.

Hoping for miracles had only gotten Maddie into trouble. If she had been at all to blame, then it was here, when she was talking with Justine and newly convinced that Vincent had healed her. Maddie had believed that she had been part of a miracle, but she had believed lots of things. Once when they were ten, she and Kelly Cox, minds teeming with Nancy Drew novels, tried to discover mysteries to solve in their Pittsburgh suburb. The girls were committed to the notion that Michael Pulaski, the thirty-something across the street who sold used cars and still lived with his parents, was a cat burglar. Which, of course, he wasn't.

It takes no psychologist to demonstrate that the emotions of teenage girls are powerful things. From an adult's perspective, Maddie could see this clearly. It was enough to be driven by hormones, to be amazed by Vincent's demonstrated remorse, to be hit by a car. Any teenage girl in this situation could conjure the notion of miraculous healings, especially at the hands of a boy like Vincent.

Now she liked to imagine that she had asked him, that she had put to him the question Justine had encouraged her to ask—and other questions, too. Why did you touch me, Vincent? Why didn't you just stay with your friends? Why didn't you leave me alone? She liked to think that the very next day found her striding up to him in the hallway before their language classes, calling him by name so that he turned to face her, and questioning him without preamble as to why he had knelt next to her in the parking lot, and what exactly he was doing when he'd groped for her injury.

She liked to imagine this, but only much later, and when she did imagine it the dialogue went no further. She was never able to put the right words in his mouth, never able to envision his stunned expression, his frank surprise. Her fantasy ended satisfactorily only in leaving him wordless, while she turned her back on him and strode away again down the hall.

# 5

*F*rank knew that cancer treatment was a process; there was no
quick fix. He understood this implicitly, and how could he not,
when every day of their lives had to take into account the process they
were subject to.

But the thought persisted that he should be able to offer her
something else, something in the line of hopefulness that would help
her. Again his conversations with Father Tim came to mind, but
the specifics that emerged were topical, even theoretical. The only
practical thought he could construe was stuff about sin—which really
didn't seem at all helpful here—and yes, hope, but hope in the eternal,
in an after-life, in a glorious eternity devoid of loss or pain.

Despite the inherent hope in that, he really didn't want to raise
those issues. Not now.

What returned again and again were thoughts of his first
communion—and not the one he had endured in the first grade,
although his dress shirt's itchy collar came vividly to mind.

No, what he meant by his first communion came much later, again
during his college days and at Father Tim's little church, a Sunday
morning Mass that Tim hadn't expected Frank to attend, as Frank
never—up until that point—had attended Mass there. And in truth,
Frank was somewhat surprised to be there himself.

It was April and unseasonably warm for Pennsylvania, and Frank had awakened early that Sunday with a strong compulsion to go to Mass. He dressed in a hurry and almost ran down the street to the church. For all his rushing, he had nonetheless arrived late, and he sat in the back and watched The Priest do what he presumably did multiple times a week—though Frank had never seen him at it.

When it was time for communion, Frank had thought he'd remain in his seat. He had reasoned there should be something more to this: some hoop to jump through, some meeting with Tim in which he forthrightly affirmed his faith before once again—after so many months—receiving communion. But again, Frank hadn't been able to help himself: there was an unnameable joy that propelled him, behind the presumably faithful parishioners, toward the front. He was grinning like a fool by the time he reached Tim and held out his hands for the host.

On seeing Frank grin like that, Tim had tried to maintain his solemnity, but Frank could detect the smile working at the corners of his eyes. Later Frank had teased him: Would it have been so wrong, he asked his friend, for Tim to smile back? After all, it wasn't a private joke the two of them were concealing—at least, no joke they could name. Could the laughter that both of them worked to stifle have somehow misled the congregation?

But Tim had argued that there aren't words for some things, that it would have been impossible and perhaps inappropriate for him to have held the parishioners captive to the obligatory explanation that here was laughter for the best reasons: Frank was a lost one, found; the two of them were brothers of the best kind; the bread and wine were everything they believed them to be, and therefore likely signified more than either one of them, or anyone, could understand. Frank, his back to the congregation, had smiled broadly as Tim said, with all the earnest seriousness he could muster, "The body of Christ." And Frank had said, "Amen."

Frank realized now that he could no longer muster the joy. Neither could he recall how long it had lasted, or if it ever returned to him in subsequent Masses. There had not been, in his memory, a repeat performance.

But he considered the actual first communion. Surely it had been a solemn occasion: that evening with Jesus and his disciples in a borrowed upstairs room. Frank envisioned a low-ceilinged space subtly lit by torches. A dimness matched by dim awareness in the disciples, who were satisfied to have met the teacher's instructions in securing donkey and room, products of yet another mysterious confluence of prophetic instruction and providence.

There were thirteen of them there, thirteen dusty, sweating travelers. A room full of egos, Frank thought, full of self-interest. They asked Jesus which of them would betray him—and didn't the question betray them all? Each of them had thought of it. Each of them had been given the opportunity and had at least one justification to follow through.

Jesus, moving among them, washing feet. He broke bread and poured wine. He was surrounded by friends and also profoundly alone, his acts of humility and love misunderstood.

All of them ate the bread; they drank the wine. Judas, the betrayer. Peter, who betrayed him, too. Not one of them comprehending any of it.

───── ∞ ─────

Friends had offered to sit with her; her mother had offered to come down for this first bout of chemotherapy. But Maddie only wanted Frank.

Now he sat next to her in the infusion room. He had found childcare and had taken the afternoon off work, and he avoided asking her if she was nervous. He also avoided looking for words of comfort or hope which, when attempted in his mind, sounded as hollow platitudes. Instead he said things like, "It's the big day!" and "Your chemotherapy debut!"

It was going to be merriment and joking, Maddie realized, which was not surprising: she recalled the route he used to take on their way home during the last weeks of each pregnancy, the ones with the huge speed bumps. "Pregnancy bumps," he called them, his little effort to jostle the baby out of her womb.

Maddie's cancer diagnosis had opened a new line of interest in Frank, who had lived on Pop-Tarts and Kraft macaroni and cheese in college. Now everything was organic, and the overhaul of pantry and refrigerator were only the front line of his assault on their household goods. Detergents were newly scent-free and environmentally friendly; all soaps and lotions were organic. Who knows what these chemicals do to our bodies, he had said to her and their friends and sometimes even the clerk in the checkout line. How do we know that cancer isn't connected directly with hormones in milk or some rogue food coloring?

He sat next to her while the liquid dripped into her chest. It hung on a pole above them, a weighty red bag attached to Maddie's port by its equally red tube. She watched Frank bravely watch the bag. This is good stuff, he said, gesturing to the medication. Just a little Kool-aid, he said.

---

Maddie had been remarkably lucky to find Frank, that much she knew. He was, as she often told him, her own Renaissance man: the writer, tennis player, and opera lover, who last summer built the boys a tree house of his own design. He was both passionate and grounded, and he was her best friend.

When she had told him that her parents would be upset that he was Catholic, he took this in his stride, making no apology or excuse. He wasn't changing anything but was pleased that Maddie wanted to convert and go to church with him. It makes the most sense for our family, he had said, for any children we might have, that we be of the same mind about church. And her heart had warmed at the thought of a family.

Sometimes it occurred to her that she might have missed him; she very nearly did, turning him down after he asked her out in the library. She had dismissed him as too bookish, maybe, too intellectual: all she wanted to do in that first semester was to blast high school's memory from her mind. Frank, wearing glasses and distributing microfilm, didn't seem relevant to that plan—which required, for starters, a whole lot of drinking.

So she had been surprised to see him leaning against the bar at the Landmark, a popular dive at the edge of town. It was her first time there, and everything about it was a study in extremes: the dark, the loud, the grit, the crowd. She was following a friend who was pushing aggressively toward the band at the back, and Maddie had been jostled into Frank by a stream of people coming the other way. She glanced up and recognized him immediately, and then, to her extreme discomfort, remained pressed into his side for some time: the stream was a long one, seemingly endless. She kept her head turned away from him, hoping that he hadn't identified her.

But he had, and apparently was not made at all uncomfortable by this forced interaction. Of course he wouldn't pretend he didn't know her and had also to immediately bring up the source of her discomfort: that she had turned him down for a date. "How'd that test go?" he'd yelled to her over the noise, grinning.

Maddie felt unaccountably offended by his asking, as though he were implicating her in a lie (she *had* had a test that Monday), but she felt forced to yell back anyway ("Fine!" terse and dismissive), while continuing to face out into the (still streaming) crowd.

For his part, Frank continued talking to her. He yelled to the back of her hair, "I was really disappointed when you said no."

She couldn't have fallen in love with him at that point. She was too embarrassed, her mind too much in the way of wanting to keep her distance from him. But she was caught nonetheless on this confession: any other guy might have asked about the test and left it there, or said something snarky, or ignored her altogether.

The least she could do, she thought, was try to impress him. She turned so as to give him her profile and shouted—bragging—that all she really wanted was to get mind-numbingly drunk, failing to realize that this goal might actually be banally familiar, the senseless objective of legions of college students. But Frank was still interested, and he drew her out. Soon the two of them were leaning into the bar side by side, their heads inclined, their voices nonetheless, necessarily, raised. Over a glass of beer (Frank insisted on paying for it) she eventually related the cause of her rebellion: the hide-bound strictures of her church upbringing. Frank was fascinated: he had recently done some soul-searching of his own in terms of religion, had explored a handful of options—both foreign and domestic (he chuckled)—and had settled on the Catholic faith of his childhood.

At about that point Maddie's friend returned for her, having long since achieved the enticing back of the room. But Maddie was too engrossed in the conversation—or was it Frank?—to leave. Feeling herself something of a legitimate expert, she was giving him her full-on critique of Christianity: all doctrines, disciplines, denominations. Frank mostly listened, but he gave bold answers where he knew more than she did—which was, to her mind, surprisingly often. Maddie's fondest memory of the evening was Frank's explanation of the Immaculate Conception, shouted at her over the noise of the band.

She did not get drunk that night, but she found she didn't mind this as she drove her drunk and stumbling friend back to the dorm. The next morning, she was glad she wasn't suffering from a hangover, gladder still to remember that she needed to go to the library. And unwittingly blushing when she saw that Frank was in his station at the microfilm desk. She thought she remembered that he worked on Saturday mornings. When he asked her out this time, she said yes.

They would tell the story in the way that all couples do, reliving it in fast-forward motion behind their eyes. Maddie would always punctuate it by repeating, "The Immaculate Conception," and Frank would always smile, the skin crinkling up around his eyes the way it did even back in college.

It had been different with Vincent. She had been much younger then—not yet sixteen and truly naïve. Justine was the one to tell her. "You're next," she had said.

Maddie had no idea what Justine was talking about, despite Vincent's instant and near-constant presence in her life. She couldn't remember when she hadn't known who he was, and since that display at the church altar, he had become a fixed part of the Bethel Hills congregation, enfolding himself into this part of Maddie's world. But Maddie didn't take the hints that were his frequent phone calls and sitting next to her at lunch; Justine's "You're next," fell on innocent ears. For all of his attentions and presence, she was confident that he would never choose her for anything beyond a friend, and she attributed his attentions to his conversion and his acquaintance with her through church.

And then she *was* next, just the way Justine promised. Word was all over school that Vincent Elander had dumped Jennifer Imhoff, that he had ended his partying ways, that he had become a church-goer and a Bible-beater. And Maddie found herself his new girlfriend, not entirely comprehending, sort of lifted and tucked under his arm in the way he would take hold of a football.

She finally realized it when she noticed her picture: he had cut it from the yearbook and stuck it inside the door of his locker. "Hey, that's me!" she said, leaning in to focus.

"Yep," he said without looking at her. He was reaching to get a book from the shelf.

"Why do you have my picture in here?" she asked him, incredulous, blushing.

"Why do you think, silly?" he had asked her, and slammed the door so suddenly she had felt the breeze of it on her face. Then he had walked her to class.

∞

It was that sort of thing that could change a life. Walking side by side down the hall, stopping at the door of your classroom when he himself isn't going in. Sitting with you at lunch every day, even inviting his friends to join him, because he's no longer sitting at his table; he's sitting at yours.

Or holding hands.

It had such significance when, walking out of church into the late spring sunlight, Vincent had taken her hand and held it. He had continued to walk; the gesture—the taking and holding of her hand—had been sudden and also casual; it depended on an understanding, one they hadn't discussed, and so Maddie wondered in retrospect how it was he knew that enough of her affections belonged to him that he could also claim some proprietary regard for her hand.

No, she hadn't wondered that. Not, at least, until much later. That kind of reflection rooted itself in indignation, and it was nothing like indignation she felt on that spring day when he first took her hand in the church parking lot and she tried to act nonchalant, following his lead, his presumption that taking her hand was perfectly natural, even what was expected of him.

Yet for some time it had the continuing power to surprise her. Walking down the hall at school, standing outside the locker room after a football game, Vincent casually took her hand, their fingers loosely touching or even intertwined. A life can be changed when things like that happen, when other people see something like that, and Maddie saw them see—saw the girls she knew but had never spoken to take in at a glance Vincent Elander standing next to Maddie, not even standing closely, not even talking to her necessarily, but their hands just touching, just holding like that. Something so small as this changed everything.

Including Maddie, of course. She would think of herself later—much later—as victimized or preyed upon. But then, at the beginning, she didn't think of such things. What she knew then was the contour of his hands, the length of his fingers, the calluses of his palms. She came to know the perimeter of her own hand by the perimeter of his; she came to know the comfortable distance between her own fingers as determined by the width of his. And she came to know, too, the power of his hand on her untouchable center, the solidity of her core.

But she didn't marvel about it at the time; she didn't wonder at the power of that hand in hers to make her untouchable solid core turn, bend, cave slowly in upon itself so that she felt she was composed of liquid.

—∞∞∞—

The vomiting had started at about one o'clock in the morning—no, earlier. It was one or so when Frank heard something in the bathroom and then turned, confused, to discover that Maddie wasn't in the bed. He found her squatting in front of the toilet bowl, gripping the seat with both arms, her hair falling around her face. Crouching behind her on the floor, Frank tended to her hair, holding it away at the back of her neck.

Already there was nothing left. The toilet was empty of all but its standard water and what looked like saliva. Maddie heaved and heaved again, and afterward spat at the strings of mucous still clinging to her lips. Frank looked about him for a washcloth, then pulled his bath towel from its bar and tucked it toward Maddie's face. Breathless, she thanked him, and then the heaving began again.

With every pause in the retching, Frank thought this would be the end. The tension in Maddie's shoulders eased. She sat back on her heels, eyes closed, lungs gasping for air. There was nothing left in her stomach; surely it was over.

And then it started again, and Frank remembered what he was dealing with. This was no virus. This was nothing her body would readily be rid of. Who knew how long it would continue? "How long have you been in here?" Frank managed to ask. He was afraid of the answer. The nausea's abatement was long enough to have given him hope: for the first time, Maddie had leaned against him, her back full against his chest.

Her answer came after a long pause: "I have no idea."

Then Maddie lurched away from him and Frank marveled at her instinct: she may have been here like this for hours; did she think there was anything left in her stomach?

He struggled to his feet, legs cramping from their prolonged crouch. He stumbled toward the cabinet, found an elastic band and clumsily tried to work it into her hair. He could wrap it well enough but couldn't figure out how to make it stay in tightly, and then Maddie was pulling away from him again. He finally gave it up, leaving some of her hair loosely coiled in the elastic while thick strands still swung toward her face. These he occasionally tried to tuck behind her ears when he wasn't otherwise stroking her back, but all of it struck him as futile.

Exhaustion interfered with consciousness. Half-awake, eyes open, Frank hallucinated: the towers of San Gimignano were etching themselves unprovoked in varied order across the bathroom wall. He and Maddie had visited the town on their honeymoon, but he hadn't the energy now to wonder why this should be the vision that accompanied his vigil. Mindless, he stroked Maddie's back and gazed at the towers against a bright blue morning sky and then washed in red against a sunset orange—always only the towers and not the lower walls of the city. Just that many-pinnacled skyline, the architectural remains of medieval ambition lined solemnly along wall and shower curtain. After that, those towers—their varied heights, their persistently haunted sense of abandonment—were always linked in his mind with cancer.

Finally they dozed: he slumped with his upper back against the bathroom wall, and Maddie spread out over him, her face on the cool linoleum floor. Occasionally, the nausea would force her mouth open and the dry retching would convulse her body, but she no longer sat up to the toilet bowl for this. She lay there crookedly without opening her eyes, a small spot of saliva pooling under her cheek.

# 6

*O*n her good days, Maddie could be impressed by cancer's power to reshape her life. There were the obvious daily changes to medication and diet, and then there was her hair—or *had been* her hair—which she decided not to think about.

But cancer was even more assertive than this, reassigning the calendar to something of its own choosing. No longer did Maddie think in terms of months or weeks, the standard weekends, seasons and holidays in their course. Instead, she had to organize her thinking around the three-week periods between her chemotherapy treatments. Listening to a friend discuss holiday plans, Maddie ran the dates through the gauntlet of her treatment schedule. She couldn't attend this party because her white blood count would be at its lowest at that time; she couldn't meet friends for lunch because she had to avoid restaurants, crowds, the world in general.

This was routine for cancer care, nothing to complain about. Others had endured these circumstances with prognoses far worse.

She reminded herself that she was receiving the best treatment. Never mind that most of her discomfort was due to that treatment and not from the cancer itself: currently she was taking medications for several chemotherapy side-effects, the results of which made her tired most of the time and ruined the taste of her food.

Endurance was the name of the game. Maddie knew that. Chemotherapy was poison, plain and simple, and it was her task to survive it, to outlive the cancer with as much of herself intact as possible. Her hair and her fingernails seemed almost obligatory sacrifices. Everyone lost at least this much in cancer treatment. So she told herself.

She didn't do the research; she left that to Frank. For Maddie, survival meant taking care of herself and also of her sons—to the best of her ability—and keeping at bay those thoughts of Vincent's year in her life, memories useless, vague, and vexing nonetheless.

Lately it wasn't Vincent she was thinking of but the people he had prayed for: Mr. Pavlik, Mrs. Senchak, little Joey Amoretti on the parsonage lawn. She thought of Susan Sweet and her high, soft voice, thanking Vincent for praying for her there in the church reception hall.

All of them had wanted to be healed, whether they asked for it or not. This much she knew, and that knowledge filled her with an unaccountable defiance. Maddie, too, wanted to be well—although she was willing to wait for it, to endure the treatment and all the time and energy it took from her. She was willing *not* to ask to be healed.

And she thought of Matthew, Justine's little brother. She remembered him sitting in the pew between his parents, his legs sticking out straight on the pew bench, the heels of his shoes extending just over the edge. He had lived and died years before any of them knew Vincent. His casket had been very small and was covered in white flowers.

---

Frank kept a watchful eye on the calendar. From diagnosis to right now, cancer had taken seven months of their lives. Only seven months. What was it in the scheme of things? They were spending their lives together. He told himself that this cancer ordeal was manageable. Give it a year. Let it take every bit of a year. And the boys were fine. They were doing fine, and they were so young. By the time Maddie was better, they would scarcely remember it.

But he worried about his wife. The treatment was taking its toll, and he was sure the fatigue frustrated her. Yet he never had a word of complaint from her—as was her way.

In truth, he never had much in the way of any conversation from her these days. He would have liked to hear her thoughts, even if they weren't pleasant ones. But she was often silent. She seemed absorbed with something outside them all. Sometimes, thinking she was asleep, Frank might quietly enter their room to check on her and find that she was just lying there, staring at the wall. She would barely register his presence.

She had let him help her with her hair when it started falling out. Frank had tried to add levity to the process: he had fetched his electric clippers from under the bathroom sink and announced they'd have a head-shaving party. Maddie had agreed to it, and they had laughed as her hair fell in clusters to the floor. Frank insisted on doing the clean-up while Maddie examined her newly exposed head in the mirror, and he thought they had cleared the danger nicely, that she had accepted her new look with pluck. But when is anything of this magnitude so simple? She had cried into her pillow for a long time that night, immune to his efforts at comfort.

Seven months in. Only seven months, and there was no changing course, there was no remedy, no experimental process that might be the escape hatch Frank sometimes thought of longing for.

The urge to call Father Tim was sudden and also the only thing to do.

"How's it going?" Tim asked.

"It's going," was Frank's reply.

"Cancer sucks," Tim said.

Frank brought him up to speed, and Father Tim's response was reassuring: deeply sympathetic and unsurprised. He had known his share of cancer patients. He had visited them at home, in hospitals, sometimes at their deathbeds. He knew the right questions to ask; he knew the terminology.

He also knew the theology but didn't utter it. Instead, he said, "You're living the dream, my friend."

That was it, of course. The reminder—the kick in the pants, really—that Frank was needing.

And hadn't he known it, even from the earliest days of Maddie's diagnosis? This was the dream—this was it, what he and The Priest had talked about all those years ago, when they had moved on from theology and Catholic doctrine and started talking about marriage.

"A good marriage," Tim had clarified, "is absolutely where it's at." And then he had gone on to paint a vision of marriage that was both stunningly beautiful and also somehow familiar: a friendship bound by sacrament, the mysterious union of husband and wife; unparalleled intimacy. Fierce, unbreakable commitment—no matter the circumstances.

Frank had been taken by this vision. He had really been enchanted. Around him, news reports were of divorce rates on the rise; his own parents had split when he was eleven. In a culture of potential societal decay, the thought of a sound, committed, "good" marriage struck him as a form of fantastic rebellion.

And he was buoyed in his thinking by romance—smitten, for example, by the sight of an elderly couple holding hands and walking feebly down the street together. Presuming them to have been married since their twenties, Frank saw in them something to strive for. His casual relationships with former girlfriends suddenly felt silly to him; Francesca's eschewing marriage seemed the height of immaturity and foolishness.

Over the first months of dating Maddie, Frank recognized in her a woman who would be willing to do the sometimes "hard work," as Tim had called it, of marriage: she wouldn't look at frustrations or obstacles as reasons to quit; she would persevere through them. With Maddie, Frank realized, he could "live the dream."

Now, after this phone conversation with The Priest, Frank felt both chastised and strengthened. "In sickness and in health," that was how it went, right? Maddie needed him now, more than ever. And here they were, Frank and Maddie, working through the hard times together. Living the dream.

Frank felt it was fine to let his conversation with The Priest rest there. It was enough to have heard that much.

⁙

When their son was not yet two years old, Maddie and Frank took little Jake to the top of Mt. Washington in Pittsburgh. It was night, past his bedtime, and for that reason alone Maddie hadn't thought it was the best idea. But they were returning to North Carolina in the morning, and Frank knew that Maddie loved the view of the city at night. They wouldn't have to stay long; they could stand there for as little or as much time as they wanted to. And didn't Maddie want to do this, even if it was just for a few minutes?

Maddie had yielded her practicality to Frank's enthusiasm, to his ardent belief in the value of a great experience. In truth, she wanted it, too. They had both grown up in Pittsburgh, but on the opposite sides of town, and it was an early delight of their relationship to discover that the view from Mt. Washington was—for each of them—their favorite thing about the city. Maddie had assumed that Frank's would be the stadium, but no, he told her. On their earliest date to the city he had surprised her with a picnic on one of the overlooks.

Of course it was a popular view with everyone: the mountainside disappearing under the feet and the rivers sliding past the city, which shot up from its widening slit of land in peaks and pinnacles. Maddie liked its contradictions: the glass and concrete against the glassy rivers, the whisper of the trees on the mountain against the drifting sounds of traffic. The city, so far below, simultaneously seemed within reach: if she wanted to, she could break one of the towers away between her fingers.

At night the city's lights were softened in the black rivers. Folded over and through the landscape, the lesser lights of houses and buildings hugged the ground and pressed close to the city, growing up as they got closer in. And around it all and through it, the lights of the cars crawled along the city's edge, slipped in and out of it, and poured, streaming, over the bridges. It was as if, Maddie once told Frank, everything around it—pavement and parking lot and tired steel mill—was a living thing, sustained by the bright heart at the center.

And so they took little Jake to see it, parking at the edge of the sidewalk and walking him between them to the overlook. It was a warm summer night, and a gentle breeze came up the mountain and gusted at their hair. There had been a baseball game that night; the stadium was still ablaze. The little family stood at the fenced edge and gazed out at the city.

Jake hadn't lasted long. He began shrieking almost immediately, in such terror that Maddie felt certain he'd been injured somehow. Frank picked him up and held him close while Maddie peered at his extremities, looking for signs of what? She thought maybe a bee sting? And still Jake screamed, clinging to his father, his legs working as though he would climb higher on his father's chest.

"What's wrong? What's wrong?" Maddie was asking, trying to be soothing while also trying to suppress the panic she felt rising within her.

But then she realized Frank was laughing, a low chuckle. "He's fine, Maddie," he said. And he made her understand that Jake was simply terrified: he was trying to climb away from the city, to get back to the safety of the car.

Later, this was a moment in their parenting that amused them: the opposed efforts they hoped would help their son. For Maddie, the solution was obvious: get Jake back to the car and buckle him safely in his car seat, then get him to bed.

But Frank was all about helping their son overcome his fear. Walking deliberately with him back to the railing, he held the climbing, screaming Jake in his arms and pointed out to him the beauties of the view: "See the boat? That's a barge. And look! There's the stadium where the baseball players work." All of it in his soothing, confident voice, and all of it effective—were it not for the terror in their little boy's mind.

Yes, they could laugh about it later. But for Maddie, it now gained some significance. It was indicative, she felt, of the sometimes opposing ways she and her husband approached things. Take healing, for example, take God. Maddie knew that if she breathed a word to Frank about Vincent, her husband would say they should try it, ask for healing, pursue this remote chance.

Maddie understood it differently. She could see what Frank had, perhaps, not bothered to understand that night with little Jake: That the mountainside beneath their feet was lost in the darkness, and then there was the glowing river below them and the even more glowing city, burning like so many coals. Jake hadn't known what was beneath them; perhaps he feared that, at any moment, the concrete would give way and he and his family would go sliding down, cascading into the river—or worse, into the hot bright center of the city.

Frank had taken Jake's fears and tried to help him see beauty. And there was beauty, Maddie knew, in faith, in asking to be healed. But she wouldn't ask, ever.

All too clearly, she understood Jake's fears that night on the mountain. More and more often of late, she felt that she was standing on the edge of a precipice with a dark and plunging void below her. There was again the sound of sliding stones, faint but clear, like shale worked loose in a mine.

No, Maddie thought. She thought again of Mrs. Senchak. She thought of Mr. Pavlik. She thought of Vincent, and then—wasn't it simply a matter of practiced self-discipline?—she forced herself not to.

# 7

*D*reams are unfair—that was Frank's thought as he stepped into the shower. A person can't possibly be held accountable for what he dreams about. Sure, Francesca had come to mind from time to time, but these were thoughts he had immediately rejected and would continue to reject. A vital discipline.

They had been in college again, making out on her parents' sofa—not that he had ever been to her parents' house (Francesca had hated Cleveland; she had hated going home; she never wanted to take Frank there). But dreams broke those rules, too. It didn't matter that he'd never been to the place. In the dream it was all completely plausible: her parents' house in Cleveland (a split-level); the two of them making out, naked on the couch and not remotely alarmed when her dad walked in to adjust the thermostat. Also plausible was the fact of the llama bleating (do llamas bleat?) just outside the basement door and Francesca's crossing the room to feed it (still naked, of course. He watched her cross the room).

He felt guilty when he woke up, and the guilt was a second injustice. He had done nothing wrong, and he told himself this as he squeezed shampoo into his palm.

But on his way to work, there she was, haunting his thoughts before he was fully aware of them. It was her hair he found himself thinking of, long and curling, the golden highlights glinting in the sun. He had loved how long it was, how it almost reached the small of her back.

—⁂—

That was the same morning of the boys' check-ups, the annual visit to get reassurance of regular growth and weight gain. Frank offered to take them: he had no pressing deadlines; it would be no problem. And Maddie—he knew without asking—was tired of hospitals and doctor's offices. Wouldn't she like to have a morning out on her own, maybe?

No, Maddie did not want this. She was well, she said. Well enough, anyway. And she had enough in the way of mornings on her own. That much she said aloud, her voice lined with irritation. But Frank could read the subtext of the ensuing silence: she was well until next Monday's chemo infusion, after which they would start all over again with symptoms old or, if they were especially unlucky, new.

Frank's response was to sigh and smile at her, and she deliberately ignored what she detected as controlled exasperation. She ignored it until she couldn't, because she didn't take her mind off it when she should have, and it was when he was on his way out the door that she brought it up again and explained to him that *she* wanted to be the one to take the boys to the doctor; she had always taken them and there was no reason for her not to, she felt perfectly fine. She might have cancer, but she was still their mother.

He went out. She remembered that he was just trying to be kind to her, and she felt sorry for the way she had talked to him.

But there was residual annoyance, too, leftover from the night before. She didn't remember why at first, but she had awakened in a tempestuous mood that lay over everything like a fine dust. Maddie only recalled the reason on the way to the doctor's office, at which point she sighed audibly, leaking her exasperation into the otherwise silent car. Eli, ever sensitive, said, "What's the matter, Mom?" To which she had answered, "Nothing."

It was the way Frank had kissed her in bed the night before: not an affectionate peck but something more hopeful. She had lain motionless as he kissed her—her mouth, her face, her neck—not knowing how to tell him she wasn't interested, but also incredulous to think that she should have to. At best, it seemed profoundly insensitive of Frank, and at worst, completely blind.

The boys were pronounced healthy, their growth rates normal, and she drove them back to school. She remembered the way her very center used to fold in the crushing tenderness of Frank's kisses in the early days of their relationship, the way he would be rushing, surprised, trying to keep up with her sense of urgency.

Now all of that seemed foreign, and she felt a twinge of guilt for this—which quickly turned to anger. How could anyone expect more of her, she thought, arguing with no one but imagining Frank on the receiving end. She had suffered an amputation and now was carrying on with treatments that impacted every system in her body. She couldn't think about sex now and she shouldn't be expected to. Resuming a sex life was somewhere down the line, well beyond the unknown day when she hoped to be declared in remission.

The last thing she wanted to do was think any more than she had to about her body. Frank, of all people, should understand that.

---

Maddie had never given much thought to her body before Vincent. There had been adolescent awkwardness when she was conscious of change, and the dominant feeling then was shame, or a fierce embarrassment at the very least. Middle school boys with their sidelong looks and humiliating comments made her consider going into hiding.

Later intimations of her sexuality went largely unanswered. She envisioned kissing a boy or two, but these intriguing exploits remained fixed in her imagination. And long before any of that, there was the presiding censure against giving into any sexual urges, a warning not spoken, per se, at the Bethel Hills Church of Holiness, but one that was abundantly clear: chastity before marriage, monogamy within marriage, sexual purity always. These were given.

It wasn't until middle school that these concepts acquired something of a concrete vision: a vivid picture of a fenced-in swimming pool, an image painted in one of her earliest days as a member of the church youth group. The conversation had been mortifying. They were all together—boys and girls, grades seven through twelve—when the topic had turned to sex. Maddie's first thought was that she was way too young for this (she was only twelve at the time), but Nicky Tedesco, their youth group leader, was easily in his thirties and had led the youth group forever. Surely he knew what he was doing.

It was brief; it was embarrassing; it made sense. Think of sex like a swimming pool, Nicky had said, matter-of-fact and grinning. Pools are fun, he said. Sex is fun. And both of them are dangerous.

They all knew the dangers, meted out to them via their parents, maybe, or after-school specials. Nicky didn't need to go into the many pitfalls: pregnancy, sexually transmitted diseases, God.

Nicky went on. Sex was like a swimming pool, and by law a swimming pool had to have a fence around it because you want to keep people from accidentally falling in. But even inside the fence, Nicky pointed out, you generally have some space before you get to the pool's edge—some decorative rocks, the pool deck, something. That way, even if someone should scale the fence, the next thing that happens *won't* be that he falls into the pool.

Clear image so far, and Nicky went on to say that their approach to sex should be like that: they should erect a fence around the pool, so to speak. They should set boundaries as to what they would and wouldn't do in terms of physical intimacy with a boyfriend or girlfriend. And those boundaries should be *well outside the pool,* he emphasized. That way, in case you should go too far, you won't find yourself falling in, if you know what I mean.

Maddie did know what he meant, or thought so, anyway, and thus was armed to defend her virginity. The word even now made her shudder. It was one of those awkward words, one that wanted its own bastion of defense about it. And so it was an unassailable bastion she had built. She knew, long before even the hint of a boyfriend was on the horizon, what she would and would not do with a boy before she got married. There was no doubt in her mind.

And then Vincent had come along, and despite the good sense of the swimming pool metaphor, Maddie had unbuttoned her blouse that day. Just a little bit; not all of the buttons. An invitation—or not. Maybe, eyes closed in the bliss of feverish kissing, he wouldn't even notice.

In chemistry class, Mr. Uzelac had explained the structure of the atom: the nucleus, containing its protons and neutrons. And buzzing all around the outside, negatively charged electrons. Negatively charged, he said again. "This means," he went on with his eyebrows raised as if attempting to highlight the significance of his words, "that nothing ever really touches anything else."

Maddie was taken aback. What? She reached for the metal leg of her chair. Ice cold. She asked without raising her hand: Then how can we tell that something is hot or cold? Soft or hard? Mr. Uzelac said something about repulsion and the force of that repulsion, the density of the atoms or their structure. All the negative electrons repel all the other negative electrons. It was that simple.

For the rest of the day and sometime after that, Maddie had felt unnerved. Is it not the knob of the door I am feeling, but electrons pressing against my hand? Not the page of my textbook? Not the water from the faucet? Not my own hair?

She had pinched Vincent's arm hard in the cafeteria. "Ow!" he exclaimed, pulling away. "What are you doing?"

She explained to him what Mr. Uzelac had said—that everything always ultimately repels everything else.

Vincent laughed. "So? What's the big deal?" he said.

"It means that nothing ever really touches anything else," she said.

"Oh," he mimicked, "Nothing ever really touches anything else," he said, teasing, his voice in a whine. And then he seized her sandwich from her hands and took a bite out of it.

"Vincent!" she'd yelled, and slapped him. But he took another bite and said with his mouth full that he hadn't felt it because she hadn't really touched him.

"Eat your own lunch," she said, more quietly because people were looking at them.

"I didn't *touch* your lunch. I *can't*," he said, smirking. "I didn't just eat your lunch because I can't touch *anything*." Justine was rolling her eyes at them; Vincent's friends were laughing.

But later, when he walked her to Spanish class, he stopped her outside the door and took her books from her, setting them on the floor. Then he put his arms around her waist and hugged her tightly, holding her there for a long time, even though people were noticing, even though he never hugged her in public, even after she said she really had to go, after the late bell rang. When he finally released her, he picked up her books and handed them to her, then pecked her quickly on the cheek. "See what I did?" he asked her, walking backwards, calling to her down the hall. "I touched you!" He almost shouted it; he gave her his smirk again, then went into his German class.

∞

Vincent did indeed notice the unbuttoning, and his reaction was almost immediate. He stopped kissing her. Then he reached up and closed the buttons again.

"I love you," he said.

Now she could not imagine willingly exposing her chest. She dreaded when Frank saw her and, despite all the exams, was not inured to the exposure at the doctor's office. It was months before she would allow herself to look, long after the mastectomy had healed.

The scars might have been worse; they had tried to be careful. But how careful should you be when someone's life is at stake? Her left side, from her armpit across her chest, was flat now and rivered with thin gray scars. They slid down her side and then across her chest; where her nipple had been, the scars rose in a slight twist. Sometimes she ran her fingers over these scars, following the lines where they had cut into her skin, tracing them like she might a road on a map. The skin here was numb, the nerves having been taken in sacrifice, her body refusing answer to her finger's touch.

Frank still said he found her beautiful. That was kind, Maddie thought—but she couldn't imagine it was true. The weight gain, her bald head, one hemisphere of her chest hemmed ragged and uneven. She knew she was repulsive, no matter what Frank had to say about it.

∞

The boys earned stickers from their visit to the doctor, and each bore the badge of honor in his own way: Jake's was on his forehead; white traces of Garrett's adhered to the front of his shirt; and Eli had laid his, still attached to its backing, on the kitchen counter, where he had promptly forgotten it in the interest of playing with Legos.

"How did it go today?" Frank asked.

"Good," said Jake, and Eli said, "Fine," and they barely looked up from their play on the living room floor. Garrett, only peripherally involved in the building projects, bounded up to his father.

"The doctor says we're all better, Daddy!" and Frank enfolded him in a hug, wondering how much of that was a four-year-old talking and how much was wishful thinking: the boys all wanted their mother to be well.

Maddie was asleep on the sofa, one arm up behind her head and the other at her side. One small move and she would knock down a variety of Lego constructions, laid like offerings along the length of her body. Frank saw her wig was slightly askew, but he knew that when she awoke, she would adjust it before she sat up. He stood there holding Garrett, watching the bent heads and listening to the quiet chatter of his older sons, the rattle of the Lego pieces as they ran their hands over them. He thought of them admonishing one another to be quiet, of their tender awareness of their sleeping mother, of the gentleness of their gifts, deposited one after another next to her.

Still holding Garrett in his arms, he headed into the kitchen, saying low into the boy's ear that the two of them would make some dinner together.

———— ◈◈◈ ————

More and more, Frank found himself thinking of Vincent. He had never met him, of course, and the scene his name conjured in Frank's mind was somehow neither that of the episode with Willy in the pouring rain, nor of Maddie lying in the school parking lot, but rather of the football game. The game was a lesser-known event in the Vincent saga, not one that Maddie was given to repeat. It was less fantastic, less striking, less clear in terms of credibility. But it was the story that Frank saw most vividly. He imagined what it might have been like had it been true: that Vincent had actually healed one of his opponents. Frank would have liked to write about it.

He sees Vincent now out near the fifty-yard line, where he bends on one knee over the injured kid on the football field. Frank himself stands on the sidelines, the chill of a Pittsburgh November seeping through his jacket as he watches the coaches clustered on the field.

Then suddenly the knot loosens and expands, and the injured boy is on his feet, moving, walking away from Frank and toward his team. The stands erupt with cheering; coaches watch him go and then follow suit, moving slowly over the field. Only one figure remains: Vincent Elander, standing with his helmet under his arm, his right leg slightly bent, watching the boy he has just healed walk away.

Frank imagines all of this, then sees himself walk out onto the field. Vincent's back is to him, and Frank calls him by name as he reaches him and reaches for him. He takes hold of Vincent by the arm and Vincent turns and looks him in the eye.

"Vincent," Frank says to him without hesitation, "I need you to come heal my wife."

# 8

*F*rank told Maddie he had a surprise for her, then presented her with the sheet of paper, the printout from Facebook. Pittsburgh's skyline was spread across the top and, in the square where his face should be, sat the symbol for the Pittsburgh Steelers. It was in black-and-white, and the name was "Vincent Elander."

"What's this?" Maddie's voice was cold.

"I found him," Frank said, his tone less exultant than he had felt when, chuckling, he printed out the page at work. A little levity would be good for them both. "I found the Superhero," he said. This was his sagging effort to bring the joke around, their age-old joke about forgotten lovers. They had laughed about this together, right? Frank remembered that, or thought he did—though now, standing in his kitchen with his wife, he wondered if he remembered it wrong.

"What in the world," Maddie said, her gaze on the sheet of paper. Then louder: "What in the world, Frank," she said.

"It's a joke, Madeleine," Frank said. Clearly she didn't get it.

"How's that?" Maddie asked, looking at him. The piece of paper trembled slightly in her hand. "Were you wanting to contact him, Frank?"

"No," said Frank, suddenly uncertain of his intentions.

"Were you thinking that maybe we ought to give him a call?

Maybe we could pay him a visit?"

Frank said no, no that was not what he was thinking. He didn't know what he was thinking. It was a just a joke.

But Maddie persisted in *not* getting it. She persisted, instead, in guessing his meaning: that he had thought maybe Vincent could be of help to them, that maybe he could pray for Maddie, maybe send a little healing her way—which of course would be pointless, because she had told Frank a thousand times if she had told him once that Vincent Elander couldn't heal people. He never could. He never could, Frank.

It was most definitely an outburst. She was yelling—and this was not at all what Frank had thought would happen. Then there came a pause, during which Frank decided not to say anything and Maddie stared at him, eyes cold.

Then, more quietly, she said, "He's just an accountant, Frank. He's a stupid accountant."

As if it were impossible that gifts like healing would ever be imparted to a humble accountant. Or to a boy in high school. Frank thought that, but didn't say it out loud.

Anyway, Maddie had left the room and left the printout from Facebook where she dropped it, lying face down on the kitchen floor. Frank picked it up and threw it in the trash.

———— ∞ ————

He should have known she wouldn't like it, Frank thought, and then he wondered why. They had most definitely laughed about this together. They most definitely had—many times. But all and any of that seemed like a long time ago now.

He felt like he needed to justify himself to Maddie, but didn't want to raise the issue again. What would he say? Vincent had just been on his mind lately. Why that should be the case was obvious to him. Why was it not obvious to her?

But it *had* been obvious to her. It had been more obvious to her than it had been to him, he realized now, and he felt embarrassed by his ignorance—his inability to see what he had been thinking. In the guise of an old joke, he had been raising the possibility—er, rather, the impossibility—that she could be healed. Which he wanted, desperately. But he had also, thoughtlessly and unintentionally, called her a liar. Wasn't that the argument, way back in the beginning? She had always insisted that the Superhero couldn't heal anybody, and she had been there. She had seen it—or rather, hadn't seen it—with her own eyes.

It didn't matter that some of it actually seemed plausible to Frank—and not just plausible because he had a penchant for believing in the miraculous, but plausible because, in some of the stories she told, it really did seem as though Vincent had healed people.

It seemed that way. But Maddie insisted it didn't happen, and she had been there.

Then he remembered San Gimignano again, with its abandoned towers against the sky. He and Maddie had missed the last bus back to Florence, and so they had time to see the towers from every angle, in every light: from the maze of bricked streets running through the town; from the olive groves on the hills surrounding it.

This was their honeymoon. Frank had always imagined taking his wife to Italy on their honeymoon, even before he met Maddie. Tuscany was their favorite part of the trip, and the quiet streets of San Gimignano had felt like a refuge from the Florentine crowds.

Still, around the middle of the afternoon, when more buses deposited their tourists and the sun's heat radiated from the streets, Frank and Maddie felt the need for an escape—and that was how they came to discover the statue, tucked in a shaded corner of a remote piazza, not far from the city's north wall. Here, next to a fountain bubbling out of a building's side, was the statue of Mary, her feet badly deteriorated.

Maddie had expressed concern: How old was that statue? And how could they let it reach such a state of decay? Weren't they afraid she would topple over? The statue's toes were long gone; the feet shorn off—not broken—but sloping from mid-arch to the supporting pedestal, completely worn away.

Frank had offered what he knew of such things, a potential explanation, probable: People believed the statue offered help or healing of some kind. You pass by it, you touch Mary's feet, you say a prayer.

Maddie sat on the lip of the fountain's pool, silent for a moment. Overhead, swallows swung through the sky.

"Still?" she asked.

Frank didn't know what she meant.

"I mean, do people still believe that? Still *do* that?"

Which marked a new conversation about healing, one less charged with emotion than when she had first told him about Vincent, but marked—Frank thought afterward—by a difference between them he hadn't been aware of, a difference, fundamentally, in faith.

Frank said he supposed they still did, and Maddie had questioned the practice, defending her incredulity with respect for the statue's age. Couldn't they see they were damaging it?

He replied that it was a difference in perceived value. What made the statue valuable wasn't so much its age or artistic merit, but rather its spiritual value. Here was a connection to God.

Maddie said that sounded medieval to her, and Frank chuckled; they both chuckled. The town's medieval towers were everywhere around them. Everything seemed medieval in San Gimignano.

But Frank had pressed the issue. Yes, maybe it was a type of faith that was more dominant in the Middle Ages. But didn't she agree that God could also work that way now? God—merciful, all-powerful, unchanging. If he chose to heal people in the ancient world, if he chose to heal people during the Middle Ages, even through a statue, could he not—*would* he not—do the same thing now?

The fountain bubbled, the swallows wheeled, and Frank looked at his bride, waiting for an answer. He was interested, almost curious. He didn't need her answer to be anything in particular; he knew what her answer would be: she would agree with him.

Except that she didn't. She told him with certainty that she just didn't think God did things like that anymore. God didn't go around doing miraculous healing. He didn't do miracles these days. God worked through science; he let people figure it out. The problem came, she said, when people expected him to work magic, or when they looked at him as a means to an end, like they could use him to get what they wanted. Meanwhile, the Bible was clear on this: God was concerned with our souls, not our bodies. That was the whole point of the church, wasn't it? Saving souls?

Frank had been taken aback. He had honestly been surprised—and he hadn't known exactly what to say. Some of what she said rang true to him; it was most definitely true. But some of it seemed empty or hollowed out, as if her words—were it possible—had dulled just a corner of God's glory.

Now, once again, Frank aligned this conversation with the others about the Superhero and Maddie's adamant position on all of it. Souls, not bodies. In which case, of course, contacting Vincent while she was in this condition would be nothing but cruelty.

He hadn't meant it that way. Of course he hadn't.

———

Later, Maddie told him more gently that the cancer was on its way out. It was the most she could do in reference to the Facebook fiasco and whatever Frank had meant by it. She felt she needed to say something; one of them did, and Frank seemed so sad.

I'm getting better, she told him. Really, she said, I know I am. She laughed: If I'm having all these symptoms from the chemo, I think we can be sure it's working! We just have to be patient.

But she didn't tell him what she actually thought, what she saw and heard in her head every time it occurred to her to call on Vincent just this once, if he could just do this one enormous favor. She couldn't think of asking without seeing him there, leaning over his car in the parking lot, asking his question, receiving the silence that was his only answer: "Do you want to be healed of a paper cut?"

———

Mostly, Maddie really did think that the cancer was on its way out. But there was a fear lurking that countered that idea, and this was the power of cancer to skip the bounds of its diagnosed site and make its way to other parts of her body. Her lymph nodes were clean: this was good. But who was to say when they would suddenly cease to be so? Who was to say when cancer would invisibly and silently slip past the porous membrane of her breast tissue and invade lung, liver, brain?

The only help for these thoughts was deliberate focus on the immediate: to tell herself that she was doing all she could, that she was undergoing excellent care, that the cancer was under attack. But at the end of the day, no one could promise her anything. She understood that.

And maybe that was some of the appeal in the mothering, she considered. Here were three lives in her keeping. She had painted the boys' rooms herself and had chosen the bedding. Their drawers were neatly organized by her hand, their meals and snacks prepared with her wisdom. Even their schedules were planned and then closely monitored by her eye. She knew who needed more sleep and who needed to spend more energy. There was some real enjoyment, she recognized, in caring so completely for these lives.

There had been that terrifying moment when the boys went missing, when, absent her watchful gaze for only a few minutes (she had been washing the dishes; she was on the phone: Go in the other room and play, boys. Mommy will be done in a minute), Jake and Eli had wandered out of the house. How long does it take for a child to disappear—even two of them together, even if they are only four and two years old?

She had gotten off the phone. She couldn't have been on the phone for very long in the first place, but already the boys weren't in the living room where she had sent them. And they weren't in the playroom, or in their bedrooms. They weren't in the backyard on the swing; they weren't in the front yard.

Maybe they were with the baby. With a start, Maddie raced up the steps, eager to prevent the boys waking Garrett from his morning nap. But he was sleeping soundly, no big brother in sight. Maddie even checked under the crib, then made a more careful run through the house, this time calling for the boys, checking closets, checking Frank's office. Where could they have gone?

Outside? But the yard, front and back, was empty. She scanned the neighbors' yards, the street. She walked to the end of the driveway while new fears arose. Their street wasn't busy, but it wasn't far from busy ones. The grid of roads appeared in her mind. Maddie began to call, loudly: Jake! Eli! Even now she could still conjure the sound of her voice in the silence. Jacob! Eli! Her voice broke, but still she called. The roads were far too busy out there and the boys were so little. Eli was still in his pajamas.

Plucking Garrett from his nap, she then went from house to house, ringing the doorbells, constantly scanning the street behind her. How was it possible, on this day of all days, during this sudden emergency, that no one else was home?

She called Frank: The boys are missing. Then Frank was on his way, but not before he asked her the question, and somehow his saying it out loud made it a thousand times more real and therefore worse than the thought of it had been: Had she called the police? She would call them, she would describe what they were wearing, she wouldn't care that she sounded like an over-protective parent, or distracted, or neglectful.

The waiting was the worst part. Waiting for Frank. Waiting for the police. Listening without meaning to for the sound of a siren. She could not bring herself to go inside the house. Please God. Please. Please. What else can one say?

It couldn't have been much time (the police hadn't yet arrived) when the boys appeared at the top of the street, walking toward home, one on each side of a man she had never seen, a man who said he'd been cleaning gutters on a house one block away, and he'd seen these two little boys (one still in his pajamas) and he'd thought that something didn't seem right. So he'd asked them where they lived and they had told him, and now he was walking them home.

That was a terrifying moment, Maddie thought, standing there in the morning light in Jake's bedroom. She was staring at the heap of dirty clothes he had stashed by his bookcase, and she was thinking that he had doubled his life span since that September day when he was four. That day shortened my life, Maddie thought to herself, and remembered once again that her life span had been newly threatened by cells growing beyond reason in her breast and the potential of their venturing outward. And she thought again of her imaginary knitting, the invisible blanket constantly spilling from her busy hands. On that day, when the boys went wandering, had the blanket followed them? She couldn't have sent it after them; she'd had no idea where they were.

⁂

Frank hadn't just found Vincent on Facebook; he'd found Francesca, too. He hadn't quite meant to. He had typed her name as a joke on himself: an old boyfriend of Maddie's, an old girlfriend of his. He typed her name, knowing for certain that she wouldn't have an account. Francesca wouldn't be the type. Nothing so pedestrian, so quotidian for Francesca.

And then there she was, and he would know her anywhere with her long, curling hair and her glowing smile. She was living in Seattle, and Frank was a little surprised. Given a guess, he would have chosen a locale more cosmopolitan: New York, at the very least, or somewhere international, like Milan. But Seattle was cosmopolitan enough, he supposed, and likely it was only a home base. Likely she was constantly jetting off from there to New York or London and places like it. Likely she was never home.

He had heard nothing from her since her sudden disappearance from campus that day. Once or twice he had thought to troll the Internet for her. Occasionally when he picked up something like *Harper's Bazaar* or *The New Yorker*, he half-expected to see her name listed among the contributors—and then he laughed at himself for somehow maintaining belief in the superiority of her writing skills. He had been so young and inexperienced when he knew her; he'd had no idea, at the time, whether she was really a good writer or not. And who could know if she'd even pursued a career in writing?

But he didn't care. He couldn't care. After their break-up, the one leaving him no recourse because she simultaneously left to "pursue her education at a school more suited to her ambitions" (or something like that), it had taken too many months of his life to get over her. It was Tim who was able to help him see Francesca's absurdity. Her ambition, her pride, the smug overestimation of her own intellect. Her resolve to "find herself," to never marry but take on numerous lovers, to never "settle down." It was The Priest who had helped him see how much better a real relationship could be, a relationship with someone like Maddie.

Father Tim was right, and Frank wasn't about to contact Francesca. He had stopped needing her—or imagining he needed her—a long time ago. But there was a lot to remember as he stared a moment longer at the image of the woman he used to know. He thought it best, most likely, if he didn't start remembering at all.

# 9

She was tired all the time. Winded by loading the dishwasher or making up the boys' beds, Maddie would sit down suddenly, frustrated that she needed to. She sat on the sofa, the edge of Jake's bed, the stairs. But where in the past a few minutes' sitting was all she needed to recover, the revival now seemed never to come. Sitting there Maddie only became more aware of the dead weight at her center, a weight that pulled at all of her limbs, her fingers, her jaw, her eyelids. She would will herself to stand, then would sit staring at a task across the room (the books piled right next to Eli's bookcase, the Matchbox cars spilled out of their storage bin, a wayward tissue balled and resting under the ottoman), and would marvel at her inability to rise to her feet. She hated her body's defiant needing, its relentless demands. It was pitiable, and on her good days Maddie tried to laugh at it. She could and did tell herself that her body was hard at work, doing other, more important things. It's no small thing, she told herself, what her body was hard at work on: fighting itself, fighting disease. The tissue under the ottoman could wait, could even decay there. It didn't matter.

But maintaining this spirited conviction required endurance of its own, and at night she was faced with a maddening irony: sleeplessness. Lowering herself gingerly into bed, releasing her weight to the mattress, Maddie asked her body to remember the fatigue of the earlier afternoon. But sleep would not come. She lay in bed, listening to the clock's tick on the dresser, to Frank's steady breathing beside her. His digital clock cast a bluish light across his nightstand, and occasionally Maddie would raise her head to read it: 1:17, 2:43, 3:31. Time's passage seemed indiscriminate: unlike the day, when the shadows of the trees or the angle of the light could educate her guess, the night's solid darkness left her no clues.

She would wander. At first she confined herself to the downstairs, roving from room to room in listless discontent. But as her illness grew worse she remained upstairs, moving from bed to bed in the rooms of her sleeping children. Exhausted, she would sit at the edge of a child's bed and look at the room in the yellow glow of the nightlight. Or she would gaze at the child himself: this time it was Jake in his predictable sweat. She had him wear summer pajamas all year round, but it made no difference. Little bubbles of perspiration spread like freckles across his nose and cheeks. The oscillating fan pushed at a few dry curls, but otherwise his hair wetly adhered to his head. His eyelashes were thick and black, much darker than his sandy-blond hair. She leaned in close and studied his face.

Mothers should know. A mother should know her child's face, she thought. She knew that Garrett's left ear was just the slightest bit bent at the top, that Jacob's whorl of hair was just to the right of the center back of his head. And Eli had his father's nose: straight and, even at this young age, elegantly shaped. It was like a little ski-jump, Maddie always thought: dramatically steep with just the slightest inverted angle at the end. He would be handsome when he grew up.

She knew their faces before they were born. Frank had chuckled at how she studied the ultrasound pictures, the slick squares of paper printed in the doctor's office and then proudly displayed on their refrigerator. To that day, she claimed she could distinguish Garrett from Jake or Eli based on sonogram image alone. Frank teased that it was because she had memorized them, but she said she would know those profiles anywhere. And it wasn't just that, she always said to Frank. She remembered each one from before he was born: Eli's spine on her right side, Garrett's on her left. It was Jake who had kicked her, mercilessly, in the ribs.

In each pregnancy, Maddie felt almost desperate to get those ultrasounds: the early months had been torturous for the withheld knowledge. Until she got the pictures, the babies were frighteningly remote and anonymous: silent, shut up in the dark, their eyes sealed shut. Unknown and unknowable.

Mothers should know, she thought, and shuddered.

These hours were the worst of all, when fatigue and sleeplessness both plagued her. During the day it was easier to keep the thoughts at bay. But at night, the silence, the dark, and the clock taunted her with what might be coming: cancer insurmountable, an agonized and drawn-out death, three boys motherless and Frank grief-stricken, grimly seeing to the needs of the day.

Her mind raced relentlessly ahead: How to meet the demands—the practices, the games? The boys would only be involved in more things as they grew older; schedules would conflict. The school supplies, the school clothes, the shoes. And she always knew where to find things, not Frank. She knew for instance that right now the ketchup sat at the back of the refrigerator's third shelf on the left-hand side. Garrett loved ketchup, but Frank could never find it.

And her mind went on: one parent at Open House at school, one parent for teacher conferences, one parent at the sports banquets, at graduation. Frank might marry again and that brought waking nightmares: if the boys didn't like their stepmother, if she didn't like the boys, if she had children of her own and Frank being pulled somehow between them.

She talked herself through it—or tried: lots of kids were raised by single parents and were happy and well-adjusted. Blended families, too, abounded. And why needlessly worry it like this?

But her mind was unrelenting. She was their mother; she had known them before they were born. She wanted to give them the gift of a mother—even if it wasn't necessary.

She remembered a girl in third grade whose mother had died, whose clothes didn't fit her and were stained, whose father packed in her lunchbox a slice of cold pizza and a piece of cheese wrapped in cellophane. The girl always seemed sad, Maddie remembered, and nothing the other girls could do would draw her out.

Frank was a good father, but Maddie imagined anyway a vivid and terrible emptiness for her sons without her. It wasn't that she was the best mother; it wasn't that she was anything like a perfect mother, but the love of a mother, that covering (and here again the vision came of the knitted blanket) that she was forever drawing over and around her boys would be stripped away. She saw them exposed, lonely, colder. The girl she knew in third grade—the one whose mother had died—always had bare legs, even in the winter.

---

Frank felt at a loss. He had tried, and he was resigned to continue to try, but he had also—consistently—failed to reach his wife. Sure, he did what he could for her: took care of the boys, did the errands, managed laundry and cooking—but only when Maddie needed him to. Moreover, those aspects of shouldering the burden might be what one performed for a spouse who had a bad cold. There were no heroics here.

Neither was he looking to be heroic. What he might have said is that he'd like to feel useful to Maddie. He'd like to sense that he was somehow essential to her recovery or, even short of that, essential to her fight against the sickness in the first place.

Instead, Maddie continued to turn inward, and in doing so, had shut him out. Without it being actually true, Frank felt fairly constantly that his wife's back was turned to him, that she was distracted by something so absorbing she didn't even know he was in the room.

The closest he had felt to Maddie was some weeks ago when, fast asleep in the middle of the night, he had suddenly become aware of a chill. He reached down to the foot of the bed to pull up their extra blanket and felt Maddie doing the same thing. Although he was only half-awake, this small gesture had consoled him: their feeling was the same, the remedy identical. He had slept well after that, and it was only on waking in the morning that he recognized his comfort in it as somewhat pitiful. Rather than being an example of their connection, his pleasure in this small gesture only underscored the lack of such gestures. It highlighted their failure to connect rather than symbolizing some success.

He had promised "in sickness and in health," but he hadn't known what the "sickness" could mean. It wasn't the treatment or the side effects. It was the loneliness. He had promised to endure it with her as long as it lasted—and he absolutely intended to—but it would be nice to feel that she wanted him along in the first place.

———— ❦ ————

Despite her constant awareness of cancer in her life and body, Maddie didn't immediately think of the disease when suddenly she was coughing all the time. Several decades' worth of the common cold told her subconscious that her ailment was nothing more. But the feverishness set in soon afterward, and Frank reminded her to be concerned. Already she had been sick for a full day when he declared he would be taking her to the doctor.

His insistence brought her to her senses, and then the fear struck: the cancer was in her lungs. She stood unmoving in the upstairs hallway, her hand curled and bracing her against the wall. She was breathing hard, almost hyperventilating when Frank found her there, ready to take her to the doctor.

"No, no, honey," he said, and his words were the only thing that could have incited her to move, because in that instant of paralyzing fear she was almost ready to give everything up, she was so tired. "It's not cancer in your lungs. Cancer doesn't give you a fever. You have an infection, sweetheart. You're sick. You have an infection."

Then Maddie released the wall and seized his neck, holding on to him as if he had just rescued her from drowning.

Maddie didn't want an infection, of course. Neither of them did. Neither did they want the diagnosis of pneumonia, or the week in the hospital that followed, or the sense that this was dragging on too long.

Frank would have admitted that he hadn't been certain it *wasn't* cancer. He hadn't known for sure. The infection wasn't good news, either—but he sure as hell would take pneumonia in her lungs over more cancer.

And he was grateful for that moment in the hallway. She had felt fragile to him; there was an unfamiliar lightness in her limbs, as if her bones were hollow. But she had seemed to gain strength from his holding her, and soon enough she was able to draw herself together and walk down to the car. In truth, he had held her longer than he'd needed to. They had stayed there like that for a long time, which had made them late for the appointment.

∞∞∞

The boys arrived and Frank brought them by the bedroom door. The four of them stood there, looking in, and then Eli ran off. There was something he didn't like about it: the seeming ceremony or the limitations. But Jake was delighted to see his mother and waved an orange sheet of paper at her from the doorway.

"Look, Mom," he said. "We're learning about the states. I picked Pennsylvania!" Clearly it was some kind of research project, and Maddie wondered if second-graders were old enough for such things. But she asked him if he chose that state because that's where his grandparents lived, and he said yes, and also because they had bears there. Maddie laughed—delighted—and said that yes, Pennsylvania had bears. She told Jake that she couldn't wait to learn more about Pennsylvania with him, and then Jake moved off, satisfied by this interview with his mother and interested now in the possibility of an after-school snack.

It was Garrett's turn. He was four and had a hard time understanding the limited visits with his mother. Frank held him in his arms and helped Garrett talk about his day. He had played at the water table and the sand table, and now he clung to his daddy and stared at his mommy. Maddie smiled back, focusing on the dimples on the backs of his hands.

The doctors had allowed her to come home: she was through the pneumonia. But enforced rest was the new prescription; she was to be more careful now than she had been. The doctors declared that when her counts were down, she was to be confined to the bedroom. And because the boys were exposed to God knew what all day at school, the doctors further declared that—on those days—she was allowed absolutely no physical contact with her sons.

Through the open door, she could hear them down in the kitchen. Frank was making up a song about peanut butter and Jake was punctuating it with the word "banana." The house was too quiet all day while they were gone; she loved to hear this singing and laughter.

She let her head drop back against the pillows. She was not close to crying today; she was getting better. But someone stirred at the door and she raised her head again, eager not to miss him. It was Eli, leaning into the room. His hands rested on the door frame, one on each side, and he let his weight swing from those hands; but his toes were clearly still within the margin of the hall. He was remaining where he was supposed to—no one could say he wasn't—but his grin told Maddie that he knew—and she knew—that he was in the room.

Then, with a thrust, he pushed off and his body disappeared into the hallway. He'd given Maddie her visit.

———— ∞∞ ————

She didn't know where he lived. Somewhere in Pittsburgh. She had thought of looking him up before—countless times, before Frank had done it, even before the cancer—but always decided she didn't want to know.

Still, she thought of it. Pulling out of her driveway in the moonlight, backing out and then making the left-hand turn. The interstate was only a few blocks away, no more than three miles, and she envisioned the road and its orange streetlights, the drugstore and dry cleaner, the car-wash.

On the interstate, both sides of the road would be lined with trees, but these would appear as shadows at this time of night. She'd have to drive for a while before the landscape opened and the sleeping farms would spring up, silos glinting silver. After a time, the mountains would come and the road would curve between their split sides. She saw her headlights alone cutting the darkness, gaining the pavement just yards before her car. Miles of road between here and Pittsburgh, but all of them connected, each one touching the next, one after the other in a long line that extended mysteriously to that place so long ago.

She thought she could see it: the roads, the turns. They had made the trip many times. She could drive right into the city, right up onto the mountain and stand looking down at the cathedral that was Pittsburgh, sitting bright astride her rivers, for all the world like a shining church in a medieval darkness. And the bridges that spanned the rivers, that stretched across the darkness, and the cars that flowed over them, their headlights like chains or diamond necklaces drawn steadily over the dark.

And somewhere in it—there or in the wrinkled skirts of the suburbs—Vincent would be sleeping, oblivious to her standing there, oblivious that she needed him at all.

# 10

*M*addie had been raised in those wrinkled skirts, in among multitudinous folds that were an irregular system of hills and valleys—one that required curves and climbs to navigate. She knew nothing else. That the sun didn't hit her living room until it had been up for some time did not register for her—not early on, anyway—as a disadvantage. She had always lived in a valley and many of her friends did the same; many others lived on hilltops and more still on the sides of hills, their homes planted improbably into the tilted landscape.

In the early morning she stood cold and slit-eyed at the bus stop, first hearing the bus and then watching its halting descent down the hill. The brakes screeched and the transmission churned, and Maddie boarded through the stiffly flapping doors, indifferently inhaling diesel fumes. She was accustomed to the bus's grinding climb up the next hill, and to getting her first glimpse of the sun only when the bus had reached the top.

At most then, the landscape of the Bethel Hills of Pittsburgh was to her an arbiter of sunlight. But not even that, not really. She wasn't aware of these things. Pittsburgh, with its winding and weary roads, was home to her.

The fact of its weariness, too, made little impression. To Maddie's inexperienced eye, the suburbs of all cities were like this one: buckling, potholed roads; small businesses housed in tired buildings; pitted and gravelly parking lots. Renovation never would have occurred to her. Such things were reserved for places like downtown, which was, at the time, in the very process of remaking itself. But the world of the suburbs—Maddie's world—was in the business of daily life, of doing what had to be done.

Which is admirable. And the people of Pittsburgh's Bethel Hills were cheerful about it. Maddie was raised among cheerful people, by cheerful people. What is the relative weight, anyway, of a neglected pothole in the scheme of life? Pittsburghers seemed to keep these things in perspective.

Maddie's life turned on three specific plots in that landscape: her home, which was in the aforementioned valley; her school, which was on a hill; and her church—the Bethel Hills Church of Holiness—which was about three-fourths of the way down an uncommonly gentle slope. In the early spring, the neighborhood's melting snow ran to the church's parking lot.

Like the rest of the neighborhood and that hill-ridden suburb, the church building was a tired one, but like Maddie's house and neighborhood, it was somewhat newer than what was planted around it. Constructed sometime during the 1960's, the architecture suggested that attention had been given to its design. But a low budget and persistent flaws in that design (the church basement flooded at least twice annually) relegated anything beyond basic maintenance to the realm of the inaccessible. As a result, the Bethel Hills Church matched the fatigued appearance of its neighbors—which likely helped it fit in.

But fatigue did not characterize the people—neither the suburban dwellers nor the congregants of Maddie's church. The people of the Bethel Hills Church of Holiness were, in fact, an energized congregation, having taken to heart long ago that which they claimed to believe: that God, in his mercy, took human form in the person of Jesus Christ and died to save his people from their sins. Moreover, they took seriously that this same Jesus had been raised from the dead, an impossibility that served to galvanize their faith: if God, because of his love, would do something like this, invading the world for its own salvation, forgiving people of their sins, and performing innumerable miracles besides, then his continuous acts of mercy were not to be doubted. They ardently believed that one could and should expect God to act at any moment: communicating to the faithful, hearing and answering prayer.

Such potential, if truly believed, was staggering, diminishing issues such as leaky basements. Belief such as this generated tremendous energy, reflected in myriad ways: multiple services held weekly, annual community outreach programs by the dozens, and an unrelenting willingness to consider and re-evaluate the church's own tenets—not its fundamental doctrines, but those rules and bylaws which might, from time to time, be found to have been in error.

The advent of HBO, for example, had been problematic, as the church had historically held a hard and fast rule against its members seeing movies. Hollywood, said church founders, apparently held to moral boundaries far removed from those at Holiness. On seeing a movie, the faithful might readily be confronted with ideas and images offensive and potentially corrosive to their beliefs, tempting them away from moral purity. But the rule had been made long prior to the ubiquitous presence of HBO and, more recently, VCRs, and so had to be reevaluated.

The upshot was a reassessment of the film industry in general, which led to the acknowledgement that some movies were, in fact, good. This meant a new freedom for the church: see and enjoy movies, but use discretion when deciding which ones. Everyone felt good about this. It discouraged the view that Hollywood—or any amoral cultural entity—was the bad guy, and it allowed for more of what the church said it wanted in the first place, which was understanding from God—not simply rules—of what one should or shouldn't do.

Other rules, too, had been revisited. There was, for instance, the rule about swimming: persons of the opposite sex were not to swim simultaneously in the same body of water. This was a rule that had been nearly impossible to enforce on the various shorelines of the continent, but which became a plain hassle in backyard swimming pools. Church leaders rethought the issue and decided that the temptations afforded by bathing suits in aquatic proximity would not irrevocably lead to sexual engagement. And so it was that, for Maddie, the rule about swimming was only a rumor of a long-dead law, and she and her friends enjoyed respite from the summer heat in any number of pools in any number of backyards—with both boys and girls, men and women in the water at the same time.

Which, again, wasn't to say that church leaders or congregants shifted their attitudes toward moral law. These beliefs were intact. One ought to be wise about what one read, listened to, watched—all of which had the power to influence. And one was responsible to avoid temptation, to keep one's behaviors right and good. Which included sexual purity: fornication, promiscuity, any sexual behavior outside the bounds of marriage was sin. It was rarely preached on, but it went without saying.

Yes, the people of the Bethel Hills Church of Holiness were striving after God, who could not and would not abide sin. If one desired to know this loving and gracious God, then one's behavior ought to reflect that desire; one's life ought to be transformed by that desire—and by the active, engaged God they sought.

It was in this context that Maddie spent a significant portion of her waking life. Her parents, her lifelong best friend Justine—this was their world, too. The church community was like Maddie's extended family. It was hardly something that she could get away from.

But of course she did not think of getting away from it then, any more than she thought about climbing out of the folds of Pittsburgh's skirt and living elsewhere.

Nonetheless, the Sunday evening altar-going experience—apparently a common way in which church members pursued God—eluded Maddie. She didn't know why most people—people without ailments or evident struggles of some kind—knelt at the altar to pray; neither did she feel the need to pray there herself. Her questions to her parents about it ("What were you praying about?" "Why did you go to the altar?") were met with a pleasant and confounding vagueness ("I'm just listening to God"); her questions to Justine (asked only a time or two) were met with a chariness ("That's none of your business") that seemed decidedly annoyed. She found both off-putting. Moreover, just as had been the case since she was very small, before she could even name why, the whole altar thing was not entirely to her taste. There was a showiness about it that made her hesitate. It was far too public.

The result was Maddie's understandable sense of exclusion when it came to the expected interaction with God, but not—not yet, anyway—a sense of impossibility.

Maddie looked for him elsewhere. As a very young child, she imagined he could be anywhere. She had been told as much. Entering an otherwise empty room, Maddie was careful with doorknobs and silence: she thought she might come upon him visibly present, and swept the room for a glimpse of a retreating sandal or the edge of a departing robe. She thought she'd found Jesus one day when, age five, she took refuge during hide-and-seek in the D'Angelos' rhododendron hedge next door. He was smaller, certainly, than she had expected, and Maddie was disappointed, coming around to his front, to find it was not Jesus but rather his mother. A statue of the placid and beautiful Mary, arms lowered, hands extended in blessing. Lovely—but not him.

She was certain that she'd found him a few days later, hiding in yet another corner of the D'Angelos' garden. This statue was decidedly male, and why wouldn't Jesus have a bird perched on one shoulder and another in his hand, a small fawn pressed against one knee? But his face was bare and his hair wasn't quite right: she didn't know until she was much older that it had been a statue of St. Francis.

Maybe these early interactions were what drew her to her family's nativity set, that familiar Christmas-time decoration. The flaps of its box were soft from repeated folding and unfolding, and Maddie removed the tissue-wrapped figures slowly: shepherd, wise man, sheep. She palpated each in its wadding, identifying it before opening and saving for last the holy family themselves: the overlooked Joseph with his lantern; Mary and her impenetrable air of unassailable peace; the baby.

They were so like statues, this little set. Like the statues in the D'Angelos' garden, they were pure white. They looked like they could have been exhumed from ancient Greece, except that they were so small. Jesus was her favorite: his swaddling clothes confined to his waist, knees bent, hair curly, hands open and reaching. Perfectly formed, but with his back forever adhered to his manger. She studied his face. What was that expression? It was more open than that of his mother, his chin raised. He looked up at her from her palm; up at the sky from the stable floor. What did he see, she wondered? There he lay, God incarnate—she had been taught to believe. What miraculous powers were lent him even here at the beginning? Did he see through the roof to the chorus of angels? Did he already long for home? Could he see Maddie, two thousand years later, her hand cradling him in the living room?

Year after year she gazed at him, making multiple visits over the course of the Christmas season, bringing her face close to his. Unlike the altar calls at church where people knelt before an invisible God, she held him here, in a way, enfleshed. She had got hold of the body—almost. And there is something, isn't there, universally accessible in a baby, something fresh and unfiltered? If God were to interact with her at all, it seemed most likely he would do it through this unassuming infant. She craned her ear, listening: the world was almost magical at this time of year. Please, God. Surely, if she was still and quiet enough, she would find he had something to say to her.

But in the end—always and every time—the infant Jesus was as impenetrable as his mother. Figures and faces as of stone, mute and faintly smiling, in the otherwise empty room.

# 11

*W*hen finally Maddie heard from God, it wasn't what she expected. Neither was it what she would have wanted: a scene far more public than a response to the altar call, in front of what felt like the entire school. One moment she was walking with Justine across the parking lot, the next she was lying flat on her back, her view of the cloudless sky partially impeded by the bumper of Tommy MacDonald's Camaro.

She told herself that it was all Tommy's fault. That was what Justine said, as did the principal and the baseball coach and several of the bus drivers who had witnessed the incident and come running to her aid. It was Tommy's fault for going so fast through the parking lot just minutes after school let out, when everyone was walking to a bus or waiting on one or crossing the parking lot to their cars or baseball practice. And besides (Justine said this more than once), Tommy MacDonald was an idiot. Anyone could see that he was an idiot. ("Idiot" was a signature word for Justine; her world was rife with idiots.) This speeding in the school parking lot, showing off his new Camaro, served as the latest example of Tommy MacDonald's idiocy.

So Maddie armed herself with the fact of Tommy's culpability and told herself repeatedly—quoting Justine—that he was an idiot, but she remained unconvinced. Justine hadn't been hit by his car. Justine had had the excellent sense to get out of the way when she saw one coming, while Maddie herself had just stood there and then paid for it by what should have been a broken femur, far too much attention, and the embarrassment of exiting school property in an ambulance.

Of course she couldn't tell anyone why she hadn't noticed the car. What was there to say? That for the first time she had seen Vincent Elander looking at her? That after almost a week of covertly seeking him out, his gaze had met hers?

She wasn't spying, and she didn't have a crush on him. It was innocent curiosity. Anyone would be curious—anyone should be curious—after that last Sunday night. She wondered, frankly, why her parents didn't talk about it, why everyone who had been at the church that night didn't talk about it. Vincent Elander, local football hero, partier and wild run-about, suddenly shows up in church—their little church—on a Sunday evening and then makes his way to the altar, prostrating himself before what was generally agreed to be God. And there he proceeds to go into a kind of convulsive weeping in a prayer lasting so long that Pastor McLaughlin has to dismiss the congregation before he is finished.

Anyone would be curious. Everyone *should* be—or so Maddie thought. And she certainly was— despite Justine's reaction.

"Wait and see," Justine had said. She knew Vincent Elander's reputation better than Maddie did. She had been to a party or two where Vincent had been in attendance. In her opinion, the staying powers of altar-going repentance—especially and perhaps even most of all for those under-exposed to church tradition—were weak. "Time will tell, Maddie," Justine had said.

But Maddie had looked for him anyway, and had studied him in the limited way that was available to her: watching him talk with his girlfriend in the hallway and laugh with his friends at lunch, get books out of his locker, head to class. There was nothing striking in any of it. Nothing different from the life of any high school student. On Wednesday she heard he had broken up with his girlfriend—Maddie had even seen her crying in the girls' room. But this, too, seemed within the realm of normal. It all seemed like a typical day in high school.

And maybe that was all there was. Maybe in this case, as it would seem in so many others, experience with God amounted to this: public, perhaps weeping, prayer, and then back to the business of every day.

Part of the business of Vincent Elander's every day—so far as Maddie could see—was baseball practice. And part of the business for Maddie was riding home with Justine, which brought them to Thursday afternoon.

Tracing their path's trajectory, she could see that she and Justine were going to walk right past him. It would be the closest she had been all week. She held her breath: he was standing there in his white practice uniform on the corner of the sidewalk; he was pressing the tip of a baseball bat against his toe; he was wearing his red baseball cap. He looked directly at her, and she had never until that moment noticed that his eyes were blue. He had seen her looking at him and she hadn't looked away, and that was when she was hit by the car.

Of course, on impact all thoughts of Vincent Elander were instantaneously shoved aside. It was a screech of brakes, a blow to her leg, and a bounce off the hood of a car, followed by a face-first confrontation with the asphalt. All of this diverted her nicely in the short term, a distraction sustained by searing pain in her left thigh and the less notable but insistent pain from multiple abrasions on her face. These things were all she knew for a time, and they were enough to make her only dimly aware of the rushing and panic around her, the careful turn of her body so that she was staring at the sky, the cries for an ambulance and that Tommy MacDonald please shut off his car. Justine was crouching next to her and asking her how she was, and all Maddie could contemplate was the violent pain. In rapid succession, the faces of Tommy and the principal and various bus drivers swam into and then disappeared from view. The baseball coach appeared and tucked something under her head; soon her body was covered by the slick polyester jackets of the baseball team.

This was in the first few minutes, and then Maddie shut her eyes and kept them that way, thinking only of the pain and trying not to cry. At one point she managed to ask Justine if she would just take her home. But Justine's answer was disappointing: it was best that they wait it out until she could be seen by somebody.

Maddie was confused. Wasn't she being seen by somebody? Someone was close by her left side and beginning to tend to her injured leg. She released a low moan.

"What do you think you're doing?" she heard Justine ask, and then Maddie opened her eyes and raised her head. There he was, reintroducing himself to her consciousness: Vincent Elander was kneeling next to her on the pavement, gently moving the jackets and then—she could hardly believe it and wanted to cry out against the pain—placing his hands on her thigh.

"What do you think you're doing?" Justine asked again. Vincent didn't answer. He just knelt there with his hands on Maddie's leg. His head was bent, and he had taken off his baseball cap. His hair was pressed into a ring.

"Vincent Elander, you had better stop that. What do you think you're doing?" Justine tried yet again. When he did not respond, she loudly informed him that he didn't know what he was doing, and she insisted they wait for an ambulance. She told him again to stop that, he shouldn't be allowed over here, and he might make Maddie's injury worse. Her voice grew shrill.

But Vincent still didn't answer, and, strangely, no adult interfered. Vincent just rested his hands lightly on Maddie's throbbing thigh, kneeling on the pavement as so recently he had knelt at an altar.

This was when Maddie discovered her embarrassment. It was seeping through her like the pain seeped through her leg and face. It reached for her from the crowd of onlookers who stood at the periphery of her vision. She couldn't make out who they were and she didn't want to know. She closed her eyes. She lay there between a stranger and her best friend and closed her eyes against them both. She closed them against the principal and the baseball coach, against Tommy MacDonald and the students who were looking at her, against everything but the pain.

And she kept them closed. Even when the ambulance came and they transferred her to the body board, when they lifted her inside and shut the ambulance doors. Even when Justine, riding next to her in the ambulance, asked her how she was feeling and Maddie answered in all honesty that the pain in her thigh was subsiding. Yes, she said, her eyes still closed, she was definitely feeling better.

She wished she could say she was not feeling better. She protested to her parents that, despite the doctors' confident encouragement, she really ought to stay home for at least one day. She had been hit by a car! Surely that was enough to grant her a day propped on the sofa.

But her parents insisted. She was feeling fine. She walked without a limp. Even the scrapes on her face were better than anyone would have expected. You could barely see them. There was no reason at all for her to stay home. They called her recovery a miracle. She had been divinely protected! Her father called the church to spread the word.

But Maddie didn't like to think of the incident as a miracle. Instead of feeling gratitude for benevolence from the divine, she was full of dread at the bus stop. Passing through the halls at school, she perceived herself the subject of whispered conversations and the object of unfriendly stares. And when, on entering the cafeteria at lunchtime, she was greeted with a chorus of ambulance sirens, she burst into tears and fled to the girls' room.

Justine—dutiful, faithful, best-friend-Justine—followed her.

The girls had been best friends since they were in the church nursery together, since (both of their mothers loved to talk about it) little Justine stood beside Maddie's baby swing and poked Cheerios into Maddie's mouth. They had ascended together through the ranks of Sunday school classes, sung together in the children's choir, labored over crafts during uncounted Vacation Bible School sessions.

And they went through the same public school system—which wasn't true for all of the kids at the Bethel Hills Church, which drew its congregation from various neighborhoods and school districts throughout that region of Pittsburgh.

This overlap and other mundane commonalities (both of them loved to read; both had brown eyes; in the first grade, their favorite color had been lime green) fostered the bond between them. But it was primarily the overlap that knit them, that provided them with a shared gaze. At school, their perception of others was filtered by what they had learned at church (so-and-so behaved badly, was in want of moral improvement); at church, so-and-so couldn't understand how it "was done," what things were like at their school. Which wasn't, in all likelihood, terribly different from how things were elsewhere.

At fifteen, Maddie believed this bond to be unyielding, even stronger than the one she shared with her parents. She and Justine had been friends all their lives. They stood by one another through everything. Not that there had been much in the way of "everything"—Maddie's own life had been quietly safe, and the death of Justine's four-year-old brother to leukemia (when the girls were six) was very much in the rear-view. Still, Maddie had been around when it happened, and so they shared that traumatic experience and everything else besides.

Had she thought about it, Maddie might have allowed little Matthew's death as the perpetuator of Justine's slight but definite superiority in their relationship. Despite its being long behind them, Maddie implicitly understood that Justine had known a darkness and loss inconceivable to her, and so therefore had a greater wisdom. Not that they talked about it. Instead, there was Justine's opinion, confidently and sometimes loudly proclaimed. And there was, too, her family's long history at the church (her great grandfather had been a founder) and her more outgoing nature. People knew Justine at school: she ran the box-office for the theatrical productions; she played the clarinet in the marching band; she was on the newspaper staff. And Justine knew people. She was always providing Maddie with the lowdown on everyone—both at church and at school. She knew the gossip, knew who was dating (or dumping) whom, knew who was suspended and why.

Maddie frankly acknowledged Justine's superiority. It was undeniable. Never mind that, between them, Maddie had the collateral of superiority (prettier face, better hair, thinner body). How could such things matter between friends? There was an uncommon bond between them, one that set them apart from all others when the need arose. As it did that day in the girls' room.

It was there, during the first half of their lunch period, that Justine helped Maddie put things in perspective: she wasn't getting nearly the attention over this that she imagined. The ambulance sirens were only coming from one part of the cafeteria, namely a small group of their friends who were trying to be funny. Besides, didn't Maddie remember the incident with John Griffin? The defensive end who split his pants in the middle of a football game? *That* was the whole school.

*That* incident had been *much* worse. And nobody even remembers that anymore.

They were standing in the girls' room, in front of a bank of sinks that stood in front of a bank of mirrors, and Justine had presented these reassurances to her own reflection.

Maddie listened, leaning against the wall and staring at her shoes, until she said with a suddenness that surprised her that she certainly *did* remember John Griffin splitting his pants—as did Justine. What were the chances that people would so quickly forget her ambulance incident?

Despite the fact that this point didn't argue in her favor—from an overall perspective anyway—Maddie had nonetheless felt a little pleased with herself. The argument was sound.

But Justine sustained this without flinching and told Maddie that even if people remembered it, nobody talked about it anymore. Which was the point.

Maddie silently wondered if it was, in fact, the point, and also considered that John Griffin had graduated and maybe that was why nobody talked about him splitting his pants anymore. She pondered this briefly and decided to change the subject. She told Justine that she hadn't even wanted to come to school that day.

Justine had been working on the pores of her chin, leaning over the sinks to get a closer look, a posture that appeared uncomfortable in every way. She said yes, it was impressive that Maddie was at school that day. She couldn't believe it, in fact. Maddie's presence at school was almost more surprising, if possible, than the accident had been in the first place.

Here Maddie explained: her parents had made her come; and she mentally reviewed the events of the night before: the long wait in the emergency room, the x-rays, the conversation with the doctor. "They think it's a miracle," she added.

Justine snorted impatiently. Despite her continued devotion to their church, she had been distancing herself from it in some ways. Within the last year, she had refused to attend church twice on Sundays ("The morning service is enough," she said). And she had become impatient with the willingness—on the part of many congregants—to attribute coincidence to acts of God ("*Relax*, people," she said).

"It *is* impressive that you don't need crutches." She turned away from the mirror and came close to Maddie, scrutinizing her face. "You were a bloody mess yesterday. I thought you were going to need stitches."

Maddie laughed at this. "Maybe it's a miracle," she said. She was unmoved by Justine's newfound sense of coincidence. She would have loved a miracle—but she wasn't terribly pleased with this one—if that's what it was.

But Justine wasn't laughing. "The accident seemed bad," she said, "but I guess it actually wasn't."

Maddie found this vaguely insulting. "Yes it was," she answered. "It *was* serious. I could have broken my femur. That's what they did the x-ray for."

Justine acquiesced: "True," she said, and then silence.

This felt shallow, so Maddie underscored it for good measure: "You saw it happen."

"I saw Vincent Elander fussing over you, that's for sure," Justine said. She was nonchalant, fluffing her bangs.

Maddie was confused. She had forgotten about Vincent Elander, and she suddenly didn't know what to say. "Yeah, what was *that* all about?" she mustered, while inside she courted the question: Why had Vincent, of all people, come to help her?

"Tell me you didn't enjoy that," Justine said.

Maddie was incredulous. "Enjoy *what*? Being hit by a car? Lying on the ground in front of everyone? Enjoy what, exactly?"

But Justine only smiled at her in that knowing way she had. "Tell me you didn't like that Elander attention," she said.

"You think this was about attention?" Maddie said.

"Well," Justine said, still smiling, "why don't you need crutches?"

Maddie found herself facing off with her best friend in the girls' room, but she wasn't sure why. She dreaded that somehow Justine knew there was more to the story—or that there was a story at all, one Maddie knew nothing about. But Justine just grinned at her until Maddie knew she was teasing.

They left the girls' room together, and Maddie was relieved that the ambulance sirens did not have a reprise on their re-entrance to the cafeteria. At the lunch table, she found some comfort in hearing

Justine regale their companions with the story of the accident. But when the bell rang and everyone went on to class, Maddie found that the sense of ostracism—worse than her previous anonymity—had taken on a new loneliness.

———— ⊸∞⊶ ————

It was the last period of the day when she was headed to Spanish class that it happened. In the normal clamor and busy-ness of a high school hallway, she felt and heard it nonetheless: a hand intentionally and briefly clasping her elbow, a low voice speaking directly into her ear, "You shouldn't worry about what other people think."

It was then that Maddie reconsidered. Sitting in Spanish, her book open on her desk, she awaited her turn to conjugate a verb and revisited Vincent's attentions to her. She saw him kneeling next to her, saw him watching her before that as she walked past him in the parking lot. Saw him smirking at her, moments before, at the other end of the hall.

Maybe her parents were right. Maybe it was a miracle. Vincent Elander—recent convert, pray-er at altar and on parking lot pavement—had healed her.

She didn't mention it to anyone yet, but by the end of class she knew for certain what had happened.

———— ⊸∞⊶ ————

And that was the beginning of Vincent. After that, he waited for her bus to arrive outside the school every morning; he walked her to class. Soon enough his lunchtime entourage was crowding her table in the cafeteria. And there he was at church, too. Sunday morning at 9:30 for Sunday school, walking into the class without hesitation, making his way through the rows of aluminum chairs to the empty one next to her, even asking Justine, when he needed to, if she wouldn't mind scooting over so that he could sit by Maddie. There he was for Sunday school; there he was for the worship service. There he was again on Sunday evening and at Wednesday evening youth group and at school the following morning and also on the phone at night.

If she had been the sort of girl who was wise to this kind of thing, maybe she would have known what was happening. Justine seemed to.

"You know you're next," she had said in their World History class. The bell had rung; Maddie had just sat down. She was opening her notes; she was smiling without realizing it; Vincent had walked her to class.

"What do you mean?" Maddie's question was innocent, perhaps unbelievably so.

"Are you kidding me?" It was Justine's tone, her signature inflection of faint ridicule that took under survey all the idiocy around her. "Are you *kidding* me?" she asked again, but she was smiling.

"Next for what?"

"For Vincent Elander, God's gift to the female world."

"What are you talking about?"

Then the late bell rang and Mr. Carson resumed yesterday's lecture, the one for which he had prepared the corresponding outline and in which Maddie was dutifully penciling notes. Justine sent her a note of her own as means of explanation: *You are Elander's next girlfriend. Obviously.*

Maddie had felt her face turn red, but less with embarrassment than pleasure. She wanted to pursue this line of reasoning. At that point, she couldn't imagine it to be true. But she couldn't discuss it with Justine because Vincent had been waiting for her after class, and then he walked her to lunch.

---

The days ran together, and who knows exactly when it was? Sometime after the school year had ended, certainly, sometime early in the summer.

Maddie had fixed it on the Elander's back porch. Of course it could have happened elsewhere. The summer had been long. It could have happened as they were sitting on the wall next to the roller rink where they went many times. Or it could have happened as they walked together back to the trolley stop after a baseball game. Or sitting in church, waiting for the service to start. Standing on the top of Mount Washington and looking down on the city. Sitting on the front stoop of her house, not his.

But Vincent's back porch is where she set it, where she would say it happened. A leaning plum tree extended branches between them and the streetlight; its leaves cast their moving shadows over them, shifting with the continual breeze. She was sitting with Vincent on the top step; the night was balmy: summer, crickets. And they could also hear the cars going by on the street in front of the house; maybe they heard a trolley sliding past.

The television was on inside the house. Mrs. Elander had the window open, and the canned laughter of a sitcom drifted out to Vincent and Maddie, but they weren't listening. Vincent was holding her hand; she rested her head on the firm round of his upper shoulder. He smelled like bath soap and clean laundry, and all of it was ahead of them: Willy's changed appearance, the coming school year, the football game, the incident on the parsonage lawn, and everything that would come after that.

Maddie didn't raise her head from his shoulder to ask him, but studied the way he held her hand, his fingers thick between hers. She asked him what she'd been wondering for weeks now: why he picked her, of all the girls he'd had before, of all the girls he could have.

His answer: something about that day in the school parking lot. The mystery's evocation stilled them both. For a moment they seemed to observe the strange incident as though it were occurring once again, this time on the Elander's back lawn all encumbered by crabgrass. Then Vincent breathed a low chuckle and Maddie winced, remembering: she thought of the chorus of ambulance sirens in the cafeteria and how she had shivered, lying there on the pavement.

What were they to make of it, aged fifteen and sixteen, so new to life and to each other? They could speak of it now, the flirtation (his) and shyness (hers) of their earliest days, but it would take some nerve for Maddie to inhale and then speak her suspicion. He was the first she told: "Vincent, I think you healed me."

It all felt like magic—that first time, perhaps every time people fall in love. Coincidence becomes destiny: unstoppable forces are at work. Why not, too, a miracle thrown into the metaphysical wonder?

Vincent said yes, he had thought that before. The idea had occurred to him.

He had seen the accident happen; the only thing he could think to do was to pray for her. Newly acquainted with God, flooded with newborn devotion, he had gone to her immediately (and wasn't that what it meant to follow Christ—to be present in the midst of suffering?) and prayed for her. He couldn't tell her how he knew to pray for her leg; he just knew. And when the coach and the principal and everyone else had been sent away, he had—another miracle?—been allowed to stay, overlooked almost, as he knelt beside her. He hadn't known she was being healed, he was just praying for her. What else was there to do?

They were silent for a moment, the crickets singing. And the vision of it lingered in the yard as Vincent spoke again, offering a question of his own. He asked what good it would be resisting her? He knew it; he was certain: God had chosen them—Maddie and Vincent—for one another, because why was it Maddie who was hit by Tommy's Camaro? Vincent knew he had a gift when he had knelt next to her in the parking lot. Maddie was the gift, he told her, and he said he had never known a girl like Maddie—untouched, unsullied, and committed—as now he was—to God.

Maddie had asked why me, and God was Vincent's answer, spoken into the top of her hair as they sat together in the lamp light. God was his answer, which would preempt any argument. Not that Maddie would ever argue, for here was the answer to her prayer: *Please, God.* He had brought her a miraculous healing, and he had brought her Vincent.

Then Vincent said he loved her, and in the subsequent kiss Maddie could no longer distinguish whether Vincent loved her because God had chosen her or God had chosen her because Vincent loved her.

She supposed it didn't matter.

# 12

*H*er father washed the car at the top of the driveway, close to the house, and his spare use of water slowly turned the driveway's lower half into a patchwork of narrow waterways. As a child, Maddie would make a world of it, naming the rivulets and rivers that every time made a different map of the macadam. Sticks and twigs, piles of small stones placed strategically in this miniaturized landscape were bridges, aqueducts, fortified cities; here were trade routes and alliances, and this gray patch, untouched by water, was a vast desert.

She could play at this for hours, her hair and back growing warm in the sun. She forgot the neighbors and their life-sized yards around her; she brought kings and kingdoms to life on the blacktop. The sound of the lawnmower dissolved in the bustle and clamor of the civilizations at her feet. She wished it bigger. She wished that the shallow rivers of her landscape would bear the boats she'd made of furled leaves, for here was a queen and her minions on a barge, a floating mission to a neighboring land.

It always came to the same end: tired of the game, she stood at the top of the driveway and, with a blast from the hose, forced the known universe to succumb to the deluge. In short time, the points of the map were driven to the gutter; the cities and bridges were reduced to flotsam in a heap by the mailbox. Maddie loved this, too. It was part of the game: distinctness reduced to uniformity, all of it washed clean. She no longer played like this, of course. The driveway had long been nothing other than a means to the street, and more recently the means by which Vincent often entered her world. His was a little car—a Pacer or something equally humble—something old and beat up, because Vincent's family didn't have much money, not that this mattered to her. What mattered was that Vincent was arriving in her driveway, coming to the house, chatting with her parents and taking her away again. They were headed to church, school, the plot-points on which her world turned, but also now to the trolley stop, because they were going downtown to a baseball game, or to get ice cream at the Dairy Queen, to the Tedescos', to the roller rink.

Like the driveway at the end of her childhood game, the whole of her life was now colored and filled by Vincent. He left no corner untouched; nothing remained to her that did not also belong to him or was not also inhabited by him, which was fine with Maddie. She couldn't say—even now in the summer when they sat on the back steps of Vincent's porch and, later, when Willy stumbled across the intersection—that she had seen it coming. She had been just as surprised as the villagers would have been—the tiny, imagined inhabitants of her driveway civilizations—when the flood came blasting over the paved rise and washed them all away.

Of course, a flooded landscape is no landscape at all, but this did not bother Maddie. Why should she be bothered when her only reaction to this change was new and whelming joy? Her identity as Camaro-victim and ambulance patient was lost in being Vincent Elander's girlfriend. And while that new identity came with considerable school-wide fame, it also came with the comfort of his near-constant presence, making her lost anonymity somewhat less of a loss.

Moreover, her parents loved him. Not only was he a good athlete (Maddie's father was a huge football fan), but his commitment to church life (he never missed a service) was impressive. And he was very respectful—Maddie's parents commented on this with some frequency—to their daughter.

Maddie was happily adrift on this flood, and she assumed the same of everyone else because she was young; because when you are in love, everything looks beautiful.

Who could be bothered, in the radiance of this transition, by the lesser details—that, for example, Vincent's friends must become her own, must also become Justine's friends? Certainly not Justine, whose lunch experience now included Vincent and his glut of loud companions. Justine handled it even better than Maddie; she kept pace with their banter and business. Her rise in social standing was meteoric. It couldn't matter that it came through the tether of Maddie's friendship.

No, Maddie had no inkling of dissatisfaction in Justine, with the exception of a singular conversation early in that only summer— Vincent's summer. And even then it was merely Justine's raised eyebrow. That was all.

It was in the Tedescos' backyard at some informal youth group gathering. The sun had gone down, the grass grown cool underfoot. Teenagers clustered in groups here and there on the patio. Some were shooting hoops in the driveway, others tossed a Frisbee on the lawn. Nicky, Vincent, Maddie and Justine sat together at the picnic table, holding disposable cups of warming soda.

They had likely been talking about summer plans and jobs, about the freedom of the months stretching ahead. And then—who knew why?—Vincent flipped an invisible switch, turning their casual conversation into an earnest debate on church doctrine.

He had asked a question about Communion, of all things—an honest query that marked him as still "new" to church life. What was with the restrictions on who could or couldn't take Communion?

An odd question, especially from a teenager. But this was Vincent.

Except that it made Maddie uneasy. She remembered Justine's words after his apparent altar-call conversion: "Wait and see," she had said.

Justine had a mind of her own. Maddie was accustomed to how carefully she weighed things and came, sometimes rather over-confidently, to her own conclusions. Now Vincent was innocently asking questions about church practice. Despite his apparent commitment to follow up on his conversion experience, Justine might remain unconvinced. He couldn't know this, but Maddie thought he shouldn't be giving Justine fodder for her doubt.

As the present adult and a minister, Nicky might have answered him, and Maddie wished he would. But he crossed his arms over his chest and waited for the conversation to unfold, smiling as if he had been hoping through years of youth ministry for a debate about Communion on his backyard patio.

Of course, Justine enthusiastically took up the subject. This sort of thing was fascinating to her. She perceived herself as something of an expert—which might have been a fair assessment for a person well-churched as she was.

Communion wasn't just for anybody, she said. It would lose all meaning if just anybody could take it. If you did it that way, then you might just as well take it anytime, anywhere. Which would make it into another meal. A snack, even—which would be wrong. The whole thing was deeply meaningful, she said. You can't take Communion until you understand and accept that meaning.

This was the right answer, but Maddie nonetheless felt a rising sense of protectiveness for Vincent. How could he be expected to understand that Communion was only for saved people, for people who accepted the sacrificial death of Jesus? She saw in her mind's eye the wide brass plates, bearing flat discs of Communion bread, passed down the rows of pews.

Vincent apparently was unsatisfied. He countered that nobody really understood Communion, right? Who could? And the disciples—the first people to take Communion—were the best example of this. They didn't get it at all. They hadn't even understood that Jesus was going to die. Vincent said that much was obvious— and yet they were "allowed" to take it. Besides, he said, if people were really and truly ingesting the body and blood of Jesus, then couldn't one expect it to have an impact—even without their understanding it?

Here Justine was quick to point out what Maddie had immediately thought: the body and blood were *symbolic*. It wasn't actually the body and blood. That was just for Catholics.

But Vincent had shrugged off what seemed to him inconsequential distinction. Symbol or the real deal, Vincent said, Communion was Communion. Taking Communion, whether or not you really understood it, would change a person, might even convert, might even save a person. In which case, everybody should be allowed to take it. Heck! Everyone at church should want everyone possible to take it. He spoke with emphatic conviction, and Maddie was impressed. For someone so new to this, he clearly thought and felt deeply about it— far more than Maddie ever had. But the protectiveness surged again: Justine thrived on argument. She wouldn't be gentle with him.

Justine doubled back. She said that the disciples hadn't gotten it because the Last Supper was before Christ's death and resurrection. She said that, in the church today, we understand Communion. We understand it now, Vincent, she said, gently repeating herself.

Almost condescendingly, Maddie feared, and she reached for Vincent's hand.

Vincent took her hand across the table, mindlessly lacing his fingers through hers, and he laughed out loud. "*Do* we understand it?" he asked her, and he leaned toward her over the table. "*Do* we?" he said again.

Maddie cringed at the laughter. She could see that Vincent was enjoying the conversation, but she wasn't sure Justine felt the same.

That was when Justine raised her eyebrow. "Yes," she said. Curtly. Smugly? Maddie didn't like it.

But the taut dialogue between them had been broken by Vincent's laughter, and then Nicky spoke. He said there was lots they still didn't understand, lots no one understands—and the three of them waited on him, hoping, perhaps, that he could parse it for them. Maybe he could itemize what, exactly, they—meaning the church or even Christians in general—could list as comprehensible and firm.

Nicky didn't. Years later, Maddie would still wonder why he hadn't resolved the debate, reasserting doctrinal truth as Justine had so carefully explained it and putting their questions to rest. Maybe—as it seemed—he had simply enjoyed the conversation, believing that it was good for Vincent to ask and Justine to answer. Maybe he expected that God would intervene subtly and, as ever, in his own time.

What Nicky did say was that theirs had been an excellent conversation, the best one he'd heard in weeks. He said he was proud to know them, proud to know that they thought about such important things, and that they should think about them some more.

Then he invited Vincent to help him find the leftover pizza, and the two of them left the table, leaving Maddie with a rare Justine: one who had not clearly won an argument.

Maddie waited for her to speak, as she wasn't sure what to say. She thought that Vincent had actually made some good points. He had questioned things she hadn't thought possible to question, and what he had said made sense.

And there sat Justine with centuries of church tradition just over her shoulder—tradition, Maddie thought, that certainly stood for something, even if she herself couldn't articulate what.

"Nicky sure likes Vincent, doesn't he?" Justine said. She was watching them across the yard, smiling.

Maddie followed Justine's gaze to where Nicky and Vincent had joined a game of football, each with a slice of pizza in his hand. "Yes," she said aloud. "Yes, he does."

---

And what wasn't there to like? Maddie had a close-up view to all of it: Vincent playing catch with his little brothers in the backyard or helping them with their homework; Vincent carrying the groceries inside, the laundry up from the basement. He teased his mother; they laughed together a lot. She chased him around the kitchen, making to whip him with the dishtowel. Or he got hold of the dishtowel, and then their roles were reversed. He was trying always, he told Maddie once, to make up for the fact that his mom was doing all of the parenting alone. His dad had left when Vincent was seven.

No one else, really, was privy to that view. But Nicky—and Justine—and everyone else knew his involvement at the church: Vincent voluntarily took on the task of mowing the lawn that summer. He helped collect the offering on Sundays. And he met regularly with Pastor McLaughlin in his study.

"Forget God's gift to women," Justine said. "Your boyfriend thinks he's God's gift to the church."

Maddie suppressed immediate irritation. "They're studying the *Bible*, Justine," she said.

"Then he thinks he's God's gift to God," Justine answered.

When Maddie didn't laugh Justine told her, "*Relax,* I'm kidding!"

But Justine wasn't kidding the time she gave her warning: "You be careful, Maddie," she said. "You know that Vincent Elander is used to having sex with his girlfriends."

Maddie was shocked. This was, at the very least, an intrusion into her privacy and, even more so, an assault on Vincent's character. Everyone knew that Vincent Elander had changed. He hadn't had a drink since he'd become a Christian. He had completely quit swearing. His friends at school even teased him for being a "Bible beater." And he had sworn off sex until marriage.

That conversation had also been an unexpected one for Maddie who, until very recently, had seen sex as a forbidden swimming pool lost behind insurmountable concrete walls topped in loops of barbed wire. And then Vincent had talked with her almost like it was a confession, sitting across from Maddie at the Pizza Hut, holding both her hands across the table. In a low voice, he had gone through the list of girls he'd had sex with: when, where, how many times. And while the list was a good deal shorter than legend or even speculation might have credited him for, Maddie felt some of her innocence lost in this uninvited divulgence.

She hadn't liked it; she couldn't quite articulate why. But she managed to question him. Why did he need to tell her? Didn't he realize that she would be thinking about this now, that she would think about it every time she saw one of those girls (two of them still went to their school)? And didn't he already know that she planned to wait until marriage to have sex? Where was the urgency in talking about it?

But Vincent wouldn't apologize for telling her. "It's important, Maddie," he said. He needed her to know.

"Why?" Maddie asked him. What happened before didn't matter. He was different now and she knew that.

They were in her driveway now. He had turned off the engine and was looking away from her, out the window on the driver's side, searching, perhaps, for a way to explain himself.

"Maddie," he said, "you're different from the other girls—all the other girls. You're the real deal," he said, looking at her now. "You're special. I don't want to treat you like them. I don't want us to be like that. I just don't," he said.

How to translate that to Justine—as if it were any of her business? Should Maddie tell her how there were honest-to-goodness tears in his eyes when he said that, how he took her hand and kissed it, like something out of a fairy tale?

She could guess what Justine would say: it was too good to be true. And then Maddie realized that Vincent's sincerity was beyond Justine. For all her years of Sunday school and knowledge of doctrine, Justine had a seam of skepticism in her, and when it came to Vincent Elander, skepticism won out over faith. Who knew why? But telling Justine about that conversation with Vincent, his pledge of sexual purity, his earnestness about God, would be (the strange biblical simile took on practical meaning) throwing pearls to pigs.

"Oh, yes, well, he's different now," Maddie said, trying to sound casual and not too confident, when in fact and in both cases, the opposite was true.

Justine had scarcely waited for that reply. "I heard that Tracy Delaney had to get an abortion her senior year." She said it almost lightly, as if tossing it at her, but Maddie received it as a challenge. Tracy Delaney had been Vincent's steady girlfriend when she was a senior. She was the former captain of the high school cheerleading squad and was now a rising sophomore at Penn State.

"That's a lie, Justine. It's a lie and a mean rumor, and I hope you haven't said it to anyone else."

"How do you know it's a lie? What if it isn't?" Justine said.

"Because Vincent would have told me," Maddie answered, now glad of his confession.

Justine was quiet for a moment.

"He's really different now, Justine," Maddie said, more gently.

Justine answered quickly, hanging her words on the end of Maddie's sentence. "Oh, I know," she said. "I know he is. I just felt like I should say something, you know. As a friend. That's all."

Maddie thanked her. It seemed the only thing to do.

Yet, for a while anyway, she was angry with Justine. She'd had no right talking to her about sex. Maddie knew the rules; she knew right from wrong.

But the timing of it was uncanny, as if Justine could actually tell, as if she knew things impossible for her to know. That, just last Sunday afternoon, kissing Vincent had taken on unanticipated power. There was no denying that Maddie liked kissing him, that sometimes—

sitting next to him in church or talking with him and the Tedescos—
she was mentally racing ahead to when she could be alone with him.
But there was always a resolve within it. Kissing, holding hands: that
was all. Hands never straying from waist, neck. The rules were simple.

And then, that Sunday afternoon as he kissed her, as she received
it, returned it (acts surprisingly both novel and instinctive), she felt
her resolve soften. It was a small collapse, the sort of thing no one
would notice.

Vincent must have sensed it—and how? She didn't act on it, not
that she knew of, anyway. But he had stopped her. He had broken
away from her abruptly and had taken hold of her face with both
hands and kissed her, firmly, on the forehead. And then he had taken
her home.

Two days after that, he took her out for dinner so that he could
confess his sexual history to her in a booth at the Pizza Hut.

It was as if Justine had surmised what Maddie had never told her:
that the defenses she had built against sexual temptation were not
quite so resolute as she thought.

But it didn't matter. After his confession, Maddie was newly
resolved—with Vincent—to do what was right. And certainly Maddie
would never tell Justine about any of this. She would never tell anyone.
Nobody—not in her world, anyway—talked about these things.

# 13

$\mathcal{V}$incent's summer meant baseball, and so came the first professional baseball game, all the way downtown, just the two of them on a weekday evening. That was when Maddie met Willy, and even that—she decided as they walked away—was a little bit exhilarating.

Vincent walked with a kind of lope: there was a smoothness to his stride and a slight lift in his step. When the crowd pressed nearer at the gate, Maddie held his arm and felt the muscles grow taut under her fingers. He scanned the faces of the people around them and looked briefly down at Maddie in almost absent-minded reassurance. But he smiled broadly as he showed her their seats: behind home plate, the best seats he'd ever had, he said. They didn't notice that the clouds had come in. The night sky was eclipsed by stadium light, and they weren't looking up. Vincent was showing Maddie the game; she hadn't cared about it before and now was determined to love it. He was teaching her to keep score in the game program. The first drops of rain surprised them; rain hadn't been in the forecast. Who would have expected this sudden downpour that had them all scrambling up the steps to the shelter of the stadium?

Already drenched, Vincent and Maddie watched through the rain as groundskeepers unrolled tarps on the field. It was only the bottom of the fourth. How long could the rain go on like this? It would stop soon enough. Vincent and Maddie—and most of that night's fans, so it seemed—would wait it out.

But when an hour passed and it was still coming down, the crowd shifted its weight. Having turned away from the edges of the field to the concrete walkways and concession stands of the stadium, the waiting fans finally acquiesced to the weather. Maddie and Vincent felt the population thinning, and still the rain came down. The tarps were pocked with puddles.

And so they left too, and soon stood among many others waiting for the light to change. They were seeing dimly in the dark rain, their backs to the stadium. Miracle or mere coincidence, they had waited on the game long enough to be exactly there, poised on the edge of the curb, to see Willy stepping down into traffic and then stumbling his way toward them across the intersection.

The accident happened fast. Amazement, impact, the collective cringing gasp. Before anyone might plunge toward the victim, he was grasping for the curb, seizing on the toe of Vincent's shoe, crawling into standing and then, inconceivably, walking away, heedless of expressed concern, promises to call an ambulance, that he ought to be seen by a doctor.

Afterward strangers might have muttered to one another about what ought to be done. They stared behind them, squinting in the rain and the stadium light, watching the retreating figure of the man in the parka who soon disappeared into shadow. The driver of the car stood with hands limp in the whiteness of his own headlights. He was being talked to by someone, but he wasn't listening. He was staring toward the stadium; his jaw hung loose.

But there was nothing left to do. With the others, Vincent and Maddie recalled that their hair and clothes were soaking wet. They stepped down into the street and headed home.

That was all there was to it: an accident they witnessed after a rained-out baseball game. Maddie wasn't horrified by it at the time, not really. The brief event was a shocking, would-be tragedy that, happily, wasn't: clearly Willy was fine. It was a story to be told to their parents when they got home, to their friends, to Nicky and Amy Tedesco.

And of course they told it.

⁂

The summer of Vincent became, also, the summer of the Tedescos. Maddie came to know their house by heart over the course of those months. Before then, she had been to their home a handful of times, and mostly for youth group events in the backyard.

And now she was there all the time, and the floor plan, even twenty years later, was locked into her memory: a small, somewhat enclosed entryway held a coat closet on the right and a sign reading "Bless this House." The entry opened to the living room, which then joined, under a narrow arch, the dining room—the room to which they had fled on an evening in late June when a thunderstorm had put an end to their backyard picnic. The dining room rather predictably gave on to the kitchen, a room so small it had no space for a table but which had once housed Nicky and Vincent's glee over the brand new microwave. The TV room was at the back of the house and was large enough only for a narrow couch, the television stand, and a recliner.

The detached garage was where Vincent and Nicky would lean under the open hood of Nicky's car. Their driveway was where they would shoot hoops. On that back patio (where Vincent and Justine had discussed Communion) Nicky taught Vincent how to grill the perfect hamburger. And late at night in that living room, he instructed Vincent as to the finer points of Billy Joel's earlier albums and the music of The Cars, all of which he played very loudly.

It was a simple floor plan, probably the same as many of the other houses in the neighborhood, but for Maddie it was singular.

Vincent was her point of access. Vincent, whom the Tedescos loved and had taken under their wing like an adopted little brother, pitying him, perhaps, for his background, for coming from the other side of the tracks. Or maybe it was something of the shared experience blooming into friendship: twenty years prior, Nicky's football coach was the same man who coached Vincent's team now. Same high school, same locker room, same plays. Amy said that Nicky relived his glory days in Vincent.

Not that they needed a reason to love him. Everyone should love him because he was Vincent.

Vincent loved them, too. He had asked about them early on, when he was brand new to the Bethel Hills Church—and Maddie had let go all she knew about them: Nicky and Amy had been at the church all their lives; he had played football and she had been a cheerleader in high school; they had been the youth group leaders for nearly forever; they were so cool. Everyone at the church loved them. And also they couldn't have kids.

Here was a story she knew by heart, failing to comprehend that Nicky and Amy had opened intimate details of their lives to the congregation so that she could have such knowledge. Amy had had five or six miscarriages and those kinds of pregnancies where the egg gets attached to the fallopian tube (and wasn't she brave and also maybe somewhat cool herself, to so casually mention such a thing as a fallopian tube to Vincent Elander!). The whole church had been praying for them for years—for *years*—and one time, when he was sharing his testimony about it in a Sunday evening service, Nicky had even cried about it. *Nicky* had cried. In front of everyone.

Her mother had taken them a meal that week, and Maddie had gone along for the ride (because everyone loved the Tedescos), and Amy had told her later that it was the best baked ziti they had ever had.

Maddie finished, a little breathless, oddly pleased.

"Wow," Vincent said quietly. "That is really, really sad," at which Maddie felt something within her fold slightly. Moments before, she had felt almost exultant. She wasn't sure why. But Vincent, of course, was right.

"Yes," she said, and she felt sad.

"I mean, they would make really good parents," he said.

It was the first time Maddie had considered this. Always it had just been a question of Nicky and Amy Tedesco becoming pregnant. It had been miscarriage after miscarriage and fertility treatments or adoption and their ability—or inability—to afford either of them. Now she could see it: Nicky and Amy and a laughing baby between them, and she felt suddenly and passionately that these two, of all people, should have children.

She might imagine, then, that she and Vincent were of some comfort to this childless couple, maybe even that Vincent's friendship with Nicky was somehow a gift to them. But that wasn't what she was thinking when she and Vincent dropped by or were invited over, when, once again, Nicky and Amy made room for them in their busy lives. Instead, her thoughts circled around the church altar-call, that realm of Maddie's inexperience. Before Vincent, she had felt left out of church life in some indefinable way. The Tedescos were a reminder of Vincent's words to her: God had chosen them for each other.

Maddie understood, too, that this friendship was good for Vincent. Her own mother had commented that Nicky was like the father Vincent had lost, and Maddie was glad of that.

Nonetheless, there were moments of discomfort in it—or one anyway: that awkward conversation, maybe the first or second time that Nicky and Vincent had headed out to work on the car. Maddie and Vincent hadn't been together for very long, and Amy had asked how it was going. Maddie had never had a boyfriend before, right?

"No," Maddie answered. "Vincent is my first boyfriend," a phrase that suddenly struck Maddie as odd. Was Vincent merely the *first*? Were there to be more? Vincent was her boyfriend; he was the only one she ever wanted or could want. Vincent had said—and Maddie believed it—that God had chosen them for each other. Would God choose this only for a period of time? Didn't God's choosing it mean it would last forever?

And were these the kinds of things she could talk to anyone—Amy—about?

Yes, she had answered. Vincent was her first boyfriend. Had Nicky been Amy's first?

Amy smiled. Yes, in fact, he *was* her first boyfriend. But they had still waited until after they graduated college to get married. Amy and Maddie talked for a while about those years: dating in high school, breaking up when they went to college, getting back together again. It was a long time, Amy said, between their first date (the homecoming dance in tenth grade) and their wedding.

"It's the waiting that can be difficult," she had said, looking at Maddie without the hint of a smile.

Then and years later Maddie wondered if Amy had meant something more by that, if even so early in Maddie and Vincent's relationship, Amy had been gently trying to pry the lid off the taboo topic of sex before marriage, if—had Maddie allowed her—Amy might somehow have been of help.

Maddie hadn't wanted her help. That lid was firmly shut. She and Vincent were devoted to God and would, therefore, remain innocent—wasn't that obvious?

On an afternoon in late August, Maddie and her mother took the trolley downtown. They had come through the tunnel and were rattling along the level slip of land next to the river when Maddie caught sight of a familiar parka moving along the sidewalk. The trolley made a stop there and Maddie stared as Willy walked towards them, pushing a shopping cart laden with bags.

Certainly she and Vincent had talked about Willy. The accident and Willy's stunning reaction to it were topics of frequent conversation, and they had looked for him every time they had gone to a game. In truth, not seeing him since had worried them, but how to find a homeless man in a city as big as Pittsburgh? They hadn't really tried.

Now here he came, and as he drew nearer, Maddie realized he wasn't holding one arm against his chest. Maybe it wasn't Willy. But he and Vincent had talked for a while; she had had time to study him, and now she recognized his face. He had been none too clean in their earlier encounters; here, in the full light of a summer afternoon, she saw that his face was still dirty, his hair greasy and matted. It was definitely Willy pushing the cart, and the atrophied arm that had been folded and useless in front of him was now normal, functioning in tandem with the other.

He was nearly parallel to her window when the trolley started up again, but she got a good look at the grip of his hands on the handle, the fingers curled around it like they should be. She rose up in her seat and stared as the trolley pulled away, confirming the vision to herself.

All afternoon while window-shopping with her mother, Maddie was preoccupied with the two accidents, laying them beside one another in her mind. Vincent had held his hands to her thigh, and later he told her he had been praying for her. The healing had seeped through her body during the ambulance ride, the pain had slowly dissolved. The X-rays dismissed her without crutches. The bruises and cuts on her face and body disappeared.

Vincent had grasped Willy by the shoulders, trying to help him to his feet. Did he have the presence of mind, even in the shock of the accident, to pray? She hadn't asked him; he hadn't said. And how had Willy experienced it? Drunk as he was, was he aware that night of a change? Or did he wake to it blinded by a hangover, only later in the day coming to realize that his useless arm and hand had been functioning normally all day?

Had it happened to anyone other than a homeless man, this would have been in the papers: *Accident Causes Miraculous, Overnight Transformation!* There would have been doctor's visits, x-rays, maybe even studies exploring connections between car accidents and rare recoveries from long-standing disability. Vincent would have been found, contacted, interviewed—this much, at the very least.

As things stood, the miracle didn't appear to have altered Willy's life at all. There he was: parka, garbage bags, dishevelment—and now the normal use of both hands.

Maddie told Vincent about it in a rush: "You will never believe who I saw today!" followed by the flood of details. She hadn't considered what his answer might be or what it ought to be, yet when she finally gave in to waiting, his reaction was unexpected: "What does it mean?" he said.

"It means that you can heal people. It wasn't just me—a one-time special event. You can heal people!" She surprised herself. It was a little audacious, wasn't it, to declare with such confidence something that, really, wasn't proved. But that was the substance of faith, right? Believing where one couldn't see? Saying it aloud affirmed her conviction. She had stepped out in faith; she had done what the church—what God—wanted her to do, like going forward for prayer during the altar call. Vincent could heal people. She had said it, and it was truer now than it had been even seconds before.

Vincent returned to what Maddie had seen, pressing her again to retell it; and with him, Maddie compared the evidence: Willy's healing and her own. Then Vincent fell silent for a while, considering, she supposed. Certainly it was a leap of faith—but not a huge one. Vincent would see it, too.

Finally, he spoke: Did she know others who could heal people?

Was this something that happened to Christians? To church people? Had it ever happened before at the Bethel Hills Church?

Vincent's questions did—just the slightest bit—rattle her confidence, but she held firm.

"No," she answered. But people in her church had been healed before, she went on. And she reminded him that her parents believed she had been healed—or divinely protected, anyway—when she was hit by the Camaro.

"Well then," Vincent asked, "what does it *mean?*"

Maddie felt that she ought to have an answer, and the fact that she didn't gave the smallest tremor to her faith. She was the traditional church-goer, product of a life-time of Sunday school. Mentally, she cast about for a reply. It occurred to her that Justine might have one, but this she immediately rejected. Certainly Pastor McLaughlin would know. Or Nicky. Vincent should ask him, and she said so.

But Vincent said he didn't want to ask anyone about it. He didn't want to talk about it with anyone—not yet, anyway, he said. He needed time to think about it, and to pray about it, too.

So for a time it was something they kept between them like a secret. Vincent joked with her: sure he could heal people, but only if they'd been hit by a car. Maddie laughed—but she also found herself watching for car accidents. She had been quiet about her own healing: that tacit yet indelible mark of God's blessing on their relationship. But this with Willy clearly, to her mind, signified something more. It suggested something in the line of God's expansive movement through Vincent. It demonstrated—better than she had seen in any other Christian—God's approval of Vincent himself. It was an amazing revelation, and while she believed it, the silence and lack of further confirmation (if only they could talk with Willy; if only Vincent had seen him, too) haunted the periphery of her faith.

She hadn't planned on telling the Tedescos, but then Nicky brought it up one day, when they were talking about going to a baseball game. "Whatever happened to that guy?" he said, and they all knew he was talking about Willy.

Maddie spoke without thinking. They spent so much time with the Tedescos that it seemed natural they should know. It had been weeks, anyway, since she had seen Willy; it was early September now.

She and Vincent had been quiet about it long enough.

And so it wasn't Vincent she was thinking of when she told them—shyly, quietly, not looking at anyone but studying the tabletop. And then she didn't say too much. She just told them what she had seen from the trolley window.

"What are you saying?" Nicky said, and Amy asked for clarification such that Maddie had to go over the details and connect the dots for them (the atrophied arm that was no longer atrophied), a verbose paragraph or so that gave her time to meet Vincent's eye. He was just looking at her, mouth closed, not necessarily (she decided) in disapproval.

For a time, the conversation was focused on Maddie—what she had seen, and when, and where. She was relieved when the Tedescos sought confirmation from Vincent, who willingly and without annoyance candidly affirmed his experiences with Willy and then expressed full credulity in what Maddie had seen, while also confessing he had not laid eyes on him since the accident in July.

This gave rise to more questions. Nicky and Amy fired away: Was Maddie sure it was the same guy? And were they sure he'd had a gimpy arm? (that was Nicky's description). Could she have made some mistake? How could they know that something else hadn't happened—some other intervention for Willy between the accident and, months later, Maddie spotting him on the sidewalk?

Maddie found herself growing defensive. What had become of the faith she had been raised with, the sense that, at any time, one might experience God's tangible intervention? She knew what she had seen—and didn't questions like these suggest doubt in Maddie herself? The slender peninsula of faith onto which she had boldly stepped was under siege—and the attack was coming from friends.

Vincent came to her rescue. He took them all back to the accident in April—Maddie's accident. The Tedescos had known about it. The whole church knew about it and regarded Maddie's protection from injury as a miracle. Maddie's father had given a testimony about it in the Sunday evening service. But no one knew what Maddie and Vincent knew, which was what had actually happened: that Maddie hadn't been protected at all but had been badly injured—and Vincent had healed her.

The Tedescos were silent for a moment, looking from one of them to the other. Finally, Nicky said, "You healed Maddie."

Vincent nodded.

"And this guy Willy?"

Vincent nodded again, and then quickly added, "Well, God healed them. I was just there."

"You were just there," Nicky repeated, smiling. He looked at Amy, who was smiling back. And then to Vincent and Maddie: "And you told no one about this because…?"

Vincent answered: Who were they supposed to tell? And what good would it do? The thing with Maddie was—he thought—an isolated incident. Who was to say that this with Willy wasn't the same way? Telling people might make them think it could happen again—and was that something they could—even *should*—assume? Two miracles. Gifts from God. It was enough.

This was revelation even to Maddie: Vincent believed it more ardently than she did.

"Vincent," Amy said, "people have been given gifts of healing before. If you've been given a gift, then you should use it." She spoke gently, wanting to tread lightly, perhaps, on ground that was so uncertain.

"Well," Vincent answered, looking across the table at her without smiling, earnest. "I guess I have then. Twice."

All of them were silent for a moment, regarding one another. Unwittingly, Maddie held her breath, waiting as if for a verdict.

Then Nicky stood up. "Let's go," he said.

Where?

Downtown. To find Willy. Obviously.

———&—

The night was beautiful: unseasonably warm and clear-skied. Summer's last hurrah. They drove with the windows down, and warm air beat around the car. They had to shout over it to be heard, wondering aloud what to say when they found Willy.

And that was it—that was the gist. Not whether they would find Willy, or in what condition they might find him, but *when* they would find him—and the certainty, in that discovery, that he had been healed.

Nicky was especially enthusiastic. He was grinning, watching Vincent in the rearview mirror as if fearing he would miss something. "What!" Vincent yelled finally, meeting Nicky's grin in the mirror, smiling and exasperated, embarrassed.

And, "What!" Nicky shouted back, as if Vincent had been healing people constantly for the last several months and so had long ago become accustomed to people staring at him, waiting for the next dispensation of wonder.

Amy told Nicky to leave him alone, and Nicky shouted back to her that he couldn't help it, what was he supposed to do? Vincent could heal people! He didn't want to miss anything!

Maddie had imagined multiple scenarios in which she and Vincent talked with Willy again, but always she was unable to move past the moment of discovery; she was never able to fill Willy's mouth with faith or gratitude. Now, as they made their way through the suburbs, it occurred to her that none of her visions were likely to be realized, that the actual encounter would be something else entirely.

She closed her eyes and felt the warm wind buffet her. She felt Vincent's fingers locked through her own and the warmth of his bare arm resting against hers. She listened to him shouting to Nicky in the front seat, to Amy scolding that they needed to turn the music down, to Vincent laughing at her for scolding him. Maddie opened her eyes when Nicky drew her into the conversation: "Maddie, how have I always told you to listen to The Cars?" and Maddie answered him: "Loud!" Laughter.

Then they were in the tunnel, where the increased noise forced them to speechlessness. Their faces glowed orange from overhead lights that hung in strips like a road's dotted lines.

Their car was packed with faith, Maddie thought: the four of them believing that Vincent had healed two people and also that Willy could be found, overtaken in some lightless alley, maybe, or sitting on his blanket near the stadium. Each scenario was equally unlikely, but improbability, she realized, was essential for faith. What was it to have faith if everything was certain? Maddie's years of church teaching, of watching fellow congregants kneel at the altar were aligning themselves in her mind, exposing an architecture she had never noticed before. Faith—God Himself—was making sense to her. Invisible in the wind-blown car, God was taking on a tangible shape. Maddie squeezed Vincent's hand.

And then the darkly lit tunnel spit them out. In all the excitement over Willy, Maddie had forgotten this moment was coming: the shocking emergence into open air. It had always conjured in her a brief but fearsome sense of inevitability, for there was the tunnel's abrupt end and then suddenly there was Pittsburgh: all vertical lines, shining glass, light. The bridge itself obscured its foundation: it rose before them out of nothing and consumed the horizon. And in both directions, other bridges also crossed the river's span, laid out like arms to pull you in. After hurtling through the mountain, she was now flying—unimpeded, helpless—into the city's burning heart, a heart made of glass, concrete, wire, light. There was no helping her.

But happily, Maddie wasn't needing help. This was a harmless city, a safe one. One praised in the papers as great for families. A place where, for example, two teenagers could wander unaccompanied to a late afternoon baseball game and come home again, safe and sound, after dark. The breathless fear at the end of the Fort Pitt Tunnel was only a game, some residue of childhood. She knew that now.

And tonight she rode through that city in a faith-filled car. In no time they had crossed the bridge and were headed toward the stadium. They were driving slowly over ground familiar and less so, each of them trolling sidewalks and squinting down side-streets for a figure that might be Willy's. All the while they talked of Vincent's gift or other things, the normal and the miraculous sifting together as if all of a piece.

It was late when they got back to the Tedescos' and significantly later when Vincent kissed her goodnight at her front door. He wasn't bothered that she had told them. He was relieved, he said, that these friends should know. To *not* tell them felt a little bit like a lie. It was good that they believed in the healings, too—even though they had no proof.

Maddie laughed, delighted. Of course they would take it this way. The Holiness people, she knew, were faith-filled people. She had known this all her life.

They hadn't found Willy that night, and they never did. Maddie's imagined possibilities were lost in memories of what actually took place: the long, slow car-ride over the thoroughfares of the city; the sense of sitting beside Vincent in the late-summer, God-filled air; the Tedescos joyful and laughing in the front seat.

# 14

$\mathcal{M}$addie had to wait for the next healing until a cold night in October. She was not expecting it. There were no cars in sight, first of all, reducing the potential for accidents, and there was the excitement of the football game to distract her. There was watching Vincent down on the field, and the group of youth group friends to surround her. Moreover, they had spotted the Tedescos sitting a few sections away, and so had scrambled over the seats to join them. Theirs was a noisy cluster, watching the game among the grown-ups.

It was a very cold night, and the stadium's thin metal seats drove the cold through their bones. Most spectators had taken to standing. From her position just to the right of the fifty-yard line, Maddie had a great view of the field, could see Vincent's every move, and could make eye-contact with Justine, where she sat in the stands with the marching band. But Maddie had nonetheless missed the bad tackle, always wondering where exactly to be watching during football games, learning again and again that it wasn't always adequate to keep her eye on the ball, that things could take place elsewhere that were equally— if not more—important.

And so it had happened this time that, watching the ball or watching Vincent, she had heard the crowd react to something she hadn't seen: the crack, the thud, the whistle and the end of a play. The lull between plays was different this time though, the atmosphere stilled by communal fear. The boy was lying there motionless and already had lain there too long; he hadn't emerged as he should have, as they usually did when surrounded like that by coaches and players and others who had run on from the sidelines.

Maddie's hands were curled into fists inside her mittens, while next to her Nicky and Amy and the others were quiet, their breath clouding in front of them.

Nicky murmured, "That was awful. That was bad," and Amy said, after a moment or two, "Vince is there."

She was right. Maddie had missed it but now recognized Vincent's frame bent over the boy, helping the coaches from both teams to surround him, while the other players hung back in pairs or threes or alone and looked toward the motionless player.

"This could be serious," Nicky said in a low voice, turning as he did so to look around. Involuntarily Maddie turned, too, and saw the stricken faces of the adults. The students in their section had fallen silent, standing still on the bleachers. Maddie caught Justine's eye. She looked solemn and shook her head.

"What happened? I didn't see what happened," Maddie said, and Nicky explained in a low voice, gesturing with his gloved hands to show the way one boy had hit the other boy and how his neck had snapped back. He had landed on the back of his head while the rest of his body was in the air. Clearly the force of his body slamming into his head at that speed, at that angle, could do serious damage.

"Might have a broken neck," Nicky said, and Amy murmured agreement while Maddie entertained unsolicited visions of paralysis in its varying awful forms.

The small crowd around the motionless player shifted. A stretcher was carried in from the sidelines; on the track, the lights of an ambulance flashed. The few players around the boy stood back, making room. But Vincent remained, kneeling there near the boy's head, his helmet next to him on the ground. Maddie could recognize his profile and the fall of his hair even at this great distance, would know, even from this far away, the shape of his arms.

The medics closed in, and still Vincent remained by the boy. Then suddenly the injured boy was standing in their midst, upright and not needing the stretcher after all. He was standing and then walking to the sidelines of the opposing team—not walking with a limp but walking carefully, gingerly for all that he'd been through, as if he himself couldn't quite trust the miracle despite the fact that he was the center of it.

Cheers came from all sides. What a relief! What a gift they'd been given, and in the face of such terrible potential loss! The game was resumed, and Maddie never remembered which team won.

Then there they were, the four of them at the Pizza Hut, and Nicky blew past any discussion of the game or major plays and closed in on the injury in the third quarter.

"I can't believe he walked out of there, man," Nicky said, and Vincent said he could hardly believe it himself. The boy couldn't have—shouldn't have—walked away.

"He couldn't move," Vincent was saying, "It was really scary." They had brought the stretcher; they were getting ready to strap him to the body board, and then the kid had bent his knees and rested his feet on the ground. Then he was sitting, and then he stood up.

"Amazing," Nicky said.

Vincent said, "Yeah," and smiled. He took a bite of his pizza.

"Vincent," Amy said, prodding him for more.

"What?"

"Aren't you going to tell us what happened out there?"

"I think you saw what happened out there," Vincent said. He was eating, wiping his mouth with a napkin as if he were a normal person, a boy in high school eating pizza after a football game.

"Come on, Vincent," Maddie said.

"We want to hear about it from your perspective," Amy said.

"I've told you my perspective."

"You healed him, didn't you," Nicky said.

Vincent sighed and stretched his arms high over his head, his body arched away from the table. "Who knows?" he said, mid-stretch.

"You said it yourself," Nicky said. "You said he couldn't move."

Well, Vincent said, it was true. It was scary. But that was all Vincent knew. All he knew for sure was everything he had already told them. What more did they want him to say? He hadn't seen the tackle, but the play ended and then the game stopped because the guy was lying there on the ground, and the coaches were running over to him. Vincent had gone to him, too. It used to be that he wouldn't go anywhere near an injured player; he always left that to the experts. Not that he was an expert now. But if someone's in trouble, shouldn't we do whatever we can to help? That's all he was doing. He went over to the kid to pray for him, that was all. It wasn't a big deal.

"Same as you did for me," Maddie said.

"Same as you did for Willy," Nicky said.

"Yeah," said Vincent. He shrugged, and they were all quiet for a moment, waiting, Maddie thought, for Vincent to make the obvious connection.

But it was Nicky who finally said it: "You healed the kid."

"Well—" said Vincent.

"Vincent," said Amy with some delighted frustration. "You of little faith," she said.

Maddie was glad she said it. She didn't want Vincent to make light of it—and that seemed to be what he was doing.

"What," said Vincent. He was straight-faced and serious. "I have *faith*, Amy," he said.

Amy blushed, as if he'd scolded her. "Well, I know that," she said quickly.

"Yeah, but it's probably important that you yourself believe you healed the kid," Nicky said.

Maddie agreed with Nicky, and said so.

"Important to who?" Vincent asked.

"What do you mean, 'Important to who?'" Nicky asked.

"I mean, who does it matter to that I have faith here?"

They were all quiet for a moment, and in the silence, Maddie felt herself somehow implicated. She knew that Vincent trusted in God. The Tedescos knew it, too. So why were they telling him, of all people, to have faith?

Amy's eventual response shed no light. "God just wants us to have faith, Vincent," she said.

Vincent sat back, smiling. "Yes. And I think we've already established that I *do* have faith. So what's the problem?"

"I just think it's pretty important that you believe in what happened," Amy said gently.

Maddie agreed with her. That was it: they knew Vincent had faith, but did he believe his own miracle? And didn't he need to? Wasn't that how it worked? With faith you can move mountains, or something like that.

"What exactly do you want me to believe?" Vincent asked. "I was there. I saw the kid get up. But I don't know how badly he was hurt in the first place."

"Well," Nicky said, "I think there is every reason to believe the kid was hurt badly. He might have been paralyzed, Vince."

"Right," Vincent said. His tone wasn't annoyed; he sounded remarkably self-assured. He spoke as if he was simply explaining to his friends things he expected them to understand, believing they would come along eventually. "But I don't know exactly what happened out there, and that's fine," he said. "Isn't that fine? Isn't that okay? Not to know?" His question was sincere.

"I think it's pretty important that you believe in what happened," Amy said gently. "God wants us to have faith." She was repeating herself, but the words were comfortingly familiar, and Maddie waited for Vincent to agree. She wanted him to agree, because Amy and Nicky were offering a trustworthy framework for Vincent's apparent gift, a framework Maddie understood: we believe, we have faith, and God works through us. If Vincent didn't believe it, then it wouldn't keep happening—and Maddie felt keenly that healings were something that should definitely keep happening.

"Okay, but here's the thing," Vincent said. "*I* didn't heal him. *I* haven't healed anybody. If anybody is doing any healing around here, it's God doing the healing."

Nicky leaned toward him, as if Vincent were in want of comfort. Vincent had been vehement, but still he didn't seem perturbed. He helped himself to another piece of pizza.

Nicky said, "We all understand that it's God who heals, Vince, but you need to understand that you have an incredible gift here. It's important. And to use your gift, you're going to have to have faith."

Vincent was listening carefully. He focused on Nicky's face, and when Nicky was quiet, Vincent still waited as if digesting his words.

Finally, "Okay, fine. Got it," he said. "It's just that I want my faith to be in *God* and not in healing people, you know? God will do what he wants to do—and if he wants to heal people, then he's gonna heal people."

"Yes," Amy broke in, almost exasperated, "but Vincent, this might be a really powerful gift."

And Nicky said, "You have a responsibility, Vince."

"Okay," said Vincent. "That may be. But I don't know what God is going to do, do you? I think the only thing I can do is pray about it. And if someone is hurt again or sick or whatever, I'm going to be praying. What else should I do? What should anyone do?"

What more could any of them say? Maddie and the Tedescos both agreed with him: Who would disagree about praying? All of them could—and should—pray.

It was the bit about what God wanted that eluded Maddie. Was that possible to determine? And anyway, didn't God always *want* to heal people? Wasn't it always a lack of faith that prevented people getting healed in the first place?

Maddie decided that Vincent had far more faith than most people. Regardless of his opinion as to how it worked or even what he did or should believe, he had healed three people now.

Why shouldn't she believe this to be a miracle? What, in all honesty, had she managed to retain from sophomore-year biology that might convince her otherwise? Her knowledge of actual biological functions was understandably limited, her comprehension of muscle, nerve, ligament and sinew was, at best, tentative.

Meanwhile, the Bible was rife with miracle. She had been taught to live in expectation. And then, below Amy's ribcage, was the certain abdominal swell—a pregnancy advancing where it had once seemed impossible.

Nicky announced it during a Sunday evening service in November: Amy was three months along! A collective gasp and the church erupted in applause. People stood to their feet with shouts and cheers; they left their seats and surrounded—as best they could, in the middle of the pews—Nicky and Amy both. The service was delayed for a long time by all of this, and when the congregation finally managed to resume some decorum, Pastor McLaughlin stood before them wiping his eyes with his handkerchief, and commented that this was one of the best worship services he had ever known.

Nicky had let Vincent and Maddie in on the news the night before, informing them in a roundabout way by asking what they would be doing in June.

In June? Vincent would be graduating. They would both be finding jobs for the summer, and in August, Vincent would head upstate with a scholarship to play football.

They were standing in the Tedescos' kitchen; Amy's back was to them where she stood at the sink. Vincent had his arm around Maddie. June was a long way off.

"We were hoping you could babysit," Nicky had said casually. He was replacing the garbage bag in the trashcan, and Maddie hadn't understood what Nicky could possibly be talking about.

It was Vincent who understood, scarcely missing a beat before he let out a whoop and hoisted Nicky off his feet, and then he was gripping Amy in his arms and trying to spin with her around their far-too-little kitchen.

That was when Maddie got it, the realization dawning slowly, a little light for her blind eyes.

Amy was smiling so hard it almost looked like she was crying. Nicky said he was absolutely positive it was a boy. Maddie was jumping up and down and clapping. Vincent wiped tears from his cheeks, and everybody laughed at him.

---

"I just hope she doesn't lose this one," Justine said. They were coming out of history class. Nicky had announced the pregnancy just days before, and it was all anyone at the Bethel Hills Church was talking about.

Maddie's response was pure confidence. "She won't," she said.

But Justine told her not to be too sure. "It's dangerous," she said, "telling people this early."

Maddie's answer was that the Tedescos had waited three months. That's how long you're supposed to wait, she said. She had learned a lot about pregnancy in the last few days.

"Still," Justine said, "They've had so many miscarriages. Anything could happen."

Maddie said again that Amy Tedesco wouldn't miscarry. Everything was going to be fine, she said.

Vincent had said so, too, when she had asked him, coming home from the Tedescos on the night Nicky had told them. Maddie had raised the question: What if she miscarries, Vincent? Because in the few hours they had known about the pregnancy, the thought of this baby's loss had already become unbearable.

Vincent answered, "She won't."

She looked at his profile, his face brightening and then going dark again with the passing cars. He was focused on the road ahead; the line of his forehead, nose and chin was strong.

"Well," Justine was saying, "of course I hope they don't miscarry. Of course I hope they don't. But you never know."

"They aren't going to lose this baby, Justine," Maddie said. Once again, just as it had when she first told Vincent about Willy, the assertion of her own confidence had a strengthening effect. Maddie felt more reassured than ever.

Justine was quiet in response to this, but the halls were crowded and each of them was maneuvering around people. It wasn't the best place for a conversation.

As Maddie made her way alone to sixth period, she reflected on how far she had come, how much she had learned about faith since those whispering days with the nativity Jesus cradled in her palm. How could she explain it to Justine, who didn't yet know that Vincent had healed Maddie or Willy, who couldn't be expected to have seen or believed the miracle during the football game?

And now Vincent had healed Amy, and that was why she was pregnant. None of them had talked about this; if the Tedescos were thinking it, they weren't saying anything. But could it be otherwise? All those years of miscarrying babies, and then the Tedescos befriend Vincent, and within months, Amy is finally pregnant.

No, Maddie wanted to say to Justine, the baby was going to be absolutely fine. But Maddie knew, too, that she couldn't make Justine believe it. Faith, she was discovering, was something learned and then practiced. It took time. Justine would come to understand.

# 15

$\mathcal{A}$my had a new book on her coffee table: photographs of unborn babies. At every visit, Maddie would leaf through it, sometimes reading the brief text, always studying the images that glowed yellow and orange against a black ground. Baby after baby—or maybe it was all the same one—photographed over the course of nine months' gestation. Maddie was fascinated by the images, the tiny fingers and tiny toes, the translucent skin, the sealed eyes.

The baby in this photo was very young, hardly human. The curved head was elongated in its extension from spine to forehead, and then came the bulge of the nose. Veins traversed the skull, thin red lines that branched and extended like roads on a map. The ribs were regular pleats along its side but not nearly long enough: they came to a stop just at the rise of the abdomen, looking more like gills than protective bone. The fingers and toes were stubs; the appendages of hands and feet drifted in front of the baby on foreshortened arms and legs, unused or useless.

Several pages further and here was a baby farther along. The fingers of an open hand extended toward the camera, attenuation evident in joints and fingernails. The thumb rested just inside the mouth, as though pressed against the upper gum. Maddie could see downy hair on the baby's face, thicker at the eyebrows, and the indentation at the center of the upper lip.

What was it like in there, she wondered, before knowing began? All sounds would be muted in the water. Floating like that, there might be no sense of gravity, no necessary sense of direction. All motion would be comfort, a kind of rocking, and the darkness would be absolute.

In that case, Maddie thought, these pictures must have been stunning to the unborn baby: the obligatory use of light, the intrusion of the camera. How to take pictures like these? How to ensure that it was safe?

Any baby she had ever known would be frightened by something like that. Such a surprising experience would be sure to bring terror and tears. But the babies in these photos seemed unamazed. Their expressions were the picture of peaceful calm and uninterrupted repose.

Or were these expressions of dismay and fear? And if that were the case, Maddie wondered, then in the moments just before the camera's flash, what had the peacefulness looked like?

Vincent teased her about the book. He said she was obsessed.

"Looking at it again, huh?" He sat down close beside her and grinned.

"It's a beautiful book, is all," she responded, and turned the page.

"I wouldn't call it beautiful," Vincent said. "That book is plain weird."

"Why do you think it's weird?" She didn't look up at him, but continued leafing through.

"That doesn't even look like a baby. Look at it!" and he pointed to the five-month-old fetus with stubby fingers and eyes tightly shut.

"Yes it does, Vincent."

"Not like any babies I've ever known."

Maddie laughed. "You generally don't see them when they look like this."

"And why is that?" Vincent straightened, mocking interest in a spirit of "now-we're-getting-somewhere."

"Because when they look like this, they aren't born yet."

"Ex-ACT-ly," Vincent said, and relaxed his posture: he rested his case.

"What do you mean, 'ex*actly*'?"

"I mean, you're not *supposed* to see babies when they look like that, and that's why that book is weird."

"I think it's weird, too," Nicky said, coming in from the kitchen. He tossed Vincent a bottle of Gatorade. "Amy!" he was calling to her in the other room. "Vince thinks the book is weird, too!"

"You two are peas in a pod," Amy answered. She was laughing.

Maddie didn't try to explain or defend her fascination. She didn't fully understand it herself, but knew that Vincent's comment hit close to home. The secrecy of it appealed to her, that sense of spying. There was pleasure in this circumvention: through these pictures, she gained a view onto something that, until recently, no one had ever seen.

Moreover, here was an education, something that made high school biology concrete. She had not remembered much from that brief introduction during her sophomore year to the mysteries of the reproductive system. How seriously could she be expected to take into account a body's biologically driven urge to further the species? What, to her, were mitosis and meiosis? What were those winding ribbons of DNA?

And what, in truth, was pregnancy to her but a happy announcement made about someone else? It was something to be observed from a distance, a mystery responsible for the steady population of the church nursery, of the world.

But this book—and Amy's pregnancy—cast all of it in life-sized terms, making imaginable not only the Tedescos as parents, but also, somewhat more remotely, herself. Now Maddie realized she would likely someday become a mother, and that she wanted to be one. As she leafed through the book's glossy pages, she imagined a new life taking shape within her. She could almost conjure inside herself the sensation of what, for now, she felt only by stretching a palm over Amy's abdomen: the gentle pressure of a knee, a foot, an elbow. This child, as yet unseen, gaining life in the dark.

Yet all of these revelations seemed formalities in light of what she had been learning already for some time, those ways of her body taught her by Vincent. Those ways, she now knew, were the reason for the swimming pool conversations, the warnings about sexual purity and the temptations that would assert themselves against it. Maddie now understood that one had to construct the boundaries before the fact, because when the passion came—those biological, natural, primal, and necessary urges—it was nearly impossible to withstand them. Her own body, Maddie realized, was truly a force of nature.

What flummoxed her was that these impulses should somehow be wrong. Confronting them for the first time in her life, she was hard-pressed to accept that acting on them was sin. Why should it be? She could discern no practical reason. The fortress she had so carefully built against fornication was, it turned out, nothing more than chicken wire. She found she could deconstruct a fence in so small a gesture as an unbuttoning.

And yet there was Vincent, resistant. Closing buttons again, returning her hands to his waist. Experienced and also opposed to this sin. If anyone could instruct Maddie in the mysterious ways of God, it was Vincent—and in this regard, Vincent stood firm.

Except, of course, when he didn't. Increasingly, he didn't. Incrementally, by degrees, they moved together past the fence's boundary, dipped their toes in the pool's shallow end. And always it ended—without real satisfaction—in Vincent's call to repentance.

He held Maddie in a grip lacking all sensual tenderness, her face pressed to his arm, his chest, and in a broken voice or one filled with confidence, he called on God to forgive them of their sin and strengthen them to withstand further temptation. He might pray it in a whisper, he might—with tears reminiscent of that night at the altar—plead in a choked gasp. And if Maddie was certain of anything, it was that Vincent was convinced of their sinfulness, of their need for God.

In light of this, she found herself consistently relieved that their relationship should persist. After all, she had lured him into sin (wasn't it always at her initiation?) countless times. Her knowledge of the Bible implied—if it didn't directly mandate—that their best course of action would be to break up. How did the passage go? "If your right hand causes you to sin, cut it off," or some horror equally conclusive. And yet, post repentance, Vincent could look at her clear-eyed, could—and did—tell her again that he loved her. The adequacy of his contrition or, more distantly, God's forgiveness, seemed absolute.

And Vincent would occasionally remind her that his faith was planted in the school parking lot, where, Vincent said, God had made it clear that he had chosen them for each other. "He gave us a miracle," Vincent chuckled, "as if he wanted to be sure we'd notice." As if Vincent wouldn't have noticed and loved Maddie otherwise, Vincent would say. And Maddie would add that she had noticed Vincent before that.

They talked about temptation, of course. There were moments of objective discussion, merciful moments when, somehow, they had circled wide of the danger and could again assert their posture of purity. They could stand circumspect and thoughtful, together studying the landscape of temptation, the swimming pool behind its concrete and barbed wire. They could laugh at the lie of stolen intimacy, that the union of their bodies would mean anything other than the potential destruction of their souls. They could affirm in blind faith that God's plan for sex only within marriage had ramifications beyond what— so limited, so young—they could be expected to understand. Maddie affirmed all these things with Vincent, reciting by rote what she had been told all her life, what he had only so recently and so fully adopted. If Vincent believed it—Vincent the miracle-worker, newborn child of God—then Maddie was sure it was right.

But there were those other moments, too, when Maddie knew they were pitted against forces beyond their strength or comprehension. At those times, even what Vincent said he wanted was not reflected in his behavior. Who was to say whether, in his car on this abandoned street or in that empty parking lot, Vincent would draw them to prayer or instead to the marvel of skin on more skin—each experience bearing something of the holy about it, something indefinably beautiful.

But no, the skin was better. Who could argue that anything but skin was better?

And then Maddie was again in Vincent's grip, her face pressed into his chest, the tears of his remorse dampening her hair. Vincent prayed aloud and then fell silent, continuing to hold her, and Maddie wondered if he was waiting for her to say something, to join her words with his in looking to God for help.

Always she was silent, listening—for what, exactly? For God to move her, to bring her, like he had Vincent, to an attitude of remorse? But if God was speaking, then she never heard him, hearing instead only Vincent's breathing, that gentle pressure which moved her with the rise and fall of his chest.

# 16

*P*ittsburgh Children's Hospital was in the heart of the city's downtown. Constructed of steel and concrete, it was nonetheless designed to let in light: from both inside and out, it appeared to be made of plate glass. There was not a room on any exterior wall that did not have one length composed of window. Thus designed and situated on the Monongahela River, the founders' hope was that the children undergoing treatment should have a view of the world around them, and the hospital's sickest patients would have rooms with a view of the river and the mountain beyond it.

Seeing beauty like this could only aid in the healing process.

Such was Maddie's imagination, anyway, of the famous children's hospital in her city, but she had never actually seen it. Had she known its actual design and setting, she would likely have been disappointed that it wasn't actually downtown, that it enjoyed only regular views of a rolling, house-dotted landscape, and that these were obtained through standard-sized windows. No river, no mountain, no plate-glass.

This might have required reassessment of her assumptions; but as they were untried, she could carry on with the images that, more and more of late, were readily coming to mind. Most vivid was the oncology ward, home to the sickest of the hospital's patients. Maddie imagined it as a long room lined with beds against one wall; and opposite the beds, providing the children with their first and last sights of the day, a wall made of windows. The windows were sloped, dropping away from the ceiling at a seventy-degree angle, coming all the way to the floor. Through them the children watched birds, planes, helicopters, traffic moving across the top of Mount Washington, and the city's famous incline making its way up and down the steep hill.

Maddie's imagination provided further details: sun streamed into the room through these windows; the beds were covered in sunlight. Each bed was different, bearing gifts sent by friends and worried families: over-large teddy bears, and Mylar helium balloons that glinted in the sunlight. Each bed was occupied by a child in some degree of terrible illness. They were bald. Their eyes were large and haunted or pinched behind swollen cheeks. Some of them had tubes attached to their arms. Some were too weak to sit up.

But hope was there, too. For Maddie imagined Vincent among them, tall and handsome, walking slowly from bed to bed, touching each child on the head or the arm, bending down to speak to them. Tousling heads where hair might once have been. He would talk to them, sit on their beds, make them laugh. And then after sitting with a child for a while, he would just tell her that he was going to pray now, and that this prayer was going to make the child better, that soon after this she would be able to get rid of the tubes forever and grow her hair back and play in the backyard just like she used to.

Vincent would move through the ward and the children would love him, and within days the news reports would be about how every child in the oncology ward at the Pittsburgh Children's Hospital was recovered, discharged, sent home. She could see the photographs: empty beds, wrapped tightly in sheets and a single blanket, walls clean of ornament, all of it soaked in sunlight that poured through the plate-glass.

To Maddie, and given what she had seen in Vincent, this vision was not unreasonable. Though she would not be likely to admit this—never aloud and not even to herself—it was somewhat of an expectation.

∞

It was a Sunday, this time in January. The day was cold but snowless, and a handful of children escaped outdoors after the church service to play on the parsonage swing set. Some of the youth group, too, had come squinting outdoors, Vincent and Maddie among them. They were standing on the church steps when they heard the ear-splitting scream. Maddie was confused but Vincent reacted immediately, racing toward the parsonage lawn, and then the rest of them followed.

The child was still struggling to his feet when they got there, but the blood was already dripping down through his hair and over his forehead. Little Joey Amoretti was no older than three, and it was his sister Hannah who was screaming, standing up on one side of the glider-swing, her knuckles white around the handles. The other seat was also occupied, and that child stared back over his shoulder, horrified at the bleeding on the lawn behind him. The glider-swing itself was still in motion, coming slowly to a stop.

Vincent went straight to Joey, who reached up to wipe the blood out of his eyes and, seeing it on his hands, also started screaming. Maddie didn't think to close her eyes against the blood, and so she had a clear view of Vincent's hands along the top of Joey's head, making a seam of the split in his hairline, pressing closed the cut in the skin over his skull.

This was the next miracle: the skin fusing the way it did, coming together tidily and binding instantly, stopping the blood, canceling the pending emergency room visit and the stitches that would have inevitably followed.

Mrs. Amoretti was there in an instant, lifting Joey from the lawn, soothing the child and, as she hurried toward the parsonage, taking under her arm the inconsolable Hannah, who blubbered on about the accident and how Joey had insisted on crawling under the glider-swing even though she had told him not to. It was a few steps and then they were gone, disappearing behind the aluminum and screen door, with Mr. Amoretti and Pastor and Mrs. McLaughlin hastening behind them.

The rest of them were left on the lawn: the small number from the youth group, the few congregants who heard the news when, breathless, it had been carried to the Amorettis. There was a brief silence among them after the door closed. Maddie stood still with Vincent, who studied the blood on his hands for a moment, then wiped them on the grass.

Around them, the small crowd divided into various circles and ellipses of concern, one of which—comprised of teenagers—gathered around Vincent. What happened? What did it look like? Vincent described the injury and exclamations erupted, followed by more questions or stories of their own.

The adults, too, put questions to Vincent, who again described the accident as he had come upon it.

Thoughtful, they recalled incidents requiring stitches for their own children; they retold stories of their own children's swing set accidents and moved on to those involving bicycles and trees. They recounted visits to emergency rooms. They discussed who might accompany the Amorettis to the hospital; they determined who might take Hannah Amoretti home with them for the afternoon so her parents would only have to worry about Joey.

Then, armed with purpose or even the simple awareness that they needed to get out of the way, the clusters redistributed themselves and most of them dispersed. The teenagers, called by their parents to waiting cars, moved off. They went home to pot roasts warm in timed ovens, to afternoon naps, to plans for casseroles quietly delivered later in the week to the Amorettis' kitchen table.

Cars were still starting and pulling out of the parking lot when the parsonage door opened and the Amorettis emerged. Hannah and Joey were no longer crying, though their faces were still red, and each of them was enjoying a lollipop. Joey's shirt was bloodied but his face was clean, and he seemed unaware of the blood matting his hair or even that he'd been hurt at all. He rode peacefully in his father's arms and busied himself with his candy.

The Amorettis thanked Vincent for trying to help them out, for comforting Joey when he got there.

"No problem," Vincent said, "no problem at all." Despite the remnant of blood along his palm, he shook Mr. Amoretti's extended hand.

And then the abbreviated and relieved conversation. They would not be going to the hospital: the bleeding had stopped; the cut seemed to be closed. It was amazing, really. Like a miracle. And now—here, with laughter—everyone could go home and get a nap, and Mr. Amoretti could watch the Penguins game from the comfort of his living room.

The family was moving away now. Vincent and Maddie were walking toward his car. Behind them, Pastor McLaughlin emerged from the house and said something about getting rid of the swing set, something about it being nothing more than a rust heap, anyway.

That was the end of it—and who would have expected anything more? It was merely a playground accident, the unfortunate result of a child's foolishness. Yes, there had been a lot of blood, but the bleeding had stopped on its own. Clearly the cut wasn't all that deep.

Except that it wasn't right. Not at all. Not to Maddie, anyway, who had seen it with her own eyes.

"What's not right about it?" Vincent asked. It was Monday or Tuesday and they were talking on the phone.

"It's not right that a miracle took place right there in front of everyone, and all Mr. Amoretti can say is that he's glad he can watch the hockey game at home."

Vincent chuckled. "There's nothing wrong with enjoying a hockey game, Maddie."

"That's not my point, Vincent. This has nothing to with hockey."

"So what's the matter, then?"

"You healed his son and he's not even grateful."

"How do you know he isn't grateful? He seemed grateful. He said thank you."

"Yes, but Vincent, he's not grateful that you *healed* him."

"I didn't heal him." This quiet reply from Vincent was vexing. In the split second between their two sentences, she knew he was going to say this. She knew, too, that Vincent knew what she meant, and now she had to steer around her annoyance.

"Fine, okay. I know. God healed him. But he's not *grateful* that God healed him."

Vincent was quiet for a moment, giving Maddie time to consider that Vincent was attending less to her words than to what her words said about her. She didn't like this thought, and reassured herself of her intentions—which were, of course, good.

"You know, Maddie?" he answered her. "I think there's lots God does that we don't thank him for, that we don't even know or recognize he does. I'm not saying we should necessarily celebrate that, but we don't have to make it our mission in life to make sure that everyone is paying attention, you know? And anyway, Joey's okay, right? And Mr. and Mrs. Amoretti are really happy that he's all right. So is everybody. They are grateful. Why isn't that enough?"

Maddie couldn't articulate why it wasn't enough—but it wasn't. Over the ensuing days, her irritation with the Amorettis spread to the congregation members who had stood waiting on the lawn, to the teenagers who had come up right behind Vincent, even to the Tedescos. They hadn't been there, but certainly they should put two and two together.

It was almost enough to make her tell Justine who, like everyone else, had heard about it. Justine would be sympathetic to Maddie's frustration. Injustice, deception, willful ignorance: Justine had no tolerance for any of it.

She didn't have tolerance for a lot of things. "What possesses a kid to crawl *under* a glider? *While* it's moving?" She refrained from calling Joey an idiot—he was only three—but suggested that he should be taken to the hospital. "Might be a good idea to have him checked out," she said. "You know, get that kid's head examined."

No, Maddie knew her friend was an unlikely candidate in championing Vincent as healer. For starters, she had increasingly found fault with her congregation's claims of a miracle—or any tangible act of God. Short of watching one unfold before her eyes, Justine was unlikely to believe that any healings had actually taken place.

More problematic was her persistent mistrust of Vincent. She spent time with him, certainly—but as Maddie's best friend, she might have found this obligatory. And she was certainly friendly towards him. But she really didn't seem to like him.

There was, for instance, a game Vincent played at school, one he had made up. He was the only one who *could* play, as the fun lay in the element of surprise. Maddie had seen him at it once or twice before they had ever spoken, and it had made her laugh even then: Vincent would choose his "victim" unawares, someone he knew most of the time, but occasionally someone he didn't. He would spot this person at some distance down the hall and then, at breakneck speed, would run the person down, his feet loudly pounding only in the last few steps of his approach. He would come to a windy and sudden halt mere inches from his victim's face, and he would shout, "Ha!"

That was it. Brief and shocking. It wasn't what one could call violent; he never touched his victim. But the recipient of his attentions was invariably startled, sometimes terrified, and would often respond with a scream, a shout, a dropping of books and papers.

Justine hated it. He had done it to her several times, and every time it made her furious. But she was angered, too, in defense of his other victims, about whom, Justine pointed out, he didn't seem to care at all.

"You're going to make somebody pee themselves, Vincent!" she shouted at him once. She hadn't been the victim that time, but was helping an unfortunate soul retrieve scattered papers. "What if someone has a heart condition?"

Vincent laughed this off, and Maddie tried to help her see the humor in it, but Justine wouldn't hear it. "It isn't funny, Maddie," she said. "He should watch out. One of these times, somebody's going to get hurt."

No, Maddie couldn't imagine Justine promoting Vincent's gift at all.

She couldn't be sure that Vincent would want her to tell Justine anyway. He seemed perfectly happy never to speak of these things—a fact Maddie didn't understand.

There was a lot about Vincent that Maddie didn't understand, and his attitude about healing people was only the beginning. His attitude, Maddie thought, was a kind of assent, submission to something that he hadn't chosen and wouldn't have chosen, if asked. He seemed to regard his gift with disinterest, as if it were a gift equal with his many others, and one he didn't care to foster.

Vincent was interested in sports and friends, Maddie, and church and God, not in any particular order, but in some strange Venn diagram of contentment.

Maddie had to correct herself. There *was* an order: it was God first, and then came everything else.

How had he expressed it? Here was a new gambit, a surprising tactic to defeat the temptation facing them in every private moment. Vincent explained it to her, and she, of course, did not comprehend it.

"It's not that I don't want you," he said. "It's not that we don't want each other. It's that we want God more."

This also had been a conversation over the phone, safely distant from one another, where they were able to regard the swimming pool and its enclosure with rational scrutiny. Maddie had agreed with Vincent at the time. It didn't sound very different from church-talk and discussions of sexual temptation in the youth group. Of course we want God more! We want to obey him because we should. Because it pleases him. Because it's right.

Maddie had hung up the phone warmed by the conversation. Their mutual affirmation of this truth fortified her; their shared commitment to obedience felt like confession and redemption both. She was awed by a sense of renewed devotion to God, awed, too, by Vincent's faith and their being chosen for one another, by the unique blessing of their relationship: its maturity, strength, wisdom.

All of which was lost days later, thrust somewhere under the car's dashboard along with Maddie's sweater and—would have been—her jeans, had not Vincent reasserted his new-found wisdom, that of their wanting each other, yes, but wanting God more.

And here the solution failed her. Vincent's formula broke into meaningless pieces. He had stopped kissing her and was in every way resisting her, urging her to God as if believing that Maddie understood and wanted him, too. But God, in that moment, was nothing to Maddie; she couldn't countenance the possibility of his presence or even, were she honest, his relevance.

Vincent could and did. Again he was the repentant one, asking forgiveness for both of them, and telling Maddie on the way home that they had to be strong for each other, that neither of them could expect to be strong every time and that this time he was glad he could be strong enough for them both.

Later Maddie felt glad of that, too—or, at the very least, that she ought to be. External restraint—in the form of Vincent, in the form of anything—seemed the best she could hope for when it came to resisting temptation. The verse again skirted the back of her mind: "If your right hand causes you to sin, cut it off and throw it away." It was something terrible like that, and she didn't have to think hard to see how it applied in their situation, how Vincent, full of God, might be better off without her.

She was glad she didn't know exactly where to find that verse in the Bible, and she wasn't about to go hunting for it. Neither would she mention it to Vincent—ever. Were Vincent to contemplate that verse about cutting off your hand, Maddie feared he would end their relationship.

Yes, sometimes her Sunday school education felt like more trouble than it was worth. But it was those years of church, too, that served Maddie now, bringing to mind what bothered her about the Amorettis' ignorance: the glory of God. They were all supposed to be about praising God, about acknowledging and, where possible (it was rumored to be everywhere possible), celebrating Him—His words, His works, His goodness. This was what they taught you in church. This was the purported ambition of every Sunday gathering and, supposedly, their lives.

She told Vincent, "It isn't that they aren't grateful. It's that they aren't aware of what God has done. You said it yourself. *You* didn't heal Joey. *God* did. People should be praising God for that miracle."

Vincent was quiet, and his apparent thoughtfulness fueled her certainty. "God should get the credit for this," she went on, "and if no one noticed it at the time or knows about it now, then he isn't really getting any credit, is he? Not much, anyway. Not enough."

That was how they left it for a while. Maddie's confidence contented her for the time being, and meanwhile there were no more incidents or further opportunities for Vincent to miraculously heal anybody. He seemed to feel this was fine.

But Maddie began watching for opportunities, almost hoping someone would cut himself opening a can of mandarin oranges at lunch or stumble when walking down the stairs. Sometimes as she sat next to Vincent in church, she pointed to the list of prayer requests in the church bulletin—not saying anything, just pointing. See? She was trying to say. You could heal all of them.

They were leaving church one Sunday when Vincent was the one to bring it up: "You're right, Maddie," he said. "There are a lot of sick people in the world."

This was what she was hoping for: Vincent was ready to put his gift of healing into active—not simply *reactive*—use. Maddie was very pleased and tried, in a quiet moment, to articulate to herself why. She reconsidered Vincent's words about the Amorettis. She told herself again that their complacent appreciation was not enough. A gift like Vincent's shouldn't be hidden; it shouldn't be overlooked. Vincent's gift was evidence of God himself—of God's choosing Vincent, of his choosing Maddie and Vincent for one another.

She wanted everyone to know about that.

—⁂—

It wasn't until she was getting ready for bed that night that Maddie found herself revisiting the episode with Joey Amoretti. She remembered it all: Vincent's familiar hands around that dreadful cut; the stout fingers and square fingernails, bloodied as they closed the wound.

But she saw it, too, from a distance. Some kids had been talking about it again after church that evening, revisiting their recent history as teenagers are wont to do. Lisa Wells mentioned that she was standing with Maddie when they first heard the screaming, that she and Maddie had hurried together to the parsonage lawn, and Vincent had gotten there ahead of them.

Standing at the bathroom sink, Maddie remembered. They arrived at the scene, but she hadn't run to Joey. Horrified by the screaming and instinctively fearful of the blood, Maddie had hung back and watched Vincent with the boy. She saw him standing over the child, his hands curved and resting on the top of his head. And then Mrs. Amoretti coming, and the retreat into the house. That was it.

She hadn't actually witnessed the miracle at all.

# 17

$\mathcal{M}$addie didn't think through how things might play out. How to skip from convincing Vincent to visiting the Children's Hospital cancer wards?

But apparently there was to be an order. There were chains of command, or lines of communication, anyway. Vincent wasn't to be a rogue healer hitting the streets of Pittsburgh with his stunning blessing. To Maddie's displeased surprise, it wouldn't be done like that. Rather, Nicky Tedesco must—with Vincent's permission— have a conversation with Pastor McLaughlin, which resulted in Vincent's subsequent conversation with Pastor McLaughlin, which then resulted in a conversation with the elders and deacons. Vincent requested Maddie's presence in both of these and she—how could she say no?—complied.

The upshot was no heroics (yet) in the oncology ward, but definite expressions of quiet astonishment, some of bold belief and none of doubt. "Proceed with caution" seemed to be the order of the day, by which was meant that Vincent's gift would be kept—for now—a secret.

What this did *not* mean, apparently, was starting small, testing out the miraculous in doses, where there wasn't much at stake. Instead Vincent was to join an already-planned prayer for a man very nearly on his death-bed.

And why not? This was the Bethel Hills Church of the Expectant, after all.

Maddie didn't like the smell of hospitals, and she had a vague discomfort at the idea of entering the room where Mr. Pavlik lay with a tumor expanding in his brain. There was something unpleasant about the whole thing: the body making something destructive to itself, the tumor growing beyond control, pressing against the brain, making the head swell. She imagined the inescapable closeness of a tumor in her own head. It was distressing.

Vincent teased her about this aversion: "It isn't contagious, Mads," he said, and she answered him swiftly and annoyed:

"I know you can't catch a tumor."

He had asked her to come along, had promised her silly things like a ride in the first vacant wheelchair they could find or going out for ice cream afterwards even though it would only be ten o'clock in the morning.

She gave in, because when did she not want to give in to Vincent? But she agreed to go, too, because she felt their coming here was her fault, borne of her confidence. Yet so quickly it had taken on a life of its own, with players she hadn't intended to include: Pastor McLaughlin and the elders would be there. And, again, when she had imagined the hospital visit, it had been for sweet little children in an oncology ward—not for an old man's brain tumor.

They stood shoulder-to-shoulder around Mr. Pavlik's bed, a wall of resolve built on cautious hope, and Pastor McLaughlin had asked if Vincent would reposition himself up by Mr. Pavlik's head, there by his right shoulder. Maddie had been summoned from her position at the window: Pastor McLaughlin called to her, and Mrs. Pavlik beckoned, smiling, gesturing with her plump hand.

Gathered in this way, they reached for Mr. Pavlik's covered body, finding limbs through the blanket. The elders and Pastor McLaughlin flanked his sides, Mrs. Pavlik gripped his right foot, Maddie rested her hand lightly on his left. Then they bowed their heads and closed their eyes—except for Maddie, who raised her head to watch Vincent lay both of his hands on Mr. Pavlik's shaved head.

She hadn't wanted to look at Mr. Pavlik when she entered the room. He had come to church after his last surgery, months ago now, confined to a wheelchair, his head mercifully wrapped in a bandage and then covered in a hat. But she thought for certain today when finding his head bare that she noted swelling near his ear, and the thought frightened her. Pastor McLaughlin prayed aloud, and Maddie wondered how Vincent could bear to put his hands on that venous head where pink scars traced its contours and then disappeared into the pillow.

Next to her, Mrs. Pavlik sighed. Maddie stole a glance at her face to see it red and tear-streaked. Her eyes were closed, but tears spilled from them nonetheless, and her lips were moving. Maddie considered the Pavliks' partnership. He was tall and thin; she was short and heavy-set. He was quiet, given to making one laugh with his dry humor, but only if you hung around to listen. Mrs. Pavlik, on the other hand, talked constantly, so much that you found yourself tuning her out. She was the busy sort, always doing something. She was responsible for the kitchen at church and for many of the decorations in the church building. Even there in the hospital she was constant motion, always fussing over her motionless husband, adjusting his blanket or his bed sheet, patting his leg, stroking his arm. During the prayer she rubbed his foot vigorously, and briefly the blanket came away and exposed bare toes, long and somewhat yellowed.

This unanticipated nakedness, innocent as it was, shocked Maddie. Suddenly she had a vivid sense of Mr. Pavlik's body there in front of her—all of it. His long limbs motionless, their muscles flaccid and sagging, his torso and the organs at work inside it: spleen, liver, lengths of intestine. He was unconscious—or maybe only sleeping— but his heart continued its mindless contractions, pushing the blood out to his extremities and drawing it back again. And what other crucial fluids pulsed among the membranes of tissue and bone?

She marveled at the body as container, grotesquely complex and having far too many distasteful needs. Yet here Mr. Pavlik wasn't making use of his body at all: something had taken root in the brain, had grown there and now was commanding his stillness. For a moment, the idea that he should be living—lying there mute, blind, unmoving—seemed absurd.

And yet she had seen that his toenails were neatly trimmed.

Maddie could imagine Mrs. Pavlik bent over her husband's bare foot, wielding the nail scissors. She would have chatted away as she cut his toenails for him, now accustomed to his silence but talking to him nonetheless, tending to the heedless growth of these nails. She would have thought nothing of the length of those toes and their hairlessness or the yellowing of the flesh. To her, Maddie supposed, it was all familiarity, as customary to her as her own two feet. She probably didn't find it disgusting.

Maddie did. She couldn't imagine fondness over such a thing. She couldn't imagine an aging lover; she couldn't imagine loving Vincent in any way other than the way he was now. Even if he were to age—which was almost inconceivable—he wouldn't age like this.

Through the blanket, Maddie could feel the bony thinness of Mr. Pavlik's left foot, and she closed her eyes as if to shut the image away. She thought instead of Vincent's toes, which she had seen often enough. They were strong and brown, like his whole body had been during the summer. She remembered swimming with him and the tautness of his torso and the bulk of muscle in his arms.

He had swum up and caught her from behind. He was pinning her arms against her chest, teasing and threatening to force her underwater, and she had screamed and struggled against him but hadn't failed to sense his chest against her back. She had been acutely aware of that naked contact between their bodies, more than she was aware of his arms around her shoulders or his hands on her wrists. Even then, when everything about him had been new to her and when every physical interaction felt alive, she had wanted more.

The prayer was over. She hadn't heard the closing words, but everyone around her was straightening, withdrawing the hands that had taken hold of Mr. Pavlik's body. There were exhalations and clearings of throat, bleary-eyed blinking as the room returned to focus.

Before she knew what to do with herself, Maddie found that Mrs. Pavlik had taken her hand.

"Oh, you young people are just so wonderful," she said. "It's so good of you to come. So good of you."

"We're glad to do it," Maddie found herself saying.

"Just wait until Dean finds out you were here," she said, and she gripped Mr. Pavlik's left foot, the one Maddie had instantly released at the close of the prayer. She clasped his feet with both hands and went on: "He doesn't know now. He doesn't know you all are here. He's sleeping now. But when he wakes up, I'll tell him. You were in his Sunday school class, weren't you, Maddie?"

"Yes. Fourth grade." She remembered his retelling the story of the Genesis Joseph: it had been compelling the way he extended the saga from one week to the next, this Sunday leaving Joseph in the bottom of an abandoned well, next week in the bottom of a prison, and the next as second-in-command over Egypt. For the first time in years, Maddie had been interested in going to Sunday school; attending Sunday school had been, prior to the fourth grade, decidedly old hat: she knew every story they were going to teach her; she'd been going to Sunday school since she was two.

Mr. Pavlik had made it exciting again.

"Well, Dean will be delighted that you were here. He talks about you, you know. He talks about all of you. He hasn't forgotten a single one of his Sunday school students," she said. She was still holding on to both of his blanketed feet, and now she was smiling at his face: the closed eyes, the sallow complexion, the loose skin that hung down in folds below his jawbone.

---

The news was not good. Mr. Pavlik had taken a turn for the worse; the tumor had grown. That disappointment came on Sunday morning, the first day after their hospital-beside prayers, and it continued trickling out after that, day after day of bad news. He was drifting in and out of consciousness. He would be home and in hospice care before the week was out—and after that, maybe he had another week left. Family was coming in from out of town.

Maddie found this incomprehensible. What could it mean? Had there been some mistake? Her mind stabbed wildly at guesses, and time and again she returned to the same fears: they should have kept Vincent's gift a secret; or worse, they had been mistaken from the outset—Vincent had never healed anyone.

She traced the history. Her own healing hadn't been immediate— not quite. The pain hadn't dissolved right away. The healing had taken time—much of the ambulance ride, at least—to sink in. And

Willy's healing hadn't been instantaneous either—or had it? When he stumbled away from them, he had still clutched his crippled arm to his chest. She tried to reconstruct the memory, but always his retreating image dissolved in the rain, his back turned against her.

She asked Vincent about it, pressing him for answers that she inexplicably believed he could offer: "Do you think maybe it just takes time, Vincent? Do you think it will still work?" The healing had to work. It had to. If Mr. Pavlik's tumor continued on the way it seemed to be doing… The ramifications were too many. Maddie didn't like to consider them.

Vincent answered gently but without encouragement. "I don't know, Maddie," he said. "We can keep praying, I guess."

Which is what the whole church had been doing for years, Maddie thought with some resentment. Mr. Pavlik had been diagnosed over two years ago. No one had done anything more or less than pray for years.

This was all Vincent could muster? If he couldn't produce miraculous results, then he might at least show more concern. Worry, maybe, or a sense of pending loss. He seemed immune to fears of failure and all that it would mean.

Justine was more sympathetic. She, too, had known Mr. Pavlik her whole life. But she was nonetheless somewhat surprised by Maddie's distraction over it. After all, the church had known its losses over the years, and neither she nor Maddie was terribly close to Mr. Pavlik. "Why are you so concerned about him, Maddie? I mean, he's a nice guy and everything," she said.

This was a lunchtime conversation, and as usual, their table was crowded. At Justine's question, Maddie stole a look at Vincent, who didn't appear to be listening. He seemed blissfully unbothered by Dean Pavlik's plummet towards death and therefore was able to enjoy his lunch, his friends. At that moment, he was creating goalposts with his fingers on the tabletop, waiting for his friend Brad to send a paper football flying between them.

Maddie felt exasperated, and also, suddenly, profoundly alone. Other than the Tedescos and the group who had prayed in the hospital room last Saturday, no one knew about Vincent's gift. Within that number, perhaps only Nicky and Amy truly believed it, while

Vincent, gift-bearer himself, didn't really seem to care about it one way or the other.

Maddie wanted desperately to tell Justine everything. She wanted that matter-of-fact approach to weigh in on all of it. She felt sure that, better than any of them—Nicky and Pastor McLaughlin included—Justine would know what to do.

And then Maddie corrected herself: What was there to do? No one, it seemed, could stop Mr. Pavlik from dying. The latest report had come to her mother via phone that very morning: Mr. Pavlik had been unconscious for two days. The end was certainly near, likely in less than a week.

So instead, Maddie tried to feign nonchalance. She agreed with Justine that Mr. Pavlik was a nice guy and said something about how she had loved having him for Sunday school. But she didn't actually remember details of that year; she just remembered the lessons. It was Justine who reminded her of the candy jar he kept in the classroom as incentive to memorize Bible verses. In a sudden burst of laughter, she recounted the story of the Sunday when Tim Douglas had gagged on a butterscotch, and a panicked Mr. Pavlik lunged across the room to give him the Heimlich.

"Remember that, Maddie? Do you remember that? Mr. Pavlik was hilarious. I can still see the look on his face. I don't think I've ever seen anyone so scared in my life."

Maddie recalled the incident and laughed with Justine, but inside she felt sick. She thought through the previous Saturday morning, all of them around his body, with Vincent standing by his head. Was it because she herself hadn't prayed? She hadn't meant *not* to pray, but she had been distracted. Was there a secret to how it was done? Were there hoops to jump through? Right things to say—like a magic trick?

Worse still, she recounted *how* she had been distracted during the prayer. It had been Vincent's body. She hadn't meant to think about it. The thoughts and memories were always empowered by wills of their own: thoughts of him kissing her, touching her.

She was suspended by sudden horror, hearing Mrs. Pavlik's cheerful voice bubbling on and on. Her house would be empty: the hospice nurse, their family, Mr. Pavlik gone. Who would she talk to? She talked all the time; who would Mrs. Pavlik be without her unceasing chatter? Maddie imagined it, heartsick: Mrs. Pavlik would continue to talk; her voice would fill the silent rooms of the house, percolating in kitchen, bath, bedroom, and no one to hear her.

"God doesn't always heal people, you know," said Justine, who believed that Maddie's interest in Mr. Pavlik turned on butterscotch and peppermints in the fourth grade. "Think of Mrs. Moorland. She was on the prayer chain for years, and she died."

Mrs. Moorland had indeed died. What was it? Congestive heart failure or something like that. Maddie knew that Justine was right, and besides, no one lives forever. But given Vincent's gift, there was something vulgar in mild acceptance. Maddie had seen four people unaccountably healed—none of whom had needed healing the way that Mr. Pavlik did. If healing was a possibility, then it was wrong for it to be withheld. Mr. Pavlik's dying smacked of cruelty.

"It's true," Vincent said. "People pray for people to get better all the time, and they die anyway." It was his turn with the paper football now, and he hunched down to align his eye with its projected path. Maddie was amazed by his apparent indifference. He had laid his hands on that scarred head. He was the one with the gift. How could he be so casual about this?

But she wouldn't question him about it. Not now, in the middle of this terrible situation, and not at the lunch table filled with their friends. Maddie would sooner pick a quarrel with anyone else.

"Doesn't it make you kind of wonder about God?" She ventured the thought quietly, surprising herself. She hadn't realized that she *was* wondering about him, and now that she knew, she wished immediately she hadn't said so aloud.

"No," said Justine and Vincent, simultaneously. Impressive, really, their coming together like this now, of all times.

"It depends on what you believe about God. I mean, you have to believe he's good," Vincent said.

Of course Maddie believed he was good. She had been told all her life that God was good. It was wrong to think otherwise.

"Yes, God is good," Justine answered Vincent. "It's not a question of him being good. But there's evil in the world. Bad things happen. People get sick. People die. It's part of life."

Maddie digested this. Justine was right, she reasoned, but it was a terrible state of affairs. Again she heard Mrs. Pavlik's voice going on and on, unanswered. And she thought, too, of Matthew, Justine's little brother. They had prayed for him to be cured of leukemia. They had asked for wisdom for the doctors. They had said all the things they always say, she was sure of it. She herself had prayed for him at the time, lisping six-year-old that she was, when her parents came to tuck her in at night. He was only four years old when he died.

Maddie remembered his funeral. The coffin had been small, engulfed in white flowers. *Was* God good?

"So are you saying that stuff happens without God in control of it?" Vincent was asking.

"All I'm saying is that there's evil in the world," Justine said. The other conversations at their lunch table had grown quiet, and Maddie caught sight of the absurdity: high school students, some of them church-goers, some completely disinterested, entertaining this conversation in the cafeteria.

"I know there's evil in the world," Vincent was saying, not dispassionately, but with something reserved, his energies given to reason. "I'm asking is God in control of the evil?"

What is evil exactly, Maddie wanted to know. Death seemed a likely suspect. She had one strong memory of Matthew: he was sitting in church next to Justine, his legs straight out in front of him, his heels coming just to the edge of the pew. He was driving his toy pick-up truck over his knees and making puttering sounds with wet lips.

Did God make Matthew die? Did God let evil make Matthew die? What was the difference?

"God doesn't make bad things happen, Vincent," Justine said. Maddie had missed something. The shift was almost imperceptible, but she knew they had squared off—or Justine had, anyway. There was a defensive edge in her voice, her gaze locked on Vincent. Their common ground had evidently been a very small territory.

"What I'm saying is, is God in control or isn't he?" Vincent maintained his conversational tone, as if this debate over God's authority was suitable for casual banter.

No, Maddie thought. Not always, anyway. He hadn't been in control on Saturday night—the very same day she and Vincent had prayed for Mr. Pavlik. On Saturday night, God had been nothing but a pitiful afterthought, while she and Vincent had been alone in her living room, her parents gone to bed.

And then a new thought came: the church altar on Sunday evenings, people kneeling there weeping. Sin was evil, Maddie realized, and you had to be sorry for your sin—or else suffer and be punished for it.

Was that what this was? Punishment? God was taking Vincent's gift away—Mr. Pavlik was dying—because of their sin?

"No, Vincent. You are saying that God makes people sick and he makes people die." Justine was angry now, and Maddie felt that familiar impulse to defend Vincent.

"But Justine," Maddie said, "You yourself said that people get sick and people die. Remember Mrs. Moorland—"

"Right," Justine said. "Because there's evil in the world. That's not what Vincent is saying. Vincent is saying that God *makes* it happen."

Maddie didn't need the summary. She got it. She had arrived there along with Justine, but to say so would be—wouldn't it?—to make some terrible accusations. How could Justine's words possibly be true—about God? About Vincent? And yet she couldn't bring her own growing realization to the conversation: evil, punishment, death—all of it as consequence.

"No," Vincent said. He was quiet a moment. "I'm not saying God *makes* it happen…" His voice trailed off, but Maddie nonetheless felt some relief in his words. Surely Vincent would have an explanation.

Justine wasn't waiting, and she wasn't mollified.

"Then what?" she asked, and Maddie again remembered Matthew. Would Vincent argue that God allowed Matthew's death? That he let it happen? Even that he wanted it to happen?

Vincent, rational, quiet, seemed determined to meet Justine's anger with calm. "I'm just saying that God has bigger things on his plate, is all," he said.

Justine expelled a stunned gasp. Maddie grasped for meaning. This was appalling! Matthew had died, Mr. Pavlik was dying—and God had bigger things on his plate? How could Vincent say that? Didn't he know that Justine had lost her baby brother? Surely Maddie had told him. Hadn't she told him?

"What?" she said, shocked and in unison with Justine.

"I mean—"

But Justine cut him off: "'His eye is on the sparrow,' Vincent. God cares about everybody. Everybody. Even sparrows, and even Mr. Pavlik, who is dying, as we speak, of a brain tumor."

"That's not what I mean," Vincent said.

"Really? Then what do you mean by, 'God has bigger things on his plate'?" She was furious, her voice lined with contempt.

Vincent remained calm, but he seemed to be reaching for words. "Not on his plate," he said. He was looking around him as if trying to find a way to explain himself. "That's not what I mean."

"What do you mean, then?" Maddie asked, and she heard her voice, coaxing, a little desperate, trying to make peace and also trying to understand.

Justine answered for him. "You mean that God is busy dealing with other issues," she said. "Maybe like world peace? Or the arms race." Her words were coated in sarcasm. "Is the arms race on God's plate, Vincent? Is that what it is? He has so much on his plate that he can't be bothered with human life. He can't be bothered with stuff like Mr. Pavlik. That's what you mean."

Maddie wanted to break in. She wanted to defend Justine's anger, to remind them all about Matthew, to defend Vincent's defenseless position, to defend Vincent. But she was afraid to try. She was afraid to say anything. Her situation—in every way—felt frighteningly precarious.

Everyone else at the table was frozen, listening, surely horrified at the ramifications of Vincent's words, because anyone would be horrified at Vincent's words—even an atheist.

"No, Justine. Give me a minute to say something," Vincent said.

"I've given you more than enough minutes, Vincent Elander," Justine said. "Everybody has. And I'm more than just a little tired of you thinking you know so much." She was gathering her lunch things. A dramatic exit was in the making, and Maddie couldn't blame her. She herself wanted to walk away, if only to collect her thoughts, to mentally align Vincent's words—so empty of compassion—with his ability to heal people.

*Couldn't he heal people?*

Justine stood to her feet, a stack of books in one arm and the remainder of her lunch in the other. Maddie braced herself for the parting shot.

"I'll remind you of something, Vincent," she said, "or maybe you don't even know: Mr. Pavlik is a really good man. I've known him my whole life. Now he's dying. And everybody is sad about that— including God."

They all watched her go. She walked quickly, swerving between the round cafeteria tables and their occupants, never looking back.

No one said a word.

Maddie surveyed the table: a chocolate bar wrapper, two crumpled lunch bags, a few folded paper footballs, crumbs. And there, lying potent if invisible among them, an invulnerable brain tumor, God's caprice, Vincent's inscrutable theology, and sin—insistent, unavoidable.

Maddie didn't know where to begin, but she thought she might try in defense of Justine—someone who had never, until that moment, seemed in need of defending. "You have to be more careful, Vincent," she said.

"I *am* careful," Vincent answered, his voice heavy with an unfamiliar frustration. "She wouldn't even let me talk—*Ow.*"

The paper football had hit him in the cheekbone. Bryan had thrown it, or maybe Brad—two of the lunchtime entourage who had silently suffered through this loaded philosophical debate, now clearly looking for a little levity. Maddie was sure they were glad Justine had swept up her anger with her lunch.

The dutiful thing was to follow her friend, but how to move toward resolution? She herself was reeling with confusion and a dreadful fear.

She found Justine fuming in the Student Commons, sitting on a bench against the wall, her arms and legs both crossed, right foot twitching at the ankle. There she sat, her church and family history inextricably combined and wedged against her chest. There was no room for Vincent in that complicated knot, no room for him or his unconventional—and disturbing—ideas.

"Sometimes that boyfriend of yours is a real asshole," Justine said, staring stonily over the room. Maddie sat down.

Surprising, yes. Confusing, absolutely. But asshole? Maddie was perplexed by Vincent, but she was also perplexed by Justine, by her friend's persistent mistrust of Vincent. And now they'd had this terrible conversation. Justine wouldn't want to hear anything spoken in his defense. Frankly, Maddie couldn't think of anything, except the unexpected memory of her asshole boyfriend in Pittsburgh's pouring rain, helping a drunk and crippled man stand to his feet. Maybe if she could get Justine to see Vincent differently, then she could hear—they could both hear—whatever it was he was trying to say.

"He cares about Mr. Pavlik," she said.

"I'm pretty sure he doesn't care about anybody but himself."

"Justine," Maddie said, as gently as she could, "I don't think he even knows about Matthew."

"What does Matthew have to do with it?" Justine's eyes filled with tears. They never talked about Matthew.

"I just mean that Vincent was talking—he was probably talking—you know, in *theory*. Theoretically. He didn't realize—"

"It doesn't matter," Justine cut her off. She was searching in her pocket.

Maddie tried again. "He doesn't realize how this feels to you."

"It's not a question of how it feels to *me*," Justine said, wiping angrily at her nose with a tissue. "It's a question of what he's *saying*."

"About Matthew?" Maddie prodded.

"About Matthew, about Mr. Pavlik. About anyone." She raised a hand in a gesture loosely resembling a wave. "About God," she said.

Maddie was quiet for a moment, again wondering what Vincent meant. In her mind, she saw him running through the church parking lot toward screams on the parsonage lawn, leaning over the football player lying on the field, kneeling beside her—when was it?—almost a year ago now. He hadn't even known her name.

And so Maddie felt she had no other choice but to tell Justine. She told her all of it—about how he had prayed for her that day in the school parking lot, about Willy, about the football player, about Joey Amoretti. And then she told her about Mr. Pavlik and how Vincent had spent a Saturday morning in prayer for a man he hardly knew.

It seemed a wise choice. *See?* She was trying to say. *See?* Vincent does care about other people.

This was not Justine's take.

"So you're telling me that your boyfriend can *heal people?*" Any sadness over Matthew's mention, any softened edge, was gone.

"Yeah." There was nothing left to say. Maddie's small hope began to dissolve.

"Vincent Elander can heal people," Justine said, flatly, sarcastic, annoyed.

"Yeah," again. Maddie didn't want to mount another defense, and it occurred to her that she wouldn't be able to. Where was the proof?

"And Nicky and Pastor McLaughlin and all the elders believe it?"

"Well, yes, I guess so. They were beginning to." She paused. And then a last, feeble effort: "They think it's possible, anyway. Nicky does. And Amy."

Justine sighed. She straightened. She uncrossed her legs and looked around the room, taking in a couple making out on a bench across the way, a loud game of ping-pong, two members of the boys' basketball team sauntering through the room. Then she looked squarely at Maddie.

"I think that everyone needs to think long and hard about this, Maddie. Everyone. Has anyone even bothered to notice that Mr. Pavlik is dying? He isn't healed, Maddie. He's dying." She took a deep breath and sighed loudly, slowly, then bent her head to her open palms.

Maddie waited a long moment. The music was loud in the Student Commons.

Justine spoke again, looking at Maddie earnestly, her anger set aside. "Vincent can't heal people, Maddie. It's great that he's coming to church. It's great that he seems to have become a Christian. And he's a great athlete and fun to be with and all that. But like everybody else, he's a person. He's just a normal person." She looked away from Maddie again, around the room, addressing these final words, so it seemed, to anyone. "For God's sake, everyone needs to wake up."

And she stood and walked off—to the bathroom, maybe, or the student store, abandoning her books and her lunch. This time, Maddie felt no obligation to follow her. She was glad, even in the din of the Student Commons, to be alone with her thoughts for a moment.

Steeling herself against Justine's words, Maddie took stock of what she knew, reciting it as she might a Bible verse in fourth grade Sunday school. Vincent had most certainly become a Christian. Vincent *could* heal people. Vincent *had* healed people. Maddie said it to herself as much as to Justine's retreating back. Regardless of what Vincent had *said* in the cafeteria, regardless of how he had *sounded*, she knew that he cared about them all.

And Maddie decided that she knew—or thought she knew—that God also cared about Mr. Pavlik. Certainly he did. And also Mrs. Pavlik. Here again she heard the cheerful, bubbling voice going on and on unanswered.

It wasn't that God didn't care, Maddie reasoned. It was simply that he cared more about sin, maybe, and it was sin he was punishing.

God punished sin.

She felt the realization, heavy and true, an ache in the middle of her chest. That was it. God was punishing her sin—and Vincent's— and he was doing it by taking Vincent's gift away. Which meant letting Mr. Pavlik die.

That must be how it worked.

<hr />

The adult Maddie, weak from cancer and its treatment, sat at the computer. Its screen glowed with a satellite view of North America. The entry of her parents' address at the prompt found her plummeting toward earth, and immediately the roads and treetops of the familiar suburb rose into existence. It was a strange view, like one from a plane, stretched flat. A bird's-eye view, or God's. But the roof of her parents' house looked right, as did the lay of the land around it. There was the deck her father built during the summer after eighth grade, replacing their concrete patio.

Just down the street, inches away, was where she had waited for the bus, and now she traced the bus's route to the high school. She revisited, turn for turn, length for length, the road to church. She followed the way to the mall, the way to the grocery stores, the hardware store, even the free-standing butcher where her mother had shopped when Maddie was very young. Maddie made all these outings while sitting at the computer desk, again and again venturing out of her parents' driveway, noting by their rooflines the houses and businesses that landmarked the way.

She adjusted the satellite's view to a horizontal gaze and with it gained the sense of spying, looking into a moment of life on the street when she had not been there, watching unseen. These actual, street-line views occasionally made her gasp: the scenes were vivid and life-like, for the most part exactly as she had left them. Her house, the paved driveway; her parents were not at home. The church, its parking lot empty. She found Justine's house: it had been remodeled. Vincent's house, still tired.

Maddie shuddered with recollection. Those spring days had been dark ones. The whole congregation had been stricken spectators of Dean Pavlik's pending death. Maddie had felt pinned in the front row, and also a tragic and unwitting background player, guilty both of his demise and of a blighted effort to heal him.

Once upon a time, she had looked for interaction with God, but he had left her blissfully anonymous, sitting unbidden in her pew. Prior to Vincent, she had been chosen by no one, for no one—and so also was innocent of Justine's doubt, Mrs. Pavlik's loneliness, and the wanton, perplexing urges of her own body.

A body designed by God, purportedly given to her by God in some kind of holy game that she could never win.

She had been only sixteen years old, and she was convinced that a man's imminent death was her fault. She'd had faith in God, and she had acted on it. If God wanted holiness, then she would do what she could to muster it. How had Vincent said it? They might want each other, but they needed to want God more.

If she were to tell this part of the story—and she never had—then she would admit that here—just here, perhaps—the sixteen-year-old Maddie had been admirable.

# 18

*I*n the first place, she would try to spend more time with Justine. The memory of Justine's little brother, surfacing in the midst of that theological debate, had taken Maddie by surprise. Now she realized that Matthew was likely never far from Justine's mind. More painfully, she realized her own ignorance of this fact had been, at best, insensitive, even blind. She hadn't been a very good friend to Justine at all, and she was resolved to do better.

She was also resolved to avoid solitude with Vincent.

It was their only hope—that, or some mortifying display of repentance at the Sunday evening altar. It was making sense to her now, the light slowly dawning after a lifetime of church, that this living, interactive, and just God should not only bless the good, but punish the sinful. She finally understood this as fundamental truth in the Bethel Hills Church. How else to explain the droning organ, the protracted wait, the kneeling displays of repentance and need?

She now knew that the consequences of sin were profound and terrible. In her case—or in that of her and Vincent—it was a gift suspended. And why should it not be? The punishment ought to match the crime. They sinned with their bodies, so shouldn't bodies suffer? Never mind that it wasn't their own bodies but was, instead, someone else: Mr. Pavlik propped at death's threshold, Mrs. Pavlik's tear-streaked loneliness.

But it wasn't too late. There was room for hope, Maddie thought. If she could not bring herself to pray openly at the altar, then she could at the very least avoid temptation, which meant avoiding Vincent: "cutting off the hand that causes you to sin"—which, in this case (she was under no delusion), was herself. Vincent, at least, had made efforts toward obedience.

And yet this, too, felt like a risk. She understood too well Vincent's devotion to God. Yes, it was a devotion embattled by Maddie, but Vincent always repented and then affirmed his resolve, willing to forge ahead and—next time—to avoid temptation. If Maddie were to suggest to him that successful obedience lay only in his cutting her off from his life, she feared he would actually do it.

No, this was not a conversation to have with Vincent.

Besides, she reminded herself, this understanding of sin and consequence was a theory. She wasn't sure she was right. It was conceivable that their sin had nothing to do with Mr. Pavlik's continued decline. It was possible that something else was at play here, that Mr. Pavlik might still recover, or that he would die because it was the way of the world and, ambiguous as it might be, the evil that inhabited it. That was what Justine had suggested, anyway.

And so Maddie decided to test her theory: she would avoid sinning with Vincent, and would plead with God for Mr. Pavlik's recovery. It was her own little spiritual discipline, the first she had ever attempted.

To her pleased surprise, her efforts were eased somewhat due to the last week of basketball season and, when that had ended, the excuses Maddie could muster: a test to study for, some extra chores at home. One Saturday night, she suggested that they spend the evening at the Tedescos—something not altogether unusual, something Vincent enjoyed.

If he suspected anything, he never said so, but at the suggestion of the Tedescos he had given her a look, quick but focused, even though they were walking together down the hall. She wondered if he understood—if, without their ever discussing it, he knew what she was up to. She was grateful that he didn't ask.

And she was glad to spend more time with Justine. She had forgotten how witty her friend could be, and she found herself enjoying Justine's sarcasm, those *sotto voce* critiques that made Maddie once again feel it was them against the world. Yes, Maddie decided, she had missed her friend.

Of course, nothing was lost on Justine, who was almost unbelievably observant. These observational skills were, clearly, the foundation of those sarcastic comments. And so she would be the one to notice that Maddie was spending less time than she used to with Vincent, and she would be the one to say something.

Maddie knew that she had successfully kept up almost every appearance. She and Vincent were clearly together at school, and they sat together during youth group, just like they always did. But now Maddie stood with Justine in the church parking lot, watching Vincent drive away alone, and Justine said,

"You two okay?"

Maddie actually felt annoyed at Justine's question. Avoiding sin was difficult enough without having to endure scrutiny.

"Yes," she answered. "We're fine."

Justine pushed it—the smallest nudge. Was she merely curious? "But doesn't Vincent always give you a ride home?" she asked.

Yes, he always did give her a ride home, but what was a small lie when trying to save Mr. Pavlik's life? "No, not always," she said. "Sometimes I ride with my parents."

Justine had no idea how difficult it was. Maddie wasn't merely working to change external practice, she was trying to change her mental focus, too. She was trying to be more mindful of others, especially of Mr. and Mrs. Pavlik. She still prayed, even when hope was virtually gone, for Mr. Pavlik's healing. She prayed for Willy and thought about little Joey Amoretti and sometimes the nameless patients in the children's oncology ward.

Time without Vincent was a worthwhile sacrifice, Maddie thought, especially if it could be sustained.

But let her mind relax for any time at all, and she would discover she was thinking of Vincent again—and not just of the way he made her laugh or the things he said. She found herself thinking of kissing him, of being alone with him, of all the times they had needed to repent. And far more than usual, during those two weeks, Vincent would surface in her dreams.

She was trying to follow Vincent's wisdom. What had he said? They might want each other, but they should want God more. It should be simple supplantation, replacing want with want. In her better moments, she felt this was right: that above all things, God should be what she most desired.

She was trying with all her energy to do so, and finding that it didn't really work.

⁕

A week went by, and Mr. Pavlik had not succumbed to death. In truth, he seemed further and further from it. Uneducated guesses might conclude that Mr. Pavlik had taken a turn toward recovery— but this was really too much for even the expectant Bethel Hills Church to hope. Instead, his regained consciousness that Friday night was regarded as the body's last push, a final chance at time with Mrs. Pavlik before the final descent. This happened sometimes. The church celebrated it quietly, glad for Donna Pavlik that she could have those moments with Dean. God is so good, they said.

But Dean Pavlik awoke again on Saturday morning and was lucid for much of the day. The swelling seemed to be going down; Donna reported that he was less black-and-blue around the eyes.

No one wanted to encourage her. Why get her hopes up? Then corroboration from the hospice nurse got everyone's hopes up: the nurse had never seen such a thing before. Truly, it was amazing. The people of the Bethel Hills Church of Holiness began to wonder: It might be a miracle! They would all be on edge, waiting to see it.

Sunday's report was better yet. Mr. Pavlik was clear-headed, communicative, smiling, the edema all but gone. He said he had some tingling where once he had been numb. The hoping against fear won out: suddenly everyone was enthusiastic.

As if in payment for this faith, the good news mounted: he was energetic, the swelling was completely gone. Dean Pavlik had an appetite; he got his color back. The news from the series of MRIs was shocking: the tumor was unaccountably smaller, then was shrinking, then had disappeared. The doctor said such a recovery was not to be believed, but the Pavliks said it most certainly *was*. So many people were praying, they told the team of doctors, the nurses, anyone who would listen.

The hospice nurse was dismissed. Against all predictions, contrary to all case studies, Mr. Pavlik was given a clean bill of health. The Bethel Hills Church of Holiness had indeed witnessed a miracle—and all in a period of weeks. The church scheduled a potluck in celebration. It seemed the only thing to do.

And would the Pavliks attend? It was early for him to be out and about. Only weeks ago Dean was at death's door! But why not? Miracles often present as ephemera. They have to be leaned into, not treated with care: either you believe it or you don't. Yes, certainly Dean and Donna would be there. They said they wouldn't miss it for the world!

The fellowship hall made its potluck transformation: tables carried in from the Sunday school classrooms and, around them, folding metal chairs clanked into place. The women's ministry covered the tables in vibrant paper and centered each one with a pot of blooming bulbs.

The food appeared in its predictable and comforting array: scalloped potatoes and string bean casseroles, ham barbecue tidy on little buns, Jell-O salad, coleslaw and baked beans, salads tossed and coated in Italian dressing. There was coffee, tea, and lemonade in large thermoses, several trays of cookies, four or five pies, and a large white sheet cake with red frosting roses and "Welcome Back, Dean!" in looping script.

"Welcome back?" Justine murmured to Maddie. They stood gazing at it together, having just arrived from an afternoon at the mall. There they had browsed and talked about everything except Vincent, healing and God—subjects Maddie, these days, had been careful to avoid. Despite Mr. Pavlik's steady recovery and all it might mean about Vincent's gift, Maddie felt it best to steer clear of those topics with Justine, deciding to let her bring them up. Which she hadn't done.

Now she and Justine were at the celebratory potluck, gazing at the cake which, in red icing, pointed to every subject they avoided. "Welcome back?" Justine said again. "Where'd he go?"

Reflexively, Maddie hit upon the other story of a New Testament resurrection: "I guess it's kind of a Lazarus thing," she said. "What do you think people said to *him*?" But she wondered why she felt compelled to give an explanation: she, too, found the word choice odd.

"Mr. Pavlik wasn't exactly *dead*," Justine answered. "Vincent doesn't have you convinced that he can raise people from the *dead*, does he?"

"Absolutely not," said Vincent, taking them both by surprise. Maddie hadn't realized he had arrived, and now here he was at her elbow, the other, unspoken guest of honor at the celebration. "Vincent can do no such thing," he said.

It was his first interaction with Justine since the cafeteria argument weeks ago, and Maddie had anticipated it with dread. But to her surprise, Justine simply smiled and Vincent smirked back. There was no time for further conversation, because that was also the moment the Pavliks arrived, greeted by shouts and cheers, which then turned into a very long period of applause.

Before the Pavliks' arrival, Pastor McLaughlin had warned everyone of Dean's tendency to tire easily. He exhorted the congregation to take it easy and not to overwhelm him. But joy is difficult to restrain, and the Pavlik's arrival (Mr. Gillece and Mr. Amoretti and others rushing to the door on seeing them, each of them wanting to hold it open; Mrs. Pavlik's insistence on pushing Mr. Pavlik's wheelchair, her face aglow, plump and shining; Mr. Pavlik's long frame folded into the wheelchair, bundled despite the spring warming outdoors) was only the beginning of a sustained and elevated din.

Mr. Pavlik still seemed frail and looked a little pallid. The wheelchair was surprising to Maddie at first, and then understandable: the road to full recovery was long; already he had come so far. With some relief, she noted that his head looked normal enough: she tried not to stare; she was glad to see his hair was growing back. He smiled constantly and shook a lot of hands, and Mrs. Pavlik had always one hand resting on him or on his wheelchair, as though trying to grasp this new reality: that of his being well.

Everyone wanted to talk with them, and so Maddie and Vincent held back for a time, helping themselves to food. Vincent was happy to shout conversation, but Maddie didn't feel much like it. Instead, she watched the Pavliks from the shadow of Vincent's side, wondering what it was like to have their lives suddenly restored. Only weeks ago, they had faced the specter of lasting separation. Their grown children had come home to say good-bye to their father. Maddie herself had clung to his blanketed foot in prayer, had felt the spokes of his metatarsals riding just below his skin. She had seen him all but lifeless, had pleaded over subsequent weeks for the death verdict's reversal— and God had answered (was it him? Or chance? Or some metaphysical triumph of good over evil?), "Yes."

Now she and Vincent sat with a crowd from the youth group, and everywhere around them people celebrated or talked about things completely unrelated. At their table, for example, Vincent and the others were chatting about the upcoming baseball season, and Justine had resumed her normal role, peppering the conversation with caustic remarks. They were discussing who among them might skip school for the Pirate opener, and Justine scolded them for it and then, moments later, related a story of when she herself had done the same thing.

Maddie was only partially listening, however, thinking instead of her restraint in the past weeks, nurturing her friendship with Justine. She and Vincent seemed to have picked up where they left off: Justine with tolerant condescension and Vincent with either oblivion or honest unconcern.

Had Maddie expected more? Had she imagined there would be some earnest discourse between them in which they hashed out their differences or found some common ground? No, she realized. That was foolish. She had never in her life known Justine to apologize— certainly never when she was at least partially in the right, and Vincent wouldn't force the issue. Vincent would simply follow Justine's lead, would, along with Justine, pretend that it hadn't happened, or that it didn't bother him anymore (*had* it bothered him?), or that it simply didn't matter.

And clearly, it didn't matter. Because regardless of who had been right in that theological debate, there was Mr. Pavlik, well and sitting upright, growing stronger every day. Maddie watched him talk with Mr. Amoretti and little Joey, who stood awkwardly at Mr. Pavlik's knee. With one hand, the child held a paper plate burdened with a large slice of cake. The plate slanted precariously towards the floor, but this pending disaster seemed to bother no one.

Across the room, Maddie saw Nicky carrying a cup of lemonade to Amy where she sat with friends. Her pregnancy was advanced at this point, and Maddie smiled to see that Amy couldn't quite sit close to the table anymore. She was due at the end of May; she and Nicky had invited Maddie and Vincent to come help Nicky put the crib together. The last time they had been at the Tedescos' house, Amy had practically pulled Maddie upstairs to see the baby's room: she had painted the pale blue ceiling with clouds.

Now Maddie trembled slightly, overwhelmed by all the noise. With her plastic fork, she pried the red rose away from her cake's white icing and let it slide to the plate. It was the same kind of cake they always had at celebrations: half chocolate, half white, and Maddie's piece had apparently come from the middle, as she had some of both. She took a bite of the white half and realized that she had never liked these cakes. They were invariably dry and only remotely flavored, and the icing coated the roof of her mouth with something akin to wax. She pushed her plate away.

Then suddenly there was Mr. Pavlik. His wheelchair's footrest tapped Maddie's chair with a gentle thump, and Mrs. Pavlik was instantly effusive : "Oh, I'm sorry, honey! I didn't mean to hit you! Are you all right?"

Maddie did her best to be consoling. It hadn't bothered her in the slightest. She had barely felt it. Really, don't worry about it. Still, Mrs. Pavlik continued to apologize.

Meanwhile, there sat Mr. Pavlik, quiet and smiling, reaching for Maddie and Vincent with both hands. "Thank you," he said quietly, somehow still making himself heard over Mrs. Pavlik's continued fuss, over the noise in the room. "Thank you so much for praying for me," he said.

They had already said their "you're welcomes," and had already released Mr. Pavlik's grip when Mrs. Pavlik had to chime in, too: "Yes, thank you! Oh, thank you! They prayed for you, Dean. They came to the hospital and prayed for you!" Clearly she had informed her husband of this before, but it apparently bore repeating. Sure enough, she said it a few more times, taking their hands, too, and holding them tightly. She thanked them again and again with shining eyes.

Maddie was sure the entire room had heard her despite the din. She wanted to shrink away from them. How many times was "thank you" necessary? When Mrs. Pavlik rolled her husband away, Maddie was relieved that the interview was over.

Except that it seemed to lead to others. After the Pavliks' departure, other people came, singly and in pairs, some of them elders from the hospital that day, some of them congregants—people who should have no idea that she and Vincent had been among them. Each of them expressed their gratitude; each of them most especially thanked Vincent. And both Maddie and Vincent said, of course, "You're welcome."

But how did they know, Maddie wondered, simultaneously realizing that she had begun to hope no one would know, that this would remain a secret among those at Mr. Pavlik's bedside. She had begun to imagine that this miracle would overwhelm everything else, that thoughts of Vincent's gift would be subsumed in celebration and then, perhaps, forgotten—just as it happened with Joey Amoretti.

When had she begun to hope this?

A glance across the room at the beaming and chatting Mrs. Pavlik dissolved the hope. This time the miracle would be announced and announced again. Maddie and Vincent would be thanked for this every time they saw Mrs. Pavlik, who wouldn't be quiet about it until everyone knew what Vincent had done for them. With a growing despair, Maddie realized that Mrs. Pavlik would never stop talking about it. Should the entire world discover what had happened, Mrs. Pavlik would talk about it even then.

---

Vincent gave her a ride home that night. The windows were down, and cool, spring-scented air rushed through the car. After the chatter of the party, Maddie was glad for the meaningless noise of the wind, and glad, too, to be with Vincent. Alone with Vincent.

They stopped at the park, just to talk for a while, they said, to talk over what had happened. But they didn't talk. Not really. And once again there was repentant prayer, all of it numbingly familiar.

When she got home, Maddie's parents were already upstairs getting ready for bed. She went in the front door, walked through the quiet house and out the back door onto the deck.

The yard was dark, and the neighboring houses didn't have their outdoor lights on. The only light came from a streetlight far up the hill, and when Maddie stepped down into the yard, that light was lost behind the neighbors' roofline.

Her feet were bare; the ground was cool and faintly damp. With her back to her house, Maddie sat in the grass, and the hill that bordered their yard seemed to rise up in front of her. It seemed taller from this angle, and she thought this must have been the way it looked when she was very small.

The sky was moonless, but the stars were thick overhead. Arms straight and hands flat on the grass behind her, Maddie leaned her head back and composed a view of only sky. The borderless space made her catch her breath. At that moment, she could be anywhere, she thought, the stars and constellations so much the same over Kansas, over Indiana, over some nameless field in the flatlands of the Midwest. But then there came a small gust of wind and, at the corner of her vision, she caught some newborn, twisting leaves of their maple tree.

Still gazing at the sky, Maddie began to landmark her surroundings: the neighbors, the shrubs and trees of their property, the scale of the hill between them. She knew by heart the yards of the people on the street behind them and who lived where, the children who, in her sibling-free childhood, were her playmates. So long ago now, when she had been little, they had played kickball and whiffle ball in that adjacent cul-de-sac. On long summer evenings they had played hide-and-go-seek and ghost-in-the-graveyard, running and screaming, feeling the grass cool under their bare feet after the sun went down. Long after dark, their mothers would call them in, and families of children would disappear in reluctant obedience. Her own house would seem over-bright after those hours of playing in the dark. The light would seem foreign and the water, washing the grass and dirt from her feet in the bathtub, would be cold. Tucked into bed, Maddie listened as the crickets' song leaked through the window screen, and already it would seem a long time ago that she had run for her life to home-base: the stop-sign at the turn to the cul-de-sac.

Now she replayed that afternoon's events, starting with the potluck, because nothing before that mattered. There were Justine and her parents, the Amorettis, the Gilleces, Susan Sweet, the Tedescos, all of them part of the Bethel Hills congregation, that small but significant family that comprised so much of her life. And there was Vincent, already tanned, freshly showered, blue-eyed.

She had intended to talk with him in the car. She wanted to tell him about her theory, to confess her gamble that their sin was robbing Mr. Pavlik of life, Vincent of his gift. But Vincent had kissed her before she got the words out, and it had been so long, it seemed, since he had kissed her. One kiss wasn't enough for Maddie. It never was.

She straightened and looked around her. The sky was a better view, she thought. It was unobstructed velvet studded with small specks of light. By contrast, this lateral view was murky, impeded by strange shapes and vague darkness. Darkness in the dark, Maddie thought: an unhappy concept.

And yet it was so. Only because she knew her yard so well could she name the dark shapes for what they were: the forsythia hedge, the boxwood shrubs, the split-rail fence at the yard's edge. Beyond the fence, the earth climbed up, plateauing for the width of the next street of houses, and then it climbed again. At her back sat her own house and the street that climbed hills on both sides, while across from them the neighbor's house also had a hill at its back.

Maddie lived, she realized, at the bottom of a bowl. The whole earth curved up from here, and if it went down again (as she knew it did), it would yet again curve upward in a seemingly endless succession of pleats and wrinkles. Reflexively she reviewed the bus route, the paths to school and to church, to downtown Pittsburgh. The entire region, she saw now, was composed of climbs and plummets; the earth— coming and going—was pitched at precarious angles. Uneven ground made for uneven footing, always difficult to navigate.

Sitting there on the lawn of her dark backyard, Maddie considered for the first time in her life that she wanted to get out.

# 19

*M*onday morning, and Justine opened with this: she wanted to know if Vincent had any plans.

Plans?

"Yes, you know. Like who is he going to heal next. And when. And who is going to notify the media—because you know, Maddie, that the media will become involved at some point. That kind of thing."

Maddie felt winded: two days ago, she would have sworn that Justine didn't believe Vincent could heal anyone, and now she was looking for an action plan, even expecting a strategy. Here was a decided change of heart—and in less than twelve hours. Throughout yesterday's potluck, throughout the few weeks of Mr. Pavlik's climb toward recovery, Justine had never allowed that Vincent had healed him. And sometime over the last twelve hours, Maddie had begun to hope that she never would. Justine's matter-of-fact doubt might serve to quell a church-wide craving for miracles.

Now Maddie suppressed a growing fear: Vincent's gift could not be sustained, not at the price God appeared to be asking. She had tried. She had found small if significant success. But if their little detour last night had shown her anything, it was that her fears were spot-on: she was unable to control herself—and ultimately, she didn't want to.

"Well?" Justine was waiting on an answer. The game plan? What was Vincent planning to do?

No one had said anything about a plan. Not Nicky. Not Pastor McLaughlin. No one, so far as she knew, had a plan.

"I don't know," she said. "It's hard to know what to do, I guess." She was making this up: maybe someone knew what to do, but she herself had no idea.

Justine stared at her. "Really?"

"Yes, really." Maddie felt a little defensive. Who was Justine— recent convert to Vincent, or to his healing people, anyway—to think she knew so much?

"Because, Maddie." She breathed a short gasp and rolled her eyes. "Why is it hard to know what to do?"

"Because there is a lot to consider, Justine," and Maddie wondered what they needed to consider, steps they should take, or should have thought about taking. She hadn't envisioned this much. The revelation of Vincent's gift had never gone the way she thought it should in the first place.

Justine was already considering. "You bet there's a lot to consider. Like all the sick people in this city, or in this state. I think Vincent should heal people. Anyone, anywhere."

"Yes, well—"

"He should just go up to random people who are sick, or go to doctor's offices or hospitals or something. If you have the ability to heal people, you should heal them, right?"

Yes, Maddie remembered it now. This was what she had thought. It was what she expected would be the outcome when they had told the Tedescos. Again there was the oncology ward, all the beds deserted.

And with it an appalling sadness, the absolute dissolution of hope.

About ten minutes after the bell rang, Justine passed Maddie a note: *GOD DOESN'T WANT PEOPLE TO BE SICK!* "Want" was underlined three times.

⸻

It may be that since its founding, the Bethel Hills Church had looked for a revelation like Vincent's. If the potluck was any evidence, then Donna Pavlik's endorsement had gone some distance to broadcast belief. Yet for all her nondisclosure as to what had finally provoked her faith in Vincent's gift, Justine was far more forthright in her belief than were the church members.

For church members—post potluck—approaching Vincent was a practice in circumspection. He became the object of prolonged stares and whispering, and people went out of their way to greet him. People he had never spoken to greeted him by name; people he knew began to engage him in casual conversations about their chronic pain or frequent heartburn.

There was, for example, Bill Mews, a man known to them only as the father of Sam and Alex, two boys from the youth group. In conversation before the Sunday morning service, Vincent was given to learn that Mr. Mews had played football in college, that his team had enjoyed an impressive record his senior year, and that ever since then, he had suffered serious pain in both of his knees—pain that was always more acute when it rained.

It had been a very wet spring.

And the service was starting. Vincent expressed his sympathy and wished Mr. Mews well, and then he and Maddie went inside and found their seats.

The pattern was invariably the same with others: engage Vincent in conversation and casually raise or perhaps only hint at a malady. Wait a moment too long for this to be merely incidental, then end the conversation. Often it was Vincent who ended it, either appropriately, as with Mr. Mews, whose untimely dialogue overlapped the beginning of the church service, or deliberately and, regrettably—Maddie felt—abruptly. "I'm sorry to hear that," he would say of that person's physical discomfort, and he would wish him well. "I hope you get better soon," or "I hope it doesn't cause you too much pain."

Perhaps their caution was understandable. Perhaps they thought Vincent's gift was, at best, a rumor.

Maddie thought it best to keep it that way, and she imagined that Vincent shared her opinion. This was his way of keeping requests at bay. Why ask for anyone to be healed if you knew for certain that it wouldn't work?

She still hadn't talked with him about it. She told herself that she didn't want to force the conversation, as the cycle of sin and repentance was tiring enough. Yet their mutual silence about his gift was beginning to wear on her. She wanted to hear what he was thinking about this subject on which he had rarely, it seemed, had much to say.

And so she ventured a single, cautious question one morning after Sunday school.

"Why don't you just offer to pray for her?" she asked him as they moved down the hall, away from yet another awkward conversation, this time about a toothache.

"She didn't ask," Vincent said.

"No, but you know that's what she wants," Maddie said.

"That may be."

They had left the senior high Sunday school class when Mrs. Leland, church pianist and toothache sufferer, found them, and now they were running late for the church service again. They fell silent as they joined a few straggling classmates on the stairs, and Maddie didn't continue the conversation until they were seated in a pew.

She leaned over and spoke to him in a low voice. "Don't you think that's what she wants?"

He leaned in to whisper back to her. "I think that's what she *thinks* she wants," he said.

⁂

A month had passed since the Pavlik potluck.

"What is your boyfriend waiting for?" This was Justine, of course, and Maddie had no answer other than defensiveness—yet another familiar pattern.

Her only words were Vincent's: nobody had asked to be healed.

"He wants people to *ask* him?" Disbelief. "Why would he need people to *ask* him, Maddie? Do people need to kneel and kiss his ring or something?"

There it was, the customary derision, and Maddie wondered what it would take to convince Justine that there was anything good at all about Vincent. Oh, she of little faith.

"Sometimes you can be pretty mean, Justine," she said.

"No, I'm not being mean. I'm just saying what is he waiting for?"

Maddie sighed. If Vincent was waiting for what she thought he *should* be waiting for—that the two of them would find all sexual temptation completely resistible—then they were apparently in for a long delay. But she couldn't say that to Justine, who had a hard enough time believing in Vincent's good character and who, for now anyway, still believed in Maddie's.

"Maybe he just doesn't want to have to read people's minds," she said. And again, "No one has asked him."

∞

It was Mrs. Adams who finally asked. Mrs. Adams, who cried indifferently over news good and bad, who offered a sopping testimony of God's mercy at every opportunity. She was a widow in her sixties, always very nicely dressed, attending church whenever the doors were open. She was waiting for Vincent after the church service the following Sunday, standing at the end of the pew.

"Vincent!" She called to him around the bodies and heads of the many teenagers who stood in her way. "Vincent!" she said again. "Would you get Vincent for me, honey?" patting the shoulder of a middle-school girl who stood nearby. And when she caught his eye: "Vincent, I need to speak with you, honey," she said. "It will only take a minute."

Until that moment, Mrs. Adams possessed two primary characteristics in Maddie's mind. One was the crying; the other was a rich southern accent that defied her decades of residing in Pittsburgh. Now Maddie could add boldness to the list.

"Vincent," she said in a conversational tone. Anyone standing nearby could hear her. "I would like you to heal me," she said.

Maddie looked around for Justine, and found her smiling at Mrs. Adams. Immediately, she guessed that the two of them had had a little conversation.

"Vincent? Vincent, honey?" Mrs. Adams prodded.

Vincent raised his gaze to her from where he'd been looking at the floor and said quietly, "I can't heal you."

Maddie gasped audibly and felt a few heads turn in her direction. What would he say next? Was this to be a confession now, their sins laid out between the pews? A bleak horror spread through her, closing artery and vein. Her fingertips pricked.

And Mrs. Adams was speaking again. Chuckling, really.

196

"Oh, I do believe you can, Vincent. You healed Joey; you healed Dean." An encouraging, almost coaxing tone, but Maddie was fixed on other things. How did Mrs. Adams know about Joey? When and in what conversations had word spread, connecting Mr. Pavlik with the swing set-glider incident months before? And then she remembered: Justine knew about all of it, because Maddie had told her.

"I can't heal you," Vincent said again, a bit more loudly this time. With clammy hands, Maddie gripped the back of the pew. Then Vincent said, "Only God can heal you."

So he would put her off with this, then. He would leave it to God, and Maddie felt a rush of relief. This was a smart way to play it, she thought.

There was a pause, and Mrs. Adams chuckled again, an unfamiliar sound from someone given to tears.

"Well, of course that's true, Vincent. Of course that's true." Now she was making her way toward him between the pews. "And of course that's what I'm asking for. But God has given you an extraordinary gift." She stopped in front of him. "I am asking if you would use that gift for me," she said, quietly and gently, humbly. There was not a trace of tears in her voice; she was not beseeching.

Silence. The group of teenagers standing around Vincent was fixed now on Mrs. Adams. Maddie felt a nervous flutter in her throat and stomach, as if she were facing exams. She was duly impressed with Mrs. Adams, who clearly wouldn't take no for an answer, but she was terrified for Vincent. What was this? Some torture—the beginnings of protracted punishment. God wouldn't accept Vincent's—their—quiet evasion. He would instead put Vincent on display. It was to be a large gesture: the gift's recision and public shame.

Maddie thought Vincent should walk away. Get out now, she thought.

"What do you need to be healed of?" Vincent asked.

Mrs. Adams lifted her hands for Vincent to see them, and the small crowd stared at knuckles that had been tied in knots. They were hard and lumpy, every joint enlarged, fingers crooked. Her skin looked stretched over them, translucently thin, exposing ridges of blue veins. It was a wonder her knuckles didn't just tear through and expose the bone.

Mrs. Adams was talking. She said she used to knit; she used to play the piano. Now her hands ached all day long; she couldn't even peel potatoes for supper. It was difficult to function, she said, with her hands like this.

Vincent listened and then, without further hesitation, covered her hands with his familiar ones, almost hairless, smooth and young. His fingers weren't long, but they were straight and healthy. Beneath them, Mrs. Adams' fingers disappeared.

Then Vincent bowed his head; Mrs. Adams bowed too. It was seconds—not minutes—before it was over. Maddie hadn't had time to compose a prayer.

"Thank you," Mrs. Adams said. Tears welled in her eyes.

"No problem," Vincent said. "It's no problem," and he smiled at her.

She reached for and hugged him over the pew, then dug in her purse for a handkerchief. Maddie was trying to get a look at her hands, to see if the swelling was already going down and knowing that it wouldn't be, but Mrs. Adams moved off, full of faith. "I'll let you know when it happens," she called out, smiling.

"All right," Vincent answered, kindly but without enthusiasm. It didn't sound as if it would matter to him one way or the other.

Meanwhile, all around them, the departing congregation hadn't seemed to notice the prayer, the quietly bold request for interaction with the living God. And the teenagers who had witnessed it moved off, already talking about other things.

---

The church parking lot ran with the morning's rain. The sky had been dark with it when they arrived, and Sunday school and the worship service had been accompanied by its steady thunder on the roof. But now the rain had stopped and the sky, still cottoned tightly in clouds, was lighter. Vincent, Maddie and Justine made their way over the black rivers of rain. The air was warm.

"So what made you decide to go for it?" Justine asked.

"What do you mean?" Vincent answered. Maddie hadn't shared with him Justine's sense of urgency, and neither had she had the chance, since the prayer for Mrs. Adams only minutes before, to tell him of Justine's likely provocation.

"I mean, what made you decide to pray for Mrs. Adams?" Her question sounded light-hearted enough, intended, Maddie thought, to be free of pressure. But Maddie felt that instinctive protection of Vincent.

"She asked me to do it," Vincent said, disinterested.

"Oh, so that *is* what it takes, then," Justine said, and Maddie detected—or did she imagine it?—derision. Suddenly she felt tired. She didn't want to deal just now with Justine.

"Yes. No. I don't know. What do you mean?" Vincent's words came rapidly, as though he was responding without listening and then was hearing her, tuning her in after having regarded her conversation as so much noise.

"Well, Maddie said she thought maybe you might need people to ask you," Justine said.

Maddie blanched. Justine's saying this felt like a betrayal, and had Maddie betrayed Vincent by telling her this in the first place? But Vincent seemed unbothered, or as if he hadn't noticed, as if this had always been public knowledge. As if he was thinking about something else.

They had reached Vincent's car and he stood next to it, leaning, his arms outstretched and hands spread and resting, despite the beaded water, on the roof. He was looking out over the parking lot, barely aware of the conversation or their presence, it seemed. He sighed.

Justine continued.

"It's not good enough for you to go out there and heal people, right? They need to come to you. They need to ask you for it." Now there was a definite edge to her tone.

"No," Vincent said, abstracted, and then, "I don't know," as if, again, he wasn't really listening.

"Justine," Maddie said sharply. It was a warning. Justine had no idea what she and Vincent had been through. To Maddie's surprised relief, she seemed to get it. She softened her tone.

"It was good of you to pray for her, Vincent," she said.

"Not really," Vincent answered. Maddie tensed. What did he mean? Was it to come out now, just to Justine? Perhaps Vincent imagined that she and Maddie shared a confidence about their sin, too. Maddie felt a terror that, like so much else, was becoming familiar.

"What do you mean by that?" Justine asked.

"I mean, it wasn't good of me, Justine," he answered, looking at her now. "I mean I have precious little to do with it." Maddie wondered what he was questioning, if this was just the same question of God doing the healing, or if it was larger, if he was in fact questioning his own goodness. Which he could do. No, she thought. To be fair, Vincent could question *Maddie's* goodness. That was more to the point.

But would he? Aloud? And to Justine in the church parking lot?

The rainwater pouring through the distant drain was loud in her ears.

"I don't think that's true, Vincent," Justine said. "I think it *was* good of you, Vincent. Really."

It was strange and dreadful for Justine to be so kind now. Kindness was always inviting. Would she unwittingly lure him into confession with it, Maddie wondered. Or had she already guessed?

Maddie studied Vincent's face, trying to read what he was thinking. He was subdued, to say the least, almost sad, as if already anticipating that the healing wouldn't work.

"Well," Vincent finally said, "I hope she gets better. Her hands are a mess." There was a pause then, filled by distant conversations and more of the rainwater running through the grate.

"Of course you hope she gets better, Vincent. We all hope she gets better," Justine said with some impatience. She was sounding more like herself again.

Vincent was silent.

"*Do* you hope she gets better?" Justine asked, and Maddie felt the resurgence of that tempestuous cafeteria conversation. She could hardly remember anymore where each of them had stood. If it was to be revisited, Maddie thought, then she was fairly sure she didn't want to hear it.

But Vincent seemed unruffled. "I just don't know if it's the best thing for her," he said quietly, looking at Maddie as if she could comprehend what he was saying. But of course she couldn't, not any more than she had been able to weeks before.

"*Of course* it's the best thing for her, Vincent. Why wouldn't it be?"

Justine said, apparently doing nothing to hide her annoyance.

"Do you really think she wants to be healed?" Vincent asked. His abstraction was gone. He was engaged but again dispassionate, interested, focusing on Justine's angry face as if he could have a rational conversation with her.

"Yes. Yes, I do think she wants to be healed. Of course she does, Vincent."

Maddie could see Mrs. Adams' hands in her mind. Yes, she wanted to be healed. The question was preposterous.

"Okay, but what next, Justine?" Vincent asked. "What next? The woman is in her late sixties. Before she knows it, she'll be in her eighties. Who knows what will happen to her between now and then!"

"What are you saying?" Justine's tone was incredulous, and Maddie was appalled along with her. "Your sixties is hardly death's door, Vincent."

"Okay, fine," Vincent said, and something had caught fire within him: there was new passion in his voice. His words came fast, as if he'd been waiting for them to understand and now, full of frustrated impatience, he was being forced to explain: "But does she want to be healed when she needs a walker? Does she want to be healed of the cancer she might get when she's in her seventies? Does she want to be healed of death?"

They were all silent for a moment, Vincent staring at Justine as if expecting that she would have an answer. But what in the world was he getting at? Maddie couldn't see it. Was he saying that no one should want to be healed of anything? Or that the elderly weren't worth it? Or was this a mask, some philosophical ruse that he could wield as an avoidance tactic, never bothering to try to heal anyone again?

Justine stared back at him. Finally, "You're a jerk," she said.

Vincent didn't miss a beat; the insult apparently held no traction for him. "Fine, Justine, but that's not the point. The point is that she doesn't really want to be healed of arthritis. When she's healed of arthritis, she'll just want something else. She'll want to be cured of a toothache. Or of her aching knees. She'll just want something else. Everybody will always just want something else."

Maddie didn't know what to make of this. "What do you mean, Vincent?" she asked.

Vincent turned to regard her, and Maddie gazed back. How could he be Vincent, so familiar, the features of face and body so well known, and yet, in that instant, be so utterly foreign? "I mean," he was saying, "do you want to be healed of every little thing?" He paused for a moment, and then, "Do you want to be healed of a paper cut?"

All three of them were silent for a moment, and the rainwater thundered down the drain.

"Mrs. Adams' hands are nothing like a paper cut," Maddie finally managed to say.

Justine chimed in with raised voice: "She has a crippling joint disorder, Vincent! She's not rubbing a magic lamp here. She wants to be able to use her hands, for crying out loud!"

"People *get* things," Vincent said. He had raised his voice, too, heedless of congregation members around them walking to their cars. "People get sick. People die. People have crippling arthritis."

"Yes! And you can heal them!" Justine answered.

"No. I. Can't." Three short syllables, and Vincent separated them, making each word painfully distinct.

"Fine. Fine! *God* can heal them. God can heal them." Justine was exasperated. She lowered her voice in suppressed fury. "But he uses you, Vincent." She paused, as if trying to accept the truth of what she was about to say: "For no good reason I can think of, he uses you."

"Well, it's not up to you to think of a good reason, is it?" Vincent said, finally meeting her insult. He was angry.

Vincent and Justine regarded one another in silence. Maddie no longer felt torn between them. She couldn't care what they thought of each other. She was instead cut adrift, mentally exhausted, no longer trying to tease compassion from Vincent's hard and heartless words.

Vincent looked steadily at Justine, perhaps waiting for an answer—and Maddie wondered at this. Why did he try with her? And why did it not seem to occur to Vincent that she, too—his girlfriend—was at the very least put off by what he had to say? Did it register at all with him that Maddie herself was dismayed by his words?

Justine was silent, now looking coldly about her, refusing to meet Vincent's gaze. Finally, she turned to Maddie. "I've gotta go," she said. She began to walk away, and Maddie was more than happy to let her.

But Vincent called after her: "Justine." He didn't sound angry anymore.

She pivoted to look at him, one hand on her hip, silent.

All anger was gone from his voice. "Paper cut, arthritis, cancer," he said, "it's all basically the same thing."

That was the end of the conversation. Now Maddie sat again at the computer desk and stared at a satellite image of that very parking lot, but the aerial perspective, as ever, was disorienting. From this odd view, she had to rethink the familiar space, searching the flat gray shape on her screen for its three-dimensional parameters. She would have to recreate the details: the determined slope and the sealed cracks in the macadam that spread like random arteries, the loose gravel here and there that rolled under the feet. On the far edge was the grate abutting the strip of lawn that bordered on the auto-mechanic. All the rain in that Pittsburgh sky had poured through the grate that day— but it was rain that had dried up years ago.

For a while she continued searching, but the house she could not find belonged to Nicky and Amy. For all the times she had been there in those days, she had been unable to discover it. She wouldn't know it by its rooflines, and she was uncertain of the neighborhood. She didn't remember the address; she didn't want to look it up and wasn't sure she'd be able to. She had hunted down a few streets once or twice— her core tense with what might be described as fear—turning off the main drag and hoping a familiar street name would assert itself, but to no avail. And then she decided it was just as well. She could do without seeing that house again.

Maddie switched off the computer because she would like to switch off the images of that well-traveled suburb, but another parking lot swam into mental view: the drama of Tommy MacDonald's Camaro instantaneously replayed itself, unaided by satellite image. There was the unbidden Vincent kneeling next to her, and Justine scolding him, and the ambulance doors closing at her feet.

There were her parents meeting her at the emergency room, and already the pain was inexplicably dissipated. And here was the impressed doctor, who was explaining that she was a very lucky young lady indeed, because her bone should have been broken: from

Rebecca Brewster Stevenson

all descriptions he'd received, she should be in incredible pain and a cast to boot. It should be a wheelchair and then a slow graduation to crutches for her. He was talking about the break that—by chance—didn't happen and also another one—the one that healed a long time ago. His comment made them all lean in to study the x-ray glowing on the screen.

Here, he said to them, here is where she broke it the last time, gesturing to the faint white line etched across her femur. It healed nicely, he said to her. He told her she should know better than anyone—as she'd been through it before—that recovering from a break like this is no picnic. You, he said to Maddie, are a very lucky girl.

But Maddie knew—and her parents knew—that she never broke her femur before. She had never broken a bone before. This faint white line, this mended fracture, so fully healed that it looked like an old break, was only hours old.

Sitting there in the emergency room, Maddie didn't think to tell her parents about the boy who tried to help her. The three of them believed in a miracle, but it didn't yet include a kid in his practice uniform. As yet, it was—to their minds—a miracle extended from God himself and not through a seventeen-year-old boy. In the fuss and the wait at the hospital, Maddie had forgotten him again for now.

She left the hospital on her own two feet. No wheelchair, no crutches.

The healing was that complete.

204

# PART II

# 20

*A*nd then it was over. The days, weeks and months, bound and disguised in cycles of treatment, finally resulted in a verdict: remission. Maddie was clean of cancer.

The return to normal had been full of promise: the port's removal, her hair's regrowth, her system's slow shed of chemotherapy toxins. But until she had the doctor's pronouncement, Maddie hadn't allowed herself to accept that she would actually be well.

Now the biggest trauma of her life—of their lives—was finished, sealed with a clean bill of health and a little pill to be taken daily for the next five years. Something to ensure it never came back again. To *try* to ensure it never came back. They couldn't promise.

Maddie understood this.

Frank was jubilant. We did it, he told her, and tears came to his eyes. On the afternoon of the news, he swept their unsuspecting sons into a dance around the kitchen. Together they paraded through the first floor of the house.

Maddie stood smiling in the midst of this silliness. The boys had endured her treatment just fine; she and Frank had weathered it well—well enough, anyway, that much of the time (lately, at least) their sons were barely aware their mother was sick. The dancing parade, then, was really for her and Frank. They were the ones who were celebrating, who were still waiting for the word "remission" to sink beneath the skin. It was they who had been granted new life. Maddie joined the parade.

And she relished their weekend trip to the beach, Frank's surprise for her and the boys. It was time away from all the distractions of home, time to reconnect as a family, he said. As she and Frank sat on the sand, watching the boys flirt with the waves, Frank told her he thought she would be needing this.

He was right. Maddie told him that cancer had distracted her. She felt as if her gaze had been held for too long at something on the periphery of their lives. Now she could see their boys full-on again and had noticed, as if she had been away, their gains in height, their changes. Garrett was suddenly older, more likely to play with his big brothers, less likely to have his stuffed kitten in tow. Eli had learned to ride his bike without training wheels that spring, which made him also seem somehow older: he walked with a big boy swagger now. And Jake, who had barely tolerated tee-ball the previous summer, was suddenly looking ahead to Little League with exhausting enthusiasm: almost every day he asked Maddie how many weeks it was until the season started.

Yes, she told Frank, it was a good idea to get away. She thanked him.

She sat close to him on the sand, their shoulders just touching each other. She told him again that she was deeply grateful for his thoughtfulness, for the tenderness with which he had cared for her during her illness. But beyond these things, she could find nothing more to say, and despite his kind response and the way he gently kissed her forehead, Maddie perceived a formality in their exchange. It felt, she thought, as if they were simply being polite.

She recalled the days just before their wedding, with Frank living in Raleigh and Maddie travelling between Pittsburgh and their little college town, making final preparations. They were to be married in Father Tim's church, with Father Tim officiating.

During that wedding week, Maddie was dismayed to find herself in frequent arguments with her parents. The day before the wedding itself, Maddie's mother had a fit about the pew bows, of all things. She didn't want plain bows; she wanted them to include fresh flowers. This readily resolved dilemma had to become an ordeal, impacting several members of the bridal party and requiring no fewer than three trips to the florist and one to the grocery store.

None of it mattered anymore. Maddie's mother had long since apologized to both of them for the trouble she had caused that day. But what Maddie remembered keenly was the sense she'd had when Frank arrived. It was fifteen minutes before the wedding rehearsal, and she was standing in the middle of the aisle with her mother. The floor at their feet was covered in pew bows and a pile of baby's breath, and Maddie had felt profoundly alone. The problem with the pew bows was multiplying in her mind, becoming a complex list of problems and failings that would ruin the wedding and, likely, her marriage.

Then Frank had come in. Hearing his voice at the end of the aisle had filled Maddie with exquisite relief. She turned and saw him standing there: his curly hair and glasses, T-shirt and shorts, his bagged tuxedo flung over his shoulder, and she remembered that she was not, in fact, getting married by herself. She was marrying her best friend.

But now things felt different. Yes, Frank had been amazing throughout the cancer ordeal. Yet, as with the boys, Maddie sensed a distance from him, as though they had lived apart for a long time and now must become reacquainted.

She wondered if it was simply the fact of her illness—a persistent sense of isolation. No matter how kind Frank might be or what he might say, she knew—and he knew—that her body had harbored disease. Cancer had lived just below the surface, and the invisibility of the disease only exacerbated what she imagined—in herself—to be a kind of detachment. She had crossed a divide, and it had been impossible for him to join her there.

She understood that she should be happy now, and for the most part, she thought she was. She relished the growing strength she felt in her core and limbs, sometimes taking a purposeful inventory: a mouth *not* full of sores, food tasting the way it was supposed to. She ran her hands through her hair. Curlier than it used to be, and shorter, but she decided to embrace the change.

And mothering her sons. Preparing their snacks, reading with them at bedtime, even folding their laundry, Maddie again felt the soft weight of the yarn in her hands, the knitting that spilled from her arms and followed her active and noisy boys through their days. Yet she knew that she was also deeply sad. She didn't often feel it during the day, busy as she was. But many times she would awaken early to find herself already crying, as if grieving unaware. Her face, her hair, her pillow would be saturated by tears.

∽

Frank was eager for the return of normal. He was well-enough warned against it. Sometimes there were permanent changes for a woman when recovering from something like this. In addition to the pill Maddie was taking daily, they had been armed with resources: several books on recovering from breast cancer, a list of websites, names of support groups, a directory of services they might find useful. All of this reminded him they were still in process, and keeping this in mind was important.

And Frank did keep it in mind. Without meaning to, he had created a mental timeline and watched it hopefully as milestones rose into possibility. Already Maddie seemed like herself again—physically, at any rate. She certainly had her energy back, and (he knew she was glad of this) her hair. In terms of daily life things had definitely settled into their pre-cancer patterns of work and carpool and the boys' various needs. In many ways, Maddie seemed to have landed on her feet. For much of what Frank and Maddie had yet to weather, the guidebooks and websites said the same thing: communicate. This made sense to Frank, and he was eager to do his part. He wanted to know how Maddie was feeling, what she was thinking. He was ready to listen at absolutely any time.

But she didn't seem to share his eagerness. The inwardness that had accompanied her cancer treatment persisted. He had tried what he hoped might draw her out: setting the living room with lit candles, making dinner, surprising her with dates and the babysitter already hired. He talked with her; he tried silence. He said what the websites told him about the sex part (as if that was what mattered to him): he knew it would take time, and that was fine, and she shouldn't feel any pressure. Not from him, anyway. He told her what he knew—that she was beautiful.

Often he was visited by a memory they had always enjoyed. It had been a strange, almost marvelous experience, one they talked about with some amazement even years after it occurred: it was before the boys were born, and Frank and Maddie had had business trips at opposite ends of the week. She arrived home less than a half-hour before Frank had to leave for the airport and Maddie had been dealing with a challenging co-worker. She wanted to tell him about the most recent developments in person, and they had missed one another deeply in a purely physical way. The upshot was an intense twenty minutes, Frank greeting her at the door and then crushing her against it as it closed behind her. She commenced talking through their kisses, responding motion for motion to his desire. They removed one another's clothes as they moved together toward the sofa.

Later, Frank had been impressed at his ability to follow and verbally respond to what she had been saying; they laughed at how she had maintained her narrative. The conversation only stopped briefly when no relevant words were really possible, and then—breathlessly, at first—resumed. They had continued talking together as they dressed again, as Frank checked his jacket pocket for his boarding pass, as they headed out to the car. By the time they reached the airport, Maddie felt herself satisfactorily unburdened and understood. It was on the phone late that night when Frank called her from Phoenix that they first chuckled together at the perfection of that twenty minutes in their apartment, a vital deposit of intimacy.

Frank knew this scenario wasn't likely to be recreated. Not any time soon, anyway, as the boys were sure to impede such spontaneity. But he held it as an ideal nonetheless; it pictured precisely what he longed for: the two of them, body and soul, belonging to each other.

Sometimes it occurred to him that this was impossible, that Maddie's physical changes had made her withdraw from him both physically and emotionally.

Then he told himself that this would not be the case. That if it *was* the case, it was not permanently so. They would get past this, too, wouldn't they? Believing—no, *deciding*—that their intimacy would be restored was a kind of faith, he realized.

But he was fine with that. This restoration would surely be something God wanted. Wouldn't it?

And then Frank put the question out of his mind, because he

wasn't certain of the answer.

———

Maddie believed that looking forward was her best option. She should forget her cancer year. But what kind of mental power would it take to block out a year of her life? How, for example, to disremember the moment of discovery? The sun had been coming in the window; the steaming bathroom was lit with it. Frank had come in and felt the lump, searching her flesh with the warm pads of his fingertips. She hadn't wanted him to find it; if he didn't find it, then she would know she was mistaken.

But Frank had found it.

And how to forget the transformation of her body from private, personal, sexual, into a medical object? The poking, the prodding, the flattened stretching for mammograms? Sitting topless on examining tables while doctors read over files and then turned to her and detachedly handled her breasts, first one, then the other? Lying motionless, half-exposed and alone while waiting for the invisible powers of radiation to take their effect? How does one begin to bury such memories?

She could do what she may to block out the images. She could reject—as soon as the memory crested—those moments that wanted to relentlessly replay themselves in her mind. But no matter what kinds of mind games she employed to keep those memories at bay, she still had her body: a breast gone, skin puckered and scarred by the surgeries and, for now, darkened by radiation. She had been assured that the discoloration would resolve, but she had seen the before and after images, and she knew just how much hope to retain.

Even if she were to permanently repress all the appointments, treatments, and side-effects of the past year, she would have this body to confront daily, a reality in vivid contradiction to images on the glossy covers of magazines. She felt herself removed by infinite degrees from all that society might find desirable. And while she could and did hide her scars under clothing, she couldn't rid herself of that abiding sense of isolation.

Frank insisted that he didn't care about the scars—and he seemed to find her desirable. But her own revulsion had him reminding her: if she wanted it, plastic surgery was an option.

As if she wanted any more surgery, any more prodding at her breasts—even if the intent was to rebuild her body.

No, she told him. There was no way she was going under the knife again.

She was post-trauma, she told herself. What she needed was time. The cancer was behind them—both it and the memories that had haunted her during treatment. The untroubled future spread out ahead of them. Everything would—eventually—be fine.

But despite her resolve, her body was her enemy. There was, just for instance, a night only recently, maybe just a few nights ago. She hadn't been fully awake; she hadn't known what had overcome her, but in the middle of sleep she had turned to her husband and readily aroused him. It had been so easy. Both of them were blinded by sleep; it was no time for conversation, and although intimacy had lately been lacking, there in the middle of the night familiarity and sheer desire had been enough.

It was only afterward that Maddie had fully awakened, and then it was in a post-coital exhaustion, slipping from the slender continent of his body to the bed sheets. It was in that brief awareness, as she turned onto her side and away from her husband, that she realized it was Vincent's body she had loved in her mind, and she wondered if it always was.

# 21

*M*addie tried lying: she was unbothered by her mind's interposing Vincent in their bed. From a practical perspective, she told herself, it wasn't altogether unnatural. Vincent's body had been, in its way, her first male body. It had been the solid image of "male" against a backdrop of the concept of "maleness": the straightness of the male form and its general solidity. Prior to Vincent, she had known "male" as father, grandfather, uncle, a teeming mass of boys that filled roughly half her experience in the school-day world and the world at large.

After Vincent, it was his frame that became the point of reference for Maddie. So another boy or man was shorter or taller than Vincent, more or less muscular, more or less fat. The eyes of this one were bluer or less so; that one's eyes were brown and so also, somehow, wrong. Length of limb, jut of chin, even posture—all of this was determined by the plumb-line Vincent had set. Unwitting, she would interpret the male population by this standard. Even now the comparison was something she knew and could reflexively describe: when she met him, Frank was slightly shorter than Vincent and a touch more lean.

So it might be that her mind, returning to itself after trauma as if waking from a nightmare, would first recall Vincent.

But Maddie knew there was more to it than that. Vincent's body had not only taught her about the male body, it had taught her about her own. By Vincent, Maddie had come to know the defining edges of herself: the skin of her upper arm and the shock of its meaningful brush with another. His hands taught her the curve of her back and his fingers the span of her waist. Even the contours of her own hand had been relatively unknown to her until he held it.

That recent dream of Vincent—was it a dream? She had been, at the very least, half-awake—felt almost like infidelity to Maddie.

She told herself that this was absurd: she hadn't been unfaithful to Frank. It was Frank in the bed the whole time.

—∞∞∞—

Frank continued to wait, ready for when Maddie wanted to communicate. But this readiness was empty if Maddie wasn't interested, and she certainly didn't seem to be. As the months rolled past them, Frank's patience devolved into mute—he wouldn't call it despair, exactly, but it was bordering somewhere near that.

Meanwhile their daily lives proceeded as demand required, and Maddie seemed fine on every front but for the talking part, that whole intimacy thing that had seemed to him the reason he got married in the first place. No, not the sex *per se*, but that and, yes, everything that comes with it: the knowing that Maddie loved him in a permanent kind of way; the sense of knowing Maddie and being known by Maddie, which included knowing each other's faults. The kind of thing alluded to but never quite captured in books and movies. The kind of thing he had absolutely believed in and still did.

Which sometimes made him feel foolish.

And sometimes confounded him because they had been through the cancer together—and wasn't that kind of suffering supposed to strengthen their relationship? Weren't they supposed to emerge stronger from this?

Frank considered calling Father Tim, who had first engendered this vision of marriage within him. But he knew what Tim would say, and Frank was already covering the bases his friend would remind him to cover: that about staying committed and being loyal and simply continuing to try.

Moreover, a conversation with Tim or any good friend might

inevitably result in Frank's admitting something he never wanted to say: his needs weren't being met.

No, Frank definitely could not talk with Tim about this. Years ago Tim had willingly determined with his priestly oath that his own needs would not be met—or would be met, mysteriously, by God. How could Frank look for sympathy from Tim here?

And what, in all honesty, did Tim really know about marriage?

Anyway, Frank wasn't convinced that his sexual needs—or any of his needs at all—mattered. The last thing he wanted to be, especially after all they had been through—after all Maddie had been through—was needy.

So he resolved there was nothing for it but to press on and continue to wait it out. Maybe things wouldn't return to exactly normal, and that would have to be okay. Meanwhile there was plenty to distract him. For example, he was coaching Jake's Little League team, which meant two evenings a week and a game every Saturday. Maddie would bring Eli and Garrett to the games, and without turning around Frank would know they had arrived because of Eli's cheering, which began as soon as he was in sight of the field.

Eli loved baseball; he loved it even more than Jake did, and he cheered from the stands like a player would: "Batter batter batter batter batter!" He made the calls on the pitches before the umpire did, and he pressed his belly against the fence, his fingers curled into the chain link. Frank loved seeing Eli stand there in his baseball hat. The boy was scarcely aware that his dad was a coach because he was lost in his dreams, envisioning himself in the major leagues.

Garrett was a little bit young to pay attention, and Frank admired how Maddie anticipated this, bringing along a small cooler of snacks and a bag of toys just to get him through the six innings. She wasn't much of a cheer-aloud kind of mom, but she planted herself on one of the lower seats in the bleachers (so she could get after Garrett if he were to wander away) and paid close attention to the game. When Frank turned to look at her, she would meet his gaze and smile.

It reminded him of that time she unexpectedly showed up at his tennis match. He had been playing poorly, and it was the beginning of the second set when he happened to look up and see her sitting in an upper corner of the stands. This was in college; they were barely dating at the time, but already Frank really liked her, so seeing her there was a pleasant surprise. She had smiled and waved, just the slightest lift of her hand—which made him tease her later that it looked as though she didn't want to be noticed.

This little taunt had embarrassed her. She said it was true—she didn't really want to be noticed. Frank hadn't exactly invited her to the match, she pointed out; he had only mentioned it. And she didn't know if maybe tennis was like golf and the players needed silence for focus? Maybe fans weren't supposed to be cheering from the stands?

Frank had chuckled to himself, delighted: Maddie took everything seriously, even attendance at a tennis match, and he told her that she hadn't broken his focus at all. Instead she had motivated him to play better, he said. In a flood of transparency, Frank told her that her presence had actually colored the rest of his game. From the moment he saw her, he had been conscious of her sitting there, and more than winning he had wanted to impress her and make her believe that he was a great tennis player.

Frank said all of this as they stood together by the tennis court. They had only been on one or two dates, and for a moment after he'd said it, he blanched at this torrent of truth-telling and attendant exposure. But Frank was banking on honesty. After dating Francesca, he had decided that honesty in relationships would be a requirement.

Happily, Maddie had responded well. She smiled, blushing, and asked him to give her tennis lessons.

They played tennis often that spring, and Maddie moved quickly from Frank's few lessons to their actually being able to play—she always apologizing for not being very good, believing that her game was nothing like a challenge to Frank and deciding that his praise was mere flattery. But it wasn't, he told her, time and again. She was good.

He would tell her the same thing years later, even when they hadn't played together in a long time. He would tell her that now with no intent to flatter her—because it was true. Maddie was an excellent tennis player—or had potential to be. She was naturally athletic. He had seen it and he knew it and he was glad to see—so far, anyway—that they had passed this athleticism down to their sons.

Other than Maddie, the only person he had tried to teach to play tennis had been Francesca, and maybe it was Francesca and not

Maddie who had—by blunt comparison—made his wife's natural abilities obvious. Because somehow the former lover always informs one's expectations of the next. And Francesca had been miserable at tennis. She had been miserable when it came to athletic effort of any kind. How had he ever been able to cajole her onto the court in the first place?

It had been some conversation about tennis as an ancient game, a classic. Something about Wimbledon or tennis in Europe, he recalled, that impressed her. Because Francesca was never one to move outside her comfort zone with something like this (and tennis was definitely outside of Francesca's comfort zone: he could see her now, surprising in her shorts and tennis shoes, she who was forever clad in long skirts and sandals and jingling ankle bracelets, her soft skin pale in the sunlight), and yet somehow he convinced her that she should learn to play. And so she met him down on the courts with her long curly hair piled up in some kind of elastic band behind her head, and the lessons he tried to give were a sorry failure.

It was a lack of coordination, nothing that practice couldn't overcome. Frank had been earnestly trying to teach her, but Francesca couldn't seem to take it seriously. After an hour or so of what appeared to be half-hearted effort, Francesca proceeded, in an amused and mocking tone, to criticize it all: sports, the game of tennis that Frank loved, and then, ever so gently, Frank himself.

Frank was accustomed to this criticism—not necessarily at things so close to himself, but to the ridicule in general. He didn't actually perceive it as ridicule at the time, but rather as evidence of Francesca's intellect and honed tastes. Taken in by her beauty, he had been a ready convert to her genius—or what Francesca implied as her genius. From the vantage point of superior intellect, Francesca derided all kinds of things, and as they climbed the hill together from the tennis court, it was American sport that fell under her critique. No, she declared, American sports weren't worth her time or anyone else's. If you wanted to find a real game to play, she told Frank, then you'd be better off with something uncorrupted by American assimilation, something completely British, like rugby or polo. Yes, polo really was the game to play. Anything, she said, involving horses.

Frank couldn't help but mark the development in her argument from culture of origin to equine inclusion, as if she were making this up as she went along. But he hadn't mounted a defense. At that point in their relationship, at that point in his life, he didn't wish to mount any defense against Francesca. Instead, "Why horses?" he had asked. And then she produced a theory so fully crafted and, at the time, believable that he wondered where she had gotten it—perhaps some ancient Greek philosopher, some long-lost disciple of Aristotle? She argued that true athleticism ought to require the harmony of movement between man and beast, that athleticism within an athlete alone wasn't enough, that it was true triumph over nature if one could combine one's efforts with that of a dumb animal. Such harmony, exerted in joint competitive endeavor, she said, was true sport.

It was vintage Francesca: opinionated, virulently critical, and passionately self-assured, all done up with impressive vocabulary. At the time, Frank found the critique disheartening—and also somewhat suspicious. Could she possibly be right about it? Far too many people enjoyed sports with nary an animal in sight. And was the meaning of sport somehow bound up in a quest for triumph over nature? But Francesca was so sure of herself. She spoke with such confidence. And she was erudite; he would give her that. At the time, Francesca was the most well-read person he had ever known.

Years later Frank still considered her words. Watching the Kentucky Derby, he seriously weighed the united skills of man and horse; he attended a polo match or two. And then he had dismissed it as ridiculous. Of course it had been ridiculous. *She* had been ridiculous. Why had he put up with that nonsense, Frank wondered to himself. Because he had been in love with Francesca—or had imagined he was in love with her, anyway. But what had been so captivating? Was it merely the look of her? Her flowing clothes; her white, dazzling teeth; the natural ringlets of her hair and the way it fell over his hands. He could grasp it in fistfuls, pressing it up against the back of her head as he kissed her, and even so her hair would fall out of his hands and extend past her shoulders. There was something luxurious about it, abundant and fragrant.

Her skin, too. Fair and soft, like it had never seen the sun, like she had never done any kind of hard labor, had never scrubbed a sink or toilet, never possibly helped stack firewood or even ridden a bike—despite the fact she had grown up in a suburb on the east side of Cleveland. No, there was something impossibly exotic about Francesca. She was different: smarter, more profoundly perceptive than anyone else—and she had chosen him as her lover.

*That* was it. Francesca had chosen him and had made him reconsider himself, even to the point (for a time) of giving up tennis. Due to Francesca, Frank had begun to think that he might become someone significant. He might leave behind him what he had never—until Francesca—considered leaving behind: a middle-America upbringing; a quotidian, middle-class career; a life of mediocrity. Francesca had exposed him to possibility and had made him feel worthy of it. There, in the first semester of his freshman year, in a small college in the rolling farmland of Pennsylvania, Frank had broadened his horizons. He considered learning to read Hindu poetry, or trying to master French so he could read in its mother tongue what Francesca declared was the world's best political philosophy. He could—and should—do great, brilliant things.

All of it had been foolishness—classic college foolishness. Not the poetry or the French, but the notion that living in the Midwest was somehow inadequate, or that tennis, bereft of horse, wasn't a worthwhile game.

Then came the memory—unbidden, detached—of a time he had awakened from napping next to her in her bed. She was reading something, holding the book above her naked body, and although this was one of perhaps a dozen times he fell asleep in her dorm room, he remembered that afternoon clearly, and the way the sunlight fell across the blond hairs of her forearm.

He didn't need to be thinking about this right now.

Right now it was Maddie—and it had always been Maddie and would always be Maddie. When he met her during the fall of his junior year, thoughts of Francesca had fractured and drifted separately away, like an ice floe gone to pieces. Their recent return, ambushing him now that they were beyond the breast cancer ordeal, was an unnecessary complication in his waiting process, this hopeful time when he and Maddie were trying to get their life back.

And they would do it. Frank knew this. He claimed its reality with renewed faith. He heard the doctor's low tones and read the concise paragraphs in the guidebooks and knew that, despite the warnings, he and Maddie would be restored to one another in what had always been the best friendship of his life: a union and intimacy that Francesca never could have given him.

He offered himself what evidence he could: it wasn't much, but only a few nights ago Maddie had awakened him in the dead of night. There were no words, but she had aroused him and then taken all he had to give her. Afterward, Frank had drifted back to sleep in a kind of intoxicated joy.

Everything was going to be all right.

# 22

*M*addie had been Catholic for more than a decade, but lately she was obsessively aware that her church building seemed riddled with—how else to say it?—bodies. At the ends of hallways, in quiet alcoves, statues dotted the building: physical, three-dimensional portrayals of that saint praying and this one saying a blessing.

This had been new and slightly strange to her when she first started at church with Frank, as the Protestant churches of her experience had a statue-free aesthetic, but she had grown accustomed to it. Now she could reflexively identify this saint or that both in her own church building and in others. She had become mindless of their presence.

Yet since her cancer ordeal, the statuary had become almost oppressive to her. She knew it was irrational, but seeing the statues now felt like forced confrontation with the physical reality of the saints—as if their memory wasn't enough, as if recalling their lives, deeds, and deaths was inadequate to encourage the soul. Popular culture glorified the body for its sex appeal, and must the church also venerate the corporeal form? Wasn't it the stuff of the soul that mattered?

It was a strange collusion, Maddie thought, and she knew her perception was faulty, as was her accompanying sense that this confrontation was aimed specifically at *her* and not the general population. Again, she realized and told herself, it was the cancer that did this to her. It was that isolation, continued.

The most oppressive statue was that of Christ, the enormous crucifix at the front of the room, compelling object of her gaze during the homily, during the hymns. In the Bethel Hills Church of Holiness, the cross was also the sanctuary's dominant feature, but it was an empty cross. She had adjusted to this difference in her earliest years as a Catholic, but now she found it troubling. Why did they have the image of Jesus hanging there? Why the perpetual reminder of his torture? His shoulders forever thrust upward, his torso contorted, the knees bent and twisted to one side. Jesus had died, but he had also been resurrected—or so the Catholics, the Christian church, herself included—believed. Why portray him always so brutally broken, the picture of defeat?

She decided that, like society at large, the Catholics were fixated on the body. For the first time in years she recalled the dark church in winter and the vigil with her mother-in-law: Eucharistic adoration.

The parking lot surrounding the church had been snow-filled and trackless, illuminated in white pools by lampposts planted in snow-buried pavement. By contrast, the church was dark. It was a round, modern structure, and the sanctuary's dome, while from the inside an impressive vault, appeared low from the outside. The vellum sky glowed faintly with diffused light from the town, and the church building seemed hunkered beneath it, a dark smudge crouching within the ring of parking lot light. Only a dull glow issued from the glass doors in the foyer, and off to the right, from a source unseen, a flat rectangle of red light lay on the snow.

It was very cold and a steady snow was falling. Maddie and Frank's mother Peg didn't speak as they made their way across the unbroken whiteness of the parking lot. They held their coats closed at the necks and bent their heads against the wind. Through the foyer doors, they were met by a merciful rush of warm air, but Peg didn't pause to absorb it. A few steps took them across the tiled floor, and then together they pushed against the heavy wooden doors to the sanctuary.

The carpet here swallowed sound. The room was dark and still. Maddie sensed a looming emptiness overhead and felt compelled to veneration by the enormous silence: they should stop, remove their coats, maybe their shoes. But Peg was moving away from her. She pushed open another door and they were in a small, dimly lit side chapel ranked with pews. Only now did she pull off her coat and gloves. Maddie followed suit and then, like her mother-in-law, knelt briefly and crossed herself before sliding next to her into the pew.

Almost immediately, Peg composed herself into stillness, folding her hands in her lap and bowing her head. Maddie hadn't expected much in terms of conversation, but this instant retreat into prayer caught her a bit off guard. She herself needed more time to adjust.

She had learned of Eucharistic adoration months before this vigil, during the classes leading to her conversion. It was an ancient Catholic practice, one rooted in transubstantiation, that mystical transformation of the communion bread and wine into the actual body and blood of Christ. Adoration extended the sacrament: for a period of time, months or sometimes years, the priests left the Host exposed on the altar, creating an opportunity for parishioners to draw near to Christ. But in honor of the Host—Christ's very flesh—someone had to be praying before it, worshipping, day and night, regardless of the hour.

At Frank Sr. and Peg's church, daytime shifts in the schedule were easily filled, with various, unscheduled parishioners also likely stopping in. But the morning's small hours were the province of the ardently devoted. Peg had signed up for Friday mornings from four to five.

She had almost seemed to be joking when, at dinner the night before, she invited Frank and Maddie to join her. Frank had begged off immediately under the auspice of exhaustion: he and Maddie had just driven all day to get there. It was mid-January and the newlyweds had come for a long weekend; they would be leaving on Sunday.

But Maddie had agreed immediately, surprising everyone including herself, and pleasing her mother-in-law—which might have been part of the design. Frank had teased her about it later in their bedroom ("Trying to get in good with my mom, huh?" which had sent her into a small spiral of concern: "Do you think that's what she thinks, Frank?"), which had in turn given rise to a brief but earnest conversation: Peg loved Maddie, she didn't need to worry about that; and Maddie honestly wanted to go to the church at four a.m. for reasons beyond keeping her mother-in-law company.

She was intrigued by the practice of Eucharistic adoration, which was redolent to her of other beauties in her new church tradition, things like liturgy and the communal recitation of creeds. It rang with her vague understanding of medieval monastic life: rising before dawn in the cold, spending an hour in prayer. Surely this had been part of the earliest days of Catholic experience, and Maddie wanted to try it.

Now she sat next to Peg in the dark side chapel, and the cold pew beneath her echoed the cold in her core. The only light in the room was a single beam shining down onto the altar. It glowed dully against the red stained-glass windows and reflected on the glossy wood of the pews ahead; behind them, the back of the room dissolved in darkness. The sides of the room were composed of large blocks of stone, and in these were occasional and evenly spaced openings, small concavities in the wall. Retreating from the room like this, the openings were darker still, but Maddie could see that each of them held a statue on a pedestal, a single white figure, faintly luminescent.

It was time to concentrate. Time to focus, time to pray. She realized with some surprise that, mentally, she hadn't gotten this far: she hadn't prepared for the actual praying so much as she had prepared for the idea of it all. Now here they were, and Peg was already silently focused. Maddie began to compose her thoughts.

She was more than a little startled by movement on the far right of the room. It was a huddled shape down near the front, and Maddie recognized with some relief that it was just a fellow pray-er, maybe the one whose shift ran from three to four. She watched as he gathered his things and then slowly stood to his feet. He was an elderly man; Maddie could now see that much. She smiled at him as he made his way past their pew, and he gave her a broad grin. The door knocked mutely as it closed behind him, and then it truly was Peg's turn—and Maddie's—to adore the host.

She gave it her full attention. That only light, coming from an unseen source in the ceiling, was focused on it, shining down on the cross, which was centered on the altar. If Maddie hadn't been told it was there she would have missed it completely, but even from their somewhat distant pew she could make it out: a matte disc at the heart of the ornate silver ornament that surrounded and held it in place.

That was all it was. A dull circle of bread, maybe an inch in diameter. Even from a distance she knew it, having tasted it monthly for most of her life and now weekly since her conversion. She knew from experience its frailty, its thinness, how it would snap in two under the smallest pressure, how it melted so readily on the tongue. It seemed an insubstantial thing to summon them from warm beds before the sun was up in winter, yet it summoned Peg every Friday, and presumably also that old man, and other people before him. It summoned people every day, every hour—generations of medieval monks and other faithful through the centuries. Now Maddie wondered what, exactly, she should do—other than bow her head.

The Eucharist (had they called it that?) in the Bethel Hills Church of Holiness appeared only during the Communion service. It made its way down the rows of pews in a wide saucer, and the discs of bread slid over one another like coins. The ushers moved along the ends of the rows and sent the saucers down them, then followed them with the juice—never wine—pre-poured into small plastic cups. All of it was prayerful and steeped in meaning: "My body, broken for you."

Sitting next to Peg, Maddie contemplated it for what felt like the first time. She wondered what, if anything, she had expected from that monthly ceremony. What did she expect now from Mass, the weekly ingestion of actual body and blood?

Then, in a flash of perspective, Maddie was shocked by the strangeness of Christian belief. Whether symbolic or actual, the Eucharist presented itself as an obviously primitive ritual. More than that, it was savage. Communion, Maddie saw, was a barbaric practice, bordering cannibalism. It *was* cannibalism, in its way—but for the fact that they also believed it was the *God*-man they consumed.

What to make of that, Maddie wondered: Consuming God? They ate him and drank him—monthly, weekly, some of them daily, and they did it—Maddie had always done it, anyway—without much at all in the way of thought. Now the idea nearly panicked her; she felt she had been deceived. If there was meaning in the practice, then taking Communion was not to be taken lightly. And yet, all her life, pastor or priest had regularly instructed her in this cannibalistic practice; worse, had invited her to partake in the deliberate ingestion of God himself. And the instructions had been meted out—always, she thought—with bland deliberation, without a hint of fear or warning, as if the entire enterprise were commonplace and, on the whole, relatively insignificant.

Perhaps there was comfort in that, Maddie thought, calming herself. She had taken Communion all her life, largely innocent (until this bracing moment) of its weight. And she had been fine; they all had been fine. Who could know, she asked herself, the true meaning of this metaphysical practice? She couldn't—could anyone?—be expected to understand, to fully acknowledge or even grasp what lay behind this ceremony. Her task as believer was to accept it and to obey—and not (she reminded herself) to analyze it. Sitting there in the presence of the Host, of Christ himself, Maddie told herself that nothing would happen. Nothing happened to Peg; nothing happened to the old man who had just left the room—and this was, for them, weekly practice. No, nothing needed to happen, she told herself again, and she felt genuine relief. Nothing would happen; it was dangerous to think otherwise.

Now, some seventeen years later, Maddie was remembering this again for what felt like the first time. She had sat there with Peg and had managed to keep Vincent's year in her life behind her, the healings that had occurred and those that hadn't. In those days it had been easy to pretend that none of her history mattered. Frank was new and exciting to her at the time, and Catholicism, with its liturgy and mystery, had quickly overwhelmed her earlier Christian experience. She had been able to deny that history for a long time—but now she knew she had been pretending.

"Do you want to be healed of a paper cut?" That's what Vincent had asked, as if it were simple and straightforward, as if—in the scheme of what might be the eternality of things—arthritis, cancer, and even death were the equivalents of a paper cut. "Do you want to be healed of a paper cut?" he had said.

She was thirty-eight years old, but the answer swelled nonetheless in her throat. "Yes!" She would shout it now if she could choke the words out, if she could stand again in that early spring parking lot with the rain water pouring down the drain. "Yes!" She would shout at Vincent if she could make herself heard over five hundred miles and twenty-odd years. "I *do* want to be healed of a paper cut!" she would say. And could it be wrong to want such a thing? "I *do* want to be healed of cancer!" she would scream it. Only a person who had never suffered from it, who had never suffered at all, who had known and enjoyed only physical strength and health could suggest otherwise. She would tell him, "I *do* want to be healed of death!"

And she would also tell Vincent—if she could find him, corner him in some western Pennsylvanian shopping mall—that she *hadn't* been healed of cancer. That God—just as Vincent had intimated— hadn't done a thing, hadn't been bothered with the paper cut cancer that would have eaten her whole had she given it the chance. She hadn't been healed; she was in remission—and it was medical science that got her there.

Vincent had been right—and that had been the problem. God *could* heal. Sometimes God *did* heal. It was the *if* that had always vexed her; his inscrutable whim, his inaccessible ideal, his unattainable perfection that made her hold him at arm's length. She recalled her posture, the stance she had taken years ago when she married Frank: she would go to Mass, she would take Communion, and she would keep her distance from this capricious and terrible God.

What harrowed her anew was that old thought of ingestion, of body and blood, coming back to her: she was attending Mass, receiving Communion—real or symbolic—on a weekly basis. She was ingesting the God-man routinely, and despite the fact that she no longer had any expectations of him whatsoever, there was no way she could pretend to be keeping him at a distance.

---

On the Wednesday after Vincent prayed for her, Mrs. Adams visited the youth group unannounced, eyes streaming.

"Some of you were there last Sunday when your friend Vincent prayed for my hands." She held them up, but Maddie detected no difference. They were still knobby and knotted, the veins blue in translucent skin. "I wanted you to know that I haven't had any pain in my hands since Sunday, since, Vincent, you prayed for me," and she nodded in his direction. "I haven't taken any medication, either." Here her eyes welled again, and she dabbed at them with the handkerchief. "At first I thought I should take the medication, but then I thought that wouldn't be acting in faith." She looked at Vincent again and then at Nicky, as if asking assurance of her boldness. "And so I didn't take the medication, and I haven't needed to. The pain is gone. Gone!" She raised her hands and spread her bony fingers, and they did seem more flexible than they had; maybe her fingers looked the slightest bit straighter. She held her hands there, palms toward the teenagers, upturned to the ceiling in an attitude of worship. "All gone!" she said, her voice, strained by tears, now coming as a whisper.

The reaction of the youth group was a bit slow in coming. The spirit of expectation that dominated the Holiness Church was always watered down among its teenagers, who, in this instance, didn't know what to make of a sixty-something-year-old woman suddenly commandeering their meeting. Yet Mrs. Adams was unfazed by their delay and continued standing before them, wiping her nose and looking around at them expectantly. Nicky came to the rescue.

"Well, praise God, Mrs. Adams," he said, and he wrapped his arm around her shoulders. "Isn't that fantastic, you guys?" Someone in the back of the room began to applaud and soon the others joined in.

As she headed out of the room, Mrs. Adams turned to Vincent and said, "Thank you for praying, Vincent."

He was the only one in the room who didn't seem the least embarrassed. He was leaning back in his chair, rocking on its two back legs, and there was a kind of glowing rapture on his face. He grinned at her and said, "You're welcome."

⁓

Maddie had been silent through the youth group meeting, listening to the barrage of questions that erupted after Mrs. Adams left the room. She followed Nicky's and Vincent's answers, which curtailed understanding to recent events: Joey, Mr. Pavlik, and, of course, Mrs. Adams. And she endured Justine's smug smile, certain now that her friend had encouraged Mrs. Adams to ask Vincent directly for prayer.

Afterward, finally alone with him in his car, Maddie gave reign to her welling anger. "I don't get you, Vincent Elander," she said.

"What do you mean?" Vincent seemed surprised.

In truth, Maddie wasn't sure what she meant. But by the time the door closed behind Mrs. Adams, Maddie was already angry, and her anger had grown throughout the ensuing youth group meeting. Afterward, sitting next to him in the car, she discovered she had been angry with Vincent for quite a while, since long before Mrs. Adams had called plaintively down the pew. But words failed her; she couldn't grasp the source of her fury, and so she landed on what was nearest to hand. As they drove off church property, she practically shouted at him, her voice charged with accusation: "Vincent, you are the most confusing person I know. You are always saying one thing and then doing another. How am I expected to keep up? *Am* I expected to keep up? I hardly think so. You and Nicky handled it all just fine, almost as if you had planned it."

Vincent didn't venture a response, and in the moment she took to catch her breath, Maddie stole a look at him. His face, lit by suburban light and oncoming cars, was calm. He was listening, interested, unoffended, and perhaps still somewhat surprised.

His silence had no impact: Maddie's anger was enough to sustain the argument. She had new realizations and, alarmed by them, she went on: *Had* they planned it? Were Nicky and Vincent working this up? Had they *asked* Mrs. Adams to come and cry at their meeting so that they could then, in some half-official kind of way, tell the youth group about Vincent's gift? More realizations and accompanying alarm: Had they put Justine up to it, too? Vincent had said he wanted people to ask him to be healed—and Mrs. Adams was the first one bold enough to do it. Had Vincent asked Justine to talk to Mrs. Adams? Was that what was going on here?

"Maddie, Maddie," Vincent said soothingly, and his low tones made her recognize just how hysterical her own voice had become. He reached for her hand—but she pulled it away from him, decidedly gratified by this unkindness. Vincent sighed and returned his hand to the gearshift. "I don't know what you're talking about," he said.

Maddie was exasperated, furious that he might fail to engage her out of ignorance, and newly certain that he had been keeping all manner of things from her.

"I mean, Vincent," she said, "that I'm not even sure that you *want* to heal people, and then all *this* happens."

"I don't know what you mean by 'all this,'" he said quietly. "I was just as surprised as anyone that Mrs. Adams showed up tonight." He paused, perhaps reflecting on all of Maddie's accusations, as if wanting to be sure, in this window of Maddie's silence, to meet each of them in turn. "And I *don't* really know if I want to heal people, Mads. And what do you mean about Justine? She *told* Mrs. Adams to talk to me?"

Maddie took it in, knowing she ought to be somewhat mollified by this lack of complicity. But her fury—its source still somewhat unclear to her—was beyond any small resolution. She could push past Mrs. Adams and Justine, because she had anger enough for this.

"What do you mean when you say you don't know if you want to heal people?"

"I mean I don't know," Vincent said, still calm, even—could it be?—almost amused. He smiled and shook his head.

But his humor, even in something as small as a smile, provoked her further. What was funny about this?

"Why not?" Maddie asked. "Why don't you know if you want to heal people?" She had forgotten her own stake in it—what she had thought was *their* stake in it: sin preventing healing. At that moment she was aware only of Vincent's words and amusement as some kind of betrayal, tied ineluctably to his argument with Justine in the cafeteria and his words—only days ago—about the paper cut. Again she felt a distance between them, felt herself swinging wide of him as if they were carried on different currents. He was impossible to reach. "Why not, Vincent?" she said again. Her tone had changed; she felt it. Her anger was shifting; it was lined with sadness, and her question, hanging in the small and terrible space between them, felt to her like a last hope at understanding him.

"I just don't know what God wants, you know?" Vincent said. His words were gentle, uncomplicated by anger or, Maddie now recognized, fear. It was the tone he always took when arguing with Justine: Vincent wasn't afraid.

Was *Justine* afraid? She was certainly angry, but was she *afraid*? Was Maddie herself afraid?

Arguing like this with Vincent, Maddie realized that he talked with Justine as if, despite their disagreement, he wasn't opposing her at all. It wasn't personal.

Yet Maddie felt most decidedly that it *was*. "*Of course* you don't know what God wants, Vincent," she said. "No one knows what God wants!" and she was quiet for a moment, believing that, for once, she had the theological upper hand, that these irrefutable words would settle something in his mind.

Vincent handled the silence nicely, letting it continue longer than she liked and giving her time to see that she had simply agreed with him. He was already ahead of her; he knew what she meant.

All of this was dawning on Maddie when he added,

"It's just a question of *when*."

*When?* Maddie was lost again.

"What do you mean, Vincent?" She heard the anger in her voice, but could hear, too, that it was softer. Why must he always answer with riddles? Why always leave her in the dark?

Vincent reached for her hand again, and this time she let him take it. He held it on top of the gearshift as he drove. "I just mean that I think God wants people to be healthy and everything, but sometimes he doesn't want it when *we* want it, you know? Like some people get healed from terrible diseases, and some people die and *then* they are healed from terrible diseases. It's a question of *when*."

Maddie took a moment to absorb this. Lost again in Vincent's theology, she forgot about being angry. Why wouldn't God want everyone to be healed all the time? *Shouldn't* God want everyone to be healed all the time? "But Vincent," she said, "that means that sometimes God *does* want a person to be sick."

"For a time, yeah, I guess so," he said.

"Well, that's pretty mean," Maddie said, and she felt her anger kick in again, but not as strong as before, and she wasn't angry at Vincent.

"No," Vincent said, so quietly she wasn't certain she'd heard him. He lifted her hand and kissed it, holding it at his lips for a moment. Then, "Never mean," he said, and she didn't argue. The space between them was contracting, pulsing to a close.

Maddie was quiet, marveling at what Vincent seemed able to hold in tension: a God who could heal people but sometimes chose not to. She remembered the note Justine had passed to her on the day after the Pavlik potluck: *God doesn't want people to be sick!* That was the God she believed in—or always had, at least. But now Vincent presented her with another option, one that might be more accurate if only because it seemed to explain some things, like the death of

Justine's brother. God doesn't want people to be sick—unless he *does*, she thought. This was a difficult theology because it didn't entirely make sense, and it also made things ugly. It made God ugly.

"So that's why you don't want to heal people? Because you don't know if it's the right *time* to heal them?" she asked him.

Vincent smiled. "No," he said. "I'm not sure I want to heal people because if I do—or, you know, if God heals people through me—then people will never leave me alone."

"Vincent!" Maddie scolded. "See? That *is* mean!"

But Vincent was still smiling. "I'm kidding!" he said, and he chuckled. "That *would* be mean."

"Are you really kidding?" she asked, only half-serious. She knew he had to be kidding—wasn't he kidding? But his gift was extraordinary: what he seemed capable of offering was what anyone—everyone— would want. More than wealth, success, or beauty, people wanted to be healthy, and they wanted their loved ones to be healthy. If Vincent continued to heal people, then he was right: people would never leave him alone. The common experience of the last few weeks flashed before her eyes: this person and that stopping him in church, relating maladies, hinting at healing. It was only the beginning, and it was understandable that Vincent might not want to be able to offer it. "Really, Vincent?" she said again.

Vincent had released her hand. He pulled into her driveway, set the car in park, and then turned to face her, one hand still on the steering wheel, the other on the key in the ignition. He turned off the engine and grinned at her. "I'm mostly kidding," he said, "but praying for people all the time would be kind of a pain." He leaned forward over the steering wheel and looked up through the windshield—at what? At the stars, maybe? "I mean, it would be a pain until every sick person in the world was healed, anyway. Which would be seriously awesome."

"Awesome." It was the new word, one that had only recently crept into the collective vocabulary, and hearing Vincent use it in the context of healing and theology momentarily derailed her. The word seemed too young and immature for him—for them—somehow.

Maddie studied him for a moment, the line of his profile, his head tipped far back so he could see the sky, his shoulders hunched near his ears. Since the beginning, she had always known Vincent's seniority to herself. It was only a year's difference, but in life experience, in wisdom—even, despite its short tenure in his life, in faith—she felt he was light years ahead, vastly older somehow. And now here he sat scrunched at the steering wheel, peering up at the stars like a little boy.

"One thing's for sure, Mads. If you think about it," he said, "every time I've, you know, helped to heal somebody, you've been with me."

Maddie had to contemplate this for a moment. She ran through the short and astounding list of healings in her mind and found that he was right.

"All I'm saying is I like that," he said. He leaned away from her slightly, now peering out the side window as if tracking something, falling silent.

Maddie smiled. Her anger, potent only minutes before, was gone. She had forgotten it. "You like that, huh?" she asked him, smiling.

"Yes," Vincent said. He was smiling broadly now, still gazing out the window. She could see the soft curl of his lip in profile. "I like that," he said again.

---

Maddie sighed and shook herself. She tossed her head and ran her hands through her hair, which was long enough now to tuck behind her ears. She tucked it. Already this gesture had become a habit, a post-cancer behavior that helped her deal with the new, mild unruliness that her hair presented with. Which was fine. She couldn't care, she told herself, and meant it.

But that memory of Vincent—the one of him sitting in the car, staring out the windshield—that was a new one, or a new *old* one, rather, one her mind hadn't pulled from the annals in a long time. It was an unused memory like the Eucharistic adoration, which was, of the two of them, the memory she certainly preferred. She didn't like to think of Vincent, didn't like to see him so vividly next to her, didn't care to recall the way his hair brushed the collar of his T-shirt as he sat there leaning forward, peering up at the sky.

She shook herself again, irritated. Why should that memory be so painful? It had been nothing. An argument resolved, that was all. There were other, far more painful memories. Why should this one matter now?

It was simply a matter of processing, of that she was certain. She had been over other memories of Vincent countless times—the one of him weeping at the altar, for example. That was a memory lacking all piquancy, holding no lurking danger.

But this with the windshield. She laughed aloud at herself, again—so often—rueful. God, he was barely eighteen at the time; she was only sixteen. They had been children.

What was that game he used to play in the halls at school? The game Justine had hated: Vincent playing his joke of surprise, running down an unsuspecting student in the high-school hallway. He did it in fun, and it always ended with Vincent coming to a stop split-seconds before a collision. It ended with a startled shout, books dropping, papers spilling to the floor. He had done it to Maddie a time or two. And to Justine.

She had been right about it, in her way. Vincent couldn't know how his victim would react. For the most part, he was indiscriminately choosing someone to receive his attention. He had no idea, as Justine once posited, whether the person in question had a heart condition. It could have been dangerous.

But at the time, Maddie had laughed when it happened—either to her or to someone else. Because despite the momentary terror, in the end it was only Vincent standing there: grinning, harmless.

# 23

*M*any of the details—as significant as they might have been—were hazy. But in all of this unsolicited recollection, the adult Maddie began to recognize their selfish selectivity, and that this selection had always been her practice. Throughout those years of friendship with Justine, for example, her best friend's deceased little brother scarcely came to mind. And she was pressed to recall much of anything detailed about Vincent's family—the mother and little brothers who were always happy to see her. To Maddie they had been peripheral; they didn't really come to church; the substance of their lives didn't overlap with hers. But she had been many times to the Elanders' tattered house where it sat against the trolley tracks, and she knew that Vincent's mother held down two jobs to make ends meet.

Maddie simply hadn't cared about it at the time. She had been ignorant of parenting's rigors, ignorant (this was still the case) of what it meant to be poor. And yet being poor had been the context of Vincent's life. She knew that he shared the rusting Pacer with his mother. Maddie had been a little annoyed at how the car's ceiling fabric sagged. She had given no thought to the Elander's inability to afford repairs or to buy a new car—or to fix up their house or move to a different neighborhood or buy nice things.

Vincent's mother didn't come to church—she insisted she wasn't good enough for church people—and this had saddened him, but sometimes she let him bring his little brothers, Marty and Alex. Vincent always seemed older on those occasions. He would politely introduce them to people and keep an eye on their behavior. He was careful to teach them the ways of church, showing them to the right page in their hymnals and supervising how they took communion. When Marty turned eight that spring, Maddie and Vincent had taken him for a picnic and a game of catch in South Park. Alex had been six for much of that year, which was the same age as Maddie's Eli now.

Had Mrs. Elander known about the healings, Maddie wondered? She herself had never told her, assuming that Vincent would do so—but she was fairly sure he hadn't. Vincent teased his mother; jokes seemed to be their primary mode of communication. She couldn't imagine the two of them growing serious enough to discuss miracles. If he had told her, his mother would have thought he was kidding.

At thirty-eight years old and at twenty years' distance, Maddie saw the Elander family as if for the first time, on level ground with her rather than as she had seen them when she was a teenager: elevated by significance to Vincent, bathed in a Vincent-cast glow. Vincent had imbued them with the glory of his charisma and athleticism, his reputation at school tempered and enhanced by his faith. She saw now that they had been poor and struggling, perhaps mostly happy with one another but always straining beneath the weight of need. She never knew what had become of Mr. Elander except that he had left when Alex was a baby, and now she could imagine how Mrs. Elander had leaned on Vincent, how—with the other boys so young—Vincent would have been not only a son but also a companion to her. And how, between sports and school, church events and Maddie, Vincent had scarcely been at home.

Then, for a frightening moment, Maddie had a glimpse of Vincent as a real person, a boy of eighteen. He had done well in school on top of maintaining his three-season sports schedule. During the summers, he took a job to help pay the bills and had volunteered to mow the church lawn. What had church-life—what had faith in God, sudden and novel to him when she knew him—meant to Vincent, Maddie wondered. He had lost some friends over it, but he had explained it away: they just didn't like it that he wouldn't party with them anymore. It hadn't seemed to bother him, so Maddie had let it drop. In truth, they hadn't talked much about Vincent's faith at all, she thought now. He always seemed to assume that Maddie already knew. Yes, she thought, her memory had been selective.

And there were things of which, even at the time, she had been ignorant. She had not, for example, been consulted as to how the church should proceed once they were certain—or almost certain— that they had a healer in their midst. The fact of it was practically undeniable. Mrs. Adams did not limit her joyous news to the youth group, and there was the case of Dean Pavlik to reconsider in light of it, and the story of Joey Amoretti to revisit. Apparently Pastor McLaughlin, the elders, and unknown others had to respond to this, had to make faithful use of this gift that, through Vincent Elander, had apparently been bestowed on the Bethel Hills Church of Holiness.

No, Maddie was not privy to the plan until after it was made: a small healing service the following Sunday at five p.m., just prior to the regular evening service. And only for a few people, a select and invited number who said they would like Vincent to pray for them.

Again Maddie recognized her selfish lens on the world. For while she frequently envisioned Vincent with the anonymous children in the imagined oncology ward, she had never given real thought to the names listed as prayer requests in her own church bulletin—or to the lives those names represented. Yes, months earlier she had pointed out the column to Vincent, eager for him to see the potential for healing. But many of the names had been there for a long time, and Maddie had stopped noting them as individuals long ago.

Now the healing service was planned, and two names regained identity, their physical ailments clearly presenting urgent need.

Roland Taylor was in imminent danger of losing his second leg to diabetes. Maddie vaguely remembered news of his first amputation, which he had suffered while she was in grade school. The idea had been troubling to her, and she was relieved when he appeared post-surgery with a prosthesis, as she had feared confrontation—even hidden by a pant-leg—with a stump.

But Mr. Taylor had been cheerful about the enterprise and, other than a slight limp, seemed unaffected by it. After his recovery, he continued to volunteer in the two-year-old class every Sunday just as he had done when Maddie was two and as he had been doing, so the story went, for the past thirty years. He was in his late sixties now or maybe early seventies and was generally acknowledged as the church-wide grandfather. With regard to the potential second amputation, Mr. Taylor reportedly claimed he didn't mind it so much—but if God wanted to heal him of his suffering circulation and, better yet, his diabetes, then he was certainly open to it. He would be more than happy for Vincent Elander to pray for him.

Maddie hadn't seen Doris Senchak for a long time. The last time she had been in church—perhaps a year ago—she had been in a wheelchair. Her multiple sclerosis had progressed quickly, and now her suffering was acute. It had been Mr. Senchak who answered the invitation for this special healing prayer—he and their two little girls.

Roland Taylor and Doris Senchak were names Maddie was accustomed to seeing—or overlooking—in the church bulletin, but Susan Sweet's name had never been on the list of prayer requests. Thus she was surprised to learn that Susan was the third person Vincent would be praying for. Surprised and embarrassed. The fact of Susan Sweet was always embarrassing to Maddie, who hoped Susan had put out of her mind those days when, with her family, Susan had first started attending the Bethel Hills Church of Holiness. Maddie and Justine had been in the fourth grade at the time, hardly enough to know better—or so Maddie now told herself. Susan had made them uncomfortable and they, mere children, hadn't known how to react. Now Maddie regretted making fun of her strange walk: a severe limp and sweeping gait, her right leg swinging out to the side before bearing her weight.

Susan was the daughter of missionaries who had returned to the U.S. when Susan was a teenager. She had been born in Africa—Kenya or Botswana or someplace equally foreign to Maddie's mind—at a mission outpost with no doctor. It wasn't until Susan was trying to walk that her parents realized she had hip dysplasia, and by that time, it was too late to correct it. So Susan had learned to walk badly: her hip's permanent dislocation forced the rotation of her leg, hence the limp and sweep, limp and sweep marking every step.

Susan's response to their teasing had been to ignore it red-cheeked, and eventually Maddie and Justine had dropped it. Maddie liked to tell herself that they hadn't bothered Susan because she was so much older than they were: How could the witless teasing of nine-year-olds have any impact on a girl of seventeen? But Maddie knew that it must have hurt.

Yet Susan never confronted them about it. To Maddie's mind, Susan was the picture of accepting one's lot in life. While her peers went away to college, Susan had studied at Allegheny Community. She had a job—something along the lines of a social worker, Maddie was pretty sure—but still lived at home. She served the church in quiet ways, helping out in the kitchen for showers and potlucks and, on Communion Sundays, filling the plastic cups with grape juice. She smiled often but never said much, and on Sunday evenings, she often made her limping way to the church altar.

With her humility, service, and apparent contentment—and in comparison with Mr. Taylor and Mrs. Senchak—Susan's request for healing now surprised Maddie. "What's wrong with her?" she had asked Vincent.

"What's wrong with her? You've seen her walk, haven't you?" he said.

But that was not the limit of Maddie's blindness. There were other things of which she had been ignorant—or to which she had willingly closed her eyes. In the few weeks leading up to the healing service, what had been the general consensus regarding it? Had all of the Bethel Hills congregants been universally expectant, fine with the notion that Vincent—a boy of eighteen, a new attendee and recent convert, a relative nobody—could heal people? Yes, Maddie had been present for those hallway encounters, those halting conversations in the foyer in which belief in healing had been implied, but what of the many people who had not sought him out?

How did they feel about these upcoming, hoped-for healings when, prior to this, many people they had prayed for simply *hadn't* been healed? Yes, occasionally miracles had taken place among them, enough to stoke the flames of belief, but these were few and far between. Many hadn't been healed; many had died—and again Justine's little brother came to mind. In the thoughts of the Bethel Hills congregation, what marked Vincent as a likely minister of healing? Did they assume that he simply had more confidence than others, the kind of New Testament faith that could truly move mountains?

And did any of them venture mentally beyond this upcoming service and into the wake of its potential success? Or was Justine alone in her visions of the media and publicity and all these might mean: the descent on their congregation of television crews, the ensuing clamor for more miracles, a parking lot full of the wounded and weary, traffic winding around the block, each sufferer understandably longing for thirty seconds with Vincent?

Maddie had considered none of this. Her vision had been decidedly of the tunnel variety, true only to her own concerns. In the short days leading to the healing service, Maddie deserted her carefully cultivated concern for Justine. She set aside the theological debate that had churned in her mind and conversations. The disciplines that had so recently marked her life were abandoned by reason, she decided, of fatigue and fruitlessness. She simply hadn't liked staying away from Vincent, and even when doing so hadn't been able to keep him out of her mind—and could she be at all sure of the impact of her restraint? Her most recent conversation with him on that matter, the one that ended with his staring at the stars, certainly suggested that her actions—or those of anyone else—had precious little to do with anything. God decided on the *when* and *who* of healing. It was that simple.

Looking back on this more than twenty years distant, Maddie considered what she had long told herself about those days: of course she had been self-absorbed, and this was understandable. Maddie had not been unusual. She had exhibited thinking and behaviors that were common, normal, even expected for a teenager. She hadn't been aware at the time that the stakes were so high. But this didn't make her any less sorry for it now.

It was a Sunday, the very afternoon of the healing service, a confluence of events that didn't matter to Maddie at the time. This wasn't premeditated. Vincent's mother and brothers had been at home when they got there; it wasn't anyone's fault that Marty had a Little League game, and there wasn't time before the service for Maddie and Vincent to go along: they had to be a back at church in a little over an hour. But they wouldn't need the car. Nicky would stop by and pick them up on his way.

Alone together in Vincent's house for an hour. What could anyone expect of them? Maybe they should have spent their time in prayer. That's probably what God would have wanted, the adult Maddie thought. But was that all the help he proffered? She had looked for him in the DiAngelos' garden; she had whispered to him in the family crèche. And he had shouted his reply through a Camaro's bumper, a blue-eyed boy, and her own weak, instinct-driven flesh.

What, exactly, did he have to say?

That afternoon, alone together in Vincent's house for an hour, they had sex for the first time. Or was it the first time, when so many times before they had come so close? What difference, exactly, did fractional distance make or where, exactly, their clothes lay? Up to their ankles in the shallow end or over their heads in the diving well, wasn't it all the same? Maddie had been losing her virginity by degrees, over a period of months. This latest development, this moment of stunning satisfaction, this consummation was mere technicality.

Oddly, she thought, Maddie didn't remember much in the way of details. There was more flesh this time, that much she knew. The complete nakedness had surprised and pleased her; she had taken it for granted then that this time there was to be no stopping. They weren't even going to try.

The tears and prayers of repentance were the same, as was Vincent's ardent belief that those prayers had been heard and answered.

But God's answer to Maddie was in what came next, in the slow but certain slippage, the rock fall that found her scrambling for escape. And she *had* escaped, eventually. It had been a painful extraction, but it wasn't—not according to God, apparently—anything that she didn't deserve.

What saddened her, what pained and alarmed her, was that it still didn't seem to be over. She had put it behind her. She was a faithful Catholic now. She was married to Frank. She was a loving if imperfect mother to their three sons. Yet here was Vincent, insistently present to her beyond all reason, when she had given him up long ago.

Despite its significance, there was only a single vivid memory of that afternoon, and this came to her now. Between their gasps of pleasure and the obligatory prayers of repentance, Maddie had stood up from the sofa and walked naked to the bathroom. She knew that Vincent watched her go; she could feel his gaze; she was proud, in that moment, of her brazenness, of their now undeniable intimacy. Moments later, Vincent came to the door and grinned at her where she stood at the sink, several feet away. He didn't say a word, but she saw that he had her bra in his hand. Still grinning, he snapped it across the room at her as one might do with a rubber band, and they had both laughed.

It had been over twenty years, but Maddie could still see him standing there. Vincent, full length, naked. There were the lines and the turn of his arms and thighs, his torso, the color of his skin. The taut musculature of his calves. The thickness of his neck and the breadth of his shoulders. The vein of hair that darkened and ran down below his navel. The way he planted his feet in the hallway carpet, with the toes of his left foot over the threshold of the bathroom, touching the cracked tile, the second toe just longer than the first.

There it was: God's answer. And immediately she was angry that it was so obvious, so true and so maddeningly impossible. It was the long memory of the body, the claim on the tangible by the untouchable. Any effort she might make to be rid of it was fruitless; it was inscribed somehow in her genetic code: the insoluble, incomprehensible bond between body and soul.

Instinctively, Maddie reached for the breast she had lost. Under her shirt, under her bra strap, raising with her fingers the prosthetic pad that balanced her appearance. She ran her fingertips over the scars, following them to that knot in the field of flat skin.

Numbness answered her there, mute, honest.

# 24

*T*he request showed up in Frank's email: Francesca asking to be his friend on Facebook. He was all wry criticism. Friends? This seemed a strange proposition when they hadn't spoken in years. In all honesty, he couldn't say that he knew her even a little now, and he could definitely make the argument that he hadn't really known her in college, when they were dating, when they were sleeping together. So would he agree, through social media, that they were friends? It seemed disingenuous, at best. The entire Facebook enterprise—he had come to believe—was by its very nature disingenuous, scratching itches people didn't realize they had, itches they might do better in exploring with a therapist rather than posting their daily thoughts and impulses on the world-wide web or, worse, critiquing those of their so-called "friends."

He and Francesca weren't friends at all. Not really. They had parted amicably enough—if one could call her hasty, mid-semester departure amicable. It had been a Monday morning. Only the night before they had enjoyed a particularly amorous evening together, all candlelight and incense in her dorm room. And now here she stood under an umbrella on the sidewalk just next to a campus mailbox, calling to him as he was walking to class, telling him that she was going.

He hadn't understood what she meant as there had been no

warning, no contextual conversation that might precipitate her withdrawal from her classes, from the college, from his life. He had answered her, understandably (though later he felt foolish for it; he had replayed his foolishness in his mind more times than he cared to remember, how he hadn't carried an umbrella that morning, and then she had made her announcement and walked away, and he, absent all rational thought, suddenly absent all emotional mooring, stood there like a fool in the rain), "Where?"

And she had said matter-of-factly: "New York. Civilization."

So he couldn't agree that they were friends actually, because there was that event in November 1986 to point to and then Francesca's consistent failure to respond to any phone calls or letters he sent to her parents' house. The rumors he had of her were not entirely believable ones, considering their sources: those she had called friends and sometimes drank with and who had been victims of her vicious derision behind their backs. It was Father Tim who had helped him see that the recovery of his own life was far more likely than any recovery of this relationship and also far more worthwhile. It was just as well to think of Francesca as having fallen off the map, so to speak—a cliché not without its appealing images, and these made Frank smile.

What to do, then, with this invitation of "friendship?" He had assumed for years that she was out there, carrying on with life. But was contact worth inviting—or, in this case, accepting?

He had spotted her for the first time at the beginning of his freshman year. She was hard to miss. In a sea of baggy sweatshirts and pegged jeans, Francesca's bohemian look caught his eye. But even if it hadn't, he would have spotted her lustrous hair, all long and shining ringlets that suggested themselves as having naturally occurred— unlike the teased, overworked hair of so many of the girls he knew at the time.

She radiated naturalness, he thought. Makeup free, fair-skinned. Her complexion had a dewy clarity and seemed also full, almost buoyant. In truth, he had wondered how she could be real: so beautiful, so without artifice. Her only ornaments were jewelry, which she wore in abundance. That first time he saw her, she'd been wearing a long, flowing skirt (this was almost always the case) and a loose tank-top, and her right upper arm had been adorned with armbands, like something out of Egyptian mythology.

Frank was smitten.

The miracle (for in this instance he would need one: she was a junior, he a mere freshman; how to effect an introduction?) was that he was unable to get into the lit survey course he should have been taking, and so found himself enrolled in one at the 300 level, something on literature of the Caribbean. He wasn't terribly interested in it, but then here came Francesca, jingling her way into the room. Enrollment was low, and she was a vibrant participant in the discussion. The professor seemed to know her from other classes, and she was extraordinarily well-read, making comments about the writing of so-and-so on such-and-such, citing "seminal works" on the impact of colonialism, reading obscure but fascinatingly relevant passages aloud. Frank found himself taking extra care when preparing for the class, and soon enough Francesca took notice of him.

One day he managed to walk out of the room with her, managed to keep conversation going across the quad, told her (lying) that he had eaten and enjoyed plantains. That became a joke between them; it was their private euphemism: "plantains" became code for sex, and for years after Francesca left, Frank wanted nothing to do with them— with them or with anything having to do with the Caribbean, because it always made him think of Francesca.

For a long time after Francesca left, there had been a lot he wanted nothing to do with because it made him think of Francesca.

But it wasn't fair, he now realized, and he shouldn't have thought of it as so completely awful. Yes, there had been serious immaturity on both their parts, but it hadn't been all bad. Like himself, Francesca was a writer. She was passionate about writing, and where Frank had decided to major in journalism, it had been a decision based less on passion for writing and more on the fact that he would never make a professional tennis player, and he didn't want to spend the rest of his life giving lessons.

Francesca had made him passionate about writing. Lying with her head in his lap, her blouse open too far and exposing more of that dewy skin, the rounding swell of a breast, she read aloud to him, brilliant paragraphs by Chandler, Lessing, even Dickens. She waxed rhapsodic over aptly worded phrases and the *mot juste*, that perfect word that shaped the tone of everything. "If you can find that," she would say to him of his work, of her own, "then everything takes care of itself." It was Francesca who had gotten him reading the dictionary. At the same time, she was fiercely critical of the writing of her peers. Such criticism was the subject of much of her discourse, especially on Tuesday afternoons after her writing class met for workshops.

"God, it's awful," she would say as soon as Frank was in her sights, even if he was several paces down the hall. She processed it all aloud to him, launching immediately into complaints of miserable syntax and no ear for rhythm and subject matter that sounded like it was "to a person," she said, "coming from old men on their deathbeds recalling lost love. There's more to life than love," she said, and Frank thought she was right.

There was, for instance, travel and politics and excellent writing, which made Frank wish he had more travel under his belt than the summer-after-eighth-grade trip that his family had taken out West. Francesca disdained even that. "What good is a geyser?" she had said, and Frank wondered the same thing. It had been a long trip in a hot car and everyone had gotten cranky, and then they arrived just after the geyser did its predictable spew and so had to wait around and everyone had been hungry. What good *was* a geyser when places like Florence were in the world? Florence and all of Tuscany, for starters, or Budapest, or Nepal?

Francesca was going to all of these places. She was destined for them and then some. She, for one, wasn't going to be stuck all her life in the bread-basket of America. Pittsburgh, she said, Cleveland—these were outposts, barely civilized. Frank's offered arguments signified nothing. So what if each city had art museums and symphonies? The closest the United States came to being civilized was New York, and maybe L.A.

Chicago? Frank had suggested, but Francesca countered that Chicagoans were too caught up in football (problems shared, by the way, with Pittsburgh and Cleveland and the host of other mid-sized cities that might otherwise claim to be civilized). Football she characterized as thinly veiled brutality; sport in general lacked art. The base competition of most sports, she held, was demeaning to human potential.

Frank thought she might be among the most competitive people he had ever known, but he certainly never voiced this opinion, able to argue against it even within himself: she simply held herself to high standards; she held everyone to high standards. What could be wrong with that? On the contrary, it was admirable.

Sometimes Frank felt afraid of her. He had a prescience of her capacity to devastate him. She had claimed there was more to life than love, and in his eagerness to please her, Frank had agreed. He couldn't possibly tell her now that he loved her, but he was relatively sure it was true. He had never felt this way about someone before, but he wasn't sure she'd like it. In truth, he was never sure that she was his girlfriend in the first place. It wasn't that he saw her with other men; it wasn't that they weren't intimate in every way. It was just that she seemed— in every way—so dissatisfied.

She relentlessly begged him to let her read his writing. She had discovered his dog-eared journal where he had failed to hide it on his dorm-room desk. But there was no way, he told her, that he was going to let her. He *didn't* say what he ardently felt: it was too early in their relationship for this kind of exposure; they had been dating—if that's what it was—for less than two months.

"What do you write?" she had asked him coyly, her fingertips planted on the wire-bound notebook, wrist arched.

That had been a frightening moment. Yes, he loved her teasing him, her kittenish grin, the tendril of hair that fell in front of her left eye. But he was terrified of exposure and certain rejection, of the inevitable post-reading critique.

"What do you write?" she had asked him again, and he answered he didn't know. It wasn't a diary. It was, he didn't know, reactions to things. Responses.

"Poetry?" she asked.

"God no," he said, and she was pleased. Poetry was to be left to the experts. Real poetry, Francesca had said, months, weeks, days before, was only written by genuine talent.

It was late October when he gave in, and he saw in retrospect how absurdly foolish this was. He was less than ten weeks into his college career, but it had felt to him like a long time already, and his relationship with Francesca (discussing poetry, drinking wine and smoking pot, breathing incense and listening to Joni Mitchell into the small hours of the morning) had seemed to him remarkably sophisticated. At the time he felt he had aged a decade; he was light-years beyond the pimply adolescence of high school—and so much of this was due to Francesca's influence.

It was one of those unbelievable Pennsylvania autumn days when the sun is shining and the warm air returns and one imagines that maybe this winter, for once, won't be a hard one. They had been alone in Francesca's dorm room for a long while, and for about half an hour had been leafing through her atlas. They were plotting the course of their future travels, Francesca having told him she thought they should spend the summer backpacking in Europe.

Drunk on Francesca's assumption that they could make plans for next summer, that they would still be "together" then, Frank hadn't concerned himself with his need for a summer job or the potential expense of such a trip. Neither had he considered how very un-Francesca-like such an enterprise seemed. "We'll stay in youth hostels," she had said; "We'll eat on the cheap." He hadn't entertained the image of her skirts tangled in her ankles on the dirty floor of an Italian train station. Instead, he had fallen more completely in love with Francesca than before (if, indeed, this *was* love), his mind swelling with what his life would be with this woman: how they would live together in Europe and both of them would be writers, and the dust of their middle-America upbringing would be washed away by European rains and snows on the steppes of central Asia. Because Francesca had convinced him of this, too: middle-America *was* dusty; it had little more to offer than dust.

It was this Francesca-intoxication, the spoken possibility of a future together that propelled Frank to new heights of intimacy. Francesca suddenly announced that it was a gorgeous day and they should haul a blanket out on the quad and lie there in the sun, and Frank had immediately agreed and then gone off to get his journal. Still riding the incandescent vision of his future, basking in the gift of late October warmth, Frank had read aloud from the journal to her, who lay with her head in his lap, the glorious mane of her curls spread out over his thighs and her shoulders and the blanket beneath them both.

She had listened with her eyes closed, and then she had listened with them open, and in stolen glances Frank saw reflected in her eyes the branching articulations of the oak tree that he leaned against, their leaves already gone to rust. She listened without comment for a long time, and Frank, still intoxicated, stopped reading excerpts and instead read an entire piece, a non-fiction narrative about building a model airplane with his grandfather. After weeks of being afraid to share his writing, he was now emboldened by this very daring act he was undertaking, as if in reading to her he was showing her that he wasn't afraid of her or anything else. He would take her to Italy that summer and would impress her by suggesting they go further east: Prague, Budapest. They wouldn't just visit Nepal someday; they would live there. As he read, images of Nepal rose in his vision: the green steppes, the folds of the mountains. He would be the one to take Francesca there.

He finished reading and closed the journal with finality, laying it beside him on the blanket, on a tendril of her hair. Her eyes were closed again. She had listened, immobile. And now, without opening her eyes, she said to him, "If you can write like that, you can write anything."

Over the course of his career, Frank had certainly received praise for his writing. His professors had lauded his work; his editors loved it. He had received various awards; he had been quoted on the news and in trade journals. He had been asked to speak at conferences; he had contributed articles to national magazines; he had recently been invited to write a book. He had also made up stories for his sons, creating a cast of characters both fantastic and familiar; his sons asked for news of them by name. And Maddie loved his writing, even clipping his column regularly from the newspaper and squirreling it away in an album somewhere.

And yet this phrase from Francesca was the one he heard most often in his head. Sometimes he said it to himself, hunched over his laptop, pondering a column or article that wasn't coming. He had wrestled with it over the years: Was it okay to be encouraged—even inspired— by something that an ex-lover had said to him once? Her words—like any trace he might have of her—should have been banished long ago, right? They should be discarded as less than useless, as insignificant and meaningless compared to what he and Maddie had right now.

Besides, he had long ago decided that most—if not all—of what Francesca said was bunk. Her estimation of nearly everything had been rooted in profound insecurity; she had perceived the world through an insatiable need to promote herself.

And yet she had said this to Frank: "If you can write like that, you can write anything." There was no self-promotion there, no wry critique. Just praise.

Frank had decided that it was okay. Francesca's words, detached from the source, could resonate with as much meaning as any encouragement made by a writing professor or an editor. They were just words, and they were sometimes helpful—especially in the pits of emptiness that every writer faces, those appalling moments when he felt beyond doubt that he had nothing to offer as a writer, nothing for anyone to read at all. Those words were very helpful, especially because Francesca—vehement critic of her college writing group and the world at large—had said them.

Frank clicked, "Accept."

———— ∞∞∞ ————

They had arrived with Nicky at the healing service to find the small group cheerfully waiting for them: Pastor McLaughlin, the three candidates for healing, a few family members and elders. In truth, Maddie supposed this much. Beyond the three people Vincent was to pray for, she wasn't sure who had been there; her memory of this event, too, was vague, as if there had been many subsequent ones like it and routine had bred oblivion.

She was certain that the service itself was brief—Vincent never prayed for long—and afterward Maddie had only a few lasting impressions. The first was the sound of Mrs. Senchak's breathing, or her effort to breathe. It was low and scraping, monstrously heavy. Every breath sounded as though she was lifting something, hoisting with great strain something that clearly wasn't meant for her to carry. The thought was distressing: Mrs. Senchak didn't look as if she had any strength at all; her body was shrunken, curled crookedly into her wheelchair, and every breath came at the price of that tremendous effort. Maddie had a fierce desire to help her, a sense that all of them should be rushing to her aid, and she wished that Mrs. Senchak were fighting against something outside herself so that any of them, somehow, could help.

But all they could offer was prayer: this gathering around her, laying their hands on her frail limbs and then mentally pressing—was that what prayer was?—their best hopes toward God. Throughout that prayer, throughout the ensuing church service, it was Mrs. Senchak's scraping breath that resounded at the back of Maddie's mind. Any perhaps appropriate thoughts of guilt were submerged in the noise of that grinding effort.

And it was likely that Mrs. Senchak's breathing was what almost made her—and therefore Vincent—miss her other recollection of that event. Susan Sweet had called his name several times already before Maddie registered it. The prayer was finished; everyone was standing around, chatting casually because they had put all their most earnest and important thoughts into praying. Maddie hadn't engaged in the small talk; she wanted desperately to get out of there, and in looking toward the door she noticed that Susan was standing behind Vincent, looking up expectantly at him. "Vincent," she was saying. Her voice—Maddie had seldom heard it—was almost unbelievably soft and high-pitched.

Immediately, Maddie tugged at his arm: "Vincent," she said, smiling at Susan and nodding Vincent in her direction.

"Oh, hey Susan," Vincent said.

"I just wanted to say thanks," Susan said, and she reached out to shake his hand.

Vincent grinned and took her hand in his. "Well, you're welcome," he said. "Always glad to pray."

"Thank you," Susan said again, and Maddie, already agonized by Mrs. Senchak's strain for air, was newly discomfited by this interaction. She longed more fervently for the exit.

"You're welcome," Vincent said again, unfazed by the awkwardness, still shaking Susan's hand, still smiling.

Susan was blushing. Maddie could see it: that awful and embarrassing blush she had noticed before on certain complexions, that started all in blotches on the throat and climbed its way up the neck.

"Thank you," Susan said, one more time. In a motion, she dropped both her gaze and Vincent's hand. He returned to another conversation, and Maddie watched Susan make her limping way toward the door.

— ∞ —

This time, Maddie didn't think to wait for news. Instead, she tried to wrench from her mind the terrible memory of Mrs. Senchak struggling for air. The sound was like an earworm, an odious, arrhythmic, tuneless song her brain wouldn't release. In any break in conversation, any lull in classroom noise, or—most horribly—lying in her bed at night, Maddie found that this ragged effort at breathing was a constant in her ears.

Once or twice over the course of those days, the thought of her recently lost virginity also occurred to her, and Maddie considered that she ought to feel guilty, but this she angrily dismissed. At best, guilt seemed self-centered and, at worst, an unreasonable demand. She felt that her sin (if that is what it was), weighed together on some cosmic scale with an agonized Mrs. Senchak, was decidedly tipped in Maddie's favor. She found it inconceivable that God should demand repentance if—rather *when*—it seemed clear that he was clearly culpable for such suffering.

More calmly, she again considered Vincent's understanding, the eternal *when* which would mean resolution, health, peace. It sounded good in theory, but she found it fell short of comfort when one considered the three very real people he had prayed for. "When" in God's mind, in the perception of the eternal, was to the time-bound a rather hopeless proposition. There were no guarantees.

And if there were no guarantees, then there was certainly no safety. Yet God insisted on repentance and devotion: Vincent, Pastor McLaughlin, Mr. Gillece all agreed on that. The God of Sunday school, of lisping "Jesus Loves Me," was more and more certainly becoming—to Maddie's mind—a charade.

So she turned her mind again to the suffering ones they had prayed for on Sunday. She imagined Susan's recovery—it seemed by far the easiest. A mere realignment of the bones, just as her own healing had been. Maddie envisioned it: Susan waking, opening her eyes, remembering the prayer and still feeling the warmth from Vincent's hands on her hip. She would sit up and slide her feet to the floor; she would stand; walking would suddenly be effortless.

But there was no news of this—and on Tuesday she learned that Mr. Taylor's amputation had been scheduled for Thursday morning.

"What does your boyfriend make of this scenario?" Justine asked her, leaning in at Maddie's locker.

"Sometimes these things take time, Justine," Maddie answered her, putting her off. She knew what Vincent thought ("it was a question of *when*"), and she herself was still holding out some hope. For Justine's sake, for her own, she could point to Mrs. Adams and Mr. Pavlik both as examples of delayed reaction—until Justine clarified that they didn't know exactly *when* Mrs. Adams had been healed.

"It might have happened that very day," she said. "It's just that we didn't *find out* about it until Wednesday."

Justine would have to plague Vincent about it, too; she couldn't reserve her little comments to conversation at Maddie's locker. She talked about it openly during Wednesday's lunch.

"So, it would seem that Mr. Taylor's going to have that other foot off after all," she said, and Vincent didn't say anything—which, apparently, wouldn't do.

"What do you make of that?" she asked, and she tapped Vincent's hand twice with a sharp index finger.

Vincent looked at her blankly. "Am I *supposed* to make something of it?"

"Well, I would think you would—" Justine paused, leaning in, and Maddie detected something akin to smugness, something like I-told-you-so, "have an explanation or something."

"I guess I'm not the guy to explain everything that God does or doesn't do," Vincent said.

Justine was unsatisfied. "Well, who is, then?"

"I'm not sure anybody is," he answered her.

"Shut-up, Justine," Maddie said, surprising herself. She was sick of the antagonism, and now that she knew—if she didn't exactly *understand*—Vincent's perspective, she found she couldn't defend it. Neither did she want to. Anyway, if anyone should be taken to trial here, it was God, not Vincent. But she still hadn't the nerve to propose this, and Justine wouldn't buy it, anyway.

"Excuse *me*," said Justine, annoyed and then, perhaps, taken aback. Maddie had never spoken to her like this, and immediately she regretted it. Her voice softened.

"Besides," Maddie said, "who is to say that Mr. Taylor isn't healed already, anyway?" Again, her own words surprised her. Even as she was saying them, she knew she didn't believe them, hope as she might that they were true. Her question, she realized without looking at him, was directed as much at Vincent as Justine. Would she forever be caught between sides? She wished that Vincent would take up the argument, would offer an explanation for God, would address for all of them this question of *when*. What was he suggesting? Did one, in asking for healing, have also to be specific, to throw in the details so that God would know what you were talking about? "Please heal Mr. Taylor, and kindly do so before Thursday. *This* Thursday." Maybe that would do the trick.

But Vincent did not seem to conceive of Maddie's anger and so didn't receive the subtle dig implied in her question. Maddeningly, he simply agreed with her: "Who's to say?" he repeated.

Justine stared at Vincent, then looked at Maddie, and then back at Vincent again. Finally, "Who's to say," she said, and again left the lunch table.

Maddie decided not to be bothered by it. She was even glad to see her go. There was more at stake here than Justine's friendship, and time enough—if she had the willpower, if she could ever grasp understanding for herself—to explain it to Justine. Meanwhile, her mind relentlessly replayed Mrs. Senchak's breathing. And on Wednesday evening, when Maddie arrived for youth group, Susan Sweet still had her limp. Maddie walked a safe distance behind her into the church building, not at all wanting to follow up or engage. The limp, she observed, made every step look like an interrupted stagger; her view must pitch horribly over the course of even a few feet.

It was a question of *when*. Mr. Taylor's surgery was scheduled for the next morning. "*This* Thursday." There had been no word about Mrs. Senchak.

# 25

$\mathcal{F}$rank was taken off guard by how the communication between them blazed up immediately, like dry leaves taken to a match. He would swear Francesca posted something to his public "wall" within seconds of his accepting her "friendship."

"Hey, stranger!" it said, all breezy, so familiar. Was it possible that things should be familiar after so much time and through the artifice of social media? And they were different people now. She hadn't really known him in college; he hadn't been then the person he'd become. How familiar could they be? And yet there it was, and Frank was quietly impressed by how, yes, familiar it felt. Within the first few days of this public conversation, they were hinting at old, private, long-forgotten and now suddenly clear jokes that would be nonsense to people reading from the outside—and yet it all felt okay to him because it was right there on his Facebook wall, out there in plain sight for anyone to see. He wasn't hiding anything.

She said she was doing great, loved Seattle, worked in publishing and made time for some writing of her own on the side, had been published here and there, mostly local. She had been married once (this was surprising) but it hadn't worked out (less surprising), one daughter (aged 12) who was, she said, "very much her own person," leaving it to Frank to interpret. In fact, she left a lot for Frank to interpret. Nearly everything she said underscored his earliest intimations: she wasn't the person he remembered; they didn't know one another at all. And yet there were those old jokes, those echoes of familiarity, as though, in communicating with her, Frank was hearing strains of songs he had once been accustomed to listen to. And she was eager to hear about Maddie and the kids, so sorry about Maddie's battle with cancer. He could imagine her laughter when he told her about his adventures as the Little League coach: he hadn't thought she would be interested in such things.

But she seemed glad to tell him she had come to appreciate sports; was actually embarrassed to report that her current favorite was cricket ("I know: I'm ever the anglophile, right, Frank?" she wrote); still couldn't quite stomach the self-absorbed pageantry of the Olympics, but what are you going to do. To which he responded that her critique of self-absorption was amusing. She caught his drift and wrote, "It was that obvious, was it?"

She said she loved his articles; he was pleased to learn she had tracked his career somewhat and now read his work from time to time by way, of course, of the Internet. And she apologized for being such an "absolute fool" in college (they had moved the conversation, by this time, to the private messages because it seemed simpler; it was merely practical to do so, Frank told himself). "You were wise to be shed of me," she said. But Frank didn't respond to that comment specifically, in part because he didn't know what to say. *She* had left *him*, he wanted to argue. There had been no wisdom about it, not on his part. The wisdom had come later.

Via email (Francesca had switched it to email; it was more convenient for both of them), he asked about her marriage, and she said that it hadn't lasted very long. It was when she was living in Italy (Oh, thought Frank, so she did manage to live internationally for a while). An honest-to-goodness Italian (which, he supposed, meant *not* an Italian-American, ubiquitous in pockets of "uncivilized" American cities) whose *machismo* had turned out to be more than she'd bargained for. "Anyway," she wrote, "I'm not very good at relationships." He left that comment alone, too, and instead made some jokes about the Mafia, to which she replied, intriguingly, "Don't get me started."

He asked if her new appreciation for sports had induced her to try any. Her response, again, was full of amused self-critique: "The most I am able to muster is an occasional yoga class," she said, which he replied was fitting. "No," she replied, "there's no athlete to speak of in this body."

It made him glad—it truly did, in what he told himself was a pure-hearted, friendly way—to be in touch with her again. It was healing, he might say, suddenly wondering if he had been quietly wounded by Francesca and so, in ways he hadn't realized, had been limping along all this time. Yes, Father Tim had helped him to get past Francesca. His had been essential help at that time. But there was nothing like this contact—this friendship—to bring him past the something-or-other of pain that he was newly aware had existed all these years.

If someone had asked if they were in contact again, he would gladly have admitted it. He meant to say as much in an assuring note to The Priest, who, on seeing his friendship with Francesca on Facebook, had sent him a pithy text: "Francesca = friend?" it had said.

Frank meant his response ("Yep") to be followed by a phone call, but the kids had kept him busy that night and he had forgotten to follow through. He found that texts, emails, Facebook messages all had the tendency to drop below one's sight-line, so to speak, which was what happened with this one. The upshot: by the time Francesca had that layover in Raleigh—maybe months after initial contact—by the time he had agreed to meet her in an airport bar ("Just for an hour or so. I don't want to be too late getting home"), he hadn't spoken to Father Tim in several months.

Not that he needed to talk with Father Tim. Frank knew where he stood. And there was something (he wouldn't be smug) satisfying about Francesca's life as she described it. Simply seeing her would affirm for him—and perhaps, for her, too—what he had long ago decided was true: the sufficiency of a quiet life. One needn't live in Milan or Tibet. One could write for a more humble newspaper. And one could have a perfectly good life.

Frank was amazed at how much she looked the same. Despite the business clothes and the lines around her eyes. Despite the changed hair—considerably shorter now, but still all in curls—he would have known Francesca anywhere.

Thursday came, and Mr. Taylor's amputation was carried out as planned. Thursday—a mere four days after the prayer service. Maddie never knew if he had asked for a delay. Did Mr. Taylor want to wait on the healing that might, as yet, take effect? But doctors concerned with the gangrenous effects of lost circulation have understandable limits to their patience, and Mr. Taylor had run out of time.

He was cheerful during their visit, not quite sitting up in bed, but with the foot of the bed raised, and the lump of his legs under the sheets coming to an abrupt end just past his knees. The sight of this sickened Maddie; she grew dizzy and her vision began to blur.

It was Mr. Taylor who noticed her pallor and instructed Vincent to get her a chair. Maddie slid into it, bending her body in half and resting her head on her knees, not looking up when the nurse came in, embarrassingly, to check on her, and barely recovering before it was time to leave. Throughout the visit she remained in her somewhat crippled position, listening to Vincent and Mr. Taylor laughing and chatting together, wishing she had more strength—from what, for what? How could either one of them, disappointed by the unpredictable unkindness of their God, find room for laughter?

Within the month, they found themselves pulling up in the gravel driveway of the Senchak's raised ranch. Mr. Senchak had asked them to come pray again and Maddie had felt some small hope: Who could know the effectiveness of repeated prayers? Mr. Gillece—his altar-going issue still a mystery—came to mind. And spring was fully arrived then; the crabapples were in bloom. But Maddie had felt her hope's foolishness in the driveway, where the basketball hoop leaned at an infirm angle, its net come loose on one side.

Inside, the atmosphere was one of weary endurance. The curtains were drawn in the living room, staining everything a muted red; a hospital bed consumed the far wall, and there, in its center, lay the shrunken form of Mrs. Senchak. Her knees were drawn up, her body curled, further diminished, if possible, since the prayer service a few weeks before. There was only the sound of her labored breathing, slowed since Maddie last heard it, and cruelly heavier. The sense of any lifting was gone; her breath was something dragged now: a deep rasp like a shovel drawn over pavement.

Vincent crossed the room to her right away. He laid one hand on her shoulder and her eyes rolled up to his face; with his other hand, he stroked her hair. Maddie followed but held back, standing near the foot of the bed, pained by Mrs. Senchak's worsened state. Arms like sticks, her flesh limp. The disease was consuming her; there would be nothing left soon but the angular lines of her skeleton and the flaccid husk of her skin.

Vincent had prayed for her, and Maddie had fixed her gaze on the drawings, the construction paper tacked haphazardly to the wall. A garden, a snowman. An airplane flying through clouds and birds right up there with it, as if flying at 30,000 feet were not extraordinary for the common seagull. The inscription, in an elementary scrawl, *For Mommy Love Sarah.*

It was on their way home that Maddie had found the nerve to voice what she was feeling. She wouldn't take it to her parents or to Pastor McLaughlin, not to the Tedescos—who were preoccupied by the last month of Amy's pregnancy. It was Vincent she would ask, because he had been there with her, Vincent and his comfort with not knowing *when.* She wondered how that was working out for him. Was he unimpressed by the suffering, standing there next to Mrs. Senchak's bed? He who had helped Willy to his feet, who had healed his opponent in the middle of a football game. The *when* in each of those instances had been obvious. Was that not also the case with Mrs. Senchak? Yet he could calmly descend the crooked concrete steps of the Senchaks' split-level ranch, swinging his keys on their ring, clear-eyed and quiet.

Maddie waited until they were in the car to speak.

"So this is it," she said quietly.

Vincent asked what she meant.

"Mrs. Senchak is going to die."

"Unless God works a miracle," Vincent said.

Maddie was furious. "Vincent," she said with a raised voice, "you *asked* for a miracle, remember? And not just you, but also all of those people praying at church all those weeks ago now, and the whole church for several years, not to mention Mr. and Mrs. Senchak— and their children! They have been praying constantly, I'm sure of it. I'm sure they're praying even now. If she could breathe," Maddie was almost yelling, "if she could just *catch her breath* for even a minute, I am sure Mrs. Senchak would be asking for a miracle, Vincent!"

Vincent didn't answer her.

Maddie had spent it all. She was silent for a moment, gazing unseeing at the weary Pittsburgh suburbs lining the road. "I don't get it," she said, her voice quiet now. She studied her impassive boyfriend in the driver's seat. "Did you see what little Sarah made for her?"

"Yes," Vincent said.

"I don't get it," she said again.

"What don't you get?" he asked her, very gently, not looking at her.

Maddie marveled: impossible that he should not know her confusion, that he should not be confused, too.

With what felt like a tremendous output of energy, she offered him Mr. Taylor. "Why should it be so hard?" she asked him. "Why can't he just have his legs? Why not let him keep even one?"

"Maddie," Vincent said, "Mr. Taylor is old."

"So?" Her anger flared again. This was old territory. Here was the conversation about the paper cut and Mrs. Adams—why shouldn't she want to use her hands?

"So?" she said again with bitterness, daring him to use the same reasoning.

"So, what do you want for him?" Vincent went on, "That he gets to keep his legs? That he doesn't need a prosthetic one? That his diabetes disappears?"

"Any and all of the above," Maddie said. What could be wrong with this?

"We all want that," Vincent said. His voice was calm next to hers, so composed. "We want our hearts to work perfectly and our lungs to work perfectly and our legs and our arms and everything. And we never want to get sick and we never want to get hurt—and if we do, we want it all to go away."

"Yes. Yes! Yes, of course we do," Maddie answered. He was making sense now. He understood, it seemed. But Maddie dreaded that there was more to it. "And why *shouldn't* we want that, Vincent? It's what everybody wants. Shouldn't we want that, Vincent?" She could feel, under the vehemence, near-panic in her own voice.

He was silent for a moment, focusing on driving, perhaps, or just letting her calm down. Or waiting for the right moment to drop the next terrible thing, a new and awful truth about God. He said, "I just don't think that's what we really want, is all."

"It *isn't?*" Maddie was incredulous. What could Mrs. Senchak want more than strength in her arms to hug her little girls? Or Susan Sweet to walk across a parking lot like a normal person, to go from here to there without the entire horizon at a tilt?

"People don't really want to be healed, and *that's* why healing doesn't work, Vincent? Because they're asking for the *wrong thing?* After people pray and ask God, after they have tried all the doctors and the doctors can't help, after they're so sick they can't walk and they're shriveled up on the hospital bed parked in their living room? After they know that they have to say goodbye to their legs or normal life or their kids that they'll never see grow up—but they can't say goodbye because they can't actually talk because they can't breathe? You're telling me these people aren't healed because they're asking for the *wrong thing?* That it's not what they actually want? They don't actually want to get better?"

Maddie said these words and then knew she was finished. She knew that his answer—whatever it was—wouldn't be enough, would ask more from her than she would ever be able to muster. She knew at that moment that she couldn't track with Vincent anymore. If her aim (what *was* her aim?) was to stay with Vincent and somehow ignore or someday absorb his enigmatic God, then it was time to give up the fight.

He pulled into her driveway, and she opened the door while the car was still moving. He asked her to wait, but she was already headed to the house.

"Maddie," he called to her. He was following her, jogging, and he caught up with her as she reached the front door. "Mads, Maddie," he said, his hands on her shoulders, gently. His voice was conversational, as if their argument had been resolved, or as if he didn't know they were having one, as if he was just going to point something out to her, something in the yard, or something that had just come to mind.

She turned to face him and looked into those blue eyes.

"No matter what anybody thinks they want," he said, "everybody just wants God."

Maddie Brees was almost thirty-nine years old and a cancer survivor. She was a wife and the mother of three. Today, she waited in the van during carpool and looked at her hands. She spread her fingers; her eyes glazed over the wedding band and engagement ring that—chemo-induced edema gone—she could wear again.

A paper cut. She would have given anything, back in that April, in that spring of her junior year in high school, to see Susan Sweet walk straight. With a shudder she thought of the Tedescos. And then mercifully the school's doors opened and Eli was sprinting toward the car.

∞∞∞

Frank's first conscious thought as he drove away—because he hadn't really been thinking for the past several hours, had he?—was disbelief that it had been so easy. Was it always that easy? If it was always this easy, then it certainly wasn't practical complexity that kept people from cheating on their spouses.

But then Frank reasoned that the ease, in his particular situation, was limited to this one experience. Maddie didn't have a Facebook account. She didn't know he was meeting Francesca; she had no idea that Francesca was in town. It was perfectly reasonable that he might be detained at work. That Francesca's layover would turn into an overnight (something about thunderstorms over Atlanta; the airline had provided the hotel room) was happenstance. None of this had required strategy. He had fallen into it, so to speak. Despite what he had just done, he couldn't be accused—not fairly, anyway—of plotting or calculating.

It had been so easy.

And, for her part, Francesca had made it easy, too: the light-heartedness of her greeting, her fluent conversation, the genuine interest in him and his work. She laughed at his jokes, reminding him that he was witty. They had laughed together. He and Maddie hadn't laughed together all that much of late, not so much in the past year or so. For understandable reasons.

It felt good to laugh.

Yes, Francesca had made it easy. Her accustomed haughtiness was gone, replaced by what appeared to be genuine regard for Frank and

263

his choices in life. She said she admired his sense of commitment. It was all so affirming. It was refreshing to be with her, and also, again, familiar—and it had seemed harmless to go to the hotel with her for another drink, because the airport bar was growing so loud and crowded. Those storms over Atlanta were apparently delaying lots of flights up and down the east coast.

Francesca had even seemed to try making Frank's going easy: no asking him to stay, no implied guilt about the hasty departure (the need to leave had suddenly been an overwhelming imperative; he had pulled his clothes on as if—absurdly—he had only in that instant realized his nakedness and was now appropriately embarrassed). It was Francesca saying she understood, saying she knew he needed to get home to his family, and those words—hearing Francesca say "your family"—had offended him: he didn't want to hear Francesca, of all people, make reference to them, even when in that moment they were a hazy reality.

Now he recognized that that was how he had managed for the duration of his time with Francesca: by somehow mentally wedging his family into a remote cell at the back of his mind. The heightened emotion leading up to their meeting (he had been distracted by it all day, all week) and the charged nature of their interaction had successfully cast the rest of his life in a muted light. Even talking with her about work had felt like a stretch for him until he miraculously gained some composure.

Now, pulling onto the highway, Frank was caught on the idea of his composure. Yes, he had been composed. He had been charming. He had charmed and entertained Francesca, had, at her request, humbly revisited work that had led to some journalist awards. He had been scolded for being too humble, and then, as if to prove her wrong, he had talked about being invited to write a book. He had even discussed possible approaches to the book with her, fellow writer that she was, would-be colleague.

And in her hotel room, he had had sex with her. Despite the intervening years and the history, sex with Francesca had felt incredibly easy, as if they were back in her dorm room again with incense and Joni Mitchell and no responsibilities to anyone.

At the door of the room, clad only in a T-shirt, she had made light of it. Old time's sake, was what she had said. So good to see him again after such a long time. Composed, smiling (belying that new and powerful urge to get away), Frank had simply agreed with her: So good to see you, too.

Remarkable composure.

Composure which, Frank thought, certainly required thinking. If nothing else, composure was dependent on presence of mind—which meant he could hardly claim to have been thoughtless. There had definitely been plotting involved in this little tryst. He could have told Maddie that he was going to see Francesca, but Maddie didn't know, either, that he was back in touch with Francesca in the first place.

The thing that Maddie always said she loved the most about Frank was his honesty. Ironically, this was something he had learned to value from Francesca, who had been—in those days and perhaps even now (how could he know?)—so heartlessly dishonest.

As Frank himself had been: heartlessly dishonest.

He drove down I-40 with all the windows wide-open, wind blasting through the car to drive the smell of Francesca from his skin and clothes. He could smell it; Maddie would, too, and so he stopped at a smoke-filled bar close to home, calling Maddie to let her know he'd be later still, trying to sound more tired than he felt so that he might match any discouragement he heard in her tone. Good! The boys were already in bed; Maddie herself was tired.

I'm sorry, Madeleine, was what he heard himself saying: sorry to have missed an evening with the boys, an evening when he could help her with the after-dinner busyness. Maybe Jake had had a lot of homework; he didn't know.

Maddie, too, was asleep when he got home, and so he was glad for a chance to shower and to throw his smoke-smogged clothes in the hamper. Glad for a chance to collect his thoughts, despite the fact that they condemned him.

Incredulity. Was it possible he had done this? He couldn't believe he had given in. Years of fidelity, of committed adherence to all he believed about marriage vows and what really mattered in life. And now, in the span of a few hours, he had managed to undo it all. Amazing how easily it could be accomplished—and it was impossible to reverse.

At the very least, he would never see Francesca again. He would never communicate with her. He wouldn't open her emails; he would unfriend her (the base immaturity of such a gesture was now suddenly essential) on Facebook. Already she had lost her appeal—and for a bizarre, confused moment, he tried to catch a strain of that appeal, to see her naked back, arched, next to him. But it was gone.

Which wasn't to say that it wouldn't return. Frank knew better than to imagine that this infidelity would act as a purging. He was a man, only human. He sat on the end of the bed, his head in his hands, while his wife slept innocently behind him.

He vowed to try harder. Discipline, he told himself. Discipline and focus and commitment. And he loved his wife.

∞

Maddie had left Vincent standing on the front step. She had shut the door in his face. "Everybody just wants God," he said. But what Maddie wanted that night was escape: to enter the front door of her parents' house and then close it behind her, to get away—finally— from Vincent. She wanted to walk through the entryway, through the living room, make that hard left into the kitchen and on into the family room, ignoring her parents' greetings, the questions: Where's Vincent? How is Mrs. Senchak?

How could she have answered them without having them slow her down? Mrs. Senchak is dying, she would have said, she's holding her own but wishes she didn't have to. It looks like it's a matter of time, but hasn't it always been a matter of time? It's a long, long time that she's known this was coming and now it's killing her for certain, but slowly. Very slowly.

And Vincent? Well, thank you for asking. I hate to disappoint you; I know you wish he'd come in like he normally does and chat with you and maybe accept, Mom, whatever it was you would have offered him to eat. But he hasn't come in with me and I think he won't be coming in with me anymore.

Moreover, I'm not really home myself. I'm headed out.

All of that would have taken too long, because what Maddie wanted was to walk through the house to the sliding glass door that opened to the deck. She wanted to open it and then close it again

266

behind her and walk away from it all through the backyard—the most
readily available route for escape.

The walk would have been a long one, and hard. Hadn't she
mentally rehearsed it once before? They were in a Pittsburgh suburb,
where flat real estate is nearly impossible to come by. And so her
walk would have meant the slow climb in the crowned vetch that
comprised the McGarvey's backyard, and then walking on through
their front yard and onto the neighboring street.

Here was flatness, but only for a space. Her escape would mean
another descent and then ascent again, this time through wooded land
and through the neighborhood park. And beyond that, what did she
know? Her childhood explorations had taken her no further. Likely
more neighborhoods, as the view from the roads would suggest. At
some point, the ground would open onto a parking lot somewhere. A
strip mall, a business. But on that night, she thought she would have
gone as far as her feet would take her, as long as she could have willed
her legs on those climbs and descents.

Surely somewhere there lay land that was flatter than this, land
unobstructed by itself, by the endless succession of hills that rose to
block the view.

She did not go walking that night. She fielded, as briefly as she
could, her parents' questions, laying it all out in the mildest of terms.
How is Mrs. Senchak? Not too good. And Vincent? Well, he had to
get home.

She went to bed early, unwillingly entertaining visions of her yard,
her neighborhood, the hills that hemmed her in.

How would it be if someone could lay hold of it, just pick it up
at two proverbial corners, like a bed sheet, and shake it all out? *That*
Maddie would like to see: the hills and valleys of the landscape, in a
shocking jolt, whipped suddenly sky high and then laid down even
and flat. The dust would take a long time to settle. The rivers would
fall into haphazard lines; they would pool and then grow stagnant
or, bereft of bed, would seep into the earth. The slag and shale of
the strip mines would drift into sliding piles; the buildings (houses of
brick and aluminum; skyscrapers of steel and glass) would slam into
the earth and buckle, becoming indiscriminate mounds of rubble. It
would be a mess that a body could pick her way through; she could

make her way out of it, find the level field that existed somewhere at the outskirts of this mess.

Maddie remembered this now, more than twenty years since that earth-shaken vision. Destructive, yes, and dramatic—but she found the longing was the same: an endless field, the waving grass. The only sound would be the sighing wind and the grasses rustling like paper. No hills to climb, no presumptuous upstart comprised of the very earth itself, as if it were the plotting enemy, waiting to catch you up with the reminder that you are made of earth, of dust.

She remembered that vision of the grassy flatland, just as she remembered the glowing cathedral of the city at night, and Vincent on the football field, at the rain-drenched curb. And in the oncology ward with the sunlight falling over his shoulders—that last memory based on nothing, composed of her own imagination, because that was the one that had never happened.

And these memories, of course, informed the vision, altered by her cancer, altered by all the fearful possibilities that, once upon a time, she had never imagined: the grassy field was not so much a refuge anymore, because who knew where the pit might be, invisible in all that grass? One false step and you are gone. The hole—for all she knew—was bottomless.

---

Saturday evening Mass, and Maddie was the last of her family in the pew. Jake had led the way and now the boys sat side by side, in order of age, with their parents to their left. Out of habit, Maddie looked over Frank and checked on her sons: faces scrubbed, hair only somewhat smoothed. Jake especially was a relentless resistor of smoothed hair; he had opinions of his own on the subject. That afternoon, he had announced to his mother that he planned to "grow it out."

Her sons, for now, were behaving themselves, and Maddie settled in. She thought this might be the first time they had all been quiet together in what felt like days. Games and practices had once again upended the mealtime routine. Last night Jake had had a game, and afterward the team had gone out for ice cream, which had bumped bedtime back an hour. The night before that Frank had been so late at work, none of them had even seen him. He had come home after she was asleep.

But the stillness of waiting for Mass to begin did not feel good to her. Busyness felt good to her these days. She liked having something to do with her hands at the very least. If it was distracting enough, it could quiet the contents of her mind and displace the sadness.

And now was the hour for Mass and there he was, agonized and dying: the crucifix looming over them all. The universal image—and when *was* this, exactly, in the chronology of events that comprised the crucifixion? Was he dying? Was he dead? Last words, bowed head, then silence.

This Catholic insistence on the body. Maddie found herself wishing for an empty cross, the plain wooden cross-beams that had hung at the front of the Bethel Hills Church. But body or no, she realized, the idea was the same: the reminder of his death. And to what end, she asked herself. Catholic or Protestant, there was no escaping this inscrutable, suffering God.

Maddie couldn't help it. Her thoughts turned, relentlessly and irrationally, to Vincent. Now it was their last conversation she was recalling, and she wouldn't let him speak. She didn't give him room, as she didn't want to hear whatever he might have come up with. And anyway, what could he have said? Any argument would have been futile. She could see him still, how slowly he walked down the driveway, got into his car and was gone.

She had been abrupt and cruel; she knew that now. At the time, it had seemed her only option, but for the first time she felt that she might like to speak to him—not about healing, not about cancer—but by way of some sort of apology. She hadn't been able to stay with Vincent; did he understand that? Vincent and his impossible theology. It was God I rejected, Vincent, she would like to say, if she could find him in the Peterson's fabled shopping mall.

The sob hit like a spasm, involuntary language of heart and mind, and Maddie heard it—or imagined and feared she heard it—echo through the sanctuary. Panicked, she turned to Frank, who didn't seem to have noticed, but she couldn't believe that and so turned to look in other directions, certain to find people staring at her. No one was.

Frank must have felt her restlessness. "You okay?"

"Didn't you hear that?" Maddie was afraid to ask him, but the sound had been so loud; there was no sense in denying that she had cried out. She would have to field his questions and come up with an excuse.

"What?" he asked her. Amazed, she didn't reply. "Hear what?" he asked again.

"Nothing," she managed, and smiled at him, hiding her relief. She had heard herself sob; she had felt the cry shake her—her windpipe and chest, her ribcage and shoulders. And yet, by some miracle, she had managed to keep it to herself. She had cried, but she hadn't cried out. She hadn't, after all, given herself away.

The service was beginning. Next to her, Frank was reaching for the missal. They were all standing now, and Frank was leaning over Garrett to whisper something in Eli's ear. When he straightened again, his left arm rested against Maddie's right shoulder, and Maddie remembered sitting next to Vincent in church years ago, before they were dating. The warmth of his arm on her sleeve had been all she knew for the length of an entire church service, and she had imagined she still felt it on the ride home.

Oh, Maddie thought, this was absurd. All of this was absolutely absurd. The familiar anger rose in her stomach, and she silently scolded herself. Here she sat in church with her family—husband and three beautiful boys—and all she could think about was this boy she had imagined she loved when she herself was practically a child. It had been a brief year; it had been puppy love; it had been childish and meaningless and should be long dead. She suppressed an exasperated sigh. For crying out loud, soon enough Jake would be the age Vincent had been when his star first swung across her horizon. This was unaccountable obsession, and it was blinding her to the gifts all around her. Far worse than the cancer, this prolonged meditation on Vincent was making her miss everything else.

Sitting again, Maddie reached for Frank's hand, holding it first with one and then with both of her own. She rested her right hand inside his left, and she knew that it felt the same as it always had: the calluses on the inside of his palm, not thick; the texture of his skin. The nails, neatly trimmed; the length of his fingers; the hair on the first length of each knuckle. Even now, in the length of his fingers, she knew them as different from Vincent's. Vincent's hands had been rougher than Frank's, busy always with a baseball, a football, or healing people.

It had been so long, she thought, since she had held Frank's hand. She took it for granted that she could do so anytime she wanted to. He would gladly respond to her affection; he would gladly listen. And he would come home to them from work every night; he would make pancakes on Saturday morning. Years ago she had told him about Vincent, and while Maddie hadn't been able to tell him the whole thing, she had always known that of all people, Frank was someone she could tell.

She had wanted to tell him. She truly had. She remembered the paths around campus, the long walks they had taken after dark, the periodic pools of lamplight; she heard the clack of the empty branches blown by the wind overhead. This was before Frank had kissed her, before he had even touched her, and yet she had felt closer to him than to anyone she knew or had ever known. He told her about learning to play tennis, about competing with his older brother on the high school tennis team, about riding Big Wheels in the woods near his house when he was five. He told her about Father Tim and about why he was Catholic which, for Frank, was different from the fact he'd been raised that way. He had talked honestly about Francesca; he had said he thought he was in love with her; he had said he also might be wrong, that he wasn't sure what it meant to be in love with someone, but that he wanted very much to find out.

And Maddie had told him about being partially raised by the congregation of the Bethel Hills Church of Holiness and about Sunday night's endless altar calls. She told him about Justine and her little brother who had died when he was only four. She told him about her parents; she told him about her neighborhood; she told him that she had wanted to go to a college as far away from home as possible— in the Pacific Northwest, maybe—but that she had also been pretty depressed during her senior year and so hadn't really been on the ball when it was time for college applications.

Frank said he was glad she had ended up where she did, and Maddie blushed in the dark.

And of course she had told him about Vincent, about Vincent

and the other boys, the brief series she had dated in the earliest weeks of college, trying them on one after another like one might try pairs of jeans. Frank brought the subject back around to Vincent, and so she told him about the church's blind faith in a God who might do anything and the unarguable fact that Vincent couldn't heal people.

Over the years she had considered it. After a dinner party, maybe, when somehow the conversation had gone to car accidents or injuries or near escapes from them, and Frank had volunteered Maddie's story of the drunken man hit by a car in the rain. After times like that, Maddie had considered just telling Frank the rest of the story, but she could never bring herself to do it. And wasn't it a happier ending, anyway, to think that Vincent's going to college had brought things to a close? Everyone, Maddie imagined, was happier this way.

Except for this year. This year Maddie couldn't claim to be happier. This year she had revisited all of it, even pieces she had thought she'd forgotten. This year the whole thing had played out in her mind too many times, and now sitting in church she made mentally to turn on it, to simply confront head-on the invisible force that funneled the awful narrative again and again through her mind. Was it possible? Could she just stop thinking about Vincent? Couldn't she put it down now and be finished with it? Why couldn't she simply walk away?

No, Maddie thought. Clearly, she wasn't strong enough. She couldn't do it alone. God knew she'd tried.

Her gaze returned, automatically, compulsorily, to the crucifix. Strange outcome, this, she thought: she had rejected God all those years ago. She had deliberately torn herself free of him and of that foolishly expectant church; she had escaped his whims and demands. And now here she sat in a church.

"Everyone really only wants God." That's what Vincent had told her, and Maddie remembered standing in her parents' living room, the infant Jesus from the nativity crèche nestled in her palm. Please, God. Long before Vincent. Long before Frank. She wasn't willing to meet God at an altar; she invited him instead into her living room. She had always wanted him on her own terms.

*Please, God*, she had said. But had she meant it?

She wasn't sure it mattered. Staring at the crucifix, she considered that God had already lost it all and so was willing to wait. He would come when invited, but would take a backseat to Maddie's pride. He could sustain her exchanging an expressed desire for God for the attentions of a high school football player. He would tolerate—for a time—Maddie's abuse of Vincent's remarkable gift.

But in the end, the crucified God would take all of that away. Everything but himself—which is what she had asked for in the first place.

The sadness crowded her throat. She felt it swelling there, threatening to choke her. She had asked for this God, but in the end she hadn't wanted him. And when it came time to cut this God from her life, Vincent had not been the greatest of losses.

Maddie looked down at where Frank's hand still rested in hers. It was so casual a thing, this holding hands, wasn't it? Maddie realized she could tell Frank. She realized, moreover, that she *should* tell him, that—if he knew—he would *want* her to tell him. And it occurred to her that there might be something in it, some magic trick of honesty—like a confession.

And then it was Vincent again in their last conversation together, sitting on the sofa in her parents' living room. For a while he had met her gaze, his blue eyes had looked into hers and then, as she had talked, had begun to traverse her face. She had watched him study her—her eyes and brows, her forehead, her lips. Once or twice he opened his mouth to speak, but Maddie had talked over him, and eventually he had dropped his gaze to his hands. She saw them now again, Vincent's hands, the square nails, the ragged edges of the gnawed nail beds, the tanned skin, hairless knuckles. Vincent had studied his own hands while Maddie had talked as if reading out his verdict, and Maddie could still see—so clearly—his bent head, his brown arms, his hands dangling between his knees.

Her long memory of the body.

Sitting in church under the closed eyes of the crucifix, Maddie felt a second sob, thicker than the last, rising in her throat. Would she have to tell Frank even about that—Vincent's hands idle between his knees in the living room? Which details were the essential ones, and which would be too many? Once she started, Frank would insist on knowing it all.

Could she bear to say it aloud? She had never said it all, never heard the sound of her voice telling the rest of the story. And what would it be to look Frank in the eye afterward? And what would he say?

The sob was thicker now. This one, she feared, would out. She felt tears swelling in her eyes and blinked hard, panicked and angry that she would have to wipe them away—a gesture impossible to misinterpret. It was an essential effort at self-preservation to withdraw her hand from Frank's and press it—just subduing a cough—to her throat.

# 26

*U*ncanny, Frank thought, that after months of almost no affection from his wife, Maddie should choose the Saturday after Francesca to hold his hand in church.

Immediately, that thought embarrassed him. As if holding hands were a big deal. He and Maddie weren't in middle school.

And yet it *was* a big deal—not only because it illustrated in bold strokes the absence of his wife's affection towards him of late, but also because of the way in which she had held his hand: she had clasped it, traced his fingers, sometimes held it with both of her own, rotated her hand again and again inside his palm. She had very nearly rubbed his skin away, he thought.

Her actions had been intense and deliberate, and he wondered if it meant something. He considered feeling hopeful—but then was caught again in the irony: his betrayal was both absolute and dismayingly recent: only two nights before. Sometimes he feared he could still smell Francesca on his skin.

The weight of it appalled him. Over the past two days, trying to go through the motions of normal life, he had time and again felt sidelined by memories of his time with Francesca: her toothy grin at the bar, her naked shoulder under his palm, the fall of her hair on the pillow. In the short work of a single evening, he had succeeded in multiplying his demons; they overwhelmed him, innumerable.

Still, his tired hope was relentless: How ought he respond to this affection from Maddie? If in fact it meant something, then certainly she would tell him. And wouldn't that conversation, leading (he hoped, he imagined) to renewed intimacy with his wife, serve to frighten those demons away?

He had waited. She was quiet on the return home from church, which was not unusual. She was busy through dinner, preoccupied with what their sons were eating (it was always a battle with Garrett), and then, after the boys went to bed, it was the same quiet evening. They watched some television; they talked about nothing in particular, and throughout, Frank was waiting, afraid to ask questions lest he be accused of making too much—anything—of nothing. They read for a while in bed, and then it was lights out, backs turned.

Frank was unsurprised to find himself thinking of calling Father Tim, but the thought was paired with regret. How to open that conversation? Certainly there had been lapses in communication between them before, but this time he could link it to his reconnection with Francesca. Of course he hadn't wanted to talk with Tim. Frank had known, no matter what he told himself, precisely what he was doing.

He wondered now, though, what Tim would say. Always, before that night with Francesca, he knew what The Priest would say, and he would call just to hear him say it. Now when he thought of confessing to his friend, he couldn't imagine what Tim would say. It was a conversation that Frank didn't want to have, not ever.

Anyway, would he need to tell him? Would he need to tell anyone? He had gone to confession before Mass. He told himself that it was all over.

That night, unable to sleep, he rose from bed and went downstairs. He sat at one end of the sofa and looked around the room. The familiar room, lit only by the hallway lamp, looked strange in this light, as though it wasn't his house despite being furnished with all the right things in all of their standard places. Frank had been up late and alone before, but tonight the room felt emphatically lonely.

Across the room, the boys' toy bins were lined up carefully along the wall. Maddie had labeled them, marker on index cards, in her careful print. The boys always put their toys away before bed; Jake was particularly fastidious about this ("No, Eli, no Playmobils in this one. This one has the blue lid."), and Frank wondered what element, if any, of household life didn't somehow bear Maddie's mark, didn't somewhere reflect her attentive eye. This with the bins was a perfect example: "An opportunity to teach the boys responsibility," he could hear her say, or something like that.

Father Tim would appreciate this, Frank thought. How often he had admired Maddie's organized pantry and her color-coded calendars! Frank thought they were helpful, cute, sometimes amusing—even, occasionally, problematic (one can be too devoted to organization, he would say playfully to Maddie, because he knew how its lack could eventually vex her). But The Priest showed genuine appreciation for the way she managed things.

"You got a good one," he would say to Frank. That, and a smile. It wasn't that Tim himself was a lover of organization; it was, rather, that he looked for opportunities to praise Maddie to Frank, and vice versa. These were tacit reminders of the quiet splendors they had in one another. Tim would say, "These things shouldn't be overlooked."

Just seeing Tim's smile in his mind's eye was enough to make Frank wince.

He decided that he shouldn't call Tim. What would be the point? Tim couldn't understand what they'd been through—what he, Frank, had been through, he thought. Sure, sure. Tim thought he knew, and certainly, to an extent, he'd been right about how marriage "worked," about how you stayed true to your commitment to each other and worked it out. Over their seventeen years of marriage, Frank and Maddie had had their share of arguments that rose into genuine fighting; the seemingly irreconcilable differences that sometimes made them feel worse than strangers; the opposite perspectives that, to each of them, seemed the only possible way. Tim would say that all of these could be resolved, and they had been. True, sometimes the fighting got worse before it got better. Sometimes one of them went for a long walk, or a beer, or a coffee. Sometimes it was a good night's sleep they needed, or sex. But always, they had gotten over it or past it or through it. And that, Father Tim said, was what it meant to live the dream.

But, given their current situation, Frank now understood that Tim didn't know what he was talking about. The Priest didn't know first-hand about cancer and, in their case, its requisite mutilation, and the way that mutilation might alienate a person from her own body, from her own husband. The Priest didn't understand holding his wife's hair back so she could vomit repeatedly into the toilet, about helping her shave her head, about silence in the form of months—not hours, not days. He didn't know about Francesca and her smooth body, unmarred by cancer or anything else. Father Tim could talk all he wanted about living the dream, but what Frank and Maddie had was a nightmare.

And Father Tim didn't know about the loneliness, because how could he be expected to imagine it? The loneliness, Frank thought, shouldn't be possible. It shouldn't be possible that, sitting in his own living room, his sons and wife at home, Frank could feel this alone.

But Frank knew that he was lying to himself. He knew that Tim would understand more than he was giving him credit for. At the very least, Frank knew—because Tim had told him—that sexual temptation was a familiar demon for a priest, too. And if Tim had a wife with cancer, Frank was certain he would hold her hair as she leaned over the toilet bowl.

All that about Tim being unable to understand was guilt talking, plain and simple.

Frank had so much guilt.

Right now, Maddie's careful print in marker on index cards made his heart ache. She had used blue markers on all of the cards; she had made them match, and Frank had teased her. Well, she had said, not failing to see how it could be amusing but explaining herself nonetheless, it's a small room, she had said. This makes it, in a way, just a little bit neater at least.

Jake had come along sometime after his mother and drawn on the index cards: awkward drawings, a child's hand. On this card, a picture of a Lego; on this, a wooden block. All of them now bore a pictorial representation of the kind of toy contained within—his own effort to ensure that his less literate siblings could do it right.

Jake. Such an earnest boy. So like his mother that way. He loved a good laugh, but he was generally serious, generally trying so hard. He had been serious even as a baby, looking all about him with those wide eyes and almost stern countenance. Observing everything, taking everything in.

His birth had been the hardest. Thirty-six hours or something awful like that. Well beyond average. It wasn't surprising, the doctor had said, given that he was the first baby. She had assured them that the next births wouldn't be so difficult, and they hadn't been.

But at the time and even since then, Frank had praised Maddie's success, bragging about Jake's difficult birth. "That's almost a full work-week," he said to her of the labor, and for a moment that day she had seemed to take it in: a little pride in her own effort, when mostly what she was proud of and glowing over was their newborn son, pink, wrinkled, beautiful, and sleeping in her arms.

Maddie had chosen the difficult option: no medication unless absolutely necessary. Then the labor had kicked in and she had tried everything to manage the pain: walking, lying on her side, perched on the delivery table on her hands and knees.

Frank had hated it. Pacing, standing by, offering the best he could in moral support. She didn't want him to touch her, then she was reaching for his hand. He had remembered the mirror (in their excited birth-plan stage, Maddie said she wanted a mirror so she could see the baby be born) and was almost thrilled to realize it wasn't yet in the room. Asking for the mirror, seeing it rightly positioned—these were things Frank could do for Maddie while, otherwise, all help was beyond him.

Then Maddie got to sitting. She had asked him to set the back of the bed upright and he had sprung at yet another chance to do something. She sat at a near ninety-degree angle, knees bent and feet planted wide, and she reached for Frank. He took her hands, but she pulled him closer, wrapping her arms around his waist. She had buried her face in his shoulder, his chest.

It was natural to wrap his arms around her also, his hands sometimes stroking her back or her hair, sometimes holding for dear life to her taut body. He thought to turn and watch the doctor, to get some sign from the nurses of her progress, but Maddie clung to him, and so he held her fast in his arms. He buried his face in the top of her head and inhaled the perfume of her shampoo mixed with sweat. He tried to provide—with his hands, his arms, his murmured support—

all the strength and comfort he could impart to this woman, his wife, who was giving everything she had to this birth. She breathed into his shirt; his chest was warmed and cooled by turns with every breath; with each push she exhaled her screams into him.

That was how Jake was born: the two of them so wrapped up in one another that neither of them actually saw the moment when he entered the world.

Frank wondered now if that was an option. Was it possible to go through an ordeal like cancer in the way Maddie had birthed Jake? It was Maddie's cancer, yes, but couldn't they have done it together? Because that was what Frank had wanted. From the outset, it was what he had wanted—and he remembered the moment of the lump's discovery and the way Maddie had clung to him in the bathroom. It had been a painful beginning, certainly. Cancer was nothing but painful—but he would have endured it with her somehow, if she had let him. Instead it had felt, much of the time, as if she had labored through it alone while he waited, desperate, in another room.

But he had meant it: "In sickness and in health." And he thought again of Francesca, some twenty years before, smug, perhaps brilliant, and an absolute fool. "There's more to life than love," she had said.

What more? Frank wondered now. What good, in the end, was publishing, was sport, was political theory, was an airport—domestic or abroad? Sitting in his deserted living room, toy bins lining the wall, Frank knew that Francesca had been precisely wrong. There's no more to life than love. Love fueled and animated all the rest.

Then, with a pang, he thought again about how he had marred it. That even if Maddie had wanted this isolation, his efforts to close the gap had gone badly awry. For all those months that he had worked against their seeming separation, he had also managed to make an enormous breach between them—one that Maddie didn't yet know about.

Frank knew then that he would tell her. It would be terrible; he knew it. But he also knew that honesty was the only way forward now—or, perhaps, it was the only way back. He would tell Maddie what he had done, and he would ask for her forgiveness, and maybe it would start them toward each other again.

He was resolved. He turned off the light in the hall and made his way to his wife in the dark.

---

The adult Maddie considered that here—right here—she might have made a clean break. A short time, a little nerve, and she would have found the courage to end her relationship with Vincent. Sure, it would have been difficult. She had loved him; he had loved her. But they were teenagers; it was only high school—right? Eventually they would have gotten past it. They would have come to realize signs from God in school parking lots could mean lots of things—or nothing at all. They could have parted ways on the basis of an irreconcilable difference: Vincent's ardent trust in an inscrutable God and Maddie's mistrust of the same.

Except that there had been a new obstruction in the landscape. Maddie wasn't going to be allowed to get away, not via an endless walk through the Appalachians and on, at length, to Kansas; nor by breaking things off with Vincent and, eventually, the entire church. Maddie was pregnant, the news manifesting via the slender white stick in her hands, there in the upstairs bathroom of the house she had grown up in. She was pregnant, and the simple sign on the test couldn't possibly have carried with it all that came next, but suddenly there were the terrors: her father's anger, her mother's tears; telling the Tedescos and then the youth group finding out and all that talk revisited about the swimming pool; and Pastor McLaughlin and the entire church. They were always expectant, that church, but this they would not be anticipating. This they would not have imagined in hundreds of Sunday evening services strung together, even if Vincent or the pastor or anyone had right there at the altar called down fire from heaven.

The only one who would not be surprised, Maddie thought, would be Justine—she had known all along that Saint Vincent was anything but.

Yet these thoughts were secondary to the certainty, the stunning pressure of irrevocable truth. First, there were thoughts of a baby—the translucent skin, the sealed eyes.

---

Vincent took her out. She fled the house when he pulled in the driveway; he had only just climbed out of the car when she reached the passenger side and pulled at the door handle—strange reversal of the night only a few days before. Now she was calling to him to never mind, get in, get in, let's go, let's just go.

She hadn't cried yet (not even when she whispered it to him— the only one she told—on the phone, cupping the receiver with her hand), and she didn't mean to cry now. Maybe it was the relief of being with someone else who knew that opened all the stops. She saw nothing of the drive and had no idea where they were headed; she was just crying hard and unrelentingly, the kind of crying that means eyes and nose all running. Vincent handed her a sweatshirt from somewhere, and she buried her face in that.

He took her to see the city. Up onto Mt. Washington, where the ground dropped away below their feet and then ducked under the river, coming up again to form the glass and glowing wedge of land. For a long time they just stood and looked at it, and Maddie was grateful for their anonymity, for Vincent next to her, for the distraction of this familiar landscape that had nothing to do with why they were there.

It had grown dark already, and the lights were on below them. A warm breeze flowed up the mountain from the rivers. They stood at the railing overlooking the city, and Vincent began talking quietly, his head bent to her, his lips near her ear.

They would get married, he said. Soon. Right away. Next month, right after he graduated. Sure, everyone would know that she was pregnant, but who cared? They loved each other, didn't they? They would be married, and who cared if people were angry at them or if they thought they were too young! And she would come to his college town with him and she could graduate from the high school there, and Vincent would get a job and soon they would be going to college together. Even if they went part-time and also had jobs and the baby, that wouldn't matter, because they would be together. Yes, it would be difficult at times, but so what? They would be lying to themselves if they thought—even for a minute—that it wouldn't be difficult.

Maddie listened. She had reasons for protest but she didn't muster argument. What she knew now was what overwhelmed her imagination: the tiniest slip of an embryo, red veins, the beating heart. And then there was Vincent on one knee in front of her, indifferent to the passers-by, the people who paused at a distance to watch him—so young!—asking Maddie—too young!—to marry him. She said yes (a shy nod; a broad, teary smile) and Vincent stood to kiss her, just very gently. The small audience offered quiet applause and moved off.

Maddie and Vincent stayed for a while longer and looked down on the city, at the pinnacled glass, lights beading the bridges, lambent rivers. She stood with her hands on the railing and Vincent stood behind her, his hands next to hers on either side. He hemmed her in and she felt safe there, deliberately putting from her mind everyone but the two of them and the idea of this third, unknown.

Now mother to three children, Maddie remembered that night and all nights together that she spent looking down on the city. This one had been in spring, but there had been other spring nights—before and after—and summer nights and winter ones and fall. That night with Vincent it had been warm; the new leaves on the mountainside had rustled invisibly beneath them. But other nights (with her family, perhaps; with guests from out of town) it had been cold and she had been bundled in her coat zipped up to her chin, and the bare branches had rattled below their feet. Or it had been summer and windless, the leaves hanging limp in the close air. She had spent many nights—before and after—looking down on this city.

There was a time—was it that night or one of the others?—any of the others, all of them—that she had wanted to start running. When was it she wanted to find out where the concrete sidewalk gave in to solid earth? The hillside itself was thick with trees; it was a small forest rooted and upright against the incline of the mountain. Her legs would have worn the blood-streaked marks of her mindless descent, and yet she had felt compelled to run.

The glowing core of the city moored that madness. She had wanted to run to it, to run into it, despite the terror of the blind plunge. For just here on the mountain she could see the bottom of the abyss, and for all its being foreign—light, glass and wire—it was also beautiful.

She never let herself run to it, of course. There was certainly no easy point of access from the concrete walkway lining the hilltop road to the forest of trees below it. And eventually, the urge to run to it had faded and then altogether disappeared. She had gone to college and then had moved away. The abyss had grown deeper and fearsome. The cathedral dissolved in the dark.

∽∾∾

At her house again that evening, Vincent walked her to the door. No one would know yet; they would take the next steps carefully. And it was late; Vincent wouldn't come in. But he would stand with her outside the door; he would kneel down in front of her; he would press his face to her belly.

"Hello?" he would say. "Hello in there," he said. "This is your father speaking."

Maddie giggled. Translucent skin, sealed eyes. She buried her hands in Vincent's hair.

"You be good to your mother," Vincent whispered into her flat stomach, "and I'll talk with you tomorrow."

∽∾∾

On this side of the conversation, Frank could only ask himself how he had expected it to go. At least he had had the sense not to make a date out of it, taking her to a restaurant where the scene would have drawn spectators. Instead, by some rare wisdom (for clearly he lacked it), Frank had poured them both glasses of wine and invited her to sit on the couch with him after the boys were in bed.

"There is something I need to tell you." He wondered now if that was true. *Had* he needed to tell her? Wouldn't it have been better if he had left the tiny detail of his infidelity out of their lives? Because now, in the full-blown hindsight of that short and devastating conversation, he felt it would have been better—far better—to have left well enough alone.

It had been ugly. She had been furious. If he had missed conversation with his wife about real, meaningful things, then he had gotten it full throttle that evening as Maddie had insisted, with a kind of sick malice, on hearing every detail. She read the emails that remained in his account and then poured over the messages on Facebook; she called him terrible names—all of them earned.

"I'm sorry," Frank had said. "I'm sorry." Quietly, sincerely. He begged her to forgive him, to see how deeply he regretted it, how wrong he knew he had been, how less-than-nothing Francesca meant to him. How much he loved Maddie. And if they could somehow get past this like they had the cancer.

The silence that followed made Maddie's earlier withdrawal seem like sweet companionship. The only time she said anything was when she told him, as he was coming to bed, that she wanted him to sleep in the guest room. Of course he complied.

And he cast about him for something more he could offer, something more he could say, only to again assent to the reality that there was nothing more. How pitiful, he thought to himself, that "I'm sorry," is, after failure, the best we can do.

# 27

*M* addie was angry. She was always angry these days. No, not that, she thought. She was bitter.

Frank had told her all about Francesca—years ago, back when he was honest. He had told Maddie about her sudden going, about how he hoped it was a joke at first and had gone to her dorm room only to find it cleaned out: the books, bedding, everything—gone. The faint scent of incense and, in the corner by the bed, a thin web of her hair curled in the dust.

Maddie had listened to him talk about her, jealousy mixing with awe: awe that he would be this open and raw about how he had thought he was in love with her, but that what she offered had been, in the end, empty. He confessed sheepishly that he had written a bad poem about it once, a parallel between the incense that Francesca loved and the love that Francesca offered: both of them vaporous and dissolving. Nothing real there.

Maddie had loved him for that. The poem might have been bad, but the metaphor was beautiful, and she had said so. For a time, she had thought that maybe it was the metaphor itself that had made her fall in love with him—but that hadn't been it. It had been his honesty and what the metaphor said about him—what he wanted: he wanted his friendship with his wife to be the best of his life, and he said it would have to be built on honesty. Honesty and trust.

Both of which were badly broken now, Maddie thought to herself. Beyond repair. As if she didn't already feel fractured, sometimes barely holding the pieces of herself together, clutching them in her cracking fists as she went about the day and trying with all her might to keep afloat what he said he wanted: this joke of a suburban dream. The breast cancer had been more than enough; this infidelity was unbearable. And he had cheated on her with *Francesca*, of all people! Francesca, the insidious and conniving vapor! How was Maddie to trust him now, or ever?

She wouldn't speak to him. She found she couldn't. He had apologized once, a thousand times. Every time he caught her eye; in a sticky note on the bathroom mirror; catching her by the arm on his way out the door: "I'm sorry." As if those words could ever be enough. To accept them felt like instant complicity; it felt like acquiescence, like joining him in his crime, as though she were guilty, too.

No. Maddie had had enough with the cancer. That effort had taken all her energies; she had to focus now on staying healthy. And the boys.

Because the cancer could come again. That was undoubtedly true. And it didn't have to come in the breast; it could appear elsewhere. Daily she pressed her pill through its foil backing, swallowing it past the lump of fear in her throat. If the cancer were to come again, she was sure she couldn't manage quite so well—and she hadn't really managed it all that well in the first place.

In those days of her silent protest, other fears came. Taking the boys to school, suddenly she was overwhelmed by remote possibilities. The kidnapper lurking during recess at the edge of the schoolyard; the freak in-school accident (she filled in the blanks with spills on the stairs and a son slipping, a fight in the cafeteria, a fire). She wouldn't let Jake go on the class field trip to the natural history museum downtown, and of course this raised a ruckus that led to Frank's questioning her: Why, Maddie? Why? I know you won't speak to me, but would you just tell me why?

Jake was dismayed. He wanted to go on the field trip. Who wants to miss a field trip? And he, too, questioned Maddie: Just tell me why I can't go, Mom.

Maddie considered telling him. On the day of the field trip she almost told him when she took him, as a pitiful peace offering, to McDonald's for lunch. But in the end she wasn't willing to explain that the reason he was at home, the reason he had missed this opportunity to go to into the city with his entire class, was that she was afraid of accidents on the highways and thoughtless drivers downtown. Anything might happen—that's what life had taught her. If breast cancer could come out of nowhere, if Frank Brees would cheat on his wife, if everything in that year of Vincent had really happened the way she had so recently remembered, then absolutely nothing was safe. Yes, maybe her fears for her son sounded irrational, but the news is full of this kind of disaster, and what mother doesn't hear it with a mixture of horror and gratitude that this time, at least, it wasn't her child?

Maddie felt sure she couldn't handle another loss. Before this—before her marriage, before she even knew Frank—there was so much lost already; and now her body was mutilated in its absolute way, and Frank was lost to her, too. She could never trust him again.

Frank, who had believed so resolutely in marriage. It would be them against the world.

She had bought it. She had still been raw from Vincent and everything else, hemorrhaging on the inside and trying to stop the loss in alcohol and avoidance and the shallowest of friendships. What hope she'd had for God was replaced by harrowing memory. She practiced new narratives and dismissed the old as error and deception. None of it could be perceived as being her fault.

And then she had met Frank and his honest, unapologetic faith in her, in them, in God. She had known a kind of salvation in building a life with Frank and a home for their boys. If nothing else, this was compensation for the devastation of Vincent's year. Better still, it was an assertion of faith: that this good could come to them, to her, despite everything else.

How blind she had been! Blinded by Frank, who blindly believed in God's goodness, in healing. Fool! She hadn't been healed—that had been science. And the marriage was a lie, too. Seventeen years destroyed in a matter of minutes. It shouldn't be that easy.

She never assumed that life would be easy. Vincent's year had taught her that much.

Involuntarily Jake's birth came to mind. She had wanted to see him be born. She had written it, along with so much else, into her extraordinarily detailed birth plan—and then Frank was the one to realize somewhere in the midst of her contractions that the mirror hadn't been carried in. He dispatched one of the nurses: "She wants a mirror!"

Later, after the birth, in a rare moment of looking up from the newborn boy in her arms, Maddie noticed the mirror standing in the corner, pushed out of the way when the moment had passed. She thanked Frank, remembering his demand for the mirror even as her eyes were closed tight against everything that didn't have to do with birthing a baby, and he laughed. "Yeah," he said, "guess we didn't need it."

Neither of them had seen Jake be born. Maddie, pressed into her husband's chest, had been too busy to look. There, in those last minutes, her body had taken over. Everything in her had suddenly been subjected to this instinctive need to push, and with the only agency she had left, she held onto Frank. Clinging to him and feeling his arms around her had locked her in, she thought, securing her in herself when most of her body seemed to be all about birthing this child.

She told him that she was sorry he had missed it, too. His back had been to the baby and his head had been bent to her hair, and the two of them together heard Jake before they ever saw him: Jake's newborn, indignant squall. Later, Frank smiled at her and then at their son from where he sat exhausted, slumped in the chair at her side. "It's okay," he said to her. "It really is just fine."

Now Maddie carried the laundry up the stairs: the chores would persist in the midst of their losses. It was mid-morning, and the sunlight flooded Garrett's room and into the hall. She carried the laundry basket up the stairs and had to catch her breath at the top. Just a pause, a brief interruption in this quotidian task. And there it was: a new wrinkle in the landscape. Was she in fact to begin it all again?

They said they had got it all. Two surgeries, multiple scars, bandages and drainage tubes and they had got it all—but who can be so sure?

Gowned and masked, carefully probing the layers of her tissue, the surgeons could only do their best. Now, a year later, here she was at the top of the stairs, leaning, the laundry basket pressed between her body and the wall. No matter that she faithfully swallowed her pill: it was no guarantee that some cancer cells hadn't torn loose and made a mad dash for the nearest blindly obliging artery or vein. Caught up in the pulsing stream of blood, the cell would course with other cells through her body. It would be borne along unsuspected, traversing the lanes and highways of her circulatory system, pressed by her throbbing heart to the system of bronchial tube, pleural cell, membrane of alveoli. And here. Here was as good a place as any. A cancer cell can find a home here, can take root, can live its private hellish dream of multiplying with greedy abandon and taking up all the real estate, killing the very thing it feeds on.

Maddie imagined it. She could see it all in her mind. She forced a cough and scoped her mouth with a wad of toilet paper. Red? Please, God, don't let it be red, she heard herself praying, and instantly thought of Frank. She hadn't talked to God since Frank dropped his little bomb, his curly-haired editor bomb. The vapors of that mushroom cloud lingered in the family room, the bedroom; they hovered over the entire house. Please, God, she said again, and thought again of Frank, saw him squatting to coach their son at first base, smiling at her over the top of his glowing computer screen. Please, God, she said yet again. The mucous on the toilet paper was clear—no, maybe just tinged with pink.

She leaned against the bathroom door, waiting for the pain in her chest.

---

Maddie had wanted to cover him somehow. Were there no swaddling clothes? Newborn Dominic Tedesco lay exposed on a small, padded table under a heat lamp. Didn't they want to put a railing up, something to keep him from falling off? But baby Dominic wasn't going anywhere. He was flaccid, grounded by his own weakness, a ventilator, and IV tubes housed in the stump of his umbilical cord.

There was the pump and sigh of the ventilator, the beep of the monitor, and Amy's cry: a soft and high-pitched keen that filled the room.

Where, exactly, had the problem begun? At what point in Dominic's invisible development did the lines of communication break down and, just here, collapse, causing this little system, this little corner to set itself up so poorly? And should it matter? Why should it be that the fault of these few, microscopic cells should make such a difference in a body otherwise so flawlessly formed?

It was his heart—and then just a part of it: the left ventricle, to be precise, which meant that his blood wasn't getting to his body. His feet and hands—so perfect in shape—bore a pale bluish hue.

"What will they do?" Maddie asked Pastor McLaughlin, who stood at the far side of the room, out of the way, leaning against the window sill.

"There's nothing," he said, and wiped at tears with his handkerchief.

Vincent had called her both times: first, to say the baby had been born, and then again, to say they were wanted at the hospital. They were needed right away, he said.

Everyone had been waiting for this. Little Dominic was the most anticipated baby the Bethel Hills Church of Holiness had ever known, and next to Amy and Nicky themselves, Maddie and Vincent likely anticipated him the most. Graduation was behind them now; they were waiting until the baby came to make their little announcements (a wedding soon; a move, as soon as possible, north, to Vincent's college town; a baby of their own sometime next January). They would wait just a little while to allow everybody to settle in and be happy over the Tedescos' baby.

The night before, Vincent and Maddie had been over at their house. Vincent had helped Nicky put the crib together; Maddie had sat on their bed and listened as Amy debated what to include in her hospital bag. Later they sat out on the backyard patio. Nicky grilled steaks, and he and Vincent teased Amy's girth: "Whale!", "House!", the tired, overused expressions that delighted the men to inexhaustible ends. Maddie scolded them, mindful of her own fate, but Amy endured it with smiling patience, knowing it was in fun. She rubbed the sides of her abdomen with her fingertips.

As it grew dark, Vincent and Nicky had taken to throwing their forks into the air, luring bats. They had talked—again—about whether it was a boy or a girl, about whether they would call when they went to the hospital (Vincent made Nicky promise). They made bets on the length of the labor.

And then morning and two phone calls, early. The Tedescos' baby boy on the prayer chain.

Maddie couldn't say when the dread began, but she would venture it was before the hospital itself. She would venture that it was before Vincent's tearful embrace in the driveway (he was getting out to come to the door and she was hurrying out to meet him; it was a beautiful summer morning with the lawn spun in dew-filled webs and the air full of birdsong). She would venture that it began shortly after the news of the second phone call had hit her, that the Tedesco's baby was sick, that they were wanted at the hospital.

Of course they would ask Vincent to pray for him.

And of course he would do so. No matter the fates of those who had gone before (Mr. Taylor getting along nicely, thank you, on two prosthetic legs; Mrs. Senchak buried at the beginning of May, and Susan Sweet swaying around the church kitchen, helping prepare food for the funeral reception), the small number was gathered around baby Dominic's comfortless bed, ready to beseech the Almighty—despite his uneven track record—for this, another miracle.

Amy was in a wheelchair, wearing the bathrobe she had last night decided to pack, and Nicky stood behind her, his hands on her shoulders. There, too, were his parents, her parents, Pastor McLaughlin, each of them red-eyed, subdued and desperate, all focused on the nearly perfect new baby who breathed with the help of a ventilator. Maddie thought the room could barely contain so much faith. Was she the only one, she wondered, who was terrified of God's "when"? Or was Vincent wrong about that, after all? Maybe it was far simpler; maybe she herself had been right: maybe God's gift to Vincent was long since gone, taken in some cosmic breath of justice for the baby growing in Maddie's unwed womb.

And yet she and Vincent stood in the room with these faithful: Maddie joining Pastor McLaughlin in his station at the window, and Vincent laying his strong hands over that small, pale chest, the broken heart.

The ventilator was the only thing keeping the baby alive now. The doctors, as Pastor McLaughlin had said, could do nothing, giving them free reign for this last effort. The monitor, the IV tubes, the ventilator—all of it waited on Vincent's prayer, a last hope.

Maddie didn't like to revisit it. She forced her mind away from it; she had become good at that. But something in baby Dominic's death (coming so soon after the prayer, when they turned the ventilator off and his little chest grew still and Amy folded over into herself, wailing and crying) forced itself into her awareness as Maddie stood in the kitchen, her phone in her hand, receiving the news from the doctor: the cancer was back; it was in her lung. It would seem to be a very small spot, but it was cancer nonetheless, and all around her, everywhere, the world was sliding gravel, and she couldn't find a foothold if she tried.

⁙

The cancer was back and Frank was flying down the interstate toward home. He had scarcely believed to hear her voice on the line; it was impossible to reconcile the feelings of elation and dismay: that it was her voice calling him, giving him this terrible news.

He couldn't get home fast enough. He hadn't known about this new threat; she had made and attended the appointment alone. But now that she knew, she said, now that she knew for certain that the cancer was back, she knew, too, that she wanted him, that she didn't want to do this on her own.

He would never be able to remember that drive home. Years later, he wouldn't be able to recall seeing the road—but there is where familiarity is enough to get you, by rote, by habit, to your house again. Because the whole way home, his mind was on Maddie, on terror mixed with joy, and there was something in it of his pell-mell run to church all those years ago, his mad dash to the little Catholic church in their college-town that April, his grinning, breathless first communion.

He hadn't been able to control his joy as Tim handed him the wafer. Now he remembered what it was that compelled him that day. It was a small, frail thing, nearly translucent, that with unimaginable strength bound profound loss and the richest gain together—a body torn, again and again, in sacrifice, in payment, for all the pain, and for everything Frank had done and would do.

Maddie met him at the door and he took her again—so grateful—
in his arms. She wasn't crying, but she was shaking, trembling, her
whole body quaking against him, rattling as though she would fly
apart. Frank had felt he was holding her together, gathering the edges
of herself closer to her core, and again and again he whispered in her
ear that he was sorry and he loved her, until finally Maddie stopped
shaking and was able to let herself cry.

———— ∞ ————

"One of yours for one of mine," Frank said, and Maddie turned to
look at him from where she lay on their bed. She was curled on her
side; the white bedspread was rumpled over and around her. This time,
for this surgery, the boys had gone to her parents' home in Pittsburgh.
The house was quiet. She hadn't heard Frank come in.

"One of yours for one of mine," Frank said again, holding his open
laptop toward her so she could see a photo of Vincent's family and, a
small square, Vincent himself, smiling and older. His blue eyes. Frank
was smiling, too.

Of course he was smiling. Dear Frank. He saw no threat in letting
Maddie contact Vincent, now or ever; why should he? Wasn't that the
point all along? Tell each other everything; no skeletons in the closet.
They could be the other's best friend that way. They could drown
their temptations in the tangled sheets of their bed; they could laugh
about old loves because old loves didn't matter anymore. "Frankie and
Frankie." They had laughed about that; it was ridiculous.

And Frank had been right about the honesty. Maddie could see
that now. She had seen it, or known it anyway, when she stood in
the kitchen with the phone in her hand and the diagnosis coming
through the signal. Somehow, hearing that the cancer was back had
brought a concurrent sense of her need for Frank. They had to do it
again. *They* had to do it again. She wouldn't do it without him.

He had left work and come home to her immediately and now,
post-surgery, he offered her Vincent.

Maddie shook her head.

Frank wanted to know what it could hurt? "What can it hurt to
ask him, Maddie?" he asked her. "He healed you once before," he said.
Somehow—Maddie saw it now—he had seen through it. He had

understood that Maddie hadn't told him the whole story, and he had trusted her anyway.

But he closed the laptop when he saw that she was crying, the tears rolling into the small well at the bridge of her nose and then falling into the pillow. Carefully, she told him the rest of the story, all the parts she didn't tell him all those years ago, all the parts she hadn't told him since then—even though he had asked for honesty. He had said they would be needing honesty. And then, when he had failed her, he had been honest about it.

Maddie began with Dominic's death, a fact Frank had known before. But he couldn't possibly have known its weight: that this was, for Maddie, the final straw with God. The last sigh of Dominic's ventilator was either an act of divine retribution or one of wanton cruelty: punishment for sexual sin reaching far beyond the guilty, or benevolence capriciously withheld. And how was Maddie to countenance faith or trust in a being so decidedly unjust or unkind? She told Frank all of it, searching for details and speaking slowly, skipping back sometimes to tell him things she'd left out. It was like turning over rocks; like she was walking in a quarry and turning every stone over, making sure she'd left nothing to his imagination, no detail unexplored. She wanted to make an earnest go of honesty this time.

On that awful day, she and Vincent rode home from the hospital in silence and then she told him she needed to be alone. Within hours, she had known she had to call Justine. Much to her surprise, Justine hadn't had much to say. Maddie had anticipated an earful against Vincent and she hadn't wanted to hear it; it had taken desperation to get her to call Justine nonetheless.

But Justine had surprised her. She had understood completely, even though Maddie had (she was learning to do so quickly) withheld some details. Justine could see that an abortion was the only way to go. They were too young to be married. How could Maddie be sure she wanted to spend the rest of her life with the guy? Connie Baskin, who just graduated, had an abortion last summer. Did Maddie know that? Sometimes you're just kind of trapped by these things, you know?

This exposure to Justine's worldliness wasn't even shocking. Somehow, Maddie had suspected it all along, and anyway, she was too desperate just now to be anything but grateful. She had teared up a little, sitting there in the booth at the Eat 'n' Park, and Justine had handed her a tissue from her purse.

And maybe Justine, certainly compassionate to the Tedescos, understood without discussion the impossibility of Maddie's continued pregnancy. Maddie didn't need to delineate for Justine just how unreasonable and even cruel it would be for Maddie to carry and then deliver a potentially healthy baby, when they had lost every child.

Yes, that much was enough. There was no need to go into the rest of it. Justine had her own issues with God; she didn't need the burden of Maddie's guilt over Vincent, and likely she wouldn't understand it. How could she understand that, for Maddie, the abortion was her only means of escape—both from Vincent and from God? In this final act, Vincent would know that she wanted nothing more to do with him. And Maddie would have no obligation borne of miracle to compel her toward God.

Bitterly, she reasoned further: God had given his gift to Vincent, his insight to Vincent. Shed of Maddie and the bond of a child between them, Vincent could have his gift restored, perhaps. He could have his life with God.

Maddie didn't tell Vincent until it was over. She had missed little Dominic's funeral because of it and so had Justine, who had taken her to the clinic and then brought her home again. Maddie told her mother she was sick—and she *was* sick: she just wanted to sleep and sleep forever. Vincent had come and sat at the foot of her bed for a while, and Maddie had pretended to be sleeping. But soon enough she had to tell him.

She asked him to come to the house; her parents weren't home. It was summer but there was a pallor under his tan; there were dark circles under his eyes. When she opened the door, he reached for her and held her without saying anything, weeping silently into her shoulder—she understood why—for Dominic, for Nicky and Amy and their unspeakable loss.

She kept it brief; she talked quickly; she gave him no time to answer. She told him that she wouldn't be marrying him—there was no need—and that after everything that had happened, she didn't think she loved God and she didn't think she loved Vincent and this just needed to be over.

And then it *was* over. It was finally done.

Vincent had stood and walked to her, then bent and kissed her forehead. Without a word, he walked out of the house to his car. She did not see him to the door, but after it closed behind him, she went to the window and watched him go. He walked slowly. Short strides, bent head. He didn't look at the house before he drove away.

She hadn't gone back to church after that, which her parents— since she'd broken up with Vincent—seemed to understand: perhaps they knew it would be too painful. She hadn't seen Vincent again, hadn't seen the Tedescos. Her friendship with Justine slowly faded— they didn't seem to know what to say to each other—and then they'd been off to college. And immediately Maddie had begun the reevaluation of everything, which was why, among other things, she had insisted that Vincent could never heal people.

Long before she was finished, Frank had lain down with her, behind her, his body curling into and behind hers: chest to back, thigh to thigh, knee to knee. Under the white bedspread, his hand rested over hers where it was lying on her thigh; she felt him breathing into her hair. He made no sound; he said nothing; and a long time went by before she was done with the telling. When she reached the end of the story, the sun had swung around and was low in the sky, and the shadows of the birch branches lay tangled all over the bed.

Frank never seemed surprised. Not that he had surmised what she told him, but that nothing she had done would change what was true all along. "I love you, Madeleine," was all he said. Over and over again he told her he loved her, as if those words could be sufficient, as if love—in light of death, cruelty and loss—could ever be enough.

Maddie was still crying at the end. Her pillow was drenched and still she cried into it, eyes, nose, mouth all streaming, her back warm against Frank.

# EPILOGUE

*I*t is later than that now, a Saturday, the middle of the day, and Frank is home. He and Maddie both, in fact, are in their bedroom on a Saturday afternoon. They had managed an excuse (what was it?) and the boys are satisfied and playing happily, for now, in the room below them. Maddie can hear their voices: Jake helping Garrett with something, and Garrett, loving the attention of his older brother, chattering happily, his voice coming to her like the chirp of a bird.

They'd had to be clandestine and quick: stolen moments like these in the middle of the day are risky at best, but she and Frank have discovered they love the risk. They think it's even a little bit funny, and they both are so often tired at the end of the day that the risk of an afternoon is more than worthwhile.

So it was quick but also richly satisfying, and Maddie now turns to watch Frank sleep, to watch his chest fall and see the sun make the skin of his shoulder almost incandescent. She imagines she can see the individual cells, each of them refracting the light. Frank is naked; they are both naked, and the sheet covers Frank haphazardly. His left leg hangs over the edge of the bed, exposed. Maddie's own body is marked with new scars and old, but she lets the sheet fall where it will, and her bare arm lies next to Frank's. In his sound sleep, he is holding her hand.

The voices downstairs begin to rise. An argument. Any moment one of them will knock on the door, seeking arbitration. But Maddie doesn't move just yet. Frank is sleeping soundly and he is holding her hand. Then she hears Eli shush his brothers and his voice, measured, comes in tones too low for her to decipher words. Ah, she thinks to herself. They are working it out. She feels a rush of gratitude and closes her eyes. Maybe she can get a little nap.

She is doing so well, everyone says. Despite the new diagnosis, they say, you are doing so well. And Maddie smiles, thanks them, agrees.

What is cancer, anyway? she might ask, if the conversation went that way. What is cancer in the scheme of things? A paper cut, maybe? She smiles to think of Vincent struggling for words to name his faith. He'd had remarkable vision for a boy of seventeen, a boy who had known suffering in ways she—never abandoned by her father, for instance—couldn't have understood. She had never understood Vincent; she hadn't really tried.

A paper cut, he had said, and she had been angry. Now she wonders what he had seen as he gazed across the parking lot that day, what vision of sacrifice and eternity had cast itself there, imbuing all hurt and loss with far greater significance than she had cared to see.

Again she sees the tilted parking lot, the crack-scarred macadam, the thin sheets of rainwater sliding toward the drain. She imagines herself walking toward him—she at thirty-nine years old—climbing the gentle slope of pavement and water to his teenage self. She doubts she would have much to teach him, even now, but who couldn't stand to be reminded of gentleness? She would like to tell him: let's not call it a paper cut, Vincent.

And then she realizes that he probably didn't even need that from her. Baby Dominic had probably taught him as much. Not that she could be certain: she didn't know Vincent after Dominic.

She didn't know Vincent after he was eighteen.

Eyes still closed, she sees his house: yellow brick with peeling paint around the windows. A wooden front porch, the boards split under their several coats of paint, curling downward at the top of the steps. The wooden steps themselves, cracked and softened; the bottom step gone altogether, replaced by a cinder block. The leaning plumb tree, lawn of crabgrass.

She had ridden past his house on the trolley dozens of times before she knew him, and now she wondered who else lived along that route, what other lives she had spied on, imagined, diminished while riding that electric vein into the city. Susan Sweet, perhaps. Maybe the Gilleces?

She saw Susan, Mr. Taylor, the Tedescos continuing on—as she heard they'd done—without the miraculous healings they had so boldly asked for. And yet they were content, persistent in faith despite God's answer to their requests.

Maybe they already had what they really wanted. "Everybody just wants God."

The sun falls through the window and warms her skin between the networked shadow of the birch. Half-dreaming, she sees an aerial view of her hometown, the grid of trolley lines and roadways, the branching streets and intersections, the lawns and green spaces, and the grit and dirt, the broken glass and waste of city life. The rise and fall of the city's wrinkled skirts, Mount Washington, the glint of the rivers. The city. And at night, the limitless breadth of stars.

All of it of a piece. The realization coming softly, like sleep, heavy and sweet. Roadways like arteries, like veins, the landscape of a body, torn and torn and torn again into this small plot and that, this life and that. And all fed by the bleeding heart of the city: beautiful, terrifying, enough.

# ACKNOWLEDGEMENTS

*I* owe many debts of gratitude for this project. First, my deepest thanks to those friends who shared their experiences with breast cancer. Thanks, too, to Dr. Allen Liles and Dr. Sascha Tuchman for invaluable medical insight. Ken and Debbie Tunnell, Paul and Tracey Marchbanks, Carolyn and Mike Shipley, and Emily and Byron Williams for very real support in making spaces for me to write. Thanks to Bonnie Liles and Walker Hicks, for taking the risk of an early reading. Daun Whitley, Laine Stewart, Tori Lye, Keith Newell and Annie Hawkins, for your prayers. Beth Wessels, Rachel Stine, and Lynne Liptak, for listening. The staff of Light Messages for all the expertise I do not have. Betty Turnbull for your tenacity and delightful sense of humor. Elizabeth Turnbull for insight, gentleness, and so much hard work. The incomparable Jamie Schneider, who understood and believed in this project in its infancy. Bill and Carolyn Stevenson and Linda Tulip, for your patience. My parents, Richard and Susan Brewster, for your constant love. My sisters, Meghan Bowker and Emily Brewster, for your encouragement. The South Hills Church of the Nazarene, for being my second home while I grew up into the world. And Bill, Will, Everett, and Emma Grace, who endured with laughter, dancing, and confident hope.

# ABOUT THE AUTHOR

*R*ebecca Brewster Stevenson was raised in Pittsburgh. She has a master's degree from Duke University and currently lives in Durham, North Carolina with her husband and three children. *Healing Maddie Brees* is her first novel. Rebecca can be found online at rebeccabrewsterstevenson.com.

# READING GUIDE

A discussion guide for readers is available online at:
lightmessages.com/rbstevenson

# IF YOU LIKED THIS BOOK

Check out these award-winning titles from Light Messages Publishing:

*The Particular Appeal of Gillian Pugsley* *by Susan Örnbratt*
From the shores of The Great Lakes to the slums of Bombay and a
tiny island in between, this dazzling debut takes the reader on an
intimate journey to unravel a family secret that's lain hidden for
generations.

*A Theory of Expanded Love* *by Caitlin Hicks*
A dazzling debut novel. Questioning all she has believed, and
torn between her own gut instinct and years of Catholic guilt,
Annie Shea takes courageous risks to wrest salvation from a tragic
sequence of events set in motion by her parents' betrayal.

*Tea and Crumples* *by Summer Kinard*
Welcome to Tea and Crumples where the click of chess pieces,
susurrus of fine papers, and grace of friendship accompany Sienna
when every bit of her has been poured out. They keep vigil when
all that's left is faith, tea, and love.